INSURGENCY
HARMONY

INSURGENCY HARMONY

THE COLLISION
BOOK 1

T. M. CLAYTON

Podium

For Mum, Dad, Amy, and Emma

Cover design by Podium Publishing

ISBN: 978-1-0394-1401-3

Published in 2022 by Podium Publishing, ULC
www.podiumaudio.com

Podium

DISTRICT OF THE MOUTH

NTU Sovereignty

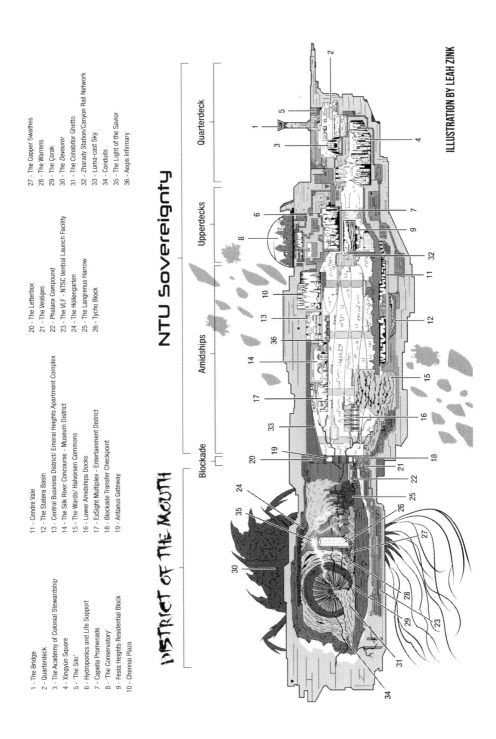

1 - The Bridge
2 - Quarterdeck
3 - The Academy of Colonial Stewardship
4 - Xingyùn Square
5 - 'The Silo'
6 - Hydroponics and Life Support
7 - Capella Promenade
8 - 'The Conservatory'
9 - Festa Heights Residential Block
10 - Chennai Plaza

11 - Cendre Vale
12 - The Statera Basin
13 - Central Business District/ Emeral Heights Apartment Complex
14 - The Silk River Concourse - Museum District
15 - The Wards/ Halvorsen Commons
16 - Lower Amidships Docks
17 - ExSight Multiplex - Entertainment District
18 - Blockade Transfer Checkpoint
19 - Antaeus Gateway

20 - The Letterbox
21 - The Vestiges
22 - Phalanx Compound
23 - The VLF - NTSC Ventral Launch Facility
24 - The Höllengarten
25 - The Langrenus Harrow
26 - Tycho Block

27 - The Copper Swathes
28 - The Warrens
29 - The Çorak
30 - The *Devourer*
31 - The Cohabitor Ghetto
32 - Zharady Station/Canyon Rail Network
33 - Luma-cast Sky
34 - Conduits
35 - The Light of the Savior
36 - Aegis Infirmary

Quarterdeck

Upperdecks

Amidships

Blockade

ILLUSTRATION BY LEAH ZINK

INSURGENCY HARMONY

PROLOGUE

ew had ventured quite so deep into the *Novara*'s sprawling sub-structure as Delilah found herself presently. The megacomplex of maintenance hubs and service ducts that lined the twenty-kilometer length of the ark ship's underbelly—now referred to as the Vestiges—had been evacuated long ago, deemed too treacherous due to its close proximity to the increasingly deteriorating ventral hull.

Occasionally during sleepless nights, Delilah's meandering thoughts would linger on tragedies past—namely, an incident in which several bulkheads simultaneously failed. A major hull rupture had occurred, and an entire residential complex was blown out into space—hundreds of souls lost to the endless night in an instant.

How fragile life is for us, the human remnant. And how terrifyingly little there is separating us all from that infinite and unforgiving emptiness outside . . .

Brushing dark curls away from her eyes, she glanced up at the plate-clad ceiling of the surrounding maintenance passage, feeling the weight of the *Novara* bearing down on her shoulders. She imagined for a moment that she could see through all one hundred and eighty decks as though they were made of glass, her imaginary X-ray vision cutting up through the densely populated wards of Halvorsen Commons to the immaculate plazas and pristine vestibules of the Upperdecks . . . The latter of the two was home, and as she pressed farther into these abandoned catacombs, she caught herself missing home more and more.

Sweeping the sleeve of her emerald blazer across her forehead, she cleared away the beads of sweat collecting on her brown, glistening skin. The Vestiges were no place for a student of the highly prestigious Academy of Colonial Stewardship. Accordingly, she had chosen to sport an anorak over her uniform to conceal her enrollment—a decision she now had to pay for by suffering the unbearable humidity, the muscles in her chest straining to expel hot, soupy atmosphere from her lungs.

"Admit it, Micah. We're lost," she said to her venturesome guide, the gangly boy leading the way just ahead of her.

"You need to give me a little more credit, Lilah," he replied, maneuvering the top half of his body out of an oil-stained engineer's jumpsuit and tying it around his waist. While toiling shoulder-deep in thruster nacelles in the docks of Lower Amidships all day undoubtedly had Micah Verhoeven better acclimated, even he appeared to be struggling in the sweltering heat. Dragging fingers through scruffy, sandy-blond hair, he continued, "I know exactly where we are. And to think I got us here on nothing but pre-Collision blueprints. We're like pioneers—I doubt anyone's been this deep in nearly a century now!"

"And with good reason too: this place is dangerous! Do you have any idea how susceptible we are to a hull rupture down here?"

Micah turned on his heel, his boyish face drawn in a vexingly charming smirk. "There hasn't been a serious breach in years. But if you're too scared to carry on, just say the word and we can turn back." He grinned, knowing full well there wasn't a chance in the Abyss she could give up now when they had come so far. She thwacked him on the arm, feigning a scowl, her mother's words of admonishment repeating in her mind.

"Mark my words, Delilah," the woman had once said. *"If I ever catch you hanging around with Micah Verhoeven again, there will be serious consequences. That boy is a leech sympathizer. It won't be long before he gets himself arrested by Phalanx for sedition—just like his parents. I won't have my daughter associated with an enemy of the New Terra Union."*

Delilah certainly didn't consider herself the rebellious sort, but the more her parents tightened their grip, the more inclined she felt to act out against them. If either knew the *real* reason she had dipped out of third period and snuck off into the Vestiges, they'd probably disown her . . .

Micah waved a halting hand at the intersection between the current passageway and a narrow service duct. Brow furrowed in uncertainty, he glanced down at his Sinegex feather—a commonly owned handheld communication device in the form of a thin wedge of tempered glass. After a moment consulting the engineering blueprints recovered from the archives of this long-forgotten region of the *Novara*, he made a chirp of recognition. Turning right and leading Delilah into stifling darkness, he switched on an LED flashlight mounted to the shoulder strap of his safety harness. A cone of glaring blue light pushed back against the gloom, lighting the way forward. Shadows rippled and danced unnaturally across the ceiling as the flashlight caught the

skeletal shapes of support structures and exposed pipework where wall cladding had fallen off or disintegrated. A cold shiver rattled down Delilah's spine
as she eyed her ominous surroundings. "You don't think we'll run into one of
them down here, do you?"

"Run into what?"

She didn't mean to roll her eyes but did so involuntarily. "Into a *leech*, of
course!"

"How many times I gotta tell you to stop calling them that?"

"I know, I know . . . I just love how much it riles you up. You're too
sensitive!"

"And *you're* dehumanizing them by using derogatory language like that."

She paused for a moment before continuing. "Yeah, but . . . they aren't
human, are they?"

"Maybe not to an ignoramus like you."

Micah quickened his pace, forcing Delilah to double her step to catch
up with him. She cast her eyes to the floor, unable to suppress her chagrin
at having seemingly caused offense. It had never made sense why the stubborn fool deemed them worthy of so much reverence, though—the plague
of hideous bipedal insectoids who arrived in a blaze of plasma and hellfire
one hundred and seventeen years ago, who crippled the *Novara* and robbed
the human remnant of its only chance of finding a home among the stars.
Those wretched creatures deserved nothing but disdain as far as she was concerned, but in the interest of keeping the peace, she supposed she could at
least appear to treat them with a little respect—if it meant so much to Micah.

"I'm sorry," she said, the words dripping with contrition. "I mean, do you
think we'll run into a co-ha-bi-tor?"

He issued a goading smile. "Well . . . the blockade only goes down as far as
Cendre Vale, and we've gone way beyond, so I guess it's entirely possible." She
felt a flutter of relief as he gave her a reassuring shoulder nudge. "But if we do
meet a cohabitor, I promise I won't let it eat your face."

Micah's path brought them to a T-intersection where the service duct
adjoined an access corridor. After a short distance, the corridor opened into a
deserted common area—a tall space cutting an oblong shape up through four
decks with balustraded balconies encircling each level. Delilah's chest swelled
as fresh air spilled into her lungs—it tasted noticeably less stagnant here than
it had in the dismal passageways behind them.

She tilted her head up to study the disc of glowing opaque glass suspended
from the ceiling—a chandelier of brutalist design—feeling the warmth of
simulated sunlight caressing her cheeks. Micah did the same, and she saw a
giddy smile touch his lips—he knew as she did that its undulating brightness,

paired with the apparent presence of operational air filtration, could only suggest a local power surge, which meant their destination drew near . . .

She moved toward the center of the chamber, where a small patch of desiccated soil, host to the brittle husks of a few long-dead shrubs, marked the remnants of an abandoned communal garden. The sunlight emanating from above would once have kept the garden lush and vibrant, but without functioning irrigation it had long since fallen to ruin.

"*Astra inclinant, sed . . . non obligant,*" Micah stammered awkwardly, reading the text emblazoned on a stone plaque partially embedded in the dirt.

"The stars incline us; they do not bind us," Delilah translated, responding to Micah's look of surprise by peeling back the breast of her anorak to reveal the same text stitched beneath the crest of her ACS uniform. "Don't tell the forbearers, but they definitely bind us now."

He responded with an exhalation through his nostrils that didn't quite qualify as a laugh. There was a moment's rumination, then the lines of his face tightened into an uncharacteristically solemn look.

"Last time we spoke you said you weren't even planning on seeing out this next semester . . . Have you had any second thoughts about it?"

"Oh, it's all just so damn pointless, isn't it?" she grumbled, digging the toe of her boot into the barren soil. "I mean, living and studying all the way up there in Quarterdeck, you'd be forgiven for thinking the Collision never even happened, the way people carry on. Why waste so much effort training the best of us up to oversee the colonization of Pasture when any chances of that actually happening were decimated over a century ago?"

Never one to shy away from expressing a borderline conspiratorial opinion, Micah replied, "It's all about maintaining control. How else is the Administration gonna stave off mass mutiny without the help of an army of mindless bureaucrats?"

Delilah felt a catch of impatience. "I'm serious—it's a waste of time! As long as the *Novara* is stranded in dark space with that *thing* attached to the hull, draining our resources, all we can really aspire to be is a bunch of caretakers. We're just biding our time until the lights turn off and the air finally runs out."

"I don't think that will ever happen," he said, adopting a tone of voice that was probably meant to reassure her. "The *Devourer* relies on our hydroponics and atmosphere processing. If it ever stopped powering the *Novara's* fission reactor, it would mean starvation and suffocation for the cohabitors too. I find it helps to think of it like a symbiotic relationship—yes, we're stranded in dark space, but we're stranded together, so we have to rely on one another to survive."

"How poetic," Delilah scoffed, mentally recounting the time she got to see the alien monstrosity with her own two eyes. All attendees at the Academy were required to undergo a rigorous induction process, an essential step of which was to spend a brief term serving on the bridge. Standing atop the helm platform for the very first time, facing stern, she recalled gazing out into the endless night, the unfathomably massive shape of the *Novara* stretching out below her like a frozen sea of nanocarbon alloy. And there it was: the so-called *Devourer*—a gargantuan mass of muscle and machinery, clinging voraciously onto the aft section of the *Novara*'s dorsal hull, wielding a biomechanical arsenal of tentacles and teeth. Imagining the sight of it now struck no less fear and revulsion in her than it did on that day. She couldn't help but shudder at the thought of it.

"You can't leave," Micah said, startling her from her grim malaise.

"And why not?"

"I know you're way better educated than me, but you've got a lot to learn about this ship and the way things are."

She gave him another thwack on the shoulder—not strong enough to cause any real pain but enough to let him know the sentiment had incensed her. "And you're suggesting staying in school is the only way I can ever hope to become as *wise* and as *learned* as you. Is that it?"

He raised a cocky eyebrow. "Well, I don't know about that, but maybe if you stick it out you just might be able to climb the ladder to a position high enough in the Administration where you can actually make a difference."

"Not this again."

"I know you don't want to see it, Lilah—nobody from the Upperdecks does. But injustice and inequality are rife on the *Novara*. We left Earth behind hoping for a new start, unbound by the selfish, destructive ways of our ancestors, only to pick up right where they left off. I know the type you mingle with up there in Quarterdeck: self-interested, uppity blowhards—the same people you can bet will be perpetuating this discriminatory status quo a decade from now."

She turned her shoulder to register her annoyance as he continued.

"But I know deep down you're nothing like them. If there's gonna be meaningful change for the future, it'll be down to bright sparks like you to make it happen."

"I don't understand why you think this responsibility falls solely on *my* shoulders. If you're so determined to break the cycle, why don't you step up to the plate?"

"I'm doing as much as I can, Lilah, but the impact I can make as a dock-yard engineer from Cendre Vale in *this* machine is severely limited—just a drop in the ocean—whereas I believe you can change the tide." He took her by the shoulders, a little more fervently than she would have preferred. "I wish I could do more, but at the end of the day, I have to think about Isaac too. Hell, things were tough on him even before our parents got carted off by Phalanx. Now it's on me to try and give him some semblance of normality. I just want things to be better for him, that's all."

Delilah took a moment to try and reconcile the hypocrisy of vowing to put his younger brother's interests first, considering Micah was the instigator of today's little excursion. She sensed, though, that bringing it up would only cause an argument.

"No matter what you do," he concluded, "just promise you'll try and make things better for people."

She pushed his hands away, showing a scornful but appreciative grin. "Get off me, you sappy bastard. I promise, alright?"

Micah set them off down another access corridor, taking the time to eagerly explain how the entire complex used to be the residential block for the two-hundred-strong team of engineers charged with the maintenance of the *Novara*'s now-defunct ripple drive. Delilah let him babble on, mustering as much enthusiasm as she could, her interest stolen by the trail of strange power fluctuations they seemed to be following: flickering ceiling lights, door hatches opening and closing, info screens flashing garbled static. Clearly something was interfering with the local power grid.

"Have you ever taken it directly from a vent before?" she asked, her excitement and unease bleeding through in her tone.

"Once or twice, yeah," Micah replied. "The headaches you get afterward are grim, but the visual stuff is way more intense. We'll be hungover as hell tomorrow, but I promise it'll be worth it."

What in the stars are you doing? she asked herself, feeling her heartbeat tripping over itself. *This is absolutely crazy. If you get found out you'll be expelled from the Academy, ostracized by your friends and family.*

But consideration of that which they sought swiftly quelled her reservations: glow—the eerie, luminescent vapor that, according to Micah, was a by-product of *Devourer* technology. When inhaled, it caused the human mind to experience waves of euphoria, unparalleled clarity, and mesmerizing hallucinations. Dwelling on its otherworldly origin nauseated her, of course, but ever since trying it from a small, disposable cap that had been passed to her at a party a few months prior, she had craved the sensation again.

She felt her respiration quicken, the pounding of her heartbeat exploding in her ears. An unsettling cocktail of warring emotions settled upon her:

guilt, lust, and fear, all vying for space in her chest cavity. Thoughts of her mother's disgust should she ever find out manifested, then capitulated to the palpable rush of recalling the sensation. Whatever glow was, the reaction her body had to the mere contemplation of it felt like a high in itself.

Possession was highly illegal, hence why such a perilous journey was necessary to acquire it. But despite risking expulsion from the Academy, imprisonment, and possibly even death, she could easily brush the potential consequences aside. A veritable desperation had overcome her now . . . She *had* to have it.

"OK. Just a little farther down this corridor and we should . . ." Micah paused. "Do you hear that?"

She did. Emanating from the darkness draped ahead of them, she heard a swelling and receding roar, like waves lapping at a shoreline or the gradual expansion and contraction of lungs belonging to some enormous animal.

"Oh, Micah!" Fear gripped her, and she tugged him back by his sweat-stained vest. "Is it one of them? Is it a *leech*?"

"Cohabitor!" he hissed. "Don't be stupid. How big do you think they are?" He turned to her, blue eyes wide in realization and amazement. "I think it's the conduit. It must be coming from the vent!"

To her sudden horror, the infuriatingly impulsive boy switched off his shoulder-mounted flashlight, plunging them both into complete darkness once again. Her frantically darting eyes took a moment to readjust, but as her pupils fully dilated, something bizarre began to emerge from the black: a gentle radiance filling the corridor—a glowing mist of swirling orange-and-violet luminescence, previously invisible in the brilliant flashlight but now strikingly vivid.

"You're not hallucinating," Micah said, anticipating her words to the letter. "I see it too."

She refocused on the space immediately before her nose, observing how the anomaly appeared to comprise millions of tiny fluorescent specks, dancing sporadically in the air, changing direction and colliding like electromagnetically charged particles. Micah extended an arm and chuckled in childish glee, watching the vibrating spores waltz and orbit around his hand in a manner that was almost playful. Delilah marveled at how the odd mist moved in synchronicity with the menacing breathing sounds—an ebb and flow in accord with each rolling exhalation that proved unnervingly hypnotic to watch.

The route terminated at the entrance to a mess hall, but the sliding doors to get inside were steel-plated, sealed tight, and the console to open them had been rendered inoperable. Here, the luminescent mist appeared to collect and congeal, funneling into a tumescent tendril that drifted up to an air vent above the doorway. They needed to get through . . . Fortunately, Micah had brought a key.

Reaching over his shoulder, he unclipped and retrieved a fission cutter from the spine of his safety harness. Gripping the power tool by its rugged handle, he swung it around and aligned it with the door.

"Are you sure it's pressurized in there?" Delilah asked, feeling the concern in her timorous voice.

Micah shrugged. "Sure enough."

Normally used by salvagers to cut apart wreckage and debris, the device expelled a ribbon of blinding fission energy, slicing through the door metal like a hot knife through butter. A perfectly circular chunk of material slid free and slammed to the ground, leaving a hole in the door about one meter in diameter, its cooling edge glowing and smooth like blown glass.

"We're going to some real lengths to get high here," Delilah joked, expecting the remark to elicit at least a mirthless chortle but instead finding Micah's face twisting in irritation.

"Why'd you have to make it sound so ugly?" he growled. "We're not just huffing solvents to get a cheap fix here, Lilah. You know it means more than that!"

Catching the faintest glimmer of desperation in his eyes as she clambered through the freshly cut hole behind him, she wondered, *How often has he been taking it?* Glow addictions were becoming more commonplace as the *Devourer* extended its reach, especially in lower-income areas like the wards of Lower Amidships where Micah lived and worked.

This was a mistake . . . If he's developed a habit, then how long before it happens to you too?"

Regret took its icy hold. She scorned herself for having ever indulged this selfish, dangerous escapade. The insatiable lust she'd felt for glow only moments prior had evaporated in an instant; all she wanted now was to get Micah away from this ghastly place and go home. Unfortunately, watching him jump and jitter in excitement as he bounded into the mess hall, it dawned on her just how difficult that would be.

They arrived in a wide space with a low ceiling stretching on about twenty meters or so, the walls lined with personal storage lockers and refreshment dispensers. Incredibly, there were coats still on hangers, plates and cutlery left on the countertop, faded Polaroid photos stuck to locker doors showing smiling faces, blissfully unaware of the devastation that would soon be wrought upon them. The mess hall was perfectly preserved—a snapshot of the moment it was evacuated one hundred and seventeen years ago.

Micah started rattling on about how the conduit in front of them was one of hundreds the *Devourer* sent burrowing through the *Novara*'s superstructure in search of air and sustenance, but his clinical explanation of the mechanism's purpose did little to temper the horrific sight of it. The conduit erupted through the floor grating, its serpentine structure like gunmetal vertebrae segmented by areas of sinew and flesh. It looped around the far side of the mess hall before plunging into an electrical panel, dividing into hundreds of wriggling appendages that fused with the breakers and terminals inside. Halfway along its spinal column–like structure, Delilah spied what she presumed to be the vent: a horizontal arrangement of gills, each about two feet in height, gasping periodically—the orifices responsible for the thrum of respiration and the source of the luminescent mist. The vent spewed billowing plumes of glow into the air, amassing in a spiraling vortex overhead as it drifted into the current of the air filtration.

What became clear, even before Micah animatedly clarified it, was how the conduit was powering the mess hall's life-support systems, then taking air from the room and siphoning protein from the refreshment dispensers in return. She hated to admit it but couldn't think of a term more appropriate than "symbiosis" to describe the process.

She stood in fearful disbelief, baffled as to how she had allowed herself to come anywhere near this complete abomination. Her insides contorted at the thought that she had once consumed even just the smallest quantity of the *Devourer*'s produce, and worse, derived pleasure from it. She felt violated. Her predispositions regarding the leeches, their culture and their technology, were instantly reaffirmed: they were dangerous, disgusting, irreconcilably alien, and she wanted nothing to do with them.

Her sense of panic increasing, she made several frenzied attempts to try and dissuade Micah from approaching the vent, each given less consideration by him than the last.

"Think of Isaac," she pleaded. "You said it yourself: your brother is depending on you now. If anything happens to us, he'll be left with nobody to rely on. Is that what you want?" But her cries fell on deaf ears; Micah had become completely transfixed. The closer he was to the glow, the more it took hold of him.

She followed as he marched toward the conduit, robbed of his will, his body like a possessed marionette. He pressed shaking hands to either side of the vent, leaned his face close to the wheezing gills, and breathed deep from their glowing excretion. He began muttering and laughing maniacally, distended eyes glazed over like two ravenous pits swallowing his crazed expression. Inhaling deeper and deeper, he pushed against the conduit, pressing the full weight of his body against its rancid anatomy until, eventually, it reacted . . . The floor shuddered; the conduit convulsed. Delilah took a cautious step back, casting her eyes to the ceiling, her neck and shoulders rock-solid in apprehension.

It started as a gradual creak, then a twang, then a groan, then a thunderous crash of metal—the cacophonic orchestra of structural disintegration erupting from behind the walls. The room began to shake violently as the conduit twisted and writhed. Micah planted his feet firmly on the ground, clutched on to viscid gill lips with rigid fingers, and wrestled to keep himself attached.

Listening to the *Novara*'s superstructure crumble around her, Delilah felt a peculiar sensation in her ear canal: an uncomfortable buildup of pressure, followed by a gentle pop. Frozen in terror, she knew exactly what it meant: *decompression.*

The mess hall exploded to life. Emergency klaxons blared while red and white strobe lights lowered from compartments in the ceiling. A synthesized voice, authoritative and cold, blurted from muffled speakers.

"EMERGENCY. STRUCTURAL INTEGRITY DECREASING. LOCAL ATMOSPHERIC PRESSURE CRITICAL. EVACUATE IMMEDIATELY."

Adrenaline flooded her system; her muscles swelled and her overwrought mind sharpened immediately. There was still time to get them both to safety, but she had to be quick, so she wrapped her arms around Micah's chest, fingernails digging into his tight pectorals, probably breaking skin. She pulled with all her might, twisting and jerking in a desperate attempt to pry him away from the source of his transfixion. But it was no use—the more she pulled, the more he resisted, caught in the deranged space between barely acknowledging her existence and viciously fending her off.

"Micah, please. We have to get out of here! This place is falling apart. You're gonna get us killed! Think of Isaac!"

Still no response.

There came another shudder, one so violent it nearly knocked her from her feet. The synthesized voice sounded again.

"WARNING. HULL RUPTURE IMMINENT. DEPLOYING LOCAL DECOMPRESSION COUNTERMEASURES."

A gut-mulching rumble came from the opposite side of the mess hall, accented by the sharp squeal of dragging metal. Delilah turned to see emergency bulkheads closing on either side of the entrance they had come through. Judging by the speed the two hulking slabs were moving toward each other, she estimated there were but seconds to get clear before they sealed.

She clasped her hands around Micah's torso, pulling him a final time, eardrums pummeled by her own bloodcurdling shrieks. She raised her open palm high above her head and slapped him across the face as hard as she could. He pivoted around suddenly, seeming for the briefest moment like he might finally have broken free from his glow-induced catalepsy, before striking her in the chest with a tightly clenched fist. She reeled backward, collapsing into a defeated, crumpled heap on the tremoring floor grating, sharp pain radiating from her undoubtedly broken ribs. She lifted her head, expecting to see him looming over her, ready to retaliate, but instead found that he had returned to the vent, hell-bent on continuing his gluttonous consumption.

Strenuously pushing herself to her feet, she glanced back at the bulkheads; they were nearly closed, but if she sprinted now, she might still make it.

"I—I'm sorry," she stuttered breathlessly, turning to Micah with tears welling in the corners of her brown eyes. "I have to go."

Gazing into the vent, he made a guttural noise of feral delight, but it was in response to nothing she had said.

It took every ounce of physical and emotional strength she had to leave his side, but she did—she had no other choice.

Heaving chest exploding in agony, she bolted for the bulkheads, turning side on and shimmying through the narrowing gap half a second before their rows of jagged teeth interlocked.

Clutching her throbbing ribs, she spun around to look through one of several portholes, gazing despairingly into the chaos that lay beyond. With Micah still clinging on fervently, the conduit thrashed and coiled like a serpent freeing itself from the jaws of a predator. Bolts of electricity jumped from the electrical panel as it detached, appendages squirming as they tore away.

The conduit reared up, then smashed through the floor, decimating all in its path. Seconds later, everything beyond the bulkheads had disappeared—atomized and consumed by the endless night.

Silence rang out, and where Micah had once stood, Delilah saw nothing but stars.

ONE

Tobias Cole Edevane stood in the en suite bathroom of his childhood bedchamber, admiring the accomplished young man beaming back from the ornate mahogany-framed mirror. He looked magnificent in a tuxedo; studying his appearance, it pleased him to notice how the steep angle of his jacket's satin lapel perfectly accentuated his sharp and clean-shaved jawline, and how the midnight-black fabric nicely complemented the dark brown of his slicked-back hair and fierce but immaculately maintained eyebrows. Doubtless he would be turning a few heads tonight, which was usually the case, given he was the respected son of Atherton Edevane, esteemed councilman to the Administration of the New Terra Union.

"Three minutes!" his father's voice boomed from the landing, a sound like crashing waves combined with the roar of some long-extinct feline beast. Even as a grown man, it struck a note of fear in Tobias and triggered a sudden snap to attention.

"Swoop's touching down in three minutes! Let's hustle up, son. You will *not* be making me late again."

A final check of his perfect pearl-white teeth for remnants of the synthesized boeuf bourguignon he'd inhaled before getting ready, then he set off, striding determinedly through his old bedchamber, which was more or less the way it had been the day he left for ACS three years earlier. Someone less aspiring and ambitious than he might have been impelled to feel a kind of reverent nostalgia, surrounded by memories and paraphernalia from simpler, more carefree times. But not Tobias. With his buzzing social life, exceptional academic achievements, and enriching chosen career path, he had far too much going for him right here in the present to be yearning after the past. No, successful people, such as him, tended not to bog themselves down by such pointless and petty retrospection.

Suited, booted, and smelling of cedar and spice perfume, he descended a lavish staircase and arrived in the parlor of the luxurious three-bed Emeral Heights apartment where he'd spent his childhood, situated just off Chennai Plaza in the financial district of the Upperdecks. His father sat perched on the armrest of a sumptuous chesterfield chaise sofa with an unlit cigar hanging loosely from his lips, decked in a navy-blue suit, and framed against a backdrop of timber and stone. On the *Novara*, using Earthen materials to furnish and decorate one's home was a mark of wealth and prosperity. For Atherton Edevane, it had become a fixation. In the years since Tobias and his older sister, Hazel, left for higher education, the man had been hard at work transforming their home into something akin to one of the museums on the Silk River Concourse, the space now peppered with timeless relics ranging from abstract works of twentieth-century art to a sparkling assortment of minerals and geodes. There were even a few unsightly clumps of rusted machinery representing each industrial revolution of the past millennia atop display pedestals. The centerpiece of this impressive shrine was the wooden blade from the propeller of an age-old aerial vehicle, which hung on steel hooks above the cast-iron hearth. Tobias marveled at the collection of invaluable artifacts as he reached the bottom of the staircase. *A little overobsessive, perhaps*, he mused, *but awe-inspiring nonetheless.*

"Oh . . . you decided to go with the salmon?" Atherton asked, acknowledging his son with a nod and striking a match with which he lit his cigar before flicking it into the hearth flame.

Tobias used the heel of his hand to smooth down a newfound crease in his shirt, suddenly lamenting the chosen color of the garment. As much respect and appreciation as he had for his father, the man had a brutally efficient method of knocking him down a rung, should he deem it necessary.

"I thought it prudent to go for something a little bolder. You did say you wanted to make an impression."

"That's true. But even still, it's a little garish, isn't it?" Atherton stood up, ostensibly to greet him but mainly to fix his slightly crooked bow tie. "This isn't just some fundraiser we're attending, after all; it's your sister's induction ceremony. I'm not sure how the highest-ranking officers of the New Terra Space Corps are likely to react to you showing up dressed like it's prom night."

Feeling a flush of annoyance, Tobias opened his mouth to riposte but was swiftly cut off.

"No matter. There's hardly enough time for you to change now anyway, so it will have to do."

Blowing rich, if slightly acrid, aromas of chocolate and creosote into the air, Atherton hastened to the kitchen drinks cabinet. He retrieved a bottle of single-malt Scotch with two tumblers and placed them delicately on the granite countertop.

"Lei-Ghannam!" rasped Tobias. "Is that from the preserves? I didn't think there was anything Earth-made left on board!"

His father carefully poured a measure of thick amber liquid into each glass, then lovingly brought the container to his face for closer inspection.

"*Captain* Lei-Ghannam was the finest to ever serve aboard the *Novara*, Tobias. I taught you better than to take his name in vain. But yes . . . it is. In fact, it may well be one of the last remaining bottles in existence. Distilled in the Highlands of Scotland, matured in virgin-oak barrels for eighteen years, and bottled over two centuries ago."

Atherton dipped his strongly defined nose into his tumbler. Tobias followed suit, taking in the overwhelmingly smoky notes of the ancient libation, then raised his glass.

"To Hazel!"

His father gave an appreciative nod. They clinked tumblers and knocked back their measures. With a mouthful of liquid charcoal, a powerful veneration took hold. Tobias considered how the combination of peat, barley, wheat, and water melting his taste buds originated from Earth—a home forever lost, separated from him by eons and unfathomable distances. If the world still existed at all, it was now an uninhabitable hellscape, courtesy of the system-wide cataclysm that sent Sol into chaos and necessitated the exodus of humanity two hundred and twenty-six years ago. Even still, he would have given anything to set foot upon Earth's shores, to set loose his senses upon the environment. He yearned to taste fresh ocean air, to hear the music of wild birdsong, and to feel the cold breeze against his cheeks . . . Depressingly, he knew the small amount of Scotch warming his belly was as close as he would ever come, which was a damn sight closer than most.

"This must have cost you a fortune."

Atherton wordlessly returned the bottle to the drinks cabinet, his softened countenance making way for the return of a hatchet-faced expression.

"We Edevanes work hard so that we need not skimp on our luxuries. While some might think it inordinate to spend so much on one's liquor, in my opinion, you just can't put a price on a taste of where we came from."

Slats of dazzling blue light swept across the parlor as the xenon headlights of an approaching swoop struck the window blinds. Father and son sprang into action. Tobias hurried to collect his beige double-breasted trench coat from a hook and followed his father closely through the front door.

Outside, a spectacular vista graced them. Stepping out onto the adjoining balcony, Tobias craned his neck left and right, astounded by the way this particular vantage point allowed surveyance of the entire length of the Canyon—a chasmic trench running from bow to stern, carved out for ease of access and to enable rapid transit to all areas of the *Novara*. The artificial sky, projected in a strip along the Canyon's ceiling, drenched the innumerable platforms and terraces on the far side of the dizzying abyss before him in the exquisite shades of dusk: gentle violet and fiery red, mixing like running watercolors and reflecting in the windscreens of the endless stream of airborne vehicles zooming by.

Truly there was no better place to comprehend the sheer enormity of the *Novara* than where Tobias stood. The vessel was the result of a planetary effort—a product of the combined resources and ingenuity of all the founding nations of the New Terra Union. Although, his father didn't seem to want to spend even a moment appreciating the surrounding grandeur, and so Tobias fell into step, quietly and completely awestruck.

A brand-new, state-of-the-art sports-model swoop hovered at the end of the private jetty—a four-seater cabin encased in a sleek exterior with a stylish chrome grill, sitting atop dual fission-drive repulsor pads. Its gleaming metallic-red finish was gaudy, flashy, and exactly what Tobias had come to expect from his father—a man with fastidiously refined tastes when it came to most aspects of life, but certainly not his choice of transport.

The passenger door swung open vertically to greet them, the hum of idling repulsor pads swelling as they approached. Tobias clambered inside and ensconced himself in a front-facing seat, grimacing slightly as the pungent odor of the synthetic leather interior invaded his nostrils.

"Destination?" a soft and slightly monotone voice inquired from speakers embedded in the dashboard.

"Capella Promenade, please, Hypatia," his father replied as he took the seat opposite, treating the swoop's integrated virtual intelligence with the same cold indifference one might show any other talking appliance.

The door sealed automatically and the repulsor pads growled as they spun up. The swoop jolted forward and took off, the sudden acceleration hurling Tobias into the back of his seat but barely eliciting a wince from his stoic father. Hypatia banked to the right and looped around to join a lane of traffic, heading in the direction of the *Novara*'s bow. Soaring along a vast, shimmering corridor of steel and glass, the swoop sped along the Upperdecks, pitching up slightly and beginning a gradual ascent toward the topmost levels accessible via the Canyon.

"New Terra News Network, please, Hypatia," Atherton intoned, removing a varnished sandalwood comb from his inside pocket and running it through the top of his graying Ivy League–styled hair.

The windscreen turned opaque and dimmed slightly. The image of a brightly lit newsroom appeared above the dashboard, luma-cast by an emitter at the rear of the cabin.

"Good evening, and welcome to the NTNN," the woman sitting behind the news desk said. *"Our top story tonight: the District of the Mouth Enforcement Department is revealing that the identity of the woman who was found murdered in the Cohabitor Ghetto earlier this week is thought to be Miss Anaya Lahiri."*

"Oh yeah. I heard about this." Tobias leaned forward in his seat. "That whistleblower got herself butchered by leeches."

"Miss Lahiri—an ex–government employee—recently came under fire for perpetrating the unsanctioned disclosure of sensitive information regarding the Administration, which officials say could pose a serious threat to NTU security."

"Eaten alive by rabid insects. What an awful way to go." Atherton shrugged and sighed apathetically. "No less than she deserved, I suppose. Such should be the fate of all who would even think of betraying the Union."

Tobias nodded his agreement. Of course, there were several theories circulating that suggested there was something suspicious concerning the timing of the woman's death. He supposed it was strange that she had been found murdered so soon after leaking drives' worth of government secrets to the public. But he didn't have the time or patience for such wild conspiracy theories. *Just a coincidence*—he felt certain of it.

"Right then." Turning his attention away from the broadcast, Atherton squared his shoulders and set narrowed eyes upon his son.

"There will be a lot of influence there tonight, Tobias—some fairly big names in attendance. I know you don't usually need help mingling with the riffraff, but there are a number of exceptional young highfliers who I think might be keen to garner your interest and who I would like you to spend some time with."

Tobias inwardly groaned. *Here we go again.*

"I know Alejandro Carmen's son will be there. Councilman Colton's daughter, Esmerelda, she'll be there too. Available as well—both are, I believe. I don't know what your *proclivities* are at the moment, but—"

"Dad, please!"

Atherton threw both hands in the air defensively. "I'm just saying: when I was your age you picked your poison and stuck to it. I never know *what* the score is with you kids these days."

"There's no *score*, Dad. And the last thing I need is for you to be my wingman."

"Nevertheless . . . handsome young go-getter with an affluent background such as yours and still single? People get ideas. Try speaking to a few of the other cadets—one of Hazel's friends, maybe. You might meet somebody you make a real connection with."

The man jumped out of his seat and sidled up to him; he wrapped an arm around his shoulder and spoke uncomfortably close to his ear. "Look . . . I know you're very fond of Miss Caleb Callaghan—I am too, and I've made that very clear. I'm just giving you fair warning that I shan't be best impressed if you spend the entire evening with her again. You know very well how it looks from the outside."

Tobias felt a flutter in his chest at the mention of Caleb's name, followed by a catch of anger at being asked to regulate his interaction with her. After a life-time of friendship, he was still uncertain about the nature of the bond the two of them shared: sometimes it felt like love, other times like a connection between siblings. While he often endeavored to be the heart and soul of any social func-tion he attended, she was the only one he was ever truly trying to impress. He could never admit to his *occasional* infatuation, of course, especially not to his prying father. Caleb, his oldest childhood friend, had been engaged for some time now, and owning up to the muddy and inconvenient feelings he'd been steadily developing for her simply wouldn't have been proper. So instead, he began mentally preparing his rebuttal, readying to sound off about what a ridiculous and laughable insinuation his father had made. It would be humiliat-ingly transparent—he had no disillusions about that. Fortunately, though, the NTNN broadcast came to his rescue and once again took the man's attention, preventing the need for an embarrassing exchange.

"The latest survey from exo-cartography has revealed that an additional thirteen conduits have been located in the past two weeks, providing further evidence of the drastic increase in the Devourer's *resource intake. Experts say that if this shocking trend continues, the cohabitors could be taking up to thirty-five percent of Novara water and protein supplies within the next year."*

The mood in the cabin changed suddenly, like a heavy thunderstorm roll-ing in over a peaceful landscape. An expression of complete and utter detes-tation swept across his father's face, bulging eyes trained on the broadcast with a seething fixation. On-screen, there was an outfit of exo-cartographers wearing hazmat suits—the men and women responsible for mapping out the vast network of leech conduits riddling the *Novara's* superstructure. They gathered around their latest discovery: a grotesque tentacle that had appar-ently excavated its way to a water-storage facility in the Statera Basin. They poked and probed at the wretched thing, holding clipboards and nodding aimlessly to one another, playing up for the camera.

"Those demons," Atherton hissed, letting his eyes fall despondently to his feet. "Look at them, sucking the life out of us."

"Thirty-five percent." Tobias shook his head, feeling a raw and primal hatred take root in his chest. "How much more can our infrastructure possibly withstand before it collapses? Surely there has to be a breaking point."

Atherton nodded somberly. "I fear we may have already surpassed it."

"I don't understand why we cannot simply search out and sever all of these conduits, seal the blockade and extradite every mutineer living in the slums beyond it, then let the leeches starve and fester among themselves. Maybe the *Devourer* will detach like a gangrenous extremity if cut off for long enough; then we can be rid of them once and for all."

"I wish it were so simple, but I'm afraid the situation is far more complicated than that." A wistful smile appeared on his father's face, his pride at hearing his son speak with such zeal on the matter shining through. It was only seconds later, of course, that he returned to his usual overbearing self. "Speaking of conduits," he said, "you make sure you stay the Abyss away from them. I hear this 'glow' stuff is really starting to tear its way through kids your age. I'd hate for you to end up like that young fool from Cendre Vale who got himself spaced huffing off one of those vents a while back."

Like many of his fellow students, Tobias knew the incident well. It had happened over a decade ago now, but since the aforementioned fool had a partner at the time who was studying at ACS, his tragic death served as a stark warning to anybody who might consider "vent hunting" as a potential pastime.

"I'm not stupid, Dad. I know to stay well clear of that stuff."

"Outstanding. Disgraceful behavior—if it doesn't get you killed, it'll certainly get you kicked out of the Academy, and the last thing I need right now is you getting expelled. That hurts *my* reputation."

"Your concern is greatly appreciated," Tobias said, inflecting just the right amount of sarcasm so as not to sound too flippant.

"I don't care how you get your kicks, Tobias, just don't get yourself killed. Or worse, caught."

TWO

arshal Eamon Wyatt's office was hardly the nicest he had been assigned in his fifteen years as an enforcer. The precinct house it sat on the top floor of was, like any other structure sternside of the blockade, a rundown salvage heap cobbled together from the reclaimed bones of the *Novara*, complete with janky, narrow hallways and infuriatingly unreliable computronics.

Sure, his workspace was claustrophobic and had a tendency to get humid as hell on warm days, but he really couldn't complain—the wide pedestal desk on which paperwork was deposited faster than he could generally delegate it was all he needed to do his job. And the panoramic windows afforded a truly jaw-dropping view of the surrounding area. He stood presently as he often did, a mug of syn-coffee in hand with a lit cigarette gripped precariously between finger and thumb, gazing into the colossal expanse rolling out before him. The locals called it the Mouth, which, if he squinted his eyes, he supposed it bore some resemblance to—a city of scrap metal constructed haphazardly in the cavernous maw of a giant.

He knew his history well: when the battle of first contact came to its fateful conclusion, the *Devourer*, like a cephalopodic predator reeling in its prey, began feeding on the *Novara*'s drifting carcass. By the time the beast had had its fill, an enormous cavity had been gouged out of her superstructure—a staggeringly vast chamber that just so happened to be pressurized and, miraculously, inhabitable. One could only hypothesize what the reason for this huge excavation effort was. Eamon surmised the cohabs were using the material to rebuild their crippled warship, or maybe just whittling out a little breathing room to stretch their weird-looking digitigrade legs. Needless to say, with the sudden appearance of a few cubic kilometers of unclaimed real estate, the newcomers began relocating in droves.

Facing an unprecedented immigration crisis, the Administration swiftly began construction of the blockade—an impenetrable dam forged of repurposed hull metal dividing the *Novara* in two, restricting the thousands of roving alien vagabonds to the ruined aft section of the ship. The quarantine itself went up without a hitch; the rub was that in all the confusion a whole mess of people found themselves stranded on the wrong side of it. What started out as a small band of disgruntled outcasts quickly grew into a larger settlement. A century later, it was a densely populated conurbation—a semi-self-governing borough independent from the NTU in which approximately ninety thousand humans and nonhumans were just about managing to tolerate one another. Eamon thought of it as a giant petri dish—an out-of-control science experiment resulting in a violent collision of culture and society.

His relatively recent appointment to marshal of the District of the Mouth Enforcement Department achieved two goals by his reckoning: historically, DMED elected its own senior officials, but by positioning him—an ex-enforcer for the government-sanctioned but privately owned security force Phalanx— as marshal, the Administration now had a man on the inside. Someone who could report back from behind enemy lines and hand down the rule of law to the disorderly masses. Secondly, it partially satiated the desires of certain higher-ups who undoubtedly would have preferred to see him hung, drawn, and quartered for a number of *indiscretions* during his time working for the Glow Enforcement Agency—the branch of Phalanx dealing with the control and regulation of alien narcotics. In truth, the move was the type of lateral promotion where those bestowing it offered a stiff handshake while twisting the knife in your side. After nearly two decades of devoted service to the Union, his reward for exposing and forcing the resignation of the two baddest apples in the history of Phalanx was immediate exile to the Mouth. As sure as the night was everlasting, the top brass was giving him enough rope to hang himself with—he'd be left to stew in the district until the day he took a bullet to the brainpan or finally offered his own resignation, but until then, there was far too much work to waste time being bitter about the injustice of his situation.

The job came with a number of headaches, chief of which was a particularly unpleasant fellow by the name of Vidalia Drexen: the self-proclaimed Governor of the Mouth. Drexen was the kingpin at the summit of a thriving narcotics syndicate. With smuggling routes in and out of the blockade, he ran a monopoly on the movement of glow throughout the *Novara*, possessing the manpower and the resources to eviscerate anyone dumb enough to challenge his status. His gang of Monarchs were a bunch of ruthless mercenaries—not your average goon-squad dipshit mobsters, mind you, but fierce, cunning loyalists. Outfitted like a paramilitary, they were tasked with defending Drexen's installations, taking out the competition, bullying business owners for protection money, and making life a living hell for those who dared refuse. The operation was so meticulously designed and so well concealed that DMED currently had no leads as to the location of Drexen's HQ. Whether it was some disused warehouse in the industrial outskirts or a facility buried way down in the Vestiges, Eamon had little hope of ever finding it. Especially not since having to divert resources away from the investigation and redirect them to the second, and perhaps more pressing, thorn in his side . . .

The organization that called itself Harmony had started as a multispecies group of activists fighting for cohabitor rights. Led by a woman under the alias of the Composer, the group held frequent demonstrations, speaking out against the Administration's segregation, with the ultimate goal of dismantling the blockade and bringing equality to all on the Coalescence—the nomenclature for the sum of the *Novara* and the *Devourer*. Eamon had been happy to let them be at first; hell, even cohabitors had the right to peaceful protest. But when the aforementioned demonstrations started producing body bags, he knew the trouble had only just begun . . . A few IED detonations later and Harmony had evolved into an insurgency—a violent terrorist cell with apparently no limit to what they considered acceptable collateral damage in pursuit of their mission. The Composer had become a corrupted symbol of hope to the most destitute in the Mouth—every day more and more rallied to her cause; her forces were growing exponentially, and each attack on the Phalanx compound—the Administration's forward operating base, situated at the foot of the blockade—could be counted on to be deadlier than the last.

Eamon knew Administrator Vargos would be chomping at the bit to declare martial law or, as much as he hoped otherwise, perhaps even deploy the grenadiers—either would only result in further escalation, perpetuating a cycle of violence that he felt woefully unprepared to break.

Somewhere in the midst of all this bloodshed and upheaval were the human and nonhuman residents truly managing to cohabit peacefully. To them, Eamon was a lawman and a protector—somebody they were relying on to restore order to this increasingly lawless place. As the Mouth's representative on the NTU council, it was his responsibility to get their voices heard bowside of the blockade. He may have initially been appointed DMED marshal to rule the district in the name of the New Terra Union, but he'd come to realize that tyranny just wasn't quite his style. As far as *he* was concerned, the denizens of the Mouth were the people he truly answered to, and he would work tirelessly to provide the security and prosperity he staunchly believed they deserved.

Now that Eamon had come to terms with his banishment, he was learning to take genuine pride in his duties as marshal. But if there was one aspect of the job he wholeheartedly despised, it was the frequent check-ins with Administrator Vargos—the head honcho herself, the big cheese, the twice-elected official entrusted with the stewardship of the governing body of the NTU. More and more he felt his own interests deviating out of alignment with those of the Administration, and these painfully arduous calls, which often culminated in a scathing review of his *"pitiful and disappointing performance,"* were a testament to that fact. Today's call was proving especially grueling due to the recent and untimely death of Miss Anaya Lahiri . . .

"I want no more excuses from you, Eamon," Madeline Vargos said, her image luma-cast above the comms terminal beside his desk. She appeared as a gaunt-faced skeleton a third her actual size, wearing a garish red suit, her silver hair fashioned in a shoulder-length bob, her expression a tightly wrung mask of impatience. "It has now been a week since Anaya was butchered and you have yet to make a single arrest. I need assurances that you and your deputies are doing everything within your power to apprehend these killers!"

Eamon stood facing the panoramic window with his back turned to the woman's projection, eyeing the look of complete despondence on the weathered, bronze-skinned face staring back through the glass.

"Like I told you already, ma'am." He ran fingers through the unruly waves of almost-black hair draped across his crown. "I've got my best and brightest on the case, but I'll be damned if the perp didn't do a stellar job of covering their tracks. There isn't a speck out of place at the scene: no blood spatter, no signs of a struggle. It's almost like Anaya fell out of the ruttin' Höllengarten."

He turned, tapping cigarette ash into his now-empty coffee cup, the golden hue of the luma-caster projection bathing his rugged features in warm, fluctuating light.

"To be completely honest, we're still struggling to fathom what business a retired finance officer had skulking around the Cohabitor Ghetto in the first place. I mean, how did she even get through the blockade?"

"I'm quite sure she had her reasons," Madeline said. "And to answer your second question, Anaya's preexisting security clearance would have given her free rein to move through the blockade checkpoint as she saw fit. We may never know *why* she chose to travel to the Mouth, but I hardly think *how* she got there is something to be concerning yourself with right now."

Eamon nodded, pursed lips signaling his dubiousness. "I suppose so . . . Guess it just feels a little serendipitous—Anaya turning up dead in a place she had zero cause to be in after dishing out a whole slew of the Administration's dirtiest secrets."

"I don't follow."

He shrugged. "You don't think it's all a little convenient?"

A frown etched itself across the deep wrinkles framing the Administrator's face. "Putting aside Anaya's unfortunate misconduct, I'll have you know she was a respected colleague and a close personal friend of mine. So, no—I find what happened to her deeply *inconvenient*, as a matter of fact."

The transmission stuttered as if the intensity of the woman's glower had somehow caused momentary interference with the communications equipment.

"What are you getting at, Eamon? Because it sounds like you're insinuating I had some kind of involvement in all this."

"There's no insinuations being made here, ma'am, just observations."

"Indeed. Well, maybe you should spend less time conjuring up wild armchair conspiracy theories and worry more about the vicious creatures who are out there freely slaughtering citizens of the NTU."

Eamon took a step toward the terminal, bringing fierce russet eyes topped by thick slugs of dark hair in line with the Administrator's.

"Ma'am, unless you're privy to information my team has yet to be made aware of, then we don't know for sure we're looking for a cohabitor suspect."

"Don't be so deliberately obtuse." Madeline flicked a hand dismissively. "Anaya was found in the Cohabitor Ghetto, was she not? I should think that's all the intel you need to put this down to interspecies homicide."

"Oh, that doesn't mean a damned thing these days." Eamon set down his mug and pressed fists against the pedestal desk, his forearms bulging beneath the rolled-up sleeves of his green plaid shirt.

"There are humans living in the Ghetto, bugs living in the Copper Swathes; it ain't so black and white anymore. I can't rule out the possibility that a human did this based on the location of the crime scene alone."

"Bugs?" The Administrator's thin lips shriveled into a coy smile. "That's not very politically correct of you, is it, Marshal?"

He sighed, indignant. "The cohabitors barely have a grasp on spoken language as it is, ma'am. They couldn't care less about what arbitrary human mouth sound we assign them."

"Enlighten me then. What is it they *do* care about?"

"Being treated with respect, Administrator—like people."

The terminal luma-caster stuttered again; even through the temporarily garbled image, Madeline's exasperation shone vividly. *Old tech. Is there a single piece of equipment in this precinct house that isn't a busted-up hunk of hand-me-down crap?*

"Enough of this! I've read the coroner's report. You and I both know that what's being conveniently ignored here are the lacerations covering Anaya's body that could only have been inflicted by a fission shank—a weapon used exclusively by cohabitors in previous incidences of interspecies violence." Vargos straightened her posture, formed a self-congratulatory smirk. "I appreciate you wanting to do your due diligence, Eamon, but you're wasting time. I want a nonhuman suspect in custody within forty-eight hours, and that will be the end of it."

Eamon considered pointing out the fact that any bozo with a fistful of nunits could acquire a fission shank from one of the cohab vendors in Tinji Marketplace, but the utter futility of making such an observation forced the words back down his throat. Instead, he gave a curt nod of acceptance.

"Excellent," said the Administrator. "Now, is there anything further you wanted to discuss before we adjourn?"

He hastened to his desk drawer and produced a data chit, then plugged it into a socket on the comms terminal.

"I'm sending over a detailed report of recent insurgent activity in the district. We managed to identify a number of—"

"That won't be necessary," Madeline said, raising a cadaverous finger. "I am kept adequately apprised about enemy movement near the compound, and what occurs outside of NTU sovereignty is, quite frankly, none of my concern."

Eamon dropped his shoulders, felt a blow of helplessness like a nonlethal beanbag round to the chest. He showed pleading hands, offering far more sincerity than the woman deserved. "Administrator, please. By abandoning these people, you leave them at the mercy of the Composer. Her foot soldiers are sweeping the desperate and vulnerable up off the street like fruit ripe for pickin'. They don't have anything to lose, and when she puts a gun in their hand and gives them flowery talk and a new sense of purpose, there's nothing they won't do in service of her crusade. I know I sound like a broken record here, but the reach of your enforcers *needs* to extend beyond the Phalanx compound if we ever want to take back control."

"Your request for reinforcement is, once again, denied. The District of the Mouth is *your* jurisdiction, Marshal. I'm afraid you must learn to keep your house in order with what support you have already been given."

"But we're at breaking point down here. DMED are a tough bunch, but we're not soldiers, and we're certainly not equipped to fight a war. If you sit on this for any longer, Harmony is gonna knock over the blockade like the thing was made of ruttin' twigs and storm the Upperdecks." He unloosed a chuckle, underpinned by just a hint of despair. "I hate to be the one to tell you, ma'am, but getting executed by revolutionaries might severely hurt your chances of winning that third term you've been campaigning for."

"Very amusing." Madeline smiled mirthlessly. "Well, if the situation is as dire and unmanageable as you suggest, then perhaps I should consider deploying the grenadiers to fortify the compound."

He took a cautious step back from the comms terminal, a runaway tram of inevitabilities barreling through his mind. Tensions between the locals and the Phalanx forces stationed at the blockade were at an all-time high. The grenadiers were humanoid killing machines, programmed with not a shred of remorse or humanity. They were commissioned after the mass mutiny attempt of 37 AC, when salvage workers, unhappy about poor pay and rising mortality rates, launched a failed assault on the council chambers in Chennai Plaza.

Mouthians would see the deployment as yet another sign of the Administration's oppression of the region, and the bots would greet even the slightest act of aggression with swift and lethal force. It would be a bloodbath, and Eamon knew he had to delay any possibility of the order being given, whatever it took.

He puffed up his chest, feigning a cavalier bearing. "Let 'Madeline's metal men' swoop in and take all the glory? I don't think so. DMED are on standby and more than ready for the task, ma'am—we'll get this place cleaned up."

"Admirable . . . Update me on your progress, Marshal Wyatt."

The comms terminal luma-caster powered down. The Administrator's projection crystallized and evaporated like liquid vented into space, then there was silence.

THREE

The windscreen of Atherton's swoop returned to its transparent state; through it, Tobias glimpsed the neon glow and wandering searchlights of Capella Promenade. Hypatia circled around before touching down on the valet landing pad, repulsor pads whining as they disengaged. He climbed out of the cabin and was greeted by the enlivening thumping of electronic music and the babble of a pleasantly tipsy crowd. Here was his favorite spot on the *Novara*—a bustling nightlife strip, nestled in a vast cavity in the Canyon's starboard wall. Lined with a plethora of clubs and casinos, this popular leisure destination ran alongside a gorgeous fabricated white sand beach; crystal clear waves rolled up and down the artificial shoreline as excess water spilled over the edge of the Canyon, cascading into the chasm below. Visitors weaved in and out of successions of palm trees, laughing and dancing in vibrant dress without care or concern. If the end of human civilization was nigh, then truly there wasn't a partygoer on Capella Promenade who knew about it.

"I've never seen this place so lively," Atherton said, maneuvering out of the swoop and straightening his suit jacket. "Have you visited recently?"

"Third time this week."

The man shook his head in disappointment. "Really, Tobias. I know you like to treat the family fortune as if it's bottomless, but it certainly won't be if you go and burn it all on private tables and cocktail pitchers."

"Which cost you more, Dad: the swoop or that two-hundred-year-old bottle of firewater?"

Atherton chuckled ruefully, conceding defeat. "I take your point, son."

Strutting side by side below a kaleidoscopic display of luma-cast fireworks, they made their way down the boardwalk. The bars and restaurants they passed were brimming with people, window fronts smeared with heavy condensation generated by the breath and body heat of the reveling masses.

In the distance, Tobias could just make out the sloped roof of the venue in which the induction ceremony was to take place—a replica Kabuki theater house, lovingly built in keeping with *Nihon kenchiku* design, paying homage to the architectural style of a culture long lost. Military personnel gathered outside the foyer with their smartly dressed entourages—the upper echelons of Novarian society, coming together to celebrate the exemplary achievements of the next generation's best and brightest.

Here is my flock, Tobias groused. *The people I am to spend an exhausting evening schmoozing with in a vain attempt to satisfy my father's desire for me to marry off.*

He sighed, subtly shook his head, and wondered whether Caleb had arrived yet . . .

Scanning the crowd, he spotted the familiar shape of his sister. Hazel stood awaiting their arrival beneath rows of spherical paper lanterns hanging from the curved eaves of the theater. She wore her brown, normally flowing hair in a tight military bun, her petite frame hardened by the rigid lines and sharp angles of her pristine uniform. Her facial features, which had once been so hilariously chubby and capable of such goofy contortion, had softened and refined into undeniable natural beauty. In the blink of an eye, the fiery adolescent who once managed to get so wound up by his devilish little-brother antics had transformed into a compassionate, courageous, and dedicated woman—a woman whom the New Terra Space Corps was about to entrust with wielding some of the most expensive military hardware in existence, charging her with the defense of the *Novara*'s airspace.

She spotted them approaching and smiled from ear to ear. His heart swelled like a helium balloon stretched to its very limits. For months now she had been away at flight academy, and only when he saw her face did it occur to him just how much he'd been anticipating a reunion. His father, evidently struck by a similar wave of love and admiration, quickened his pace. The two of them looked utterly ridiculous: lumbering toward her in a half walk, half run, not helped in the least by their restrictive clothing. She hunched her shoulders and let her knees buckle slightly—a mannerism Tobias knew all too well meant she was suppressing laughter.

She greeted them both, wriggling with excitement, and held them close in a forceful and loving embrace.

How long has it been since we were all together like this? he wondered, while his sister took a jab at the color of his shirt. He smiled. *Too damned long.*

How unfair that they should discover this newfound love and respect for each other now, just as life sought to pull them apart. Why, when they'd had countless days to get on each other's nerves, when his unending torment of her felt duty bound, could they not have taken time to show such warmth and appreciation to each other?

Of all forms of wisdom, hindsight is by general consent the least merciful, the most unforgiving, it was once written.

"Look at you, sweetheart," Atherton said, eyes gleaming with pride. "Airman Hazel Edevane of the NTSC. We can all rest a little easier knowing you'll be out there defending us from those vile leeches and their frightful interceptors."

"Thank you, Dad. Although I'm not an airman yet—I'm still just a trainee. And there hasn't been a cohabitor breach of NTU airspace in thirty years, so I doubt I'll be seeing combat any time soon, but I do appreciate the sentiment."

Tobias could tell Hazel's use of the word "cohabitor" had gotten underneath his father's skin; it had gotten underneath his own too.

Call them what they are, Hazel: they're leeches, he wanted to say, but refrained, for now was hardly the time for yet another drawn out political debate. This was a time to commemorate Hazel's superhuman triumphs, to bask together in Edevane greatness . . . or at least it *was*, right up until his father's utterance of those eight dreaded words—the wretched sentence that could bring him down from the highest highs to the absolute depths of his emotional well. A simple string of vowels and consonants with the power to whisk up sorrow and resentment like no other force in existence . . .

"Your mother would be so proud of you."

A winsome smile appeared on Hazel's heart-shaped face, his sister clearly not so adversely affected by the words as he. Not wanting to spoil the moment, he forced down the asteroid-sized lump in his throat and kept his quivering lips tightly sealed.

Why should we care whether we have the blessings of our mother? he pondered angrily. *Why is it expected of us to seek the approval of a leech sympathizer who saw fit to abandon her children at such an early age? Who did nothing, it seems, but cause scandal after scandal, moving mountains of money to antihuman organizations beyond the blockade, endangering her husband's political career, and bringing shame to the Edevane name?*

What memories of his traitorous mother did he have, other than the times when she would return home having been gone for months on end and both he and Hazel would barricade themselves in their rooms while screaming arguments erupted downstairs? How could he be expected to forgive the years of heartache inflicted upon their poor father by the woman's engineering of her own senseless death, when her mutinous actions finally caught up with her in the form of a lethal alien pathogen?

Tobias never mourned the loss of his mother: in truth, he despised her for it, and the idea that he or his sister should be striving to make that woman proud in any capacity whatsoever was, quite frankly, preposterous.

He sensed his indignation had become visible on his tightened face and was determined not to let the moment overshadow the evening. He exhaled steadily to calm himself and brushed his vexations away as the doors to the theater opened and the guests were ushered inside.

The swarm of aristocrats and adulated sons and daughters spilled into the venue, its authentic architectural style extending into its interior. Tobias arrived in a large square space with a stage enclosed by shoji screens. Above, light filtered through a lattice grid of wooden slats supported by rafters exuding the thick musk of timber rot treated with varnish. Interspersed with cylindrical paper lanterns, woven tapestries hung like banners from the ceiling depicting scenes of nature and ancient society in brush strokes of red, black, and green. The theater—a relatively new addition to Capella Promenade— signified a growing desire to be in and around spaces that simulated the lost environments of Earth. Distance, it is said, makes the heart grow fonder, which most Novarians could attest to emphatically, regarding the world they left behind and the one they would never reach. The building was a love letter to a golden era, and while the craftsmanship on display was certainly evocative, for Tobias, the novelty soon wore off, having been spoiled already by his father's historical menagerie back home.

The next hour was a blur spent sauntering about shoulder to shoulder with his two familial companions. Palms red raw and knuckles aching from countless handshakes, Tobias made what little effort he could with the parade of potential suitors rolled out before him, none of whom could he say left any lasting impression whatsoever.

Is this really the best the NTU has to offer? he lamented. *Self-obsessed, insipid airheads without a modicum of decent conversation between them?*

Standing in a huddle with Councilman Colton, discussing the recent spate of violence in the Mouth, Tobias managed to position the man's admittedly beautiful daughter, Esmerelda, so that the entrance to the room lay behind her. Affording a hollow smile, he flicked a glance over her smooth-skinned shoulder, intent on grabbing Caleb the very second she arrived, hoping to catch her before some pompous windbag swept her away for conversation.

"Come now, Miss Edevane," Colton said—a tall man in a pinstripe suit with frail glasses resting precariously on the bridge of his beaked nose. "Surely you cannot be suggesting these attacks should be allowed to go on without consequence. There must be repercussions for the actions of these savages!"

"With all due respect, Councilman," Hazel replied, green eyes sharp and sure, "the aggressions at the blockade are the work of a faction of extremists who do *not* represent the greater cohabitor population. Of course, tighter security at the blockade transfer checkpoint is critical for public safety, but to persecute an entire species for the crimes of a few would be unjust *and* unethical."

"Even still, if the leeches refuse to indemnify the Union for damages, then should they not at the very least be expected to take responsibility for the violence?"

"No more than any of us here should be expected to accept liability for the atrocities committed by Humanity First, or any of the other rising human supremacist vigilante groups."

Tobias's father cleared his throat. "*Allegedly* committed by Humanity First. Councilman Colton and I have close friends involved with that particular organization, darling. I would urge you to take care with such accusations."

Colton harrumphed. "Quite the social activist you're raising here, Atherton. Let's hope she doesn't go the way of her mother, eh?"

An intensely uncomfortable silence followed—a feculent smog ladening the air.

That's the second mention of her tonight, Tobias thought. *No matter how hard I try, I will never escape that treasonous woman and her damning legacy.*

"My apologies, Atherton," Colton said, shamefaced. "That may have been in poor taste."

Atherton smiled thinly. "Quite alright."

"What about you, Tobias?" Esmerelda chirped up—an obvious effort to redirect the conversation. "I believe some ACS students are required to undertake vocational experience at the Phalanx compound in the Mouth. Do you have any plans to go in the near future?"

Tobias sneered, growing weary of the inane and incessant questioning. He almost chose not to answer at all, but instead decided to use the opportunity to prove to the girl's imperious father how little an impact the "slip-up" regarding his mother had had on him.

"Not even the threat of expulsion from the Academy could persuade me to set foot in that rancid, festering favela. The last time an Edevane ventured beyond the blockade, she was ravaged from the inside out by a leech virus. I have absolutely zero plans of meeting that same fate myself."

Hazel furrowed her brow and tightened her posture. He wasn't sure if it was disapproval at the unabashed contempt he'd shown toward their deceased mother or disconcertment over the growing divergence of their political inclinations. He couldn't say it wasn't impressive, the way she stood her ground and managed to wrangle the discussion, even if her opinions on the subject were dangerously naive.

Just then, the moment Tobias had been anticipating finally arrived. Wearing a black sleeveless charmeuse gown that clung provocatively to her slender physique, Caleb entered the room, her lustrous coppery hair like an avalanche of fire resting on bare shoulders. Fastened to her left wrist, a luma bracelet cast white ivy vines creeping up her arm—a tattoo inked with pure light, scintillating in the crystal droplets of her silver earrings. A susurration of envy and desire arose from the throng as all eyes fell on the girl in the black dress.

Tobias excused himself from conversation, leaving his father to grandstand about the dangers and pitfalls of multispecies society, before making his way through the crowd toward Caleb.

"I'm not used to seeing you out of ACS uniform," he said, making his swaggering approach. "I almost didn't recognize you."

"I know . . . I hardly ever get dressed up like this. I look absolutely ridiculous, don't I?" She tugged awkwardly at her gown, endearingly oblivious to just how radiant she really was.

"Outrageous," he teased. "Is it just you by yourself tonight? I was expecting to see Jade hanging off your arm." He glanced around the room, pretending to search for Caleb's fiancée, using the break in eye contact to disguise his glee at finding Miss Tanaka quite absent.

Caleb shook her head solemnly. "Phalanx have their hands full at the moment with all the trouble going on at the blockade. They're pretty light on coverage, so they've started pulling off-duty enforcers to help out at the compound until things die down a little." Sadness pulled at her face. "I hate it when she gets stationed in the Mouth. It makes me sick to my stomach with worry. I can't imagine how perilous things must be over there."

A flurry of guilt tore through him. *Jade Tanaka is risking her life defending NTU sovereignty and here you are trying to shark her fiancée. Go and take a cold shower, you despicable creep.*

He shook his head in repressed self-abhorrence, then placed a reassuring hand on the small of her back, showing a heartfelt smile.

"I know it's pointless telling you not to worry, but Jade is as tough as they come. Remember, she manages to keep you in check, so I think it's safe to assume she can handle whatever the leeches throw at her. Just you wait, she'll be back, boring us to death with uneventful war stories before you know it."

Caleb breathed a sigh of relief. Tobias had, once again, demonstrated his innate ability to summon the precise combination of words to appease her fraught mind.

"Anyway." She flicked a hand to cordially dispel the unpleasantness. "How's the evening been going so far? Have you been holding your own without me around to back you up?"

He scanned the theater with contemptuous eyes. "My infernal father is trying his hardest to get me paired off with one of these vapid nonentities. Honestly, the man is relentless sometimes."

"Oh, he's harmless compared to some of the alligators in *this* swamp. I see Esmerelda Colton is here. Have you tried speaking to her?"

"Don't you start as well! Tell me I'm being overparticular, but I'd like to court somebody with at least a little conversational finesse. I've never known polite chitchat to turn so abruptly into an interrogation."

She chuckled. "You're being overparticular."

A volley of furious footsteps came pounding from across the theater, leather soles of expensive shoes screaming on the lacquered floor.

Dammit, man. Am I not allowed even a moment alone with her?

"Why, if it isn't Miss Caleb Callaghan," Atherton bellowed. "How beautiful you look tonight! Simply glowing, almost incandescent!"

"That's very kind of you to say, Councilman Edevane." Caleb greeted the man with a peck on the cheek as he flicked Tobias a fierce look of admonishment before slipping into a more congenial demeanor.

"I came to ask if you would pass along a message of thanks to your betrothed for me. I've been informed Jade's unit was recently tasked with reinforcing the transfer checkpoint at the blockade. How incredibly selfless and courageous it is of her to do the work she does. That girl's a true Novarian hero. Wouldn't you agree, Tobias?"

Tobias swallowed nervously. "Wholeheartedly."

"I'll make sure she knows you're both keeping her in your thoughts," Caleb said. "I just wish I could stop worrying about her so much. The District of the Mouth is such a treacherous place; I just hate to think of how vulnerable she is."

"Treacherous indeed." Atherton pursed his lips. "More so every day, it would seem. But since the mutineers living sternside of the blockade are so hell-bent on maintaining their little interspecies melting pot, I'm afraid they must accept these deplorable acts of violence as a simple fact of life. It's just a crying shame that good people like Jade Tanaka are the ones being made to foot the bill."

He moved in closer, speaking in a quiet and clandestine tone. "I'll ask both of you to keep this to yourselves, but I believe Administrator Vargos may be readying to deploy the grenadiers. If that's the case, I imagine Jade and all the other enforcers stationed at the Phalanx compound will soon be relieved of their duties and we can leave dealing with the violent rabble to the metal men."

Tobias turned his stare to the android presently serving hors d'oeuvres by the buffet table: a faceless nanocarbon skeleton encased in titanium armor plating with wreaths of hydraulics cables connecting its hulking limbs—one of several thousand mechanized infantry units used by the Administration to quell dissension and deter mass mutiny. Like many older models, this one had been decommissioned and reprogrammed for leisure and manual labor, although the electric-pink bowtie fastened around its neck did little to soften its fearsome appearance. He smiled grimly, envisioning the moment the hordes of leeches making trouble at the checkpoint found themselves face to face with a battle-hardened garrison of mechanized infantry.

"That's wonderful news," Caleb said, her manner brightening in an instant. "Although it does make me wonder why the Administrator has waited until now to deploy them."

Atherton sighed. "Well, some of our more liberal peers would probably deem it a little heavy-handed and unethical. But as they say: desperate times call for desperate measures."

The induction ceremony finally began. Hazel and her fellow trainees ascended onto the stage and waited in rigid formation as Admiral Coombs congratulated them one by one, hanging engraved medallions around their necks. Having forgotten his daughter's earlier transgressions, Tobias's father stood beside him, glowing with pride. The man reached over and gave his shoulder a firm, appreciative squeeze—a relatively rare moment of tenderness, but one that was certainly not unwelcomed. Both father and son watched in complete adoration as Hazel received her wings while the admiral began a grand speech, decreeing the fine individuals standing before him "the new protectors of the human remnant."

Then, a moment of disruption rippled through the crowd. Electronic tones could be heard chirping from jacket pockets and clutch bags. Ceremony attendees began removing their feathers, their shared looks of concern highlighted red by the security alert flashing synchronously on their screens. Tobias didn't know what was transpiring, but from the growing disquiet, he could only deduce that it was something terrible.

He didn't think to check his own feather because he was distracted by the sudden realization that Caleb was nowhere to be seen—despite standing next to him only a moment ago, she had now completely vanished. Leaving his father looking somewhat perturbed, he exited the theater in search of her. Outside, the carousing masses had been similarly captivated by their personal devices; people stopped dead in their tracks as an unnerving quiet descended on the Promenade.

On a nearby landing pad, he found Caleb frantically trying to hail a swoop from a terminal, heels clutched in shaking hands with mascara tears streaming down her reddened face. Tobias heard his feather chime—a notification that the threat level had increased. He didn't need to check the details of the alert to know that Jade Tanaka was dead.

FOUR

till reeling from the call with Vargos, Eamon collapsed in his seat, head cradled in his clasped hands. His dour mood was instantly alleviated, however, when the door swung open and his two favorite DMED staffers tumbled into the office. The first came bounding toward him on four legs, an excited whirlwind of scruffy brindle fur with dopey eyes perched over a handsome snout.

He'd only been in his new position as marshal a few months when a cohab crept into the reception area of the precinct house carrying a bundle of rags in its long, chitin-plated arms. He recalled how terrified it looked, as if unsure whether surrendering a mangey, half-starved puppy to the authorities was a punishable offense. It always struck him as peculiar how such formidable specimens could be so very fearful of their comparably puny primate neighbors. Even a juvenile cohab would have little trouble crushing a man's skull with their bare paws, and yet, the fearsome insectoids were generally very cautious around humans.

He recalled the cohab tenderly handing over aer emaciated cargo, taking great care not to interrupt its slumber before vanishing. With no shelters or adoption centers available, Eamon and his deputies had no choice but to accept the stray and take him in as one of their own. DMED's new fluffball mascot was given the name Abraham, paying homage to the department's previous marshal—a man who learned the hard way just how much interference Drexen would tolerate in his affairs before drawing a bloody line in the sand . . .

Abe launched into Eamon's lap, his manic tail whipping through the air like a conductor's baton.

"Alright, alright. Get off me!" He jostled to push the adoring mutt away, struggling to escape the frantic tongue and hot, smelly breath lapping at his stubble-encrusted jawline.

"I keep tellin' ya to quit locking him out like that when you're taking calls. It gets him all worked up." Deputy Jyn Sato—a fearless, vivacious Mouth native in her early thirties with wicked smarts and a mean attitude—stormed into the office. Dressed as casually as ever, she sported tight denim jeans and a white button-down shirt, her long jet-black ponytail resting on the breastplate of her Kevlar vest.

Finally managing to settle Abraham, Eamon replied, "I can't have him in the office when I'm on the caster to Vargos. Boy gets his hackles raised at the mere projection of the woman."

Jyn planted herself on the desk beside him, leaning over to ruffle the dog's ears affectionately. "Just keeping us safe from the big bad bureaucrats, aren't ya, boy?" she cooed in soft but husky tones.

Eamon caught himself staring again—an awful habit he was admittedly still in the process of trying to kick. They were just so damned striking, though—those blackish-purple veins crawling up her arms and neck, resembling thunderbolts frozen under her medium-tan skin, discolored vessels radiating like shattered glass in an intricate pattern below her wide, upturned eyes.

He wasn't one to pry into someone's past—she'd never mentioned the affliction before, so he guessed she had no desire for it to be brought up in conversation . . . Of course, that didn't mean he couldn't use his finely tuned powers of deduction to hazard a good guess. He'd been in the Mouth long enough to know that Jyn's vascular condition was likely the result of her being "baptized in the endless night," which meant that at some point she'd been with that sect of crazy space worshippers, the Church of the Abyss. They were a group of zealots who believed a bunch of sanctimonious crap about the Collision being divine punishment for the sins of humanity, and that Pasture was a "New Mecca" that could only be reached through a lifetime of penance and prayer.

Most airlocks sternside of the blockade that were still functional had since been converted into places of worship. It was here that young followers would be made to undergo a barbaric rite of affirmation—bound in a pressure chamber and exposed to the void, brought back from that dark precipice with only seconds to spare before they succumbed to asphyxiation. Like Jyn, those who survived the ceremony would forever bear the scars—a permanent manifestation of their devotion to the so-called Divine Abyss. Despite proudly wearing its mark, Jyn's faith—or lack thereof—was something she had never discussed, which caused Eamon to wonder whether she had since disavowed her beliefs. The Church of the Abyss was a cult—notoriously difficult to renounce. Emotional abuse was deeply ingrained in the tenets of the religion, and those who managed to escape could expect to be ostracized by any friends and family they left behind. It was a sore spot for her; that much was obvious. While he'd never press her on the subject, he hoped someday she would deem him worthy of confiding in.

Indeed, there were a number of question marks hanging over Jyn's past. She was relatively green on the force and wasn't subjected to anywhere near the same level of vetting and evaluation that an average DMED deputy would endure. Her expedited progression through the ranks was thanks in part to the invaluable set of skills she possessed. With the cohabitors showing a complete disinterest—or inability—in spoken or written language, understanding one another had been historically difficult. *Not difficult: impossible.* Jyn, however, was a cipher—a special breed born with the ability to tap into the cohabs' extrasensory means of communication. He didn't fully understand the mechanics of her abilities—only that it meant his department finally had a method of conversing with the nonhuman residents living in the district, which made her an indispensable member of the team.

"You get another grilling, boss?" she asked, her attention still mainly focused on the heavily panting Abraham.

Eamon rubbed the back of his neck. "More like a deep fry."

"I'm sure it wasn't all that bad. C'mon, let's hear the bullet points."

He sighed, sitting back in his seat.

"Well . . . it doesn't look like we're getting any more support in the fight against Harmony. Not unless we want the grennies marching into the Mouth and getting folks hot under the collar."

Jyn shrugged. "We don't need any extra support. Like I keep telling ya, the Composer doesn't have a problem with DMED as long as we stay out of her way. She wants to keep banging on the Administrator's door? I say we let her have at it."

"That better be a joke, Deputy." He stood up, collected his Chevesic MK2 machine pistol from the desktop and slid the weapon into his shoulder holster. He kept it loaded with armor-piercing rounds designed to penetrate thoracic carapaces. Thankfully, there hadn't been a situation yet in which the special ammo had been necessary.

Jyn cast him a troubled look. "Yup. Although not a particularly funny one, I gather. You got a face on like you've been chewin' a wasp."

"I know you're a big cohab-rights advocate, Jyn, but careful you don't go siding with the terrorists."

She tutted. "Jeez . . . Vargos did a real number on you this time, huh?"

He angrily grabbed his fur-collared aviator jacket from the back of his seat and swung it over his shoulders—a gift for his thirty-eighth birthday from the ex-wife. The marriage might have gone down in flames, but the coat still fit perfectly.

"I'm sorry . . . It's just so damned frustrating," he conceded. "You'd think with a victim as high profile as Anaya Lahiri, the higher-ups would be expecting us to keep our nose to the grindstone on this one. All the Administrator wants is the first cohab we can pull off the street thrown into a holding cell so she can get her mug shot for the evening broadcast. She's got no interest in prosecuting the real killer whatsoever."

Jyn's snide expression melted like wax as the gravity of the situation dawned on her.

"Look," Eamon said, dropping his shoulders in a show of resignation. "I know you and Keller have been putting the work in already, but if we don't get this right, Phalanx are gonna steamroll the investigation and some poor bug'll end up paying for the department's incompetence with their freedom, or perhaps even their life."

She nodded, visibly imbued with new resolve. "Where do you need me, boss?"

"I'm not doubting your thoroughness here, but there must be something we overlooked. I want you knocking on doors in the Cohabitor Ghetto ASAP. We need some answers from the locals—see if we can't figure out what in the Abyss Miss Lahiri was doing out there in the first place."

"Count on it," she asserted, watching as he marched to a storage locker to retrieve Abraham's ballistic vest.

"You taking my boy somewhere?"

"We're headed bowside," Eamon confirmed, struggling to fasten the harness around Abraham as he hopped and wriggled in excitement. "Got business with a weld and salvage captain down at the docks of Lower Amidships."

"You've mentioned her before. Holloway, right? Captain's an old balaener-class hauler?"

"The very same. Holloway can be a real hard-ass. I'm not sure what she wants to discuss, but I know it's got something to do with Drexen, so I don't expect it'll be a particularly pleasant conversation. I'm hoping bringing this heartthrob along will help soften her up a little."

"You be careful with my best bud there, Wyatt. You know what folks think of you around those parts. Don't go antagonizing nobody."

He stopped in the doorway, turned with a smug grin. "Hey, it's me we're talking about."

The department had a few modern cruisers in its fleet—sleek pursuit models with Hypatia integration and the latest in fission-injection tech under the hood. Eamon didn't care all that much about specifications or high performance; when he headed out on duty, he preferred to take the old prowler. DMED's longest-serving patrol vehicle cut a fearsome silhouette—an armored swoop with an ultramarine body, bashed to hell after decades of operation. Only half of its emergency light bar still worked, and the PA system was in a similar state of disrepair. The old girl tended to strafe to the left at high altitudes, and one day the frequent drive core stalls would almost certainly be the death of him. Anyone who asked why he was so fond of this old wreck would get the same answer: that the old-school gimbal-mounted repulsor pads provided increased maneuverability essential for navigating the narrow alleyways in tightly packed neighborhoods like the Warrens. Truthfully, though, there was something comforting about sinking into the threadbare nylon upholstery and soaking in the smoke-stained vinyl interior. It felt like sitting in a piece of history—riding alongside every marshal who had served before him and submerging himself in their collective knowledge and experience.

I wonder if any of you lot had this much trouble . . . Could sure do with the advice of a few grizzled veterans right about now.

Vectoring toward the blockade, he pulled back on the flight wheel, sending the prowler soaring high above the district, the cityscape below resembling the coral reefs of Earth's now evaporated oceans, fields of chaotic urban growth completely devoid of rhyme or reason in construction. The main residential block appeared as a towering monolith, climbing from the rusted rooftops of the encompassing slums known as the Copper Swathes. Beyond, a strange conglomeration of bubbling domes and twisted spires marked the Cohabitor Ghetto, which funneled like the head of a river, trailing up to the yawning orifice in the *Devourer's* exterior—a swirling vortex of sharpened teeth spewing reels of conduits from its gullet, the gaping machinery responsible for carving out the vast cavity wherein the district was situated.

Looking forward, the staggering edifice of the blockade dominated the view through the windscreen. An immense impenetrable wall patched together from recycled hull metal, the structure spanned the width of the Mouth, looming like a dark, oppressive storm front. The natives regarded it as an inescapable symbol of their subjugation, for there was no corner of the district from which it could not be seen. Always in its shadow, there was no respite from the reality of their internment.

His eyes fell to the Phalanx compound—a huddle of prefabricated buildings encircled by a perimeter of concrete barricades, where Phalanx enforcers in tactical gear held back a surging mass of protesters and hopeful immigrants. Those fortunate enough to have been granted transfer papers were being forcefully extracted from the crowd and ushered up a flight of low steps toward the checkpoint—a tunnel through the blockade fronted by a succession of walk-through security scanners.

Get out while you still can, folks, he thought. *When the grennies lock this place down, there'll be no escape for any of us.*

Abraham growled softly at sudden movement ahead. Two sentry turrets, positioned on either side of Antaeus Gateway, sprang to life in response to the approaching prowler. Yellow lights pulsated on their primitive rotating gun barrels while an anonymous pencil pusher, probably sitting in a comfortable Quarterdeck office, checked over Eamon's credentials.

"Do they seem extra tetchy to you today?" he asked Abe, who barked his response.

After a suspenseful moment, the sentry lights switched to green; the turrets stood down. The gateway's blast doors crawled open, accompanied by a calamitous orchestra of hidden gearwork erupting from inside the blockade wall. A second tunnel revealed itself, this one large enough for vehicular egress. Eamon pushed the throttle and sailed the prowler through the aperture, which was aglow with ultraviolet light, illuminating Abraham's toothy grin to hilarious effect. The end of the tunnel appeared as a gradually widening spyhole, through which could be seen the vast access channel known as the Canyon—extending for a dozen or so kilometers ahead, draped in a tapestry of imitation twilight and bespeckled by the red and white sequins of a thousand dashing, darting swoops.

It had been some time since Eamon had ventured bowside of the blockade. The wards of Lower Amidships had been home for most of his years, but there was something uncannily strange about coming back. When the top brass forced him out of the GEA and reassigned him to the Mouth, he left so much behind: his career, his marriage, his whole damn life. Returning felt like wearing someone else's clothes or slipping back into a coat of shed skin—he could visualize his past self hitting up the dive bars in Cendre Vale or leading a briefing in the busy bullpen of the Halvorsen Commons precinct house. Now, he felt like no more than an empty husk of the man in his mind's eye. That steely-eyed straight shooter with a fire in his belly was beaten to a bloody pulp, cast aside by an establishment that would rather see a good enforcer strung up than confront its own problems with systemic interspecies violence.

Back in the old stomping ground, he silently remarked. *Weird that I don't miss it, not even in the slightest . . . Guess it's hard getting homesick when home gets sick of you.*

* * *

The docks of Lower Amidships were a vibrant hub of commerce located in a massive starboard hangar. From here, freighters transported large quantities of goods to regions of the *Novara* that were inaccessible via the Canyon. And salvage outfits scouring the nebula of drifting wreckage known as the Debris Belt returned to unload their haul, selling useful scrap to traders and offering up recovered tech to the Administration authorities for paid requisition.

To the untrained eye, it was honest blue-collar work—good folks making ends meet with nothing but graft and gristle. Unfortunately, having put more crooked captains away for glow trafficking and illegal salvage in the last decade than he cared to count, Eamon knew all too well the rat's nest this place really was—one where most of the rats inhabiting it would probably like to see him get zeroed in the worst possible way. His persona non grata status was about more than just his arrest record, courtesy of his renown as the cop who threw his own partner under the barge as well.

There was a time when getting called a leech sympathizer or a traitor was the worst of the backlash he could expect coming to a neighborhood like this. After all, he had been Phalanx, which meant no matter how much somebody might have wanted to put the hurt on him, he was downright untouchable. Now, he wasn't so sure if his authority as DMED marshal would even be recognized, much less grant him those same privileges . . .

Setting down the prowler in a parking bay on the main concourse, he leaned over to double-check the straps on his companion's bulletproof vest, wishing like hell he'd brought his own.

Abe jumped out as soon as the passenger-side door swung open and bolted for the nearest docking bay. Climbing out of the prowler, Eamon glanced over to find the pup sniffing at the landing clamps berthing a pugnator-class freighter—possibly the ugliest damn ship ever brought into existence, its stubby, rotund nose cone and asymmetrically positioned forward thrusters creating the profile of a fat, grimacing face.

The vessel's name was painted on the side of its unwieldy fuselage.

"*The Segregator*," he read aloud, sneering in disgust. Written in ornate calligraphy, it appeared alongside the insignia of Humanity First—seven white rings interlinked against a background of cobalt blue, a symbol once used by the founding nations of the NTU to represent Earth, commandeered two centuries later by a bunch of intolerant dirtbags with too much time on their hands and syn-beer in their systems.

It wasn't long ago that supporting the group was considered a taboo—generally looked down upon and, if done, played very close to one's chest. But at a time when attitudes of human supremacy were becoming more than just a political opinion, these asinine reprobates were flying the colors on their ships, flaunting their ignorance like sports hooligans belligerently waving the banner of their favorite casterblade team.

He heard the gentle trickling of liquid and glanced down to find Abe relieving himself on the landing gear of the vulgarly named freighter. Fortunately, none of the ship's crew were around to witness the act of unapologetic defilation. He'd promised Jyn he wouldn't antagonize the locals, but that didn't mean he wasn't prepared to throw fists at anyone who might try to hurt Abraham.

"Good boy."

The pair headed past rows of docking bays housing ships of every size and class in the fleet. Those that weren't receiving maintenance were being loaded up with cargo by the framework of cranes suspended from the ceiling. Captains gathered with their crews in the shadows of their sleeping behemoths. The stench of engine fumes permeated the air, stinging the eyes and burning the nostrils, but not nearly so noxious as the venom in the glares of those who recognized him. He nodded in acknowledgment at a group of unscrupulous onlookers who scrambled to pocket evidence of their dirty dealings, watching him go with baleful expressions.

Relax, guys. It ain't you I'm here for.

The bar in which he was set to meet Captain Holloway lurked in a dingy alcove at the far end of the hangar. The Weary Navigator was the name of the place—a dimly lit hovel ideal for those who preferred to keep themselves and their business out of the limelight. A place for swapping overembellished war stories, gambling away the last of one's nunits, and picking up odd jobs, especially those too hot to be listed on the bulletin board.

Abraham skulked obediently between Eamon's legs as he pushed through a set of double doors. The joint was quiet—empty, in fact, save for one other patron occupying a booth by the far wall. Eamon took a stool by the knife-etched bar top, where billiard lights hung low and accentuated the silver wisps of cigarette smoke wreathing in the stale air. A single refreshment dispenser stood in lieu of an attendant—probably installed by the establishment's exasperated owners, sick and tired of receiving abuse from drunk and disorderly ship rabble. From the machine, he retrieved a bottle of freshly pressed cider and a ration of synthetic meat jerky. He figured it might be a while before Holloway showed up and gauged his surroundings to be safe enough to kick back a little.

"Don't snap now, you hear?" he said, ripping open the packet as Abe sat at his feet, hungrily licking his black, leathery chops.

"If you wolf down too much of this shit you're gonna start to get real pudgy. Believe you me."

The all too familiar jingle of the NTNN broadcast sounded from a panel in the corner of the room. A reporter appeared on-screen while a flurry of infographics scurried around her like pixelated insects.

"Welcome back to the NTNN. Our top story tonight . . ."

"Panel off!" Eamon snapped, quickly silencing the feed. He twisted the lid off his cider and took a long swig, eager to soothe the sudden bout of anger broiling in his stomach with sweet liquid relaxant. It wasn't the jingle that had triggered the adverse reaction, nor the image of the peroxide blonde with the freakishly wide smile. Really, he couldn't stand to endure even a second of the vitriolic nonsense that was undoubtedly about to follow. He'd come to understand the network as a cancer, eating away at Novarian society. More and more its purpose seemed to be to divide and galvanize people, to stoke the fires of their fear and ignorance. With every news cycle came the arrival of some new tragedy or scandal that would be heavily dramatized, completely misinformed, and expertly crafted to vilify the inhabitants of the Mouth. The most devoted of viewers were a scared and gullible breed: eyes glued to screens day in, day out, their appetite for outrage wholly insatiable, their loathing of nonhuman people blind and boundless. It was no wonder groups like Humanity First were gaining so much momentum when the only source of current information was basically a recruitment ad.

He shook his head to dispel his growing irritation, managing to enjoy a moment of peace before the guy sitting in the booth decided to open his mouth.

"Hey, pal! I was watching that."

Eamon swiveled around on his stool to face the stranger—a broad-shouldered, barrel-chested brute of a man with a shaved head and a long wiry goatee. He wore a denim jacket stained with Abyss knows what over a zipped-down jumpsuit. On his breast pocket were stitched two very familiar words: *The Segregator.*

"Is that so?" Eamon took a candid swig. "Well, too much of it'll rot your brain, friend. It's good to switch off from time to time. Consider it a favor."

The stranger stood up suddenly, beer bottles clinking as his gut knocked the table.

"Wait a sec . . . don't I know you?"

Eamon felt his insides plummet.

Here we go.

He glanced down at Abraham, who, sensing the beginnings of an altercation, had begun to maneuver himself between the legs of his stool. *Sorry, bud.*

"Yeah . . . I recognize you," the stranger said, pointing a grubby finger. "You're that leech-sympathizin' marshal from the Mouth, aren't ya? That dirty snitch who got those good Phalanx cops fired."

He tried to fight back the welter of distressing imagery that followed, but no amount of concentration could stave off the mental echoes of that terrible night: a flash of blood on bootheel, the head of a young cohabitor reduced to purple goddamn puree; that look of horrid satisfaction on his partner's face as he beat the living spit out of the suspect's cipher, the kid's grief as raw and intense as any Eamon had witnessed before. Not even the strongest firewater on the *Novara* could help wipe way those wretched memories. They were ingrained in his psyche like a ball and chain—one he'd lug around with him for the rest of his days.

"There wasn't anything good about them."

The stranger took a few steps forward, the bulbous contours of his thuggish face harshened by the fluorescence of the billiard lights. Up close, he looked even uglier than his ship.

"Good, honest folks—Novarian heroes—losing their jobs for doing exactly what they were supposed to be doing: defending us from the leeches. You ought to be ashamed of yourself."

"Oh, I'm ashamed alright." He let slip a rueful snicker, took another swig. "Ashamed of my Nov-Net search history, ashamed I don't call my mother as much as I probably should." He stood up, turned to put himself in a less vulnerable position. "But putting those murderous bastards out of commission and making sure they *never* worked in law enforcement again? No . . . I ain't ashamed of that."

Finally finding his courage, Abraham crept from out of cover, hackles raised, baring his teeth. The brute took another step forward, setting threatening eyes on the snarling dog.

"Why don't you take this mange-ridden vermin and piss off back to that shithole you crawled out of. You're lucky you're a cop—else I'd blow your traitorous head off your damned shoulders right here, right now."

Eamon removed his Chevesic from its holster and slammed it down on the bar top. "I've got no jurisdiction here, pal, so if you wanna make something of it, you better be quick on the draw. I got no problems putting holes in a mouth-breather like you."

Said mouth-breather smiled in an I-like-your-spunk-but-I'm-still-gonna-kill-you kind of way. "It's gonna tickle me to see you try," he said, his fat hand hovering over his own holstered firearm—a snub-nose Magnum, probably loaded with explosive-tip rounds of obscenely high caliber. If Eamon hesitated, his brains would be up on the wall among the collage of beer coasters and sports memorabilia.

Just then, he heard the double doors behind him swing open. He didn't dare break eye contact, knowing the second or two it would take to check who had entered would be all his opponent needed to riddle him with lead.

"Jonah Sinclair. Are you bothering this nice man?" a woman, whose voice Eamon recognized immediately, asked from over his shoulder. Abraham's tail began tapping the leg of his stool rhythmically, the dog seemingly disarmed by the new arrival.

"Just a spirited discussion between me and my new friend here, Hollo-way." Jonah let his guard down and moved his hand away from his Magnum. "Is this Mouth cop with you?"

Eamon whipped his head around and felt a surge of relief. Delilah Hol-loway, captain of the *Assurance*, stood by the doorway, wearing her signature long-tail duster coat, a gun-belt strapped with concussion rounds for the break-action repeater resting on her shoulder. Partially obscured by unruly curls of black, billowing hair, her brown, wrathful eyes were trained on Jonah, who shriveled in response to her next words.

"I've got business with Marshal Wyatt. Might be best if you finish up your drink and leave us to it."

"I was just leaving, Delilah. No need for a fuss." Jonah hastened to the door and fled, but not without bidding Eamon farewell with a forceful shoulder barge.

Exhaling through pursed lips, Eamon reholstered his Chevesic and slumped back onto his stool.

"Better late than never, I suppose. A few seconds more and you might have been doing business with a corpse."

FIVE

amon had always regarded Delilah Holloway as something of an enigma. Despite carrying herself like an upstanding citizen of the NTU with all the intellect and diplomacy of somebody educated up in Quarterdeck, she seemed to have done her very best to disassociate herself from her obviously wealthy background. Captaining an old balaener-class hauler with a ragtag crew of rejects and misfits, she'd taken to dressing like a brigand and worked hard, it seemed, to surround herself with naught but scoundrels, rubbing shoulders with some of the most unsavory characters bowside of the blockade. Even in the short space of time since getting her wings, she had managed to garner the respect of most of her peers—some in the docks even seemed a mite fearful of her. Eamon guessed it was all down to that commanding presence of hers—an air of regal authority that made every word that fell from her lips sound like poetry recited by a drill sergeant, irresistible and overpowering to the weak-minded.

Her ship, the *Assurance*, was outfitted first and foremost for salvage: equipped with a massive nanofiber net that was used to reel in gulping mouthfuls of scrap metal, adrift out there in the Debris Belt. She had a whip-smart salvage specialist on her crew with an aptitude for finding and extracting coveted tech, giving her an edge at digging up those hidden nuggets that most salvage outfits tended to overlook. But instead of surrendering her yield to the port authorities, as was mandated by the Administration, Delilah would load up a cargo barge with a couple tons of illicit salvage, then smuggle it into the Mouth via Antaeus Gateway to be sold on the black market. Sure, she may have been one of the more principled ship captains Eamon had regular dealings with, but, in truth, she was just as crooked as the company she kept. He wouldn't normally have given the shameless plunderer the time of day were it not for the second, and perhaps most critical, of her ship's commissioned roles . . . The *Assurance* doubled as a welding vessel, the very last in the fleet. The first thing Delilah did after sinking her inheritance into that old boat was stick a magma cannon to the underside of her fuselage. The scrap she retrieved from the belt that wasn't worth jettisoning into space was melted down into slag and fired at the *Novara*'s external shielding to reinforce the deteriorating hull surrounding the Mouth, where the *Devourer* had its claws dug in deepest. The job was tedious, dangerous, and one of the worst commissions one could take on as a skipper from a payment perspective. But Delilah wasn't stupid—she had her reasons, and though she kept them to herself, he suspected they were deeply personal . . .

The Administration, in all its bullheaded negligence, had seen fit to wash its hands of everything beyond NTU sovereignty, abdicating itself of the responsibility of the ninety thousand souls currently living under the threat of cataclysmic hull collapse. Delilah's ship was the only preventative measure in place between the folks in the Mouth and the merciless black, so he was more than happy turning a blind eye to her *less honorable pursuits* if it meant keeping her skyborne.

Bringing Abraham to the rendezvous hadn't quite had the effect he had hoped it would. The mutt was getting plenty of fussing, lying belly up, tongue hanging from his chops and legs kicking the air, but the captain's bearing was just as stern as ever.

"Are you trying to get yourself zeroed?" she asked, crouched down and rubbing Abe's stomach, her neck craned upwards, symmetrical features contorted in annoyance. "One of these days you're gonna pick a fight that I won't be there to bail you out of. Don't think these roughnecks won't take the opportunity to gut you like a fish, just because you used to be Phalanx."

"That Jonah guy looked at Abe funny!" Eamon protested, retrieving another cider for himself from the dispenser and a sweet tea for the captain. He would have joked that she was already sweet enough if he didn't think it would get him socked in the mouth.

"Pudgy bastard called him 'mange-ridden vermin.' Can you believe that? You know, one of these days you're gonna tell me how it is you have all these meatheads wrapped around your little finger."

"I'm serious, Wyatt," she groused, taking the booth farthest from the one Jonah Sinclair had been fumigating. "By bowling into the docks and behaving exactly like the self-righteous hothead they all think you are, you're putting *my* reputation on the line too. It suits us both nicely that we can do business together and I don't want that to change, but not if it means jeopardizing my status with the other ship captains or you suffering grievous bodily harm."

"I guess it wouldn't kill me to let things slide from time to time." He slumped onto the bench opposite her, perplexed at feeling simultaneously nurtured *and* reprimanded.

"It's not all your fault." She sighed, stirred her tea absentmindedly.

"Maybe going forward we should agree to meet in the Mouth: that way I don't get seen with a rat and you don't risk getting exterminated like one."

"Call Abe a rat again and see what happens, Holloway." He took a swig and watched as the dog jumped onto her bench and curled up next to her. "Meeting sternside ain't gonna happen. Phalanx are especially jittery right now, thanks to all the shit going on at the compound. They're cranking security up to eleven. Hell, even me and Abe almost got chewed up by those sentry turrets on the way here. I think getting through the blockade might be tougher for you than it has been previously."

"Under normal circumstances, I'd be inclined to agree, but this isn't your average smuggling run we're talking about here." She shifted in her seat uncomfortably, as if readying to disclose something sensitive and feeling apprehensive of how he would react. "We're taking on commissioned work. Specifically, we've been contracted to extract three industrial hydro-ionizers from the outer reaches of the Debris Belt and deliver them to a location in the Mouth."

"Hydro-ionizers? They sound big, Delilah. Big things tend to attract attention."

"Well, they aren't small fry, that's for sure. But then again, neither is our contact. This guy has the connections to make sure we won't have any trouble getting the shipment through Antaeus Gateway."

He stared for a moment, bemused. "OK . . . so what exactly do you need from me then?"

She blew her tea, took a cautious sip. "Let's just say you and your department might have something of a personal vendetta against our new employer, and I thought it best for you to hear the news of our partnership from me first."

"Is that so?"

"I need this job to go as smoothly as possible, Wyatt. I just want some assurances that you're gonna be able to put bad blood aside and do your part in making sure there won't be any DMED interference once the merchandise is through the blockade."

Eamon took a moment to mull over the possible identity of this mysterious heavyweight, the one with whom he supposedly had a score to settle. Watching Abraham rummaging under the captain's hand for a scratch between the eyes, the marshal the mutt had been named in remembrance of entered his mind. Then the penny dropped.

"So . . . you finally got yourself on the Governor's payroll, huh?"

Delilah's brown eyes were glistening and steady, charged with trepidation. She leaned forward, clasping her hands around her tea, narrowing her shoulders. "He isn't messing around, Wyatt. If the retainer he already paid us is anything to go by, I'm gonna be able to fuel the *Assurance* for the next six months. Think about it: we finally get to make some real nunits, and you won't have to worry about hull ruptures for the foreseeable future. It's a win-win situation."

Eamon paused, picking at the label on his bottle. "I'm sorry, but there's no such thing as a win-win situation when it comes to dealing with Vidalia Drexen. Trust me: he's the only one who ever comes out on top—the rest of us inevitably lose." He shook his head, a swell of dejection rising in his chest that almost felt like he was being broken up with. "I don't get it . . . I thought we had a good thing going? It doesn't make a lick of sense why you'd wanna go and complicate our arrangement by bringing that psychopath into the fold now."

"It's just business, Wyatt. It doesn't need to be personal."

"But you have to know that once you go down this route there's no coming back? There's only one way anybody gets to leave Drexen's inner circle, and that's in a body bag."

"It's just one job we're talking about here. It hardly means we're signing up with him. Look . . . you know I had the best of intentions when I started this getup, but that was back when there was a whole fleet of welding ships commissioned and compensated by the Administration. Now it's just us out there, on our own. I've got pieces falling off my ship that haven't been manufactured in a century and a crew who I'm guessing probably wants to get paid sometime this year. I'm sorry, but I'm done busting my ass for chump change when there's real work on the table." She sat back and folded her arms tightly, looking less like a ship captain and more like a moody teenager. "We're taking the job, Marshal. With or without your blessing. If you so much as think about getting in between me and my payday, then we're gonna have real problems. Maybe we'll see just how long the crumbling hull around the Mouth lasts when there's nobody out there looking after it."

He laughed bitterly, sank the dregs of his cider. "Don't talk like one of them, Lilah—like some gutless profiteer. You and I both know you'll have the *Assurance* out there shooting slag until she's running on fumes. So why don't you quit the mercenary act and tell me the real reason getting these industrial hydro-whatevers into the district is so ruttin' important to you."

The captain's solemn countenance faltered, the veneer of a ruthless corsair falling away to reveal the heart of gold hidden poorly beneath.

"Isn't it obvious?" she asked. "Vidalia's plan is to dig a channel along the Çorak."

"No, actually," he said, brow peaked in surprise. "I sure hope he's got a permit for that."

"It might just be a strip of wasteland between the Cohabitor Ghetto and the Copper Swathes now, but once those hydro-ionizers are spliced up to a conduit, they'll produce an unlimited amount of purified drinking water, the intention being to install them strategically along the channel and essentially create an artificial river."

"Siphoning from the siphoners. Smart."

"I know you're being a jerk right now, but just imagine what it could do for people in the area. The single most poverty-stricken region on the whole of the Coalescence and we might have the tools to revitalize it. It won't matter that the Administration has seen fit to condemn these people to die of thirst and starvation if we can make them completely self-sufficient."

He showed his palms in defense. "Don't get me wrong, Delilah: it sounds great—downright utopian. But I've seen enough of Drexen's 'savior of the people' hogwash fall flat to know that he's no philanthropist, just a bloodthirsty tycoon. Surely you don't really believe he's prepared to hand valuable tech like those ionizers over to charity, having paid you a small fortune to retrieve them. I promise you there's an ulterior motive here, you're just not seeing it."

Delilah's sober demeanor returned. Her expression became one of impatience, making it abundantly clear that she was done trying to convince him of what she genuinely believed: that Drexen's intentions were noble and that taking the gig was the right thing to do.

"I'll say it one more time, Wyatt. We're taking the job. Don't get in my way."

He nodded slowly, lips drawn in a thin line, inwardly concluding that any further attempts to dissuade her would be completely futile and potentially damaging to their business relationship.

"There won't be any complications on my end, Holloway. You have my word. I'm just looking out for you, that's all. Much as you might like to walk and talk like one of these brainless mercs, I know you and your flock are carrying the fire—always have been, always will. I'd just hate to see you getting taken advantage of by the likes of Drexen."

"We can handle ourselves." She smiled, melting into her seat in visible relief. "But thank you, I appreciate your support. You know, if things go smooth, there's a cut in this for you too, if you want it?"

"Naw, I don't need paying. You just make sure that ship of yours is out there patching up the hull and keeping that hungry void at bay. I reckon that'll make us about square."

She leaned over toward the snoozing Abraham, took his face in cupped hands, and pressed her nose to his.

"The *Assurance* and her crew are at your disposal, Eamon. Always."

* * *

"TRAYTOR . . . LEECH SIMPATHISER". The words appeared in angry brushstrokes of black and brown, burned with a fission torch into the paint-work of the prowler's driver's-side door—no doubt a parting gift from Jonah Sinclair or one of any number of his spineless confederates.

Outstanding . . . intolerant and *illiterate.*

Eamon set the defaced prowler to autopilot and vectored back toward the Mouth. He wound the passenger's-side window down enough so Abe could stick his head out and chomp at the air, but not enough for him to jump through—something the idiot had attempted more than once.

He reclined his seat and closed his eyes, thinking even thirty seconds of rack time might help alleviate the nagging ache in his temples, which had been steadily developing since the call with Vargos. Probably not helped in the least bit by those two ciders and his hopelessly irregular sleep schedule.

Goddamn lightweight.

Just as the maelstrom in his head began to lessen to a gentle breeze, Deputy Keller's panicked voice came rattling through the dashboard comms-line.

"Marshal! Are you still bowside? We've got trouble!"

He jolted to attention, instinctively grabbing the flight wheel. The prowler lurched forward as the autopilot abruptly disengaged.

"I'm still in Amidships but on my way back along the Canyon. What's going on?"

"Looks like protesters got through the perimeter at the Phalanx compound. They've knocked over one of the barricades and are flooding into the facility!"

"Fantastic. Just what we need right now. Has there been any lethal response from Phalanx?"

"Riot-control measures only, but I don't think it'll be long before they kick things up a notch. You better hurry."

He flicked on the red and blues and maxed out the throttle, barreling into a starfield of flashing headlights as if facing down a legion of excited paparazzi. One hand on the flight wheel and the other steadying Abraham, he sent the prowler diving and swerving to avoid oncoming traffic, narrowly missing a few head-on collisions but trading paint once or twice. He didn't have a plan and felt woefully unprepared for what was unfolding. The only thing he could be certain of was that Antaeus Gateway would be locked down if things continued to escalate. He had to get back into the district before then, or else he'd be explaining to the Administrator what DMED's own marshal was doing in the Weary Navigator of all places when the revolution began.

The gateway's blast doors opened automatically as the prowler sailed toward them, triggering a fleeting spike of hope that the situation might still be contained. Maybe, just maybe, there was still time to get things under control.

Emerging from the black light of the egress tunnel, the Mouth in all its ramshackle majesty materialized around him. He slowed to a hover high above the compound before descending as rapidly as he could without stalling the repulsor pads. In this old crate, there was no guarantee he could start them up again in time before careening into the ground.

"Keller! Is Deputy Sato on scene yet?"

"I can't reach her, Marshal. I think she's still making inquiries in the Cohabitor Ghetto."

"Let me know the second you make contact. I can see the compound now. It's a goddamn stampede. I'm gonna need all the backup you can get me."

"Roger that."

Descending lower, the hood began to obstruct his view. Holding an increasingly panicked Abraham in place with an outstretched arm, he banked to the left and craned his neck to gaze despairingly into the chaos ensuing below. One of the barricades encircling the compound had been forced over by a load lifter—probably stolen from somewhere in the industrial outskirts, now tipped on its side, smoke spewing from its engine coverings. A swarm of protesters and refugees had spilled through the new opening into NTU sovereignty: scared, angry people, driven to the breaking point by what Eamon had come to suspect himself—that with tensions between Harmony, Phalanx, and Drexen's Monarchs reaching a fever pitch, war was on the horizon, and those who didn't get out now would have no choice but to fight or die in it.

The enforcers stationed at the compound were standing their ground against the seething mob with riot shields and weapons drawn ready, sharing expressions of growing terror. Even from Eamon's altitude, he could lip-read their shouts of panic and confusion.

"Get back!"

"What are our orders, sir?"

"Permission to engage?"

"What are we doing here?"

"Negative! These are just civvies. Stand down!"

The level of restraint on display was surprising. Had the grenadiers been deployed already, he would undoubtedly have been looking at the sight of a massacre.

Just then, a scuffle ensued. Partially obscured by milky plumes of tear gas, the mob broke through the Phalanx line and rallied toward the checkpoint, reaching the security scanners like a wave smashing against a cliff face.

He dropped the prowler lower, focusing the repulsor pads downwards in hope of scattering the throng with the dust kicked up by the propulsion. But it was no use: those below him were too frenzied, too desperate to be deterred.

"Keller! They've reached the checkpoint. We need to alert the bowside authorities before they make it through to the Canyon!"

He heard the first syllable of Keller's hurried response. Then, an explosion—emanating from the checkpoint, a shock wave ripped through the crowd, catapulting several lifeless bodies like rag dolls through the air. A billowing mass of black smoke erupted from the epicenter, illuminated from within by convulsing veins of green voltaic energy. A terrible metallic squeal sounded as a piece of shrapnel tore through the underside of the prowler's chassis, screaming through the cabin and blowing a jagged hole through the roof, missing Eamon's brow by centimeters. The chunk had obliterated the front-left repulsor pad; the prowler dipped its hood and fell into an involuntary nosedive. Emergency klaxons shrieking, dashboard warning lights scintillating like winter solstice decorations, he wrenched back the flight wheel in a vain attempt to regain control. Heart belting against his rib cage, a feeling of complete helplessness overcame him as the ground continued to grow through the windscreen.

With seconds to spare before impact, he abandoned the unresponsive flight controls and scooped up Abraham, burying him forcefully into his chest. The dog snapped and snarled in a rabid state of fear and confusion; the more he squirmed, the tighter Eamon held him.

A moment later, the world went black.

Eamon got his thirty seconds after all. Although, coming to, he certainly didn't feel any better for it. He clutched his throbbing head, triggering a sharp pang in his right shoulder—*Must have slammed it into the driver's-side door during the crash.* Abraham sat in the footwell between his legs, trembling violently but seemingly unharmed. The mutt jumped into his lap, pressing two slender paws against his chest and licking the gash on his forehead.

Thanks, buddy. I'm all better now.

Eamon mentally clawed his way back to a more conscious state, gradually becoming aware of the enveloping scenes of death and destruction. The ringing in his ears subsided, capitulating to the equally piercing sound of a woman screaming. Through the shattered windscreen and beyond the prowler's crumpled hood he saw blurred shapes staggering forward—survivors with skin blackened by explosive residue, clothes torn and bloody, their faces contorted masks of horror. The stumbling figures were silhouetted by the murky blaze raging behind them, the checkpoint now like a dragon's throat, barely containing a swirling inferno and expelling a column of smoke that scaled the blockade and pooled beneath the ceiling of the Mouth.

An unusual cognitive dissonance struck him as he gazed with stinging eyes upon the smoldering heaps strewn about the compound: so mangled and so many that his brain could hardly reconcile the truth of what they were—the bodies of those killed in the blast.

How many? he wondered, figuring that since the detonation had come from right near the security scanners, in the dead center of the crowd, even the best possible outcome would still be a devastating loss of life.

Was this your doing, Composer? If so, you best make peace with the Abyss. Whether I have the jurisdiction or not, there ain't a nook or cranny on the Coalescence you can hide where I won't hunt you down.

Still standing protectively on his chest, watching vigilantly over his master's shoulder, Abraham growled softly in his throat. Eamon glanced through blood and sweat into the rearview mirror, immediately spotting the source of Abe's growing agitation: there were four individuals approaching—two humans and two cohabitors, garbed and hooded in wraps of brown cloth, moving with a calm and composed precision against the flow of the escaping masses. They were armed to the teeth, carrying rifles augmented with what appeared to be *Devourer* tech—XT-90 semiautomatics encased in gruesome sheaths of bioengineering. Eamon had never seen such weaponry before, but he recognized the sadistic bastards wielding them as the dangerously fanatical militants of Harmony. DMED didn't have an unwritten truce with the Composer like it did with Vidalia Drexen. If he allowed himself to be seen, her acolytes would swiftly execute him. Accordingly, he pushed Abraham back into the footwell, keeping a hand wrapped firmly around his snout to prevent the valiant fool from barking and giving away their position. Reclining his seat fully and turning onto his side, he listened intently to the cumbersome footsteps of the nearest cohabitor, the rhythmic thumping of its talons striking the ground growing ever louder. As the behemoth came alongside the prowler, Eamon thought for sure that he had been spotted, until aer attention was drawn by a commotion coming from deeper inside the compound.

"Sir! We've got contacts!"

"They're armed! Take cover!"

"Let's drop these assholes!"

Eamon propped himself up to peer through the web of cracks in the windscreen as earsplitting claps of gunfire rang out. Having regrouped behind an armored personnel carrier, the surviving enforcers had engaged the enemy. The insurgents quickly returned fire, although they unnervingly neglected to take any form of cover before doing so. They trudged forward with unflinching resolve, seemingly uninterested in their own well-being, caring only about inflicting as much suffering as they could before their inevitable neutralization.

Their bizarre weaponry spat phosphorescent bolts of greenish plasma, which ate through just about anything it struck: concrete, titanium plating, nanocarbon alloy—there didn't appear to be anything it couldn't dissolve like cotton candy. Even the armored personnel carrier was pocked and punctuated with glowing impact marks. Whatever this spliced tech was, it was damn formidable stuff . . .

The insurgents had now moved beyond the crumpled hood of the prowler. Having managed to stay unseen so far, Eamon suddenly found himself in the perfect position to flank if necessary. Careful to keep Abraham hidden in the footwell, he quietly opened the driver's-side door and slid out onto his knees. Unholstering his machine pistol, he crept around to the rear of the prowler, listening to the sharp whining of rounds tearing through the air above him. With his grip of the Chevesic slipping in his sweaty hands, he spun around to peek over the trunk, hoping to get a better assessment of the ongoing skirmish. Apparently, Phalanx were still churning out as many steely-eyed sharpshooters as they were back in his heyday. The remaining enforcers had already put down two of the attacking insurgents. A woman with tattoos crawling up her neck to her jawline lay in the fetal position, clutching an abdominal wound as she writhed beside her slain cohabitor counterpart.

Briefly, it seemed as though the tide of the engagement had turned, as the two remaining insurgents managed to pin down the enforcers with coordinated suppressing fire. That was until a marksman with a long-scope rifle, lying prone on the roof of the APC, sank a high-caliber round into the chest of the second human. The remaining cohab was thrown into a violent rage; in a last-ditch effort to take as many lives with aer as possible, ae began hip-firing indiscriminately, laying down a torrent of brilliant slugs at aer cowering targets.

Eamon saw his window of opportunity. The enforcers were pinned down again, so it was now or never . . . He drew a deep breath, pirouetted around the rear of the wrecked prowler, took the insurgent in his aim, and fired two rapid bursts. Beyond the iron sights of his Chevesic, the cohabitor reeled; a cloud of purple vapor exploded from aer abdomen. Ae went limp and collapsed into a crumpled heap of rags and exoskeleton. His fleeting sense of relief capitulating to nausea and shock, Eamon fell to his knees and threw up.

SIX

The Academy's main lecture hall was a remarkable structure: a striking amalgamation of Gothic and minimalist architecture, with struts and columns descending from its vaulted ceiling like rows of sharpened fangs. Tobias's private study pod was one of thirty-eight, arranged concentrically around the speaker's podium. Complete with a desk, a reading lamp, a high-spec computer pane, and a personal coffee dispenser, it had everything he needed to get through the grueling seven hours a day usually spent debating or enduring seemingly never-ending lectures.

Some of the greatest captains, administrators, and fleet admirals who had served the NTU since the *Novara* left the lunar shipyard were educated in this very auditorium. Often Tobias found himself intently studying the faces of the alumni depicted in portraits hanging on the walls, charged with the utmost certainty that one day his own face would be right up there with them . . .

Naturally, there were those who considered pursuing an education at the Academy of Colonial Stewardship entirely redundant, since the dream of interstellar colonization had been eviscerated by a chariot of demons over a century ago. Tobias tended to disagree—although he would never set foot upon the Grasslands of Pasture himself, he felt it was his responsibility to carry the torch for those who eventually would. He believed that one day, maybe many decades from now, the *Novara*'s ripple drive could be rebuilt. His descendants might find a way to cast off the *Devourer* into the empty black and finally get the voyage to the Hephaestus Cluster back under way. And so, it was imperative that the knowledge of how to build a self-sustaining society from the ground up was passed down through the generations, so as not to be lost in the sands of time.

Besides . . . as well as the absolute privilege of getting to follow in the footsteps of greats such as Admiral Coombs or Captain Lei-Ghannam, graduating from ACS would also fast-track him into a postgrad job in the Administration—some of the perks of which would be a comfortable starting salary and a luxury Emeral Heights apartment.

And why shouldn't somebody of my pedigree be rewarded handsomely for such hard work?

The hall had been dimmed for today's lecture on the fundamentals of ripple-space propulsion. Normally he found the tranquilizing low light and sound-muting surfaces perfect for putting him in a state of zen and focus, but in light of recent events, the auditorium felt more like a church of old, and Professor Delgado's soft, reverberating tones could easily be mistaken for the reading of a eulogy. It was hard not to feel sorry for the man— as engaging as his presentations usually were, of the seven students who had worked up the emotional strength to attend today, only two were paying any attention. Like Tobias, the rest were simmering in their respective study pods, scouring the Nov-Net for new details on their panes, sifting indignantly through repetitious headlines for any morsel of new information about the attack . . .

Almost twelve hours had elapsed since a group of leeches detonated an explosive device at the Phalanx compound in the Mouth. A terrible firefight ensued, and by the time the assailants were put down, twelve enforcers—valiant protectors of NTU sovereignty—were dead. Tobias wasn't sure if he'd even blinked away from the broadcast since then, but he knew at the very least that he hadn't slept. The image of the decimated checkpoint was seared into his psyche, somehow appearing even more vividly on the back of his eyelids when he dared to try and rest them. Then there was the frequent displaying of the mug shot of one of the supposed perpetrators. According to local sources, the beast was known to local law enforcement as a dissident prior to the attack and was somehow inexplicably free to go about its wicked business. With every appearance of those eight soulless eyes, his stomach churned an excruciating concoction of fear, wrath, and a burning desire for retribution—a bloodlust like nothing he'd experienced before. By no means did he consider himself a violent person; truthfully, he'd never thrown a good punch in his life. But given five minutes alone in a room with one of those depraved creatures, who wanted nothing more than the total annihilation of the life he knew and the ones he loved . . . well, he didn't know what he would do, but it wouldn't be anything pretty.

The NTNN had filled its schedule, inviting countless experts and commentators on to bicker about potential motives, even wheeling out the obligatory leech sympathizer to fruitlessly argue that not all cohabitors were terrorists—the type of callow-minded fool eager to weaponize the attack in order to fuel their political agenda; such dangerous liberal sentiments were even more of a threat to society than the leeches themselves.

"Please turn your attention to the following demonstration," Professor Delgado said as a luma-cast projection of the *Novara* as large as a swoop appeared above the podium. Tobias would normally marvel to see the vessel in all its pre-Collision glory, but he was far too distracted to take any real notice.

"By creating a ripple-shaped distortion in space-time, the *Novara* was able to skim along the crest of each wave like a skipping stone. It was by no means instantaneous traversal but drastically reduced the distance and time necessary to be crossed in order to reach its destination."

The resounding silence was oppressive; not even a whisper of acknowledgment arose from the students and the sound of the professor awkwardly clearing his throat bounced chaotically around the auditorium.

"Of course, those of us up to scratch on our history know that it was research and development into the field of localized gravity distortion at the Europa Laboratory that led to the accidental generation of a powerful singularity near Jupiter. The inner planets were gradually pulled into elliptical orbits, meaning for half the year Earth became a hellish inferno and a frozen wasteland for the rest. I think it pertinent to remember that the technological leap that spelled our doom was also our salvation."

Tobias pried his eyes away from the broadcast to afford the man a nod of comprehension, before hastily returning to his pane. The live feed had now cut to the vigil presently being held in Chennai Plaza, where mourners with somber expressions stood with candles in hand, huddled together before a wall plastered with photographs of the victims: some looking dapper in their Phalanx uniforms, others depicted in casual wear among friends and family. As the camera panned across the collage of smiling, youthful faces, Tobias felt a twinge of guilt as his eyes fell on an image of Jade Tanaka. He glanced across the lecture hall at Caleb's empty study pod. It had always irked him that she was allocated the one directly opposite, meaning she could throw him off with stupid faces or rude gestures when he took the floor—something she took advantage of during especially heated debates.

He knew choosing to attend a lecture instead of being by her side wasn't exactly a shining example of best-friend behavior. But for one thing, there were finals coming up, and while he understood perfectly well that now was a time for grieving and reflection, a blemish on his spotless attendance record was something he simply could not abide. There was also the small matter of Caleb's whereabouts. She had left Capella Promenade in such a hurried, hysterical state the previous night that he never got an answer to the question of where she was going. She wasn't at Aegis Infirmary with the families of the other victims; he'd called ahead to check. She hadn't gone home either; her mother—a woman who made no secret of her disapproval regarding her daughter's engagement to a leatherneck—was brutally dismissive when quizzed over the caster about her disappearance.

"She's probably just moping somewhere, Tobias. Don't trouble yourself too much—I'm sure she'll turn up sooner or later."

Earlier in the day her feather had been ringing out. Now, she had switched it off. The niggling worries at the back of his mind had snowballed into an urgent and impending sense of doom. As resilient and tenacious as he knew she was, it dawned on him that he really had no clue as to how she would be reacting—neither of them had dealt with anything remotely as traumatic as this, and there was little that unnerved him more than uncharted territory.

He watched the minutes tick down on his pane, physically willing them to move faster. After rambling on for a short while longer, Professor Delgado finally concluded the lecture, albeit on an exceedingly bleak note—a truth Tobias knew all too well but was still unwilling to accept: that to repair the *Novara's* ripple-space capabilities would take a tremendous workforce and access to materials and resources that simply did not exist. Without the intervention of some divine miracle, the human remnant would be stranded indefinitely, and that was the end of that . . .

The auditorium brightened; he jumped to his feet and hustled around the ring of study pods, hoping to find something in Caleb's that might determine where she was. Her desk was kept nowhere near as immaculate as his and was littered with mementos and memorabilia: everything from bobble-head pop culture figures to an assortment of hair products to merchandise for the Amidships Stingrays—her favorite casterblade team. The trophy from her time on the ACS fencing squad triggered a warm smile every time he saw it. *Trust Caleb to find a way to hit people with sharp sticks legitimately.*

Then there was the double-sided luma-frame he'd bought for her nineteenth birthday—a flat wedge of birchwood that fit comfortably in the palm of his hand, with two microemitters embedded on either side luma-casting independent moving images. On the first side he saw himself in an EVA suit, tumbling helplessly with flailing limbs against a veil of black peppered by stars, his safety tether looping and coiling around him like a white ribbon in the weightlessness. Caleb floated beside him, managing to keep better control of her inertia as a more seasoned recreational spacewalker but failing to control her guffawing at his utter lack of coordination. He shook his head ruefully, quite happy to be the butt of the joke as long as it made her laugh.

He flipped the luma-frame over in his hand. The image projected on the other side was of Caleb and Jade, depicted in a tender embrace against a backdrop of greenery. They stood beneath the pink blossom of a Japanese maple tree, noses pressed together, smiling from ear to ear. The vid had been taken up in the Center of Horticultural Preservation, or the Conservatory as it was commonly known—a vast eco-dome situated above hydroponics housing various botanical gardens that represented the many different biomes of Earth, ranging from tropical greenhouses to a desert-climate cactus garden— Tobias's favorite, given how bitterly cold life aboard the *Novara* often was.

Jade, a renowned green-thumb, had a private garden that she and Caleb spent most of their free time at, cultivating herbs and vegetables or bathing in the enclosure's simulated sunlight. If memory served, the gardens were where the two first met . . . He wrapped his fingers around the luma-frame, clutching it firmly to his chest, steadfast in his hypothesis that Jade's garden was exactly where he would find her.

Tobias watched the zoetrope of solemn-faced figures slow to a stop as the Canyon tram pulled into Zharady Station—the main transport hub for Amidships. Stepping out onto the platform, he saw in the vacant stares of those waiting to board a familiar look of defeat, like gazing into shattered glass—numerous fragmented reflections of his own fears and insecurities, all desperately seeking comfort but fervently avoiding eye contact.

The leeches hit us hard this time, he thought, striding into the main transit terminal, a large concourse sheltered by a sloping canopy of teal-tinted glass. Stoic and still amidst the fray were groups of armed Phalanx enforcers strapped with semiautomatic carbines, vigilantly watching the ocean of commuters. Such heightened security measures were unusual and an obvious reaction to the increased threat level prompted by the attack. Truthfully, he wasn't sure how he felt about it: relieved and thankful, he supposed, to have guardians in blue keeping people safe, but unquestionably crestfallen that such drastic precautions were necessary.

Is this what we are now? he wondered, heading for the succession of glass elevator pods in the foyer. *A policed state, where treating public spaces like war zones is the cost of normalcy, our day-to-day spent looking over our shoulders as we wait for our alien enemy to rear its ugly head again?*

The doors to one of the elevator pods vibrated open. He stepped inside, joining yet more glum worker bees, faces buried in their feathers, no doubt thirsting to satiate their own morbid fixations.

Tell us more about the victims, he imagined them saying. *Did any of them leave children behind? Were any due to retire soon? Perhaps one was an off-duty volunteer—a celebrated pillar of the community, dearly missed by those touched by their unwavering generosity.*

He had spent the whole day torturing himself, digging through the same Nov-Net articles in a masochistic hunt for any insight that might amplify his anguish. Such had always been in his nature—an inexplicable drive to emotionally exacerbate bad situations, always considering the worst possible scenario before even knowing the facts . . . although, now it was different. Now, a faint ray of hope had cleaved asunder the dark fog occupying his mind. He had pushed aside his leech-centric vexations and was focusing solely on Caleb; the closer he got to the Conservatory, the more certain he was she would be there.

He didn't know what he would say upon their reunion: a groveling apology for not being with her all along, he guessed. Perhaps he would say nothing at all—just reach out and pull her into an impassioned, but strictly platonic, embrace, careful not to let his thoughts travel to that unsettling realization— a door in his subconscious, keeping locked away that which he desired most but which to open would be to succumb to his most diabolical impulses. That realization being, simply, that Caleb was no longer engaged . . .

A sharp climb through Halvorsen Commons brought him and the other pod occupants into the heart of the *Novara*'s life-support block. The last few decks of hydroponics disappeared below his feet before the elevator jolted to a stop. The doors slid open, heralded by a melodic chime. A gust of warm air rolled in, fragrant with the heavenly scent of freshly cut grass. Beyond lay the atrium to the Center of Horticultural Preservation: a space that, were he the religious sort, he would say resembled the customer service desk at the pearly gates. The walls of the atrium reached up to the underside of the Conservatory itself—a magnificent glass dome that extruded from the topside of the *Novara*'s hull, enclosing the center's multitude of gardens and greenhouses within.

Doubling as an aviary, the facility was kept on a rigid day/night cycle in order to accommodate its various species of resident birds. For the first twelve hours, the dome's amino-silicate glass became opaque, turning brilliant blue to emulate the boundless skies of Earth. At night, the dome returned to its crystalline state, granting a staggering view of the enveloping cosmos, perfect for stargazers like Tobias, who took a kind of melancholy delight in reminding himself of the unfathomable distances between those lonely points of light and that this was as close as he would ever get to any of them.

He left the elevator pod and set off toward the center of the atrium. Here, encircled by a ring of curved info boards and exhibits, there stood a bronze statue of a woman on her knees, looking down glowingly at the small leafy plant sprouting from soil cupped in her hands. The pedestal upon which the statue was erected displayed the name Amara Thaddeus above a phrase of ancient poetry.

> *Nature's first green is gold,*
> *Her hardest hue to hold.*
> *Her early leaf's a flower;*
> *But only so an hour.*
> *Then leaf subsides to leaf.*
> *So Eden sank to grief,*
> *So dawn goes down to day.*
> *Nothing gold can stay.*

Amara Thaddeus was one of the *Novara's* original architects, charged specifically with the design of all environmental and life-support systems. The story went that in the early planning phases, the lunar shipyard's board of executive directors rejected her proposal for a self-sustaining eco-dome that would remain open to the public, deeming it to be an unnecessary expenditure taking vital resources from other, more critical areas of construction. But Amara knew that access to nature would be paramount to the mental well-being of the generations of spacefarers about to spend their entire lives aboard the *Novara*. Even the dangerously overpopulated megacities of her dying world maintained green spaces for their residents, and to send two million souls into the endless night without somewhere to feel a kinship with trees or the grass beneath their feet would be to condemn them to a deprived and soulless existence.

She rebelled against the other architects, fought tooth and nail with the board, even forgoing her own place aboard the *Novara* to secure planning permission to build her Conservatory. Although not without struggle, eventually Amara had her way; the facility was built as a place for horticultural preservation, but, as a young man stranded many light-years away from solid ground, Tobias knew that it preserved something far more spiritual than a simple collection of Earthen flora. For many Novarians it was a lifeline—the only remaining connection to Gaia, the mother mankind left behind.

Amara died long before ever knowing just how important her gardens would be for the post-Collision human remnant. Although, in a way, there was a part of her that lived on. The irrigation and climate-control systems maintaining the Conservatory were so complex that, at the behest of their notoriously stubborn designer, they were run to this day by a virtual intelligence programmed by none other than herself. Amara had injected her knowledge, experience, and personality into a caretaker VI, fortifying it with the most advanced encryption available so that not even the ship's captain could override its stringent protocols. In the immediate aftermath of the Collision, as he began drawing potentially lifesaving power from nonessential ship systems, the great Captain Lei-Ghannam was quoted as saying, "The specter of that blasted gardener would happily see us all suffocate if it meant protecting her prized rhododendrons."

How grateful Tobias was that Amara had been so untrusting of others to safeguard her life's work. He found transitioning from the atrium into the rolling swathes of verdure immensely cathartic, realizing that, whether he found Caleb here or not, it had been worth the trip for his own sake, and he dared not dream of the barren wastes that could have been . . .

A pathway led through various hedge-fenced partitions, cutting across neatly pruned botanical gardens and untamed meadows overflowing with tall grass and wildflowers. As the imitation daylight dwindled, the Conservatory was swaddled by the star-stippled blanket of night. Bats swooped low as indiscernible shapes of leather and bone, their membranous wings catching the argon glow of the streetlights illuminating the way forward. He passed the shadowy outline of the tropical greenhouse, skirted around an ornate stone water fountain, eventually arriving at the basin where the private gardens were located.

Maybe it was a trick of the low light or the result of being so accustomed to the luma-frame's oversaturated image quality. Either way, the pink blossom of the maple tree standing just behind Jade's plot seemed noticeably muted in color—once vibrant and full of life, now appearing wilted and dreary.

Caleb still wore her finery from the night before. Her luma bracelet was running low on battery and the vine leaves crawling up her arm were now flickering and dim. She sat with her back against the tree trunk, head hung forward, a tangled bird's nest of burnished copper draped over her tear-stained face. Tobias turned cold at the sight of her. She was a ghost—a defeated, disused husk, the light inside all but extinguished.

"Oh, Firebird," he uttered, letting slip an old pet name he was sure they'd both outgrown. She lifted her head and showed an ephemeral smile.

"You finally came."

He removed his blazer, wrapped it around her trembling shoulders, and sat down beside her.

"Have you been out here all alone since last night?"

"I didn't know where else to go," she mumbled. "I tried to get into the compound, but they weren't letting anybody through the blockade. They kept telling me to go to Aegis Infirmary, but it didn't make any sense that she would be there. This was the only other place I could think of to look for her, but . . ." She paused and averted her eyes in what looked like fearful recognition of her own confusion.

The hatred he felt for himself in that moment was raw and potent.

What in the Abyss were you thinking? he silently chastised himself. *Sitting on your ass listening to Delgado blather about space-time metrics when Caleb needed you more than ever?*

He placed his hand on the back of her head, pressed her face into his shoulder and combed knotted hair with his fingers.

"I can't put into words how truly sorry I am that you had to face this alone because of me. I'm here now, and I promise I'll never leave your side again."

"It feels like a dream." She used the skirt of her dress to wipe her nose. "Is this really happening? No! I won't let it."

Listening to Caleb's soft whimper and gazing upon the impeccably maintained garden before him, he was visited by Jade's memory. Though he'd spent years now positioning her as an adversary in his mind, it dawned on him that he had his own fair share of grief to deal with.

"Jade was the last person on the *Novara* who deserved this," he said, grasping at straws to produce words that might be even remotely meaningful. "I know what happened to her was terrible and tragic, but she would want us to be strong. She would expect us to look after each other."

"I just can't believe she's gone."

He reached into his pocket and produced the luma-frame. He placed it in Caleb's muddied palm and closed her fingers around it tightly.

"She's not gone. Look, she's right here."

It was a gamble of a gesture—one he wasn't sure would help cheer her up or send her spiraling out of control. She eyed the projection of happier times with downcast eyes, bottom lip quivering. She turned to him.

"You're a good friend, Tobias."

No, I'm not . . . far from it.

"What do you need?" he asked. "Tell me what will help take the pain away . . . Whatever it is, I can make it happen."

She tilted her head reflectively, sending the question deep within herself. He saw her gripping the luma-frame tighter, tensed fingers turning red; he worried for a moment that she might snap it in half.

"I need . . . I need to make them pay."

He nodded. "The leeches? Don't worry, they will. If my father thought the deployment of grenadiers was in the cards before, then I doubt there's any question about it now."

"No. You're not hearing me." She stood up suddenly, stared down at him with eyes scintillating like the lit fuse of a firecracker. "The Administrator is too much of a coward to do anything about this. She'll condemn the attack on the network and regurgitate all the same old, hollow condolences, but that will be it. Those wretches will get away with it again, and people like Jade will keep on having to give their lives for the Administration's inaction and ineptitude. When I say I need to make them pay, I mean personally."

He stood up to bring his eyes in line with hers, took her by the shoulders. "And how do you plan on doing that?"

"I don't know . . . I haven't figured out the details yet, but the short answer is that we sneak into the Mouth and find a way to hit back at them. Get our hands on some weapons and take the fight right to their doorstep."

"Caleb . . . I know you're hurting, but please be rational. Jade chose her line of work so she could protect us—to keep you safe. Do you really think this is what she would want? You and me launching some suicidal assault on the *Devourer* on her behalf?"

Caleb took a final look at the luma-frame, her face a twisted visage of grief. She unclasped her hands, letting the object fall to the dirt.

"She's dead . . . I couldn't care less about what she wants. You asked me what *I need* to take the pain away, and I gave you an answer: I need to make them suffer. If you aren't going to help me do that, then I guess I really am on my own."

Her gaze of fierce defiance faltered; there was a moment of tormented deliberation, then she collapsed into his arms.

"I'm sorry," she sobbed. "It's all falling apart. I just don't know what to do."

He lowered her to the ground, let her head rest in his lap.

"The only thing you need to do right now is rest. Whatever comes next, we'll tackle it together."

He glanced down at her forlornly, discovering that she had already drifted off to sleep. He rested his head against Jade's maple tree, then did the same.

SEVEN

Delilah was on pins and needles. The insurgent attack at the block-ade had sparked a ship-wide lockdown; all commercial vessels were recalled to their respective docking bays and all departure permits had been rescinded until further notice. Fortunately, the *Assurance*'s secondary designation as a welding ship would grant her emergency egress in the event of a rupture. But as fate would have it, the decrepit shielding near the seam where the *Devourer* fused with the *Novara*'s hull was, infuriatingly, holding firm, which meant that for the time being, her wings were clipped.

Meanwhile, Vidalia's hydro-ionizers were adrift in the Debris Belt, just waiting to get snatched up by another crew. Word about the score had gotten out, and at this juncture it would come down to whoever was lucky enough to receive the green light to disembark first.

Delilah had taken this job in a bid to win the Governor's favor, but nothing would make an enemy of him faster than losing such valuable commodities to the competition. Making sure not even a scrap of decent work was tossed her way ever again would probably be the least of his retribution, should she fail.

When they met in the Weary Navigator, Eamon Wyatt had tried to instill doubts in her mind concerning Vidalia's intentions with the ionizers. And while she knew it was entirely possible the Governor wasn't being completely honest about what his plans for them were, the prospect of getting a reliable source of drinking water into the desolate region of the Mouth known as the Çorak was too good an opportunity to pass up. The big payday and the steady stream of work that would come from fulfilling the contract would be wel-come remunerations, of course. But her determination to succeed was driven by something far more intangible than financial gain.

"No matter what you do, just promise you'll try and make things better for people."

Micah's almost final words were like a tattoo on her gray matter—a melody so entrenched in her consciousness that it could never be soothed or put to rest. They had informed every decision she had made and precipitated every insane leap of faith taken since that terrible day down in the Vestiges. What happened in that abandoned mess hall twelve years ago was so pointless, so utterly devoid of rhyme or reason, that it had become her life's purpose to try and find meaning in it ever since—a pledge that derailed her studies at ACS and compelled her to abandon her life in Quarterdeck in search of better comprehension of the injustices Micah once emphatically alluded to. She had to make good on her promise: that she would do everything in her power to improve the lives of others. While she knew captaining a weld and salvage ship was likely not what Micah had in mind, it was a damned good start. Her ship's dual designation meant she could divide the crew's efforts into maintaining the *Novara*'s criminally neglected hull and making sure quality-of-life-altering technologies like those hydro-ionizers ended up in the hands of people who needed them most, as opposed to the Administration, who would only strip them for parts.

She couldn't do either of those things, however, as long as the *Assurance* was grounded, which it had been for nearly twenty-eight hours by the time she decided to march into the harbormaster's office to raise hell about it.

The control tower from which Iver Polakorski lorded over his sweaty little domain was situated at the rear end of the hangar. Standing in a stuffy operations cabin chock-full of comms and radar equipment, Delilah gazed through the tower's forward-sloped windows out into the docks, having never seen them quite so full as they were presently. There wasn't a single docking bay unoccupied—haulers and freighters of every class were practically piled on top of one another, lying dormant before the hangar's egress aperture: a giant rectangle of perfect black, protected by a thin veneer of opalescent energy called a fission field that kept the endless night at bay. She felt so despondent listening to Polakorski babble about port restrictions and lockdown regulations that she had almost tuned him out altogether. Absently, she stood with her back turned, imagining the bedlam that would ensue if a sudden power failure knocked out the fission field. There were emergency fail-safes in place that would prevent the hangar and its contents from getting sucked out into space, but stars only know if they were still in working order . . .

Polakorski sat leaning back in his seat, boots resting impudently on his desk. Delilah regarded him as a sniveling little vole—revoltingly smug about the minuscule amount of authority bestowed upon him as lord commander of the proverbial armpit of Lower Amidships. The fact that many of the ship captains operating out of the docks respected her word more than his was a cause of great discontentment to him. Accordingly, the pair generally made a concerted effort to keep their interactions as brief and infrequent as possible. The current circumstances, however, had warranted more face time than she feared she could stomach.

"Am I talking to myself here, Captain Holloway?"

She spun around, hand resting on her hip, and caught the slimeball leering at the region below her gun-belt with narrow, beady eyes.

"Unfortunately for us both, no."

"How many times do I gotta repeat myself, then? The lockdown order you're asking me to flagrantly disregard here comes straight from the top. I know cuz you're highborn you think you should get priority over every other scrap crew looking for special treatment in this joint, but the fact is, nobody's going nowhere until the Administration tells me otherwise."

"But this ain't about *salvage*." She took a sharp step forward, now towering over the increasingly insolent harbormaster. "If there's a rupture sternside and we aren't on hand to assist, the resulting decompression event could rip the Mouth apart. We can't afford to be sitting on our asses waiting for you to cut through the red tape and give us the all clear. This is life and death we're talking about."

"Oh please," he sneered. "You really expect me to believe *you* of all people give a leech's ass about the vagrant scourge beyond the blockade? You're from Quarterdeck. What do their lives matter to you?"

"A vacuum doesn't care whether your hide is covered in skin or scales, Polakorski. If the shielding around the Mouth fails, the void is coming for us all the same."

He furrowed his brow, betraying annoyance at the fact that her argument had struck a chord. After all, he wasn't an idiot—just an asshole.

"My hands are tied, Holloway. If you've got a problem with it then you need to take it up with Vargos yourself. I'm sure a beacon of education and high society such as you will have no trouble cozying up to the likes of the Administrator."

A deviant's grin swept across his cherubic face, the condescension in his tone as glaring as the mustard stain on the collar of his workwear. Delilah scoffed. "Great idea. Perhaps we'll do brunch . . . Come to think of it, I imagine she'd be keenly interested to hear about some of the crooked stuff that goes on in this cesspool."

"That's high and mighty coming from the likes of you, princess. You think I don't notice that your scrap haul is consistently two tons under your ship's maximum capacity? If the port authorities were to find out you've been holding back valuable salvage, or worse, smuggling it through the blockade, they'd confiscate your ship, ya know?"

She pulled aside the tail of her duster coat, rested her hand on the stock of her concussion repeater in its thigh holster.

"Over my dead body."

"I'd remind you about the strict no-firearms policy we have on deck, but you'd probably just disregard that too."

Delilah flashed a disingenuous smile, turned, and headed for the door.

"Thank you as always for the *stimulating* conversation, Iver. Let me know the second I can get the *Assurance* starside. We've got work to do and I don't want to spend a second longer in this dump than I have to."

"Trust me, Delilah: you'll be the first to know," he blurted after her. "You think I enjoy having some uppity blue blood playing space pirate in my docks? The sooner I can get that hauler of yours outta here, the better."

The *Assurance* was an older ship—pre-Collision at least. But that didn't stop her being the most gorgeous hunk in the entire Novarian fleet. The elegant contours of her signature balaener-class design harkened back to a time when humanity aspired to soar through unfamiliar skies. A long, descending neck bridged her gently sloped cockpit to an aerodynamic fuselage, with forward-swept wings leading up to a vertical tail fin, crafting a flowing, swanlike profile. Admittedly, certain modifications Delilah had made since acquiring the vessel had somewhat diminished its sleek appearance. Namely, the gaping holes cut through each of the wings to accommodate two retrofitted impulse thrusters, providing an increase in inertial maneuverability that any ship operating in the Debris Belt would be doomed without.

Positioned just forward of the wide cargo bay door was the centerpiece of Delilah's whole operation: a rotary turret emplacement with a glass enclosure called a magma cannon, capable of firing a stream of molten slag that cooled and hardened on impact, making it perfect for soldering ruptures and reinforcing weak points in the *Novara*'s deteriorating hull.

Her heart swelled as she arrived at the docking bay, her foul mood lifted by the sight of her beloved hauler. To her, the *Assurance* was home—a refuge in increasingly turbulent times, where she and her crew of rounded-up strays could dictate the rules, where society was what they chose to make it. Getting her hands on a ship and outfitting it for welding and salvage operations had not been cheap, nor had it been easy. Her blood, sweat, and tears were seeped into the very alloy; it was a part of her now, and she a part of it—a statement that would almost certainly go disputed by her first mate: a grizzled veteran of the NTSC who just so happened to be the ship's previous owner. The *Assurance* had been in Kahu Heperi's family for generations, right up until the day he was forced to sell her in order to pay off a number of stacking gambling debts. His only stipulations for the sale were that he would be allowed to keep his place aboard and that he, and *only* he, would be permitted behind the helm. Delilah was left with no choice but to recruit the old dog as a pilot, which suited her just fine, given she needed somebody with the prowess to negotiate a particularly hazardous environment and he was perhaps one of the best stick jockeys on the *Novara*. Unfortunately, Kahu's unmatched skills came paired with a bad attitude and a strong disdain for authority. Though highly decorated, his career was marred by an eventual dishonorable discharge for drinking on the job—something he seemed hell-bent on continuing in his current position. He was stubborn and foul-tempered but also staunchly protective of those around him. Delilah found that having the added muscle on her crew far outweighed his regrettable behavior, and even with the constant boozing, there was no denying he was a maestro behind the flight stick.

She found the delinquent lounging in a hammock fashioned from cargo tie-down straps, which he'd hung from the support struts of the boarding ramp. Even in his advancing years he managed to keep himself in impressive shape, with bulging muscles stretching the timeworn fabric of his NTSC jacket. He wore the old garment zipped down over a low-cut tank top, revealing golden-brown skin blotched by faded tribal tattoos; ash-gray dreadlocks hung like curtains woven from stone on either side of his battle-hardened face.

"Something wrong with your bunk, Heperi?" Delilah asked, carefully stepping over the piles of assorted scrap metal strewn about the landing platform—the same scrap she had ordered him to load into the slag furnace several hours prior.

"It's like an oven in there," he uttered in response, eyes still shut. "I keep telling you: the *Assurance* gets hotter than a Rennaxi Junction stripper when you leave the air filtration switched off for too long."

"And I keep telling you: there's no point burning hydrogen just to keep the life support running when we're clamped up like this. You better figure out a way to cope, Kahu, because I'm sick of hearing you moan about it."

"What does it look like I'm doing?" He shot her a defiant look, took a swig from his pewter hip flask. Droplets of synthesized alcohol lingered on his unkempt mustache, which partially concealed the jagged streak of scar tissue running down his cheek—a grizzly visual accompaniment to the war stories he reveled in recounting.

Delilah sighed, too exasperated after butting heads with Iver Polakorski for yet another shouting match about Kahu's bad habits.

"Is Teo around?" she asked,

He sighed. "It's not my job to babysit the Mouth rat, Skipper. I'm here for one reason and one reason alone: to make sure you don't get my ship pulverized running your little salvage op out there in the Debris Belt." He propped himself up, gestured with a clumsy nod into the cargo bay. "You know what she's like, though. Probably scurrying about in engineering, taking the place apart bit by bit, trying to find something shiny."

Delilah stormed up the boarding ramp, seized the hip flask, and waved it forcefully before his nose.

"You'll be the one getting pulverized if you don't stop calling her that awful nickname. And for the last time, this isn't your ship anymore. You sold her to me, remember?"

She ducked under the hammock and headed up the boarding ramp, taking a swig of sickly-sweet rum as she went.

"What did the harbormaster say?" he shouted after her, stifling a yawn. "Are we still grounded?"

"For the moment we are, but I want to be ready to disembark the second we're released. So load that scrap into the furnace like you were supposed to hours ago and have your preflight checks done ASAP. Let's get prepped for a fast exit."

He nodded and performed a fumbling dismount from his hammock.

"You got it, Skip."

Most modern haulers were designed for fuel efficiency and cargo capacity, leaving little room for crew quarters or recreational spaces. Despite its streamlined exterior, the *Assurance* was deceptively roomy on the inside. Delilah climbed an access ladder and arrived in a spacious galley/lounge area, which acted as a central hub for the rest of the ship. Though she'd made many performance-enhancing modifications to core systems since her acquisition, she had chosen not to alter the interior decor; something didn't feel right about setting up shop in someone's home and immediately gutting it to suit her own tastes, especially when said person was still living there. Truth be told, she had grown rather fond of the way Kahu kept it—the galley's steel-plated surfaces were festooned in mandala tapestries and old Turkmen rugs, while a colorful collection of antique fabric lamps bathed the space in a soothing luster. It was a cozy, bohemian oasis—a stark contrast from the cold and brutally industrial aesthetic that most ships adhered to.

Although hesitant to admit the old pilot had been right about the temperature, she couldn't deny it felt like a sauna in the galley. Worst of all, after days spent marinating in the repugnant confines of the Lower Amidships Docks, her beautiful hauler had developed something of an odor.

Maybe it is time to let the air in a little.

She made her way down helm access—a long trapezoidal corridor that led to the nose of the ship. The *Assurance*'s bridge was standard-sized for a vessel of her class, with a wide, V-shaped windshield, partially obscured by the array of consoles and control pedestals encompassing the helm and pilot's seat.

She reached up to the overhead instrumentation panel and ritualistically flicked a combination of switches. A blast of cool air swept through the cabin as the gentle hum of the life support whirred up from behind the walls. The *Assurance* awoke from her slumber, the neurons of her central nervous system firing up from stasis in the form of a thousand blinking status lights, speckled like fireflies throughout the bridge.

"Told you!" Kahu hollered from the cargo bay, his voice muffled under the clangor of crashing scrap metal.

Delilah could stop to appreciate the improved air quality for no more than a few seconds before the comms console lit up with an urgent inbound communication.

What now? she groused, reaching over to accept the call. The cockpit dimmed and the windshield polarized. She then met the piercing and predatory eyes of Vidalia Drexen as they were projected by a luma-caster just forward of the helm, his smooth skin pulled tightly over an angular jawline, his face a statue of ebony porcelain. In previous meetings, the Governor had worn some variation of a fine tan suit, but here he appeared in a velvet robe—sumptuous red divided by golden strips of embroidered detail. With manicured hands clasped tightly on a stone desk space, he sat before a panoramic aquarium; unidentifiable creatures slunk like specters through the murk behind him, shadowy fins and tendrils swaying in the current of the water filtration. Delilah wasn't knowledgeable enough about Earthen or *Devourer* wildlife to guess where they originated from, which perhaps made them all the more menacing to observe.

"Captain Holloway," Vidalia said, his deep voice striking fear, vibrating the air in her lungs as if pumped through a subwoofer. "You must forgive the late hour of this call. I'm afraid there is an urgent matter we must discuss. Do you have a moment to speak?"

"Governor." Delilah cordially bowed her head, using the momentary break in eye contact to banish the nervousness from her expression. "An unfortunate excess of it, actually. Ideally, we would have been starside already and hard at work retrieving your quarry, but unfortunately, the *Assurance* is still clamped in the Lower Amidships Docks. I had a few words with the harbormaster just now to see if he could lift our docking restrictions but had no joy."

"The current lockdown measures are partly the reason for my call." He leaned forward, the irregular staccato of his speech carving out an intimidating air of gravitas. "With things the way they are at the moment, I am unable to guarantee safe passage through the blockade as was originally agreed. As it stands, it will not be possible to transport the goods into the Mouth through traditional means, and attempting to do so would be ill-advised."

"I see . . . well, it doesn't mean the plans are completely scuppered. We have space to keep the ionizers hidden aboard the *Assurance* until things die down, if needs-be."

He shook his head ardently. "While I have full confidence in your crew and their capacity for discretion in this matter, the cargo in question is far too valuable to risk losing to the port authorities. You understand what's at stake here, Delilah."

She felt a fluttering sense of hope in response to the Governor's uncharacteristic display of candor. *Marshal Wyatt was wrong,* she dared to think. *Vidalia may be a ruthless kingpin, but he does care for the well-being of his constituents. He knows those ionizers will be a lifeline for the people living in his territory and has nothing to gain from lying about what he intends to do with them.*

"Completely," she said, matching his sincerity. "I trust you've made alternate plans for delivery, then?"

"Indeed I have. I believe the only viable course of action is to expedite our *other* arrangements. As soon as you can disembark, my associates will rendezvous with the *Assurance* via landing skiff. Once you have secured the goods, they will guide you safely to the delivery point via a previously inaccessible route."

Delilah's heart sank. "Is there really no other way?" she asked, knowing she had failed to suppress her consternation from the way Vidalia ran a hand impatiently over his neatly shaved scalp. "It may be too soon for that. There are certain people aboard who I fear may react adversely to the arrival of our new crewmembers. I haven't yet had a chance to get everyone acclimated to the idea."

"If you are referring to Wing Commander Heperi then I must admit that I too share your concern, Captain. That obstinate drunkard has a troubling history of demonstrating aggression toward nonhuman persons." One of the creatures in the aquarium flicked its tail fin suddenly, seeming to match the growing irritation of its keeper. "The individuals I am sending to assist are not only very dear to me but precious commodities as well. I suggest you take a moment to apprise Mr. Heperi of the situation, because if anything unfortunate were to happen to them, know that the consequences for you and your crew would be grave, to say the least."

Delilah took a moment to deconstruct what was a very clear and serious threat.

What in the Abyss have you gotten yourself into?

"Governor, if I may . . ."

He silenced her with an austere look, the umbral circles of his eyes like tunnels leading to endless nothingness.

"If you cannot accept these new terms, Captain, then you leave me with no choice but to . . ." He paused, let a cruel smile touch his lips. "Terminate our contract."

She swallowed the lump in her throat and pushed her shoulders back in an attempt to save face. "That won't be necessary. I'll see to it your associates are treated with the utmost respect by the crew. They'll feel right at home on the *Assurance*. You can bet on it."

"Only a fool bets, Captain. You have given me your word. I expect you to keep it."

Vidalia ended the call abruptly. An oppressive silence smothered the cockpit, leaving Delilah in the frigid grip of uncertainty.

EIGHT

With the Governor's threats of repercussions still weighing on her mind, Delilah left the sanctity of the cockpit to investigate the ruckus she had heard—and struggled to ignore—during the call. Following a cacophony of raised voices and fists slamming on countertops, she found Isaac and Teodora blowing up at each other in the galley—nominally, over the logistics of the upcoming Debris Belt excursion.

It was not unusual for the pair to clash in the run-up to a job. The incessant bickering that went on between them felt more indicative of a relationship between siblings than it was shipmates. She figured the problem stemmed from the fact that they were too alike: intelligent, strong-willed, and fiercely dedicated to their respective roles. But it was that sense of kinship paired with their claustrophobic work environment that often turned healthy competition into something far harder on the eardrums.

The instigator was usually Teodora Brižan—the *Assurance*'s Mouthnative salvage specialist: an effervescent ray of sunshine—as stubborn as a mule with a predisposition for explosive temper tantrums.

Growing up with her many siblings in an interspecies orphanage sternside of the blockade, Teo learned to stand up for what she believed in and to never back down from a fight. It was there, in an environment consisting entirely of repurposed wreckage, that she became a prodigy in the field of salvage—gifted with an innate understanding of taking superstructure apart and a nose for sniffing out valuable tech. She was an irreplaceable component of Delilah's operation, violent mood swings and all. Her smile could light up the darkest of rooms, while moments of sorrow brought melancholia crashing down upon the ship.

Olive-skinned with cerulean-dyed hair fashioned in a long plait, Teo's dress sense matched her vibrant and chaotic personality: her nimble physique was kept encased in a nanofiber jumpsuit worn beneath a colorful knitted sweater. She sported a utility belt embellished with cartoon stickers of flowers and long-extinct animals, as well as steel-capped work boots spray-painted like the hide of a psychedelic zebra. Looking like a piece of industrial hardware given to a child as a plaything, the girl stood by the island counter-top at the center of the galley, flouncing her arms as if swatting away a fly. The subject of her furious gesticulation was the topographical view of the hunk of wreckage from which the ionizers were waiting to be excavated, projected by a luma-puck on the countertop.

"You come up with some insane ideas, Isaac," she said, downturned eyes bright and angry. "But this one takes the gold standard. You're not taking into account how fragile these beasts really are. They've been drifting out there in the empty black since the Collision, meaning they'll be structurally unsound. If you ham-fist this like the last time you tried to use that damn grapple, you're gonna nuke this score too!"

Isaac Verhoeven, the young man Delilah entrusted with the repair and maintenance of the *Assurance*, took a moment to prepare his rebuke from the far side of the island. She couldn't help but feel a stab of remorse as she looked at him; twenty-four years old with long sandy hair kept in a scruffy topknot, his engineer's jumpsuit tied loosely around his waist, he was the spitting image of Micah—or at least, the way he appeared in her memory . . .

Isaac sat forward on his stool, fiddling anxiously with the safety goggles slung around his neck. "That one wasn't my fault! There was no way I could have predicted that compact reactor would go into meltdown. In fairness, it was *your* responsibility as salvage specialist to let me know it still had residual power!"

"Passing the buck again. What a shock!"

Delilah pulled up a stool and positioned herself between them, ready to assume the role of mediator. She gave Isaac a reassuring nod, catching sight of the one physical attribute that differentiated him from the way his brother looked at the same age: the clouded lenses of his eyes—an indication of seri-ous and extensive glow abuse.

Isaac had followed in Micah's footsteps in more ways than one. All Verho-even boys, it would seem, had an affinity for tinkering with the inner workings of swoops and ships. With seemingly no chance of his parents ever seeing the light of day again, he had left foster care in his adolescent years and sprouted into a fine engineer—far more accomplished than his older brother ever had the chance to be. But while Micah's burgeoning glow habit was cut short, the one Isaac picked up in the wake of his brother's death had been allowed to blossom into a debilitating addiction. By the time Delilah abandoned her ill-fated pilgrimage to the Mouth, Isaac's dependency had taken over and destroyed his life. Having returned bowside, she found him in the custody of the Glow Enforcement Agency, awaiting trial for burglary and possession of a controlled substance. Thankfully, then-Detective Eamon Wyatt, taking stock of the tragedy that was the boy's life and eager not to have him end up as just another statistic, agreed to let Delilah take him under her wing. She was determined she wouldn't lose another Verhoeven boy the way she lost Micah, so she bought a ship, got him off the *Novara*, and took him as far away from the source of his addiction as she possibly could.

What followed could only be described as the withdrawal from hell, but he came out the other side dependable, resilient, and the only person on the *Novara* she ever wanted keeping the *Assurance* ticking over.

Teo and Isaac simultaneously jumped down each other's throats, realizing their captain was now present and both feeling the need to defend themselves.

Delilah raised a silencing hand.

"Start from the top. What's this about?"

"Isaac's tryna change the plan again." Teo reached over the countertop and tapped the glass surface of the luma-puck. The projection of the target wreckage zoomed in; layers of structure peeled away to reveal a cross section of an intact length of maintenance corridor. Beneath the floor grating were three discernible cubes of machinery interconnected by a reinforced lattice of pipework.

"Here you can see the hydro-ionizers the Governor's commissioning us to extract. Originally, we agreed I was gonna go EVA, slice them out myself, and manually guide them into the cargo bay using my thruster pack. But Isaac's got some crazy notion about fixing a fission cutter to one of the arms of the pneumatic grapple so he can retrieve them remotely."

"I can do it, Captain," Isaac interjected. "I know we've had some issues with remote extractions before—"

Teo scoffed. "There's an understatement."

"—but I've been practicing with the grapple and I'm way more precise with it now. We all know we're against the clock on this job—doing it this way could save a lot of time."

"I'm all up for shaving off a few minutes," Teo said, taking on a more civil demeanor, "but if Isaac cuts the coolant lines in the wrong order or botches the retrieval again, then we'll be explaining to the Governor why the bounty was delivered irreparably damaged."

Delilah looked into Isaac's milky eyes, saw the embers of a fire stamped out, pleading for a chance to reignite. She wanted to give him the opportunity to prove himself but ultimately knew the risks were too great. Still, that didn't mean a compromise couldn't be reached.

"Once the ionizers are cut free, you're absolutely sure you can reel them into the cargo bay remotely?"

"Positive, Captain."

She drew a breath, exhaled through pursed lips.

"As long as these lockdown measures are in place, we're only getting clearance to disembark under the pretense that it's for welding—this detour to the Debris Belt won't exactly be sanctioned, so every minute we can scrounge counts."

She turned to Teo, conveyed with an unsmiling expression that what she was about to say was gospel, and nonnegotiable.

"You know old tech like this better than anyone. I think it's best you go EVA and cut them out manually as per the original plan. But then, Isaac, I want you on standby with the pneumatic grapple for a fast retrieval. If we're smart about this, we can collect the quarry, get it delivered, and be back before the harbormaster even suspects a thing."

Teo opened her mouth to protest but saw the steel in her captain's preemptive scowl and retracted into her technicolor shell.

Isaac nodded, wind back in his sail. "Understood . . . and thank you."

Delilah smiled, fighting to conceal the truth that, inwardly, she felt shame. She knew firsthand the damage glow had wreaked on the Verhoeven boys, and yet, here she was taking work from the man who peddled it up and down the *Novara*. She had managed to convince herself that working for the Governor was a necessary evil in her quest to "make things better for people" while earning a hefty sum in the process. But the closer she got to the reality of fulfilling the contract, the more uncertain she became that it was justifiable.

"Next order of business," she announced, straightening her posture. "Vidalia's changing the plan for delivery. He can't get us through the blockade anymore, so he's sending two of his associates to guide us to the delivery point and assist with the installation."

Teo's sullen bearing dissipated in an instant, replaced by puppylike excitement. "New crew members? Are these our exo-tech specialists?"

Isaac looked to share some of Teo's infectious giddiness. "I was wondering when they'd be joining us. Does this mean we'll be running *Devourer* salvage from now on too?"

Delilah shook her head. "It won't mean anything if we don't nail this job for the Governor. I'm not sure how long they're planning on staying with us, but it's imperative we make a good impression. That means I can't have you two screaming at each other in the galley while they're aboard. Understood?"

They looked at each other and said, "Understood" in unison.

"Keep the peace. That's all I ask."

Teo clambered over the island countertop again, deactivated the luma-puck, and slotted it into one of the pouches on her belt.

"The *Assurance* is gonna get awful cramped awful soon. But as long as it don't mean I gotta bunk up with Kahu, then it's fine by me."

Delilah snickered. "Teo. If I made you do that, I think you'd have reasonable grounds for mutiny."

It wasn't long after the dispute in the galley that the call about a rupture finally came in. Delilah felt the *kerthunk* of the docking clamps disengaging and saw the landing pad running lights turn from red to green through the windshield.

We're free.

Like a rhino performing ballet, Kahu spun about the helm, initializing various ship systems in a tattoo-covered whirlwind guided entirely by muscle memory. The old pilot had done outstanding work as usual; the *Assurance* would be starside within a matter of seconds.

She vaulted into the copilot's seat and buckled herself in. Teo was in the cargo bay prepping for EVA while Isaac had already lowered himself into the magma cannon via the helm access ladder chute. The only problem with such a smooth and well-rehearsed takeoff was that there *still* hadn't been time to tell Kahu about the inbound skiff. In spite of what Vidalia had advised, she didn't intend on painting him the full picture—he would get the broad strokes, obviously—but she feared that revealing too much could send him into a blind rage.

The paranoid old fool might even deny docking permission or obliterate their shuttle with an aggressive ramming maneuver.

The gut-mulching vibration of the impulse thrusters rattled her bones as they fired up; she turned to Kahu and shouted over the engine thrum, "After you get clear of the fission field, hold position before vectoring to the rupture site."

"Huh? Why?"

"We're doing a quick pickup—two passengers, docking by shuttle."

He creased his brow—a hoary caterpillar sitting atop his dubious expression. "I don't like uninvited guests, Skipper."

"Duly noted. Now, get us out of here!"

"Yes, ma'am."

He maxed the throttle, sending the *Assurance* hurtling through the fission field and out into the endless night. Delilah felt her organs slam against the back of her rib cage as the windshield filled with a spiraling infinitude of stars.

"Feels good to stretch her wings a little." Kahu recentered the flight stick and brought the hauler out of a corkscrew maneuver. "She was getting cranky cooped up in that hangar."

"I'm gonna get cranky if you don't stop fooling around! This ain't a joyride. We've got work to do."

Mouthing the word "killjoy," he pitched upwards and turned the *Assurance* back on herself, leveling out as the gargantuan silhouette of the *Novara* came to dominate the forward view. The hangar they had just departed appeared now as a tiny window of teal-hued light in an oppressive, elongated absence of stars, the Coalescence of the crippled generation ship and its tumorous appendage lurking like a leviathan in the deep.

Kahu engaged the inertial dampeners, killing the ship's forward momentum. Squinting into the gloom, Delilah spotted a windowless bullet-shaped craft, creeping from darkness into range of the external floodlights.

"That's a lutra-class jump ship—ain't cheap to come by. We got royalty coming aboard or something, Skip?"

"Yeah, something like that."

Kahu turned to the control pedestal beside him. "Transmitting docking permissions now."

There came a powerful jolt accompanied by dampened noises of machinery—the landing skiff integrating with the airlock docking mechanism. He unbuckled his safety belt. "Table's all set. Time to go and meet the hitchhikers."

Delilah placed a hand on his shoulder, forcing him back into the pilot's seat. "There'll be time for that later. Right now, I need you to get us over to quadrant thirty-seven and in position over the rupture. Try and give Isaac the best angle you can. When he's finished up, set your heading for the Debris Belt."

Kahu made a face like a teenager ordered to do his chores. He reluctantly grabbed the flight controls and began accelerating toward the rupture. Delilah hoisted herself out of the copilot's seat and took a few steps toward helm access. She paused in the doorway, cast a glance over her shoulder at the storage locker at the rear of the bridge. Resting on the top shelf was Kahu's holstered Onema-77 fixed-cylinder revolver—a relic of the past probably even older than the *Assurance* itself. She considered taking it, uneasy in the realization she had absolutely no idea how he would react to the arrival of the visitors. Ultimately, she decided to give him the benefit of the doubt—a good captain kept faith in her crew, even when it terrified her to do so.

"Kahu," she said softly. "You trust me . . . don't you?"

Through the windshield she saw their target destination approaching; the old pilot expertly pulled the *Assurance* up alongside the rupture site, where a faint plume of atmosphere could be seen venting into the black.

"With my ship, Skipper," he replied. "Which I can confidently say is worth a hell of a lot more than my life."

A pane in the helm access corridor displayed a live feed from inside the magma cannon emplacement. Delilah stopped to check on Isaac's progress as she headed toward the airlock; over his out-of-focus head and through the glass enclosure, a stream of slag could be seen coiling and coagulating over the rupture like a glowing rope of white phosphorus, solidifying into bulbous mounds of silver.

"You got it covered down there, Verhoeven?" she called down the ladder chute.

"Local hull integrity back up to acceptable levels. I think we're about done here."

"Outstanding work. Report topside as soon as you can."

Having seemingly abandoned preparing for her upcoming assignment, Teodora had taken it upon herself to welcome Vidalia's associates aboard and had ushered them into the lounge. She was joined by a young girl of similar age: pale-skinned and frail of physique, with narrow, sunken eyes and a large gap in her front teeth. She wore a tulle gown the same color as her long ivory-white hair, with a brass pendant hanging around her neck in the shape of a crescent moon.

She was accompanied by a cohabitor—a towering creature, easily eight feet tall, wearing some kind of navy-blue shawl around its hulking shoulders. Delilah had always thought the aliens had a sort of equine look to them—like a horse if it was bipedal, its fur hide replaced by organic armor. Four pairs of black, almond-shaped eyes stared down in unblinking curiosity at the blue-haired human gallivanting at its feet. Teo's excitement over having a cohabitor on the ship was to be completely expected, given where she was raised. But the way the girl greeted the forbidding entity was like watching a kid open her presents on winter solstice morning.

"Oh, Captain! Can we keep aer?" She held its giant paw in a fervid embrace, buried her pixie-shaped face into the chitin plating of its arm. The cohabitor snorted from the breathing holes on its neck in what looked like a blend of fear and confusion, the mandibles beneath its elongated snout chattering manically; the poor thing had absolutely no clue how to respond.

"Teo. Please let go of our guest," Delilah said sternly. Teo feigned a playful sulk, taking a stool at the island countertop.

"Whoa . . ." Isaac stood in the doorway, mouth agape, wide eyes encircled by marks left by his goggles. Delilah had been similarly concerned about how her engineer would react to the new arrivals, considering the by-product of

Devourer biotech was the source of his dependency. Isaac had worked hard to kick the habit, and a relapse now would be catastrophic. Thankfully, in demonstration of the fact that he'd grown up every bit as compassionate and open-minded as his brother, he joined them in the lounge and collapsed into Kahu's recliner, a grin of unbridled amazement spreading across his face.

"It seems stupid now," he said, "but for some reason I thought our exotech specialist would be human. I didn't expect a cohabitor."

"Null!" the girl interjected, clutching her brass pendant nervously, her colorless hair almost translucent in the dim lamplight.

"Is . . . is that his name?" stammered Isaac.

"It's *aer* name," Teo corrected. "Cohabitors are hermaphroditic. They aren't boys or girls like we are. Well . . . in a way, they're kinda both. You use ae, aer, aerself when talkin' about 'em."

"Far out."

"Names and pronouns are not generally applicable." The girl pulled up a stool at the island, leaving her statuesque companion looking a little bit lost, standing alone in the lounge. "Cohabitors do not have written or spoken language. Their method of communication is too abstruse to be defined by human understanding. But yes. If you wish, you may call this one Null. And my name is Mercy."

Delilah bowed her head courteously. "It's a pleasure having you both aboard. Vidalia spoke very highly of you. I'm excited to see what we can achieve together."

"Hang on a second," Isaac interrupted, rocking pensively in Kahu's recliner. "If cohabitors don't have language, then how do they communicate?"

Mercy was allowed to utter no more than one syllable of her response before Teo excitedly took the reins.

"There's no need for talkin'. They can read each other empathically—feel each other's feelings, project images and ideas into each other's heads."

"I get it," Isaac said, making an expression that suggested otherwise. "Like telepathy . . . Is that why you hear horror stories about them getting inside people's minds, making them do things they don't want to, or turning their brains to mush?"

"That's a load of crap!" Teo sounded as though she'd argued about this subject many times before. "Yeah, it's true that if they try to link with *us* in the way they do one another, the result can be painful. But that's only because we're incompatible. Ain't no malice in it—they're just tryna say hello." She skipped around the island, plonking herself next to an increasingly discombobulated Mercy. "Then you get people like Mercy here. She's a cipher." Teo pointed at her temple. "It means she can access their wavelength—make an empathic connection with Null and read aer just like any other cohabitor, allowing her to convey and receive emotional and experiential information."

"Ah! So, she's like a translator?"

"Amazing, right? Ciphers are pretty rare. When I was a kid, I wanted to be one so bad. Used to give myself migraines trying to read the cohab kids at Juniper Sanctuary. Just weren't what I was destined for, I guess."

"Fascinating." Delilah took a few measured steps toward Null, who had become transfixed by one of the old fabric lamps, studiously running its shade tassels between slender digits. "Perhaps you and Null could give us a demonstration?"

Mercy let a faint smile pull at the corner of her lips. "Certainly."

There was a fizzle in the air—a soft brush of static like the kind produced by rubbing a balloon on carpet. Mercy closed her eyes, biting her tongue in concentration. When she opened them again, they were, astoundingly, illuminated. Orange and violet light burst forth from her irises as though her skull had been hollowed out and filled with brightly burning candles. Null's many eyes produced the same phenomenon, the pair jointly dousing the galley in eerie opalescence.

Mercy's focus deepened. She tilted her head and spoke awkwardly with prolonged consonants and erratic inflections.

"We feel . . . gratitude, excitement."

Teo jumped in exuberance while Isaac sank farther into Kahu's recliner, dumbstruck. Delilah glanced at Null, understanding that Mercy was now essentially a conduit for aer thoughts and emotions. Here were two species, existing on opposite ends of the anatomical spectrum—who had chanced upon each other in the void—capable of such a deep and profound connection. It dawned on her how little she really knew about cohabitors: their biology, their culture; even after all that time searching for answers in the Mouth, she had barely scratched the surface. Her awe was tempered somewhat by the sudden realization that she could no longer feel the pull of deceleration; they had arrived at the Debris Belt, which meant Kahu would come barreling into the galley at any moment . . .

"I see the *Assurance*," Mercy continued. "I see its crew, and I feel . . . welcomed." The girl paused, weighed visibly by a sudden unease. "I feel . . . fearful, alert. I see . . . I see a man. A man with a gun."

Delilah spun around and met Kahu's eyes as he lingered in the entrance to the galley, revolver drawn with Null firmly in his sights.

"You brought one onto my ship?" he hissed through bared teeth, his face twisted in rage.

Teo jumped up from her stool and raced to put herself defensively in front of Null. But with a paw that spanned her entire torso, ae effortlessly pushed her back out of the line of fire.

Kahu stepped forward, the downlight above his head casting distorting shadows over the angles of his grimacing face.

"Get clear of that thing, Mouth rat!"

"Put the gun down, you idiot! Please! They aren't here to hurt us."

But the girl's plea went unheeded; instead, he tightened his shaking hands around the grip of his Onema-77.

Delilah sidestepped into his line of sight in quiet disbelief that she had been so foolish as to leave the firearm in his possession. Evidently her faith had been misplaced. Strangely, though, she found it difficult to be angry, for there was fear in his deranged expression—the fear of a man whose only experience with beings like Null was dogfighting with them from beneath the canopy of a kestrel, watching helplessly while his squadmates were shot down by enemy interceptors, back in the days of the Antonelli expansion. She showed her palms, offered a pleading expression. "Heperi. I really need you to just take a breath and think about what you're doing right now." She gestured toward Mercy, who had gradually made her way across the galley to Null, taking cover behind aer. "These are Vidalia's people. They're here to help us with the job. Just think about what the Governor would do if either of them got hurt."

"I don't fear the Governor," Kahu said, eyes darting frantically between Delilah and his target. "Drexen is just a man . . . but this thing—this thing is the devil. You have no idea what it's capable of. It'll get inside your skull, turn your brains to scrambled protein, make you wanna hurt yourself and those around you." He flicked the muzzle of his gun at Mercy, whose eyes were once again glowing brightly.

"Look. It's already got her brainwashed."

"I am here of my own volition," the girl intoned, stepping out from behind her protective wall of exoskeleton, although her words did little to placate and only seemed to serve as further evidence of indoctrination.

"You see? I bet it wants to take over the *Assurance*. Dive-bomb her into the *Novara!*"

Isaac stood up from the recliner like a projectile launched from a slingshot. "Kahu, if you fire that hand cannon in here, the round will blow straight through the fuselage. Put it down before you get us all killed."

"Shut your mouth, boy! You don't know what you're talking about. Besides, getting spaced might be a downright mercy compared to what this leech will do to us all if we let it live!"

Delilah brought herself before him, rested her hand on the stock of her concussion repeater.

"I am ordering you—as your captain—to holster that weapon, pilot. I don't want to put you down, but I absolutely will if you make me."

Kahu's rugged features formed a look of pure desperation. "You might have to, Skip . . . I'm not gonna let it hurt any of you."

Null, the only individual present who hadn't yet attempted to calm him, suddenly made a sharp braying sound; ae began motioning gracefully with aer giant paws, like slow interpretive dance.

Mercy tilted her head back, her retinal luminance brighter than any other light source in the galley. "We are here to help the *Assurance*. Provide water! Bring new life to the Mouth! Save our people!"

"You see?" whispered Delilah. "They're not here to hurt us."

Approaching slowly with arms outstretched, ready to collect the revolver from his trembling hands, she saw in Kahu a moment of hesitation as he gave everything to defy his base instincts. He exhaled deeply, rum-reeking breath quivering through strained vocal cords. Then he let the gun fall into her hands.

She took it, emptied the cylinder, and realized the safety was on and had been the whole time.

NINE

Sorely missing the department's old prowler, which would never fly again thanks to its untimely *decommissioning*, Eamon made his way on foot into Tinji Marketplace—the beating heart of the Copper Swathes. On any other day, these awning-canopied streets would be thumping with atonal music, thronged with traders and street performers, the air redolent with the aromas of exotic spices and seared cultivated meats.

Now, the place was a ghost town—evidently deemed too dangerous for usual commerce, with fears that public spaces might be targeted for further violence growing more by the hour.

It took a lot to break the spirit of a mouthian, but the eerie quiescence that had descended upon the marketplace suggested the Composer had done just that. The days of Harmony characterizing itself as the underdog fighting against the forces of government tyranny were over. There was no disputing what they were now: violent terrorists who would kill anyone in their crusade for the emancipation and restitution of the Mouth.

Abraham stayed diligently in formation, his pace a little slower than usual. Occasionally he would glance up at his shambling human, dopey brown eyes telegraphing concern.

"I'm fine," Eamon kept telling the agonizing mutt, quietly unsure of how true a statement that was. Following his forcible removal from the Phalanx compound, he had limped back to the precinct house for a checkup in medical—no showstoppers, which was fortunate given nothing short of two shattered femurs could prevent his return to duty.

There were some things a slip of med-foam and a stim shot couldn't fix, of course, like the self-flagellation and second-guessing that inevitably followed any use of lethal force. Or the irrepressible sense of culpability regarding the truth about his whereabouts prior to the massacre: boozing it up with a crooked salvage captain on the wrong side of the blockade.

He was no stranger to coping with guilt. In fact, he'd become quite adept at channeling it into something more conducive to the task at hand. He would let it reanimate his battered husk like a shot of adrenaline, keeping him sharp and on his feet until the Composer and all her twisted sycophants were behind bars, or frozen solid on the far side of an airlock.

In his mind, the threat level the faction represented warranted the formation of a kind of joint task force—one pooling the best resources and intel from both sides of the blockade. But expecting that kind of departmental cohesion from the current Administration, whose interest in justice existed only so long as it served their agenda, was a fool's game. Just like with the Lahiri murder inquiry, DMED would be shut out completely, allowed to contribute little more than a condemning dossier of nonhuman persons of interest, who likely had nothing to do with the crimes they would be convicted of. Much of this he expected to be briefed on during the emergency meeting Madeline Vargos had frantically arranged following the attack.

Probably get a load of earache for "interfering" with Phalanx operations too . . . Won't that be fun?

The Administrator's summons would have to wait, though, for there was a matter of even greater importance that first needed tending to. Eamon could function on little to no sleep—he could cope with working shell-shocked and slightly concussed from the crash and subsequent shoot-out—but he couldn't do it on an empty stomach.

Tucked away in a dark alcove beneath the Moorish archway of the Amaali Bazaar, there was a street food place that he and the deputy frequented during downtime, where his quest for much-needed sustenance would be fulfilled. Jyn favored it for being one of the few establishments outside of the Cohabitor Ghetto that catered to both human *and* nonhuman patrons—perfect for exchanging a few quiet words with residents of an *extraterrestrial persuasion*.

What does she call it again? "Attaining resonance," that's it—tuning the dial in her mind like an old FM radio, tapping into the cohab frequency, eyes like a pair of incandescent light bulbs.

Occupying a stool by the glass counter, he watched in quiet admiration while the deputy ordered—knowing Jyn—probably enough for a family of four. The cohab server with whom she was in wordless negotiation loomed as an immovable pillar wearing a stained apron, the glowing emissions of the exchange reflecting in rakes of purple and green in aer iridescent carapace.

Eamon's limited understanding on the subject was as follows: "resonant" humans were only able to make a solid connection with a very limited number

of cohabitors. There existed an added level of compatibility that made finding a partner with whom resonance was attainable an arduous task, causing those who were successful to often form a kind of consortium. The term
"cipher" applied to someone who committed themselves to a single cohabitor
and dedicated their life to the bond. It wasn't a romantic partnership by any
means; in some ways, it was more significant than that—a permanent sharing of the mind, a melding of the soul, a psychic union transcending time
and space itself. Jyn Sato, however, was more than just an average cipher:
she was "hyper-resonant," meaning she had never met a nonhuman person
with whom she could not forge an empathic connection—a walking, talking Rosetta Stone of sorts. Hyper-resonants were of an incredibly rare caste:
generally speaking, no more than two or three existed at any given time, and
estimates were that perhaps less than a dozen had discovered and successfully honed their abilities since the Collision. DMED was fortunate to have
one at their disposal. Now, things like nonhuman interrogations without a
cipher present to muddy the waters were possible, as well as connecting with
community leaders to build public outreach with some of the most cut-off
and alienated demographics in the district. All thanks to Jyn's unique "linguistic" capabilities.

Another moment of silent back and forth passed, then the transaction
was concluded. The server stomped off into the kitchen to relay the order
to aer cipher—a squat woman in a hairnet who immediately began hurling
produce into a sizzling wok.

"Any hot gossip?" asked Eamon.

Jyn simpered, shook her head as she perched herself on the stool beside
him. "There were Monarchs poking around earlier in the week, tryna get the
'Governor's discount,' if you catch my meaning. Bastards even raided the tip
jar before they left. I didn't see anything specifically about Harmony or the
attack, but I sure felt a lot of fear and uncertainty about the situation. I think
ae's nervous about how heavy-handed the Administration's reaction to this
will be."

Eamon licked his thumb, used it to wipe away the dried bloodstain he
had just noticed on the fur collar of his jacket. "Ae and me both. Vargos was
already threatening to dispatch the grennies when we last spoke. After what
went down at the compound, you can bet she'll have them marching through
the blockade before second shift is out. I'm dreading what'll happen when
those protesters work up the courage to go another round."

"Yup. It'll be a total shit show." She began massaging her temples, fingers tracing the brilliant filigree of vessels creeping out from behind her ears.
"I might have to leave dealing with the activists and the metal men to you,

though. I've been banging on doors tryna piece together Anaya's last few hours for . . . well, I've lost track of how long. I need to clock out and get some rack before I cook my frontal cortex."

Dissatisfied with not being the center of attention for more than five seconds, Abraham ferreted his snout into Eamon's hand, gazing up expectantly. Eamon smiled. "We're just glad you could take the time out to come and check on us. It was a rough ride."

She reached over and let the adoring mutt nuzzle her palm. "You both look like you've been through hell and back. I'd tell you for the hundredth time there's no need for a marshal to go throwing himself headfirst into every situation that arises, but at this point I feel like I'm banging my head against the wall."

He shrugged and twinged at the subsequent stab of shoulder pain. "Old habits die hard, I guess."

"Yup. And you'll die real easy if you don't learn how to let other people handle things."

The server returned carrying two plates piled high with mounds of heavenly fragrant kothu parotta. The marshal and the deputy simultaneously snapped their chopsticks and began shoveling down mouthfuls of shredded noodles and charred vegetables, Abe waiting patiently by their feet for falling scraps.

"Did you dig up anything new with the Lahiri case?"

Jyn gave a noncommittal nod, cheeks like a hamster's, stretched to their fullest extent. "I know where Anaya went; I've put together a pretty solid timeframe too. But I don't think *why* she was in the district in the first place is something we can extrapolate without picking the trail up bowside."

Eamon grunted cynically. "We've got a better chance of ripple-spacing our asses to Pasture than we do of crossing the blockade right now."

"Then I hate to say it, but I think this case is dead in the water. With the crime scene scrubbed and the body already repatriated, I'm not sure what else we can do. I've gotten about as much mileage out of the Ghetto as I can already. The residents are spooked—won't even open the door to a deputy."

"Funny, isn't it?" He gestured with chopsticks through the entrance, into the bazaar—normally so overcrowded that people would be walking cheek to cheek but instead completely deserted.

"It wasn't that long ago folks were singing the Composer's praises and calling her the liberator of the Mouth, spray-painting that asinine mantra, 'Quell the Dissonance,' on every wall in the Copper Swathes. Now just look around . . . She's got people terrified, too scared to leave their homes or go about their normal business. Some savior she turned out to be."

Jyn stared down into her steaming grub, solemn and ruminative. "Do you think it went to plan?" she asked softly.

"Did what go to plan?"

"All those protesters and refugees you said pushed over the barricade, the ones who were killed in the blast. They're the same people whose rights and freedoms Harmony is fighting for, aren't they? Do you think the Composer intended for there to be so much collateral?"

He registered ambivalence with a sideways glance.

"Harmony wants two things, Jyn: the blockade demolished, and the Administration dissolved. I don't reckon they're the least bit concerned about who gets zeroed in the process."

His snappy riposte put the deputy on the back foot. She fished out a chunk of cultivated meat and tossed it to Abe, taking a long beat to ready a hopefully less spurious counter.

"I'm not saying she shouldn't be made to pay for her crimes. Even if the blockade falls and Harmony ends up getting their revolution, justice will come for her like it does for us all. The thing is, she's Mouthborn—just like me. You know how pissed off I am about the way things are: the abysmal standard of living, the oppression and strangulation we're subjected to by a neglectful government. And yet, I could never purposefully harm my own people, even if I was convinced it could somehow lead to things improving for the Mouth. I'm not discounting or overlooking the folks who just lost their lives; it's just difficult to reconcile that somebody from *my* neck of the woods could have meant for it to go down the way it did."

"But you know this isn't the first time one of her 'demonstrations' has resulted in a body count," he replied, impassioned but tempering his voice. "The fact is that the whole thing hinged on those protesters breaking through the Phalanx line and rushing the checkpoint. It was the only way the insurgents were getting deep enough into the compound to effectively detonate the IED. There was no possible version of their plan where a significant number of civilians didn't end up in the mud."

He paused, shivered at just how clinically he had described the single most heinous thing he had ever witnessed: like a historian dryly recounting war strategy.

Perhaps it's some kind of coping mechanism.

"Look. I understand where you're coming from, Jyn, but it's important we don't lose sight of who it is we're up against. She led them like lambs to the slaughter—there ain't no other way of looking at it."

"I guess you're right."

It was then as if a soundproofed curtain rolled out between them. For what felt like the longest time, they ate in total silence. Harmony had always been a point of contention for Jyn—as a hyper-resonant Mouth native, she understood the cohabitors' plight better than anyone. She struggled with the dichotomy of proudly sporting her DMED badge while finding that many of the hopes and aspirations she held for her people aligned with those of a terrorist organization. Ultimately, Eamon didn't believe there to be any real conflict of interest—the trail of destruction Harmony had left behind was peppered with the bodies of innocent cohabitors too. That was more than enough to put them on Jyn's list. She was a little green but a good enforcer nonetheless. As opinionated and overzealous as she tended to be on the subject, her heart was in the right place.

Another miserable minute of silence passed. Eamon had begun to suspect it would take a miracle to kick-start conversation again. Fortunately, he had just the trick . . .

Clandestinely scanning the eatery to make sure the other patrons were minding their own business, he reached into the inside pocket of his jacket and produced a pistol—one of the heavily augmented firearms wielded by the insurgents during the attack.

An almost indecipherable look of dread and surprise swept over Jyn as he set it down carefully on the countertop, the weapon's demonic appearance triggering a wave of gnawing revulsion. The thing was hideous: a standard subcompact handgun covered in blackened viscera, cocooned in the rotting entrails of some disemboweled creature.

"Oh, Wyatt." Jyn was aghast, the color drained visibly from her cheeks. "What in the stars are you doing with that? And where did it come from?"

He leaned toward her and continued in hushed tones, "I managed to swipe it from the compound before the crisis response team kicked me out on my ass. This is one of the weapons the insurgents were using; a couple of them even had burst rifles engineered with the same alien crap. These weapons fire standard projectile rounds charged with some kind of freaky voltaic energy—melted through titanium-weave armor like it was rocky road ice cream. I've never seen anything like it."

Jyn swallowed the lump in her throat, eyes darting manically over the weapon, running fingers over the sinew and fibers of its menacing anatomy.

"This looks like *Devourer* biotech," she said, her posture shriveling at the implications of that conclusion.

He nodded. "I'm ninety-nine percent sure that's what we're looking at. My understanding was that this stuff was so far beyond our comprehension that we might as well consider it magic, but it looks like someone's figured out how to splice it with human weaponry."

"You're right. Even the cohabitors alive today barely have a grasp on it. You don't need to be an engineer so much as you need to be a surgeon to understand it. It doesn't make sense how anyone could have ascertained the knowledge to pull this off."

He smiled coyly. "I think I know how we can find out. Phalanx are probably scratching their heads right now, trying to dig up intel on where this came from. The thing is, they don't know the Mouth like we do."

"I don't follow."

He clasped his hands over the weapon to shield it from a passerby, waited for them to leave the eatery before continuing.

"Looking past all the organic attachments, I'd recognize the existing modifications any day. The slide porting, the custom grip, the heavy iron sights—this is Devruhkhar's handiwork, no two ways about it."

Jyn threw her head back and unleashed a loud, sardonic laugh. "Devruhkhar! Really? You think that incompetent meat sack is working for Harmony?"

He signaled with a quick hand motion for her to keep it down. "I don't think it's as simple as him *working* for them. Ask yourself, though: would that unprincipled slug have any reservations whatsoever about selling weapons to a terrorist cell if the price was right? The answer is absolutely not."

Jyn took a mouthful of noodles, spoke while chewing to impudently broadcast her dubiousness. "This is a stretch, Wyatt—even by your standards. That guy is a lot of things, but a leech sympathizer ain't one of them. I sincerely doubt he'd be prepared to offer up his precious stock for the cohabitors' cause. Besides, his grubby prints are probably on one in every three guns in the District of the Mouth. Just because you recognize some of his mods, it doesn't mean he sold directly to them."

"It's the only lead I've got—you don't need to tell me how much of a long shot it is. I'm going over to his workshop after I meet with Vargos to see if I can't squeeze something out of him. Try and talk me out of it all you want."

"I'm just making sure you're not wasting your time is all. We've tried putting the pressure on that scumbag before. Even if he did sell to Harmony, there's no way he'll cooperate."

She set down her chopsticks and swiveled around to face him. She placed a hand on top of his, interlocking her fingers and squeezing gently. Their relationship had never been anything other than strictly platonic, but in that moment, he felt a flurry of something else . . .

"Consider this," she said, almost whispering. "Let's say you're right: Devruhkhar is selling weapons to the Composer. Harmony has left DMED more or less out of the equation up until now. But if they find out you've been sniffing around one of their suppliers, and worse, holding on to this prototype tech, the Composer will send everything she has in her arsenal at you."

He flashed a cocky grin. "All in a day's work, Deputy."

"Remember what I said about learning to let other people handle things? Phalanx don't want you anywhere near the compound for good reason. These are terrorists we're talking about, an armed militia! Your usual one-man band routine is gonna get you killed on this one."

Abraham brought his head to rest on Eamon's thigh, still gazing up with those giant brown marbles, almost as if reaffirming Jyn's sentiment. Unfortunately, no amount of puppy-dog eyes would dampen his determination. He removed his comparatively massive hand from beneath Jyn's, turned his head to face her, only just avoiding eye contact. "I appreciate your concern. And honestly, I wish like hell I *could* just take a back seat. But we both know the folks who died at the blockade will never get justice if we leave it to the feds. Same goes for Anaya. As stupid and suicidal as it might sound, it's incumbent on us to make sure the Composer answers for her crimes. The Administration will hijack this whole damned thing and twist the narrative to further deepen the human-cohabitor divide in any way they can. I don't know about you, but I'm done standing around while innocent people are persecuted just because they don't have the power to defend or speak for themselves. I'm not expecting you to follow me into the breach, but you can't stop me diving in myself."

Jyn's temper flared. She snatched the handgun from the counter, seeming for a moment like she might bolt for the door with it, ending his reckless, harebrained plan before it had even begun. Instead, she shoved it back inside his jacket pocket and yanked the breast closed.

"Just watch who you go flashing that thing to, you stubborn ape. There's plenty of lowlifes in the slums who wouldn't think twice about zeroing a marshal to get their hands on tech like this. Be careful."

He smiled. "Hey! When am I ever anything but?"

There was a landing platform suspended just above Antaeus Gateway that acted as the sole transit point for a facility commonly known as the letterbox. It was a rectangular indentation carved high up into the blockade, where the only thing separating the Mouth from the rest of the *Novara* was a wide plate of blast-proof glass—a window into another world. Previously used for business liaisons and face-to-face contact between separated friends and family, the letterbox had recently fallen into disuse, thanks to the increasing tensions between the two territories existing on either side of it.

It was here the meeting with the Administrator was to take place, the matters at hand evidently too sensitive to be discussed over the caster. Following a somewhat tempestuous lunch break, Jyn had dropped Eamon and the mutt off before turning in for the day. "Attaining resonance" for an extended period of time was, as she put it, "every shade of exhausting you can think of." She maintained that, despite their stoicism and apparent incapacity for facial expression, cohabitors were incredibly emotional beings. They felt joy, fear, and sorrow with an acuity that simply dwarfed the human emotional spectrum. To attain resonance with one in the throes of emotional turmoil was to subject herself to brutal physical agony. A whole shift spent brain-bridging knocked her for six and usually put her out of commission for at least a day or two. Although not much progress had been made with her current investigation, Eamon reckoned she'd earned a little R and R. He watched as her cruiser sped away and descended toward the urban sprawl beneath him, whistling sharply to recall Abraham, who had wandered precariously close to the edge of the landing platform to see her off. Before heading over to meet with Vargos, he took a moment to appreciate the astonishing view afforded by his current elevation. The letterbox was no more than ten or fifteen meters below the ceiling of the Mouth, which put him in remarkably close proximity to the Höllengarten—a dense thicket of lambent vegetation that cascaded inversely from the *Devourer*'s hull and stretched out high above the district like a carpet of fire, named for its orange radiance and lethal toxicity to humans. He didn't proclaim to be an exo-botanist, but he knew at least that the cohabs harvested the growth and refined it down to an edible pulp that provided a primary source of sustenance. Additionally, the Höllengarten pumped oxygen into the Mouth and happened to do a better job of purifying the atmosphere than the *Novara*'s own air filtration—another act of unquestionable benevolence from the alien dreadnaught, which, in his estimation, provided far more in the way of support and infrastructure for people than the Administration that insisted on vilifying it so.

He heard Vargos clear her throat behind him, her penetrating voice amplified by speakers embedded in the walls of the letterbox. He turned to find her waiting on the far side of the glass divider, realizing immediately how much the luma-caster in his office had muted the lurid color of her imperial-red suit. He almost felt the need to shield his eyes from it.

She was flanked as always by a security detail of two armed grenadiers, the status lights beneath their featureless faceplates pulsing yellow as they scanned his credentials. On the landing pad behind them, against the dazzling backdrop of the Canyon, her pearl-black hummerzine hovered on cobalt-encased repulsor pads, with enough armor plating to probably withstand a shot from one of the *Novara's* dorsal rail guns.

Abraham began pacing back and forth, hackles raised, snarling at the figures on the opposite side of the barrier. Madeline made a cluck of disgust in her throat. "Must you insist on bringing that mangy beast with you everywhere you go, Marshal Wyatt?"

"Wouldn't leave the precinct house without him. Abraham watches my six. Keeps me safe from . . . *predators*."

She flushed visibly with anger before meeting his impish grin with a cruel and calculated smirk. "Well . . . I suppose there are a great many *predators* on that side of the blockade. I'm glad to hear you're taking the necessary precautions."

"What brings you all the way down to the district, Administrator?" he asked sharply, already weary of the disingenuous verbal table tennis that usually preceded these meetings. "It must be something urgent to warrant coming here yourself. I doubt an Administrator has visited the letterbox since before the Antonelli expansion."

"I imagine not. Well, first I wanted to thank you in person for your part in neutralizing the insurgents during the abhorrent and most unfortunate events at the Phalanx compound. I am told our remaining forces were in a tight spot before you intervened. I can't say your loyalties have ever been under question, but it's good to know we still have a man on the inside who knows where his lie."

Eamon blinked, perplexed; the last thing he'd expected was a thank-you. While it made for a nice change to be on the Administrator's good side for once, he felt a creeping suspicion that it was only because she was buttering him up for something . . .

"Loyalty didn't have anything to do with it. You put me here as marshal to protect and serve these people—I intend to do just that. It's just unfortunate DMED *still* don't have the resources to put together an effective counter-terrorism unit. Otherwise, we might have caught this before it happened. Instead, corners were cut, and a lot of people paid with their lives."

"I am well aware of the death toll, Marshal Wyatt."

He clicked his tongue against his teeth. "Thing is, I'm not so sure you are. I saw that vigil in Chennai Plaza on the NTNN. It was very moving—what you said—and while I agree it's absolutely tragic those twelve enforcers died in service of the Union, it was a little disconcerting to hear absolutely no mention whatsoever of the seventeen civilians who were killed as well. Even more troubling is the doctored security footage I keep seeing in which the two human insurgents have been completely edited out!"

Madeline pinched the bridge of her aquiline nose. "Oh, Eamon. Not this again. For the last time: the NTNN is a privately owned broadcasting entity. I have little control over what they cover and how they choose to cover it."

"But surely you understand the potential dangers of how they're portraying this whole thing. Not once has it been stated that there were *humans* assaulting the compound too. They're spinning it less like the work of a fringe group of extremists and more like the damn cohabitor declaration of war! It's this type of skewed coverage that's driving so much support for dangerous pitchfork mobs like Humanity First."

The Administrator locked her arms rigidly behind her back. "I do not have the time nor the patience to stand here and discuss journalism ethics with you. And I'll warn you again about such slanderous talk in regard to Humanity First. They happen to be an exceptional and highly reputable group of proud NTU citizens—a far more civilized social movement than the unruly dissidents advocating for the dismantling of the blockade in the wards."

Civilized . . .

No less than a year ago had a handful of the "dissidents" she was referring to—predominantly students—been beaten to within an inch of their lives during counterprotesting by a bunch of thugs led by none other than Bhaltair Abernathy. This was in the early days of Humanity First, before he would go on to assume the "respectable" face of the organization: wearing fancy suits and speaking at rallies and fundraisers, weaponizing the fear and ignorance of the easily manipulated with vile rhetoric disguised as indomitable patriotism.

You can dip a rotten apple in caramel, but it will still be black at the core.

Vargos must have sensed Eamon was on the cusp of bringing up Bhaltair's violent past—she cut him off before he even had a chance to open his mouth.

"I have an engagement with Admiral Coombs shortly, Eamon, so I'm afraid I must move things along."

"Fine by me."

Her bearing became unsettlingly affable, as if she were about to ruin his whole day in the politest way possible. "As you know, the transfer checkpoint was completely destroyed by the explosion. It will take significant repair before it can once again resume operation. Accordingly, we will be taking the opportunity to make drastic improvements. The new checkpoint will be completely blast-proof and heavily fortified, with far superior biometric scanners and a more robust system for ID verification. Naturally, this will take a substantial amount of work and will require the checkpoint to remain vulnerable for a number of weeks. I have authorized the deployment of the garrison to oversee the reconstruction and keep the compound secure in the interim."

Eamon knew it was coming, and even still he was unprepared for the sheer dismay that came crashing down on him.

"Administrator, please," he begged. "I appreciate the need to step up security, but sending in the grenadiers right now will only inflame the situation further. The people here are hurting; they're angry enough as it is. If you go throwing your robotic death squad into the mix, tensions are gonna reach a breaking point. We could have mass mutiny on our hands!"

"That is precisely the reason I am sending them," she replied ingratiatingly. "Really, Eamon, I thought you would have been happy about this. You said yourself that DMED are stretched dangerously thin at present. These reinforcements will help take the pressure off and free your department up to resume your existing duties: finding Anaya Lahiri's killer, for example."

Madeline's grenadiers flinched as he took a sudden step toward the glass. "I told you already: I've got my best and brightest on it. But otherwise, my department's priority *must* be Harmony. We need to focus all our efforts on neutralizing or apprehending the Composer if we have any hope of preventing another attack."

"That won't be necessary," said Vargos as melodically as birdsong, clearly enjoying watching him squirm. "The attack happened on NTU sovereignty—Phalanx counterterrorism are more than capable of bringing those responsible to justice. The only thing I need from you is a comprehensive list of all nonhuman persons with existing criminal records for violent offences. Is that something you can provide?"

Eamon hung his head, the weight of his despair like a chain around his neck. "Right away, Administrator."

Abraham began barking at something behind them. Eamon turned, hearing the unmistakable growl of fission-injection repulsor pads disengaging. He shielded his face from the rolling clouds of dust kicked up by a cruiser setting down on the landing platform. It was in pristine condition, the red and blue of its enforcer decal as sharp and vivid as any he'd seen before. The driver's seat was empty, which suggested it was fitted with Hypatia-integrated remote autopilot. The thing was brand spanking new—straight out of the factory.

"A replacement," the Administrator said, "for the one destroyed during the attack. It's the very least I could do for your valiant efforts in defending the compound."

He turned to face her and stuttered a pathetic thank-you, feeling as though he was about to accept a bribe from the devil herself.

TEN

It was the morning after the reunion in the Conservatory. Tobias had taken Caleb back to his father's apartment to spend the night, thinking she was not yet in any state to be returned home. Mrs. Callaghan had always been a sort of mother by proxy, and he would have liked the opportunity to seek solace in the pragmatic, stiff-upper-lip attitude with which she usually met adversity. But having been so vocal about her dissatisfaction with the career prospects of her future daughter-in-law, the woman would be callously unsympathetic to the news of Jade's death—perhaps even positively gleeful about it.

As Caleb had sobbed herself to sleep in his old bed, he had taken the sofa in the parlor and dozed by the ember glow of the open hearth, finally managing to find some inner peace after a day spent fraught with despair.

Things seemed a little brighter with Caleb around, her presence like a flicker of candlelight in a dark and endless tunnel. In the morning, seeming to have had a dramatic improvement in constitution, she joined him in the kitchen wearing some of Hazel's old casuals. They indulged together in Atherton's reserves of hydroponically grown and freshly ground coffee—rich and invigorating in flavor, a far cry from the tasteless sludge synthesized in the Academy dormitory.

His father had left discreetly in the early hours, presumably to attend yet another emergency council session, which had been incessant in the aftermath of the bombing at the blockade. Atherton had always strived to make his paternal admiration of Caleb well known and treated her as no less than an immediate extension of the Edevane clan. But Tobias knew that at times like these he could be intolerable, his politically charged pontificating surly enough to send her spiraling into an abyss—one it would take many hours to help claw her way back out of.

Having the apartment all to themselves was a small blessing. Their leisurely morning was a moment of stillness and repose, a bittersweet facsimile of a norm which, sadly, would forever be a distant memory. They frittered the time away bringing Jade Tanaka back to life in their minds, swapping stories of first meetings and fond—occasionally embarrassing—anecdotes from their long-shared history together. They remembered her for the brave and selfless Novarian she was, with her endearing obsession with anything that blossomed or sprouted leaves and her immutable dedication to serving the New Terra Union.

For the most part, Caleb kept a brave face throughout; occasionally the cracks in her cheerful facade would show: a quiver of the lips, a tremble in her voice, a blink that seemed to last just a millisecond too long. He didn't suspect it would take much for the thin sheet of ice beneath her feet to give way and for the tenebrous depths of grief to swallow her whole—a fate he was steadfast in devoting all his efforts to preventing.

By now he'd accepted that his impeccable Academy attendance record was about to receive its first mark; he'd made a promise to stick by her side and, clearly, she had no intention of resuming studies any time soon.

"Where you go, I go." The words left his mouth with conviction, but Caleb's response was not one he was anticipating, nor one he was convinced represented a particularly good idea. She expressed a desire to pay her respects at the memorial in Xìngyùn Square, reasoning that Jade would have liked to see the mounds of flowers that were being left in remembrance of the victims. He aired his reservations, fearing the impact going would have on them both, given their joint *fragility*, but as Caleb's effervescence began to return, so too did her stubbornness. Within the hour, they were heading along a balustraded boardwalk toward Xìngyùn Square: the metropolitan center situated at the Canyon's bow terminus. It was the crown jewel of the Upperdecks—a vast plaza enclosed by a myriad of retail stores, galleries, and fine-dining restaurants, the upturned spires of the Central Business District looming overhead—stalactites of metal and ice sculpting a dazzling inverted skyline.

Down on ground level, the busyness took Tobias by surprise; the square was astir with people shopping, socializing, and going about their day, seemingly oblivious to the butchery that had taken place less than forty-eight hours earlier. How quickly his fellow citizens had consigned the carnage to the back of their minds and managed to reinstate everyday monotony. He found it remarkable, if a little disconcerting, but knew that to have it any other way would be to give the leeches exactly what they wanted: for fear to consume his way of life; to allow not one facet of his peaceful existence to remain unsullied by the threatening tide of extinction. There was a fine line, it would seem, between carrying on in defiance of their cruelty and showing a staggering lack of reverence for their victims.

Caleb tugged him through the crowd by the sleeve of his cashmere trench coat, picking up speed as they traversed deeper into the square. At the very center there stood a monument commemorating the founding nations of the New Terra Union and the historic collaboration that led to the *Novara's* construction. Nine arms of burnished copper climbed like the intertwining branches of a tree, reaching for sunlight. They converged to support an armillary sphere with a model of the *Novara* bursting from its core. A plaque at the base read, "Astra inclinant, sed non obligant."

A dead language for a dead planet.

He appreciated the symbolism but had always considered it a terrible eyesore; the "branches" in particular were forebodingly reminiscent of the leech conduits that now pervaded the *Novara's* superstructure. Its unsightly appearance was mitigated somewhat by the floral scenes scattered beside it. A now nearly knee-high pile of flowers surrounded a collection of canvas portraits—one for each of the twelve victims—sitting in wooden easels, white rose garlands draped between them. Eleven of the deceased were depicted looking dashing and dignified in their Phalanx uniforms. Jade Tanaka, on the other hand, had been immortalized tending to her garden in denim overalls and muddied gardening gloves, a smile of maternal pride shining down at the carrot leaves sprouting from the soil at her feet: content, full of life, blissfully unaware of her grim fate.

It was a beautiful and heart-wrenching tribute—one that, bewilderingly, Caleb seemed to completely ignore. She grabbed him by the hand and charged ahead, hardly acknowledging the touching memorial left in remembrance of her beloved.

"Wait a second. Where are you going?" He dug his feet in deep, trying to slow her down. But the more he protested, the harder she pulled, quickening her pace until they both broke into a clumsy, uncoordinated jog.

"I just want to show you something. It's right over here, I promise!"

The crowd density increased noticeably, and they soon found themselves in the thick of a rambunctious assemblage. Caleb barged her way through, leaving Tobias to sheepishly apologize on her behalf. Soon, the reason for the gathering became apparent: a stage, erected at the far corner of the square with tall vertical banners standing on either side—cobalt blue with a repeating pattern of white interlocking rings.

Immediate recognition of the symbol brought uncomfortable realization cascading over him. There had always been a certain manipulative streak to Caleb's character—a means of getting her way by virtue of pulling on his heartstrings. Normally he found it charming. But this . . . this was outright subterfuge. She hadn't the slightest interest in the flowers or the memorial as she had indicated earlier: they had come to Xìngyùn Square to attend a rally . . .

A Humanity First rally.

He stopped abruptly, shook his hand free from her grasp.

"Why didn't you tell me?"

She spun around with an achingly transparent look of surprise on her face, like a child caught red-handed and feigning innocence.

"Because I know how you feel about them. If I'd told you beforehand you never would have come with me."

"That's exactly right! And I would have done my damndest to stop you from coming too. Just think about what people might say if we allow ourselves to be seen. Associating with Humanity First in any capacity is basically committing reputational suicide."

She rolled her eyes. "You really can't do anything without fretting over how it will affect your social standing, can you? Some things are more important than how others perceive us, Tobias!"

"It's not just that." He moved in close, spoke with more force but considerably less volume. "Humanity First is *extremist*. Have you completely forgotten about what happened last year, what they did to the students who crashed that demonstration down in Halvorsen Commons? One of them is in a repulsor chair, you know? Beaten so badly he'll never walk again."

Her taut countenance indicated, if fleetingly, that her next words might have been something to the tune of *they got what they deserved.* She took a steadying breath, seeming to acknowledge just how unbecoming that would have been.

"Of course I haven't forgotten. And obviously I don't condone any use of violence, but I think it's important to remember that it was the leech sympathizers who threw the first punch. *And* that the retaliators were in no way affiliated with the organizers of the event."

"Maybe not. But doesn't it say something about the *class* of people who attend these rallies? I know you're hurting, I know you want to take action, but this just isn't who we are!"

She shrugged, made a sweeping gesture at the enveloping crowd.

"Look around you. Do the people here look like violent thugs or skinheads to you?"

To her credit, they did not. In fact, attending was what could only be described as a snapshot of mankind—people of all ages, ethnicities, and walks of life, uniting over a common cause: the preservation of human culture and society. There were even a number of individuals whom he recognized: other students of ACS, scholars, notable influencers, and politicians—people he respected. It dawned on him that perhaps his assessment of the movement they were here in collective support of may no longer be appropriate.

She took him by the hands, stared up with glistening, beseeching eyes. "I've had enough, Tobias—enough of this magnificent generation ship, which our ancestors charged us with the stewardship of, being nothing more than the host to a parasitic infestation. Enough of people getting slaughtered in defense of an Administration that's too bogged down by bureaucracy and indecision to impose the necessary sanctions. How many more atrocities must we suffer before there's real, tangible change? Humanity First is the *only* group willing to stand up and do something about it."

The crowd in front of them began to stir, the air rich with anticipation. Smiling reassuringly, she directed his attention forward as a levitating podium sailed into position from stage right.

"We're here now—let's just listen to what he has to say. If it doesn't resonate then I promise I won't try and stop you from leaving. But my place is here, and there's nothing you can say that will change my mind."

Someone's back to her old self . . .

He began an exculpatory response, but the words were stamped out by the roar of the crowd, whipped into an excited frenzy as Bhaltair Abernathy took the stage.

Tobias had never seen Humanity First's founder and self-anointed mouth-piece in person, but he recognized him from countless debates broadcast on the NTNN. Bhaltair was a regular on the network—a man he suspected avidly enjoyed the sound of his own voice and couldn't very well allow any major development to transpire without letting the whole *Novara* know his controversial take on it.

His background was in exo-cartography—the division of engineers and scientists whose job it was to map out the path of the conduits and monitor the *Devourer*'s ever-increasing resource intake. He had gained notoriety speaking out in public forums about the Administration's inaction regarding the issue, quickly amassing a legion of similarly disillusioned followers who joined him on the warpath. There was a lot of passion and dedication within his fan base but not an overabundance of intellect. It was their tendency to meet political discourse with general thuggery that gained their repute as a bunch of truculent hooligans—precisely the reason Tobias had been so opposed to rubbing shoulders with them.

It was obvious from the impressive production values on show today, however, that Mr. Abernathy was striving to dispel his organization's belligerent reputation. He sauntered across the stage toward the podium, waving ingratiatingly at his doting congregation. The fabric of his ghastly three-piece suit was embroidered with a map of Earth: ugly splotches of blue, green, and yellow delineated by contours and coastlines warped by his stout physique. He swept his pompadoured hair back, tattooed knuckles adorned with cheap, gaudy jewelry, before speaking pointedly with palms exposed, his amplified words cutting through the clamor.

"Friends! The Administration would prefer to keep you none the wiser. But make no mistake: we are at war. The threat we presently face is the gravest in the history of mankind. And yet, the people in power want to keep you distracted and pacified, blind to the truth that it is their leniency and their negligence that brought us here—to the very brink of annihilation!"

The crowd erupted in a chorus of affirmation: Caleb included. Tobias could feel the energy radiating off her, Bhaltair's poignant words like photosynthesis on her skin.

"It's true," the shepherd said to his flock. "Something must be done. And if you're here today, then it's because you know Humanity First is the *only* group prepared to do what's necessary. The sooner the politicians up in Quarterdeck recognize this as a legitimate movement, one that has the support of the Novarian public, the sooner we can put words into action and undo the damage done by a century of fecklessness and indecision on their part."

Tobias smiled mirthlessly, wondering what his "feckless" politician of a father would say about such targeted slander.

"Contrary to popular belief," Bhaltair continued, "we are not here in the name of vengeance or retribution. We stand here today in the name of love: love for the twelve valiant souls who were so cruelly taken from us not two nights ago."

A reverent murmur rippled through the audience.

"Furthermore, we stand here for truth. And the truth is that just like every other man, woman, and child maimed and murdered by those vicious savages festering in the ruins beyond the blockade, the victims will not get the justice they deserve. Our government—the people who claim to serve and protect us—will *not* respond to these aggressions with the force that is so clearly warranted. The Administration has already accepted leech control, and in turn they have sealed our fate!"

The crowd seethed—pumped fists and placards thrust violently into the air, the deafening choir of a hundred furious voices pummeling Tobias's eardrums. The zeal, the outrage—it was overwhelming, yet oddly reinvigorating.

"Those of you who know my story know that I'm all too familiar with the true nature of these creatures. Having spent over a decade working in exocartography, I have witnessed firsthand the crippling impact their resource siphoning has had on our communities: from the water shortages in the

Statera Basin to the dangerously poor air quality in the foundries of Cendre Vale. I've come to understand the simple fact that we can ill afford the burden of these parasites. If we are to avoid extinction, then we have no choice but to be rid of them!"

The mood amidst the crowd had reached fever pitch, Bhaltair's intensity and vehemence provoking rabid hysteria. Tobias was so enraptured by the unfolding chaos that only now did he notice Caleb gripping his hand, their fingers fervidly interlocked . . .

"No longer can we tolerate the persistent hostilities of these aggressors, nor go on pandering to the hordes of glow addicts and mutineers cavorting with them beyond the blockade. If we—the human remnant—have any hope of surviving, then we must dismantle the Mouth, seal the blockade, and cast the *Devourer* off into the endless night once and for all!"

Bhaltair slammed his fists on the podium repeatedly, each impact like kerosene to the flame.

"So, let the skeptics and the naysayers call us 'speciesists' and 'bigots.' History will remember those who stand against us as those who stood against humanity. Through strength and determination, we *will* restore the *Novara's* ripple-space capabilities. We *will* complete the expedition encumbered on us by our forebearers. Together, I believe we can reshape this union of great nations into the proud spacefaring civilization we once were and are destined to be again!"

Bhaltair's address concluded with vociferous applause—a ruckus so loud it reverberated off every faceted surface in Xìngyùn Square.

Looking beyond all the theatrics, it was surprising just how much of the sermon Tobias found himself in stark agreement with. This was far more than the sensationalist hyperbole he had expected to hear coming from the likes of Humanity First. In a matter of minutes, he had gone from cynical observer to willing participant, his attitude of moral superiority gradually distilling into a renewed sense of humility.

Caleb looked to have been similarly affected—galvanized into action by an inexorable sense of pride and purpose. Yet to release his hand, she stood beside him, trembling with resolve, tears of acceptance and determination rolling down her mantling cheeks. Staring wistfully into her earthy-brown eyes, he imagined that perhaps she had found some consolation in the idea that Jade did not die in vain, that there could be meaning and purpose hidden in her passing. Maybe in death she would act as the catalyst for monumental change—a spark that would ignite the fires of revolution, triggering a great reclamation of all that was lost in the Collision. Maybe, thanks to her sacrifice, there could be more to look forward to than a long and painful extinction . . .

He caught himself, finding it hard not to get completely swept up in Bhaltair's rhetoric. After all, there were a number of concerns regarding the viability of his manifesto that bore some consideration. This notion of somehow "casting the *Devourer* off into the endless night," for example, was specious at best. The inconvenient truth that everybody seemed to be ignoring was that the *Novara*—with her irrevocably damaged fission reactor—still relied heavily on her gruesome symbiote to keep almost all major systems functioning.

If there really was some way to amputate the Devourer without cutting off our only power source and subsequently suffocating ourselves, then surely we would have done it decades ago?

He kept that conundrum to himself, not wanting to jeopardize Caleb's improving disposition with rampant overthinking. She was happy—something he hadn't been sure he could accomplish ever again—and he wanted to live in that moment forever: standing there in the crowd with her hands cradled in his, feeling like they were both part of something bigger, given an opportunity to contribute to the resurgence of mankind.

Disappointingly, the moment was obliterated by the sudden appearance of Atherton Edevane. Tobias smelled the man before hearing the sonorous timbre of his voice—that assailing concoction of bergamot perfume and cigar smoke invading his nostrils.

"You don't know how proud I am to see you both here today."

They spun around to face his father, who had apparently been looming behind them for the duration of the rally.

Caleb all but leapt into his arms, yearning for what she likely knew was the only parental comfort she would find on the *Novara*.

"How are you, my dear?" he asked softly, his jawline buried in her sunset-orange locks. "I'm so terribly sorry for your loss. What wretched, unprecedented times we are living in."

She mumbled an indiscernible thank-you into his neck.

"Come now, Tobias. Don't look so shocked. By now I've made my support of this cause abundantly clear." Atherton placed a hand reassuringly on Tobias's shoulder.

"You did," he replied, realizing how much surprise he had betrayed in his gawking expression. "But I thought it was limited to having a few connections with people involved. I had no idea it had gone as far as attending demonstrations."

"My involvement with Humanity First goes deeper than vague interest. I've been trying to find the right moment to tell you this—I suppose there's no time better than the present. I am actually here as a financial benefactor.

In truth, I have been funding Mr. Abernathy's campaign efforts for several months now."

"That is . . . unexpected," he stuttered. "The man certainly had a lot to say about the Administration—he didn't speak too kindly regarding you and your ilk."

Atherton chuckled, tenderly releasing Caleb. "Yes, well . . . Bhaltair can be a little *blunt* in his addresses. But who here can deny the ineffectiveness of the current establishment? When the wolves are at the door and nothing is being done to deter or defend against them, clearly something has gone wrong."

"But what about your reputation?" Tobias asked. "Surely it's not appropriate for a councilman to be privately financing a group of activists with such an infamous record?"

Atherton shrugged, aloof. "People are angry, son. And considering the current state of things, I'd say they have every right to be. The very few instances in which supporters of Humanity First *may* have lashed out were only due to a lack of direction. Up until now they haven't had the adequate guidance or resources to channel that anger into constructive activism, which is exactly what I and the other financial backers are aiming to provide. We're fully aware of how unfavorable that might make us in the public eye, but that's something we're working diligently to turn around."

"Well, I think it's very inspiring," Caleb said, wiping tears with the sleeve of Hazel's Class of 124 AC sweater. "You're risking your career to stand up for what you believe in. I think we could all aspire to wear our hearts on our sleeves a little more as you are doing. What a sorry state of affairs it is that showing pride for your own species should be sneered at or looked down upon."

"Quite right, Miss Callaghan. It certainly hasn't made me the most popular amongst my peers, but I'm afraid we must all be prepared to make sacrifices if we are to weather the storm that is on the horizon."

"What storm?" Tobias asked.

Atherton placed a hand on each of their backs and began walking them in the direction of Bhaltair, who had now descended from the stage and was greeting people in the crowd.

"You two are both extremely bright, incredibly perceptive. I'm sure you have a number of concerns regarding the logistics of some of what you heard. But you should know that there are things going on behind the scenes that might make the idea of separating from the *Devourer* seem less like fantasy and more like our last chance for survival. By no means will it be an easy road, but rest assured it is the only one that leads to the preservation of human civilization. This is the future—it's *our* future—and I would like nothing more than to have both of you be a part of it."

ELEVEN

Had Kahu been on the bridge to witness Delilah sitting at the helm with her boots resting on the main control pedestal, he would have told her *"Get those mucky clodhoppers off the darn hardware."* But he was AWOL, still simmering in his quarters over the fiasco with Null in the galley. Given time, he would eventually resurface, either laughing the whole thing off or drastically downplaying the seriousness of it. However he chose to reconcile his actions, Delilah only hoped he would do so quickly. The extraction of the hydro-ionizers was well underway; soon they would need to set course for the delivery point, and the paranoid old fool kept the flight stick bio-encrypted to his dermal signature. Translation: they were dead in the water until he could sort his head out.

He did at least manage to park the *Assurance* directly over the mission target before obliterating his chances of receiving any captainly praise by waving a gun at Vidalia's associates. The unsightly berg of wreckage in which the Governor's prize was buried ambled beyond the windshield, a detached and relatively intact segment of maintenance corridor rotating listlessly in the weightlessness of space, its serrated surface a testament to the tremendous force with which it was ripped out during the Collision.

Beyond it, the Debris Belt stretched on into nothingness: a nebula of metal detritus, scintillating in the *Assurance*'s floodlights like a surging blizzard of broken glass. In spite of what it was—a monument to one of the most devastating and consequential battles in human history—there was an undeniable beauty about it. For Delilah, it felt like gazing out onto a field of crops: the wheat that put fuel in the tanks and the chaff that kept the magma cannon ready to do its job. The belt was by no means an unlimited resource; eventually it would be depleted, every fragment of flotsam scrapped or salvaged by outfits like hers, picking at the bones of the *Novara* until the emptiness was truly empty. Such a drought was unlikely to occur in her lifetime, judging by the current density. And so, for as long as she could keep the *Assurance* sky-borne, she could count on a bountiful harvest.

The screen on the operations console showed the live feed from Teodora's helmet cam. Through the condensation settled on her visor, Delilah could see a pair of busy hands, clad in the burgundy-tinged nanoweave of her EVA suit. She had already freed one of the ionizers from its ancient restraints and was hard at work carving away material with her fission cutter to release the second. The bridge resonated with the quavering sound of her voice as she sang an example of the twentieth-century folk music she adored so much: a somber yet strangely uplifting melody with abstract lyrics about something, or someone, called "Ruby Tuesday."

A steady beeping emitted from the vital-signs monitor. Delilah leaned toward the comms panel. "Teo. Knock it off. That's a nice rendition you're giving us, but you're burning through your oxygen way too quick."

"'Nice?' She's completely tone-deaf," Isaac snarked from the copilot's seat. Delilah shot him a scornful look undermined by the smirk she was struggling to repress—he wasn't wrong.

Straining from physical exertion, Teo replied, "Sorry, Cap. Will do. Gah! I don't know why the *Novara*'s architects were so obsessed with using titanium alloy in all the subdeck brace work. These ionizers are hemmed in tighter than a gnat's ass!"

"It's moon metal," Isaac replied. "Half the ship is made from the stuff—smelted from the ore mined from the quarries on Luna. When our forebears realized just how much material was needed to construct a metropolis-sized ark ship, they turned the whole rock into one big foundry."

Delilah closed her eyes; listening to the boy talk with such passion and vigor about something so tedious as Novarian metallurgy, she could almost swear it was Micah sitting beside her instead.

"Thanks for the history lesson." Teo stretched out an arm to prevent herself from floating away from her workspace, panning her helmet cam around to reveal the dark, derelict confines of the enveloping corridor. "Don't make it any easier to cut through though, does it? Anyhow, the first two ionizers are released and ready for you to come and fetch."

Isaac was already one step ahead. Hunched forward, tongue pinched between teeth in concentration, he had connected his portable pane up to the main control pedestal and was using the secondary flight stick to manipulate the pneumatic grapple. Outside, a metal claw drifted into view of the windshield, tethered to the cargo bay via a braided-steel cable. It would stop abruptly and change orientation as Isaac's finite adjustments translated into quick bursts from the microthrusters attached to each digit. With impressive precision, he sent the grapple drifting lengthwise along the wreckage then maneuvered it through the same entry point Teodora had used.

Soon after, the first hydro-ionizer was ensnared and headed to the cargo bay, which Null and Mercy arrived just in time to bear witness to.

"Permission to enter the bridge, Captain?" Mercy asked, demonstrating better adherence to rank and procedure than Delilah's own crew. Cautiously, she accepted; they planned to observe the extraction or monitor it on Vidalia's behalf.

Null lumbered past the helm, squatting to clear aer brow of the overhead instrumentation panel. Ae pressed the ridge of aer snout against the windshield, gazing into the Debris Belt in what might have been awe or fascination—hard to discern without any recognizable body language.

Delilah cleared her throat. "I'd like to take the opportunity to apologize, actually. I promised the Governor you'd both feel right at home with us, and that wasn't exactly the warmest of welcomes, was it?"

Mercy offered the faintest suggestion of a smile. "No. But we have had far worse."

"I'm sure you have. It doesn't excuse his behavior, of course, but I think you should know: Kahu is a veteran of the NTSC. He flew during the Antonelli expansion, and honestly, I don't think he's ever come to terms with the fact we aren't at war anymore."

Mercy brushed silk-white hair out of her sunken eyes, clutching on to her pendant as though fearing someone might snatch it off her.

"Keeping knowledge of the past is . . . difficult when you live in the Mouth: warped and obfuscated by segregation from the rest of society. I must admit that I am not well versed about that particular conflict."

"We're basically experts, the way Kahu yammers on about it," Isaac chimed in. "It all started when a freighter drifted into *Devourer* territory after suffering a major drive core failure. Cohabitor interceptors fired a few warning shots, then sank it, killing a crew of nine. The fleet admiral at the time, a guy called Kal Antonelli, responded by triggering a campaign to push back the perimeter of NTU airspace, resulting in a complete bloodbath for both sides."

"Kahu experienced some real trauma, is what we're getting at," Delilah interjected, watching Mercy's eyes glaze over from the unsolicited war history. "It might explain why he reacted the way he did. He's convinced the cohabs they fought during the expansion used some kind of psychic warfare to terrorize and torture his squad. It's had him spooked ever since."

Mercy joined her counterpart at the front of the cockpit. Turning to face Isaac, she said, "I see. Similar to your mention of Null's kind being able to 'turn brains into mush.' The girl out there—the salvage specialist—she was very quick to dismiss the idea, but the truth is that such rumors are not entirely unfounded. You know already that if a cohabitor links with a nonresonant human, it can be painful and disorienting. Well, some cohabitors have learned to harness that incompatibility and use it as a weapon." She lifted a diaphanous hand and placed it softly on the plating of Null's upper arm. "The protection and preservation of the Savior—what you call the *Devourer*—is paramount. And so, pilots like Mr. Heperi who were sent to encroach into Savior airspace will have had terrible horrors visited upon them, but only out of sheer desperation, a need to defend that which has given life."

"It makes so much sense now." Isaac furrowed his brow, focus visibly torn between the conversation and the task at hand. "A buddy of mine once worked maintenance on an old lepus-class hauler. He hated it—went on and on about it being a haunted ship. When he was alone, down on the engineering level, he would get terrible headaches and hear bizarre screeching noises coming from inside his head, always had this feeling like he was being watched by something lurking in the shadows. Turns out, one of the other crew members was secretly a cipher and was sheltering a cohabitor fugitive, keeping aer hidden beneath deck. I guess every time my buddy got close to discovering aer, ae was just using their 'incompatibility' to ward him off. Like a self-defense mechanism."

"You never told me that," said Delilah. "What happened to them both?"

Isaac's bearing sank, eyes sorrowful but still transfixed on the grapple controls. "Well, what happens to any cohab who ventures bowside of the blockade? Ae was thrown into a dark hole and never seen again. I don't know what happened to aer cipher—probably charged with sedition like my folks were. As for my buddy, he lost his engineer's post, and it was all downhill from there. He got wrapped up in some pretty gnarly stuff . . ." The thought seemed to tail off—likely because it led to something that Delilah already knew but which he was unwilling to discuss: that the friend in question was the same one he was arrested with, and the "gnarly stuff" they had *both* gotten embroiled in was burglary in possession of a deadly weapon, necessitated by the outrageous expenses of their collective glow usage.

Unfortunately, neither had made very deft criminals, but unlike Isaac, his partner in crime had been without someone like Delilah watching over him, and subsequently never managed to secure a deal with the GEA for conditional release. Isaac knew how lucky he was to have his freedom but had been plagued by survivor's guilt ever since. Thankfully, Mercy had no desire to delve any deeper into his troubled past.

"We can empathize with why Mr. Heperi reacted so adversely, and we accept your apology. However, we must stress that there can be no further altercations. I will not allow any harm to come to Null, nor ae to me, and so for the safety of everyone aboard, it cannot be allowed to happen again."

Delilah paused, fiddling nervously with one of the concussion rounds slotted into her gun-belt, unsure how to respond to being threatened by a passenger on her own ship. Before she could decide on an appropriate course of action, Isaac jumped out of the copilot's seat in a sudden panic.

"Captain. Look!" He was pointing frantically at the radar scope, which had just pinged three bogeys on hot approach. Transponder frequency and thermal signatures suggested they were kestrels—NTSC fighters out on patrol.

Fantastic. Caught with our pants down running illegal salvage while harboring an enemy of the NTU.

The *Assurance* would be impounded, and everyone aboard arrested for treason. Yet, neither of those things concerned her more than what the Governor might do after learning she'd botched the job *and* lost two of his most precious assets to the Administration.

She sprang to her feet, slammed her fist on the ship-wide intercom.

"Heperi! Quit your moping and report to the bridge. We've got trouble!"

The short time it took for the man to appear suggested he was already lurking in the helm access corridor, probably working up the courage to show his face again and agonizing over what to say. She wasn't sure what the symbolism of ditching his old blazer for a standard viridian-colored flight suit was: hopefully an offering of truce. Lingering in the doorway, bottom lip quivering, he could utter no more than a single syllable before she cut him off.

"Stow it, pilot. There'll be time to apologize later. Right now, we've got uninvited guests and I need you to give 'em the silent treatment."

He zipped his flight suit up to the collar, returned an appreciative nod, and vaulted into the pilot's seat, beginning a rapid shutdown of the ship's systems.

Having almost completely forgotten she was still EVA, Delilah hailed Teo from the comms panel. "Looks like there's some bad weather headed our way, kiddo. We need to go dark until it passes. Your oh-two is at thirty-seven percent, so as long as you keep your breathing nice and shallow, you'll be just fine. I promise we won't leave you out in the cold for too long."

A timorous voice came back through the helm speakers. "Nebula. Don't forget about me, Lilah."

"Captain. Is everything alright?" Mercy asked, the illumination of her eyeballs signaling that a direct channel to Null had been opened.

Delilah offered a resolute nod. "There's a squad of scout ships inbound. Fortunately, we have a contingency for situations such as this. We're masking our thermal signature so we blend in with the rest of the garbage, but that means powering down the *Assurance* for a spell. We'll experience some momentary weightlessness and it'll get real cold, real fast. I hope that's OK."

"Nebula, Captain. Whatever is necessary."

Before powering down the helm, Kahu buckled himself in and sent the *Assurance* into a leisurely roll to emulate the constant motion of the Debris Belt. At a distance, the hauler would look like just another hunk of wreckage, adrift in an ebbing river of the stuff.

"Okey-doke, folks. Cold shoulder engaged."

He reached up and flipped a final switch on the overhead instrumentation panel. The hum of the life support went dead, the constant roar of idling impulse thrusters suddenly silenced. The unyielding blackness outside spilled in through the windshield; the only light in the cockpit was that emanating from Mercy's and Null's eyes, which wasn't bright enough to be seen from the kestrel's current range . . . probably.

Delilah felt her insides turn upside down as the gravity emitters below deck released their hold. Feeling her feet lift from the floor grating, she wrapped her arms around the backrest of the pilot's seat to keep herself steady. Taking an alternative tact, Isaac tucked his knees into his chest and began performing clumsy somersaults in the air.

"You're gonna regret that when I switch the gravity back on," Kahu joked.

The ship began to sing, her internal support structures moaning and wailing as they contracted in response to the sudden drop in temperature. Delilah's breath appeared as icy vapor before her face as she spoke. "Great work, Heperi. Have you got visual yet?"

"Affirmative." His gaze directed her toward three distinct engine trails—thin streaks of blue extending in the distance, obscured occasionally by the looming silhouettes of debris.

They were kestrels for sure, far off but just close enough for their avian outlines to be distinguishable. They cut through the black at astonishing velocity, their trajectory suggesting they were not on course to intercept but circumventing the Debris Belt altogether.

Kahu twirled the ends of his mustache contemplatively. "Sure don't look like scout ships, Skipper. Their formation's clumsy, too inconsistent. Might be a training op."

"Keep us hidden for a little while longer. Let's not push our luck."

He grunted in agreement before turning his attention to Mercy, his weathered features and salt-and-pepper facial plumage disarmed by a look of mortification.

"Girl? Could you tell the bug I'm sorry? I get confused sometimes, forget what year it is. Spent so long with your friend's kind lined up in my sights that it's hard to forget they ain't the enemy no more. I promise I won't lose control like that again."

Mercy blinked, standing there with the paws of her imperturbable ward holding her down by the shoulders, her head surrounded by an aura of ghostly hair rising and swaying as if submerged under water. She smiled, effulgent eyes brightening. "Do not fret . . . All is forgiven."

The kestrels vacated the Debris Belt seemingly without ever detecting the *Assurance*. The gambit had worked, and with the three hydro-ionizers secured and Teodora safely back aboard, the time had come to discuss the logistics of delivery.

Delilah felt anxiety creeping in over the Governor's plan. When she posited that any alternative method of entering the Mouth would have been known to her already, Mercy gave an infuriatingly cryptic response.

"Like all things, Captain, your knowledge of the Coalescence is hindered by the boundaries and limitations put in place by the human remnant. We must endeavor to break through those boundaries: then the way forward will reveal itself."

The girl's moon-shaped pendant was, in fact, a locket, which she opened delicately to reveal an embedded microemitter that projected a set of coordinates. Once Kahu inputted the numbers into the nav console, it became immediately clear that "breaking through boundaries" meant violating the NTU perimeter and trespassing into *Devourer* airspace.

"You can't be serious about going through with this, Skip?" the old pilot groused. "They'll pick us apart like piranhas the second our nosecone crosses into their turf."

Admittedly, Delilah felt just as much apprehension about the idea, but she had to believe the Governor knew what he was doing. The assets currently stowed in her cargo bay were too valuable to risk getting seized or destroyed by cohabitor interceptors; she had every confidence he would have made whatever arrangements were necessary to ensure their safe retrieval.

"We press on," she declared. "We've come this far, and I'll be damned if we're turning back now."

Kahu's resounding protestations were many—considerably less unhinged than earlier in the galley, but there was little time for yet another showdown with him.

"Feel free to take an escape pod and drink yourself to death somewhere else, Heperi!" Delilah bellowed. "But if you wanna get paid for this job, then you will buck up and do what your captain tells you!"

"Alright, alright!" He showed his palms in submission. "At least if you're wrong about this we'll be too dead to butt heads about it."

Then, for perhaps the first time since the Antonelli expansion, a human ship made its way into cohabitor airspace. Sensors showed not even a whisper of other traffic in the vicinity. If there *were* interceptors slinking somewhere through the black-scape, they were giving the *Assurance* a generously wide berth. It wasn't obvious if this was Vidalia's doing or if it was somehow related to Null being aboard. Either way, the empty radar scope definitely helped sooth Delilah's nerves.

Their trajectory took them arching around the *Novara*'s stern, presenting an utterly stupefying view of the ancient vessel's destroyed thrusters, each stadium-sized nozzle charred and mangled beyond recognition.

"Hey, look at that!" Kahu blurted for the attention of Null. "You did a real number on us, eh, Bug? And to think those Humanity First clowns think we can just slap a lick of paint on those behemoths and get the *Novara* moving again."

"Fat chance of that," Isaac concurred, humbled and awestruck by the scale of the devastation before him.

Soon, the surface of the *Devourer* filled the windshield, an impregnable bulwark of amorphous muscle-metal, somehow both draped in shadow *and* subtly luminous. It was an unnerving sensation to recognize absolutely nothing—to have no frame of reference with which she could identify any part of its foreign composition. It spawned an implacable urge to flee, survival mode kicking in and causing every fiber of her being to scream at her to turn the ship around and escape while they still could. She blew a calming exhalation to expunge the unnecessary reaction, deeming it terribly symptomatic of her old self.

Arriving at the coordinates, Kahu zeroed out the throttle and brought the *Assurance* to a gentle stop.

"Well. We're here; we didn't get shot to hell. I'd call that a win."

"Ever the optimist," Delilah quipped. "OK, you two. What's our next move?"

Mercy smiled impishly. "You have done all you need to, Captain Holloway. Please allow us to do the rest."

Null released an acute braying noise. Ae turned to face the windshield, raised one arm, and placed aer paw against the aluminosilicate glass. The crew was simultaneously struck down by what felt like an intense and immediate migraine. Delilah experienced extreme auditory discomfort, the assailment of a piercing shriek stabbing at her eardrums but strangely accompanied by no detectable sound.

"I'm sorry." Mercy placed a hand on Isaac's shoulder; the young man was keeled over in agony. "Traversal through the Savior can be quite unpleasant for nonresonants. But I assure you the sensation will pass soon enough."

Kahu, having almost certainly been subjected to the strange neurological bombardment before, was uncharacteristically composed. He shook his head in feigned disappointment of his crewmates. "Bunch of wimps. C'mon, it ain't that bad."

Ahead, the *Devourer's* anatomy began to shrivel and divide, its shell unfurling like the petals of a flower in bloom. An opening formed, revealing a tunnel stretching deep into its core, host to a vibrant maelstrom of orange-and-violet luminescence.

Without warning, the *Assurance* lurched forward.

"Hang on, Heperi. Let's just think about this for a second!"

"It's not me, Skip! Something's pulling us inside!"

He grappled ham-fistedly with the throttle, desperately trying to wrest control of the ship back from the invisible chains that had seized her. The impulse thrusters howled and spluttered, the strain of opposing forces triggering raucous vibrations throughout the fuselage. Within seconds the ship was consumed entirely, picking up speed as it was dragged into the bowels of the *Devourer*.

TWELVE

"Edevane, do I have your attention?"

Wing Commander Mattias Luscombe stood in rigid military posture at the front of the mission briefing room, his hoarse voice and razor-sharp elocution jolting Hazel out of her reverie. She straightened up and clasped her hands attentively on her writing table.

"Yes, sir. Undivided, sir."

Hardly convinced, Luscombe lingered for a suspenseful moment in the path of the ceiling-mounted luma-caster, the electric-cyan coordinates and geometry of Delta Team's upcoming mission highlighting his hatchet-faced expression.

Hazel couldn't have let her focus wane for more than a few seconds—evidently long enough for the wing commander to deem it necessary to reprimand her in front of the other cadets. Although chagrined at having been caught out, she couldn't deny that she was distracted. Those fabled eight uninterrupted hours had proven particularly elusive in recent weeks—more so in the nights running up to a training exercise. By now she had grown accustomed to lying awake for hours, studying the underside of the bunk stacked above hers, head buzzing with wing formations and six-degrees-of-freedom flight maneuvers.

Last night, however, she had been inundated with a slew of semilucid dreams centered predominantly around her mother. In one she recalled sitting cross-legged, embodied as her childhood self, on the icy-cold floor of an Aegis Infirmary hallway. Her inappropriately overdressed father sat on a bench against the wall, slouched forward with his face buried in his hands. A doctor wearing blue surgical gloves and a respirator mask stood over him, explaining in a disturbingly clinical manner how an unknown virus had ravaged her mother's nervous system.

An infant Tobias gallivanted nearby, inexplicably decked in a toddler-sized version of his ACS uniform, too young and too innocent to fully comprehend the gravity of the situation. Through an observation window she saw her mother sitting upright on a gurney, paradoxically, alive and well—a vision of radiance, even in a drab hospital gown, the glowing warmth of her smile traveling through the glass and caressing Hazel's tearstained cheeks.

She wasn't a believer in the esoteric—not the sort to go finding patterns in tea leaves or shapes in the clouds of the Canyon's artificial firmament. Ultimately, she knew it was nothing more than the firing of synapses triggering a garbled memory-vision of her deceased mother. But just because she didn't think there was any hidden significance, didn't mean she couldn't be thrown completely off-kilter.

The wing commander barked her name a second time, trying to catch her off guard once again. "What are Delta's orders?"

As flight leader, it was absolutely her responsibility to know. Fortunately, she had the plan thoroughly committed to memory.

"Launch from the Silo at thirteen hundred hours," she said succinctly. "Complete two rotations of NTU perimeter airspace. Rendezvous at the CAP point with Charlie pending successful sweep of the Debris Belt. Form up in Vic and return to base."

The wing commander smirked, hawklike eyes fixated on hers. Beneath a highly decorated blazer he wore the same bluish-gray emblazoned NTSC flight suit as his cadets, albeit looking considerably fiercer in it. Freckled and fresh-faced with brown shoulder-length hair fashioned in a tight sock bun, Hazel felt embarrassingly green measuring up to the battle-worn militarist towering before her.

"Outstanding," he said dryly. "Now remember, this exercise will take you danger close to hostile airspace. Your kestrels will be fragged but *only* as a precautionary measure. Under absolutely no circumstances are you to engage the enemy. If leech interceptors are sighted in breach of NTU airspace, you will turn tail and haul ass. Is that understood?"

"Understood, sir!"

As Luscombe turned to address the briefing board, a fellow cadet by the name of Horatio Guzman leaned over from his desk, bringing a face as sculpted as a pile of bricks and framed by an unflattering buzz cut into Hazel's peripheral vision. She knew he was fixing to start something even before he opened his mouth. From day one he had been needlessly antagonistic with her—so bumptious about his humble working-class beginnings, as if he was the only cadet in history to get into flight academy on a scholarship.

All brazen and no brains—that's just what her father would say.

"What the hell is with you?" he whispered strenuously.

"I'm fine, Guzman. I don't need you keeping tabs on me."

"And I don't need *you* blowing this whole exercise because you're too bone idle to pay a-fuckin'-ttention in a mission briefing. Quit daydreaming and get your head in the game."

She turned, spitting her words. "Maybe as flight leader you should focus more on keeping Charlie Team in check and spend less time berating me and mine."

He smiled grimly. "It's only *you* I've got eyes for, Edevane. Remember, every one of these training exercises is a test—an opportunity to prove ourselves to Admiral Coombs. We've all got a lot more riding on this than you do, since not all of us have *Daddy* to thank for paying our way into the corps. Some of us are actually here by our own merits."

"No, Horatio. I'm pretty sure you're here because of a clerical error."

The pair snapped their attention back to the wing commander as he turned to face them.

"The birds you're in today are older models, refitted after the Antonelli expansion—some even have their original pre-Collision airframes—but that doesn't mean they don't have it where it counts. Your first instinct might be to go full burn as soon as you clear the Silo. But remember, you will *not* exceed *Novara* port speed. Slow and steady makes for better surveillance, helps avoid accidents. You are ambassadors of the NTSC now, and I expect you to act like it! Anyone who gets so much as a scratch on the paintwork due to reckless flying will be discharged without notice. I hope that's clear."

"Sir, yes sir!"

Luscombe whipped his head in Horatio's direction; the prig's bullish demeanor deflated like a gasbag the moment he fell under the wing commander's scrutiny.

"Guzman! If Charlie encounters any unauthorized commercial traffic during your sweep of the Debris Belt, just call it in—do not approach."

"But sir! What if—"

"Quiet, Cadet. It's not your job to play judge, jury, and executioner out there. You will *not* exceed the mission parameters. Is that clear?"

"Clear, sir."

He nodded and moved to address the other cadets. "Rest up, do your homework, report to the Silo for oh nine hundred hours. I want this exercise smooth and by the numbers. Let's make the good people of the New Terra Union proud and remind the admiral exactly why it is you're all here."

Maybe trying to get forty winks in prep for the mission isn't such a terrible idea, Hazel thought—easier said than done when her excitement equated to that of a child on winter solstice eve. Soon she would be set loose into the endless night with nothing separating her from that shimmering ocean of stars but the glass canopy of her kestrel—a moment she had been dreaming of for as long as she could remember, and which she sincerely doubted the sixty-two simulated flights she had undertaken successfully conveyed.

She decided, instead, to make tracks straight for the Silo with the intention of getting acquainted with her fighter, familiarizing herself with the old girl down to every rivet and bolt. But no sooner had she collected her effects and headed for the door when Horatio came back for another sparring session, apparently unsatisfied with how he had fared in the last round.

"I'm serious, Edevane. Don't get in my fuckin' way. Complete your assignment and rally Delta to the CAP point *on* schedule. If you three get yourselves into a scrape or try and slow me down, I will not hesitate to leave you in the dust."

Hazel preemptively shuffled her feet into fighting stance; she was more than capable of handling the obstinate lout. He would be slow on the swing, heavy-footed—easy enough to sweep the legs and take him out with an elbow strike to the temple, should he make it necessary.

She hardly needed any backup, but she had to blow a quiet sigh of relief when her squadmate Shiyana Hale dove in to assist.

"Why don't you cool it, Horatio?" said Shiy, who Hazel had had little interaction with, even though they had attended school together. The daughter of a renowned magistrate, Shiy had always kept her interests to herself and her focus on her studies. Truthfully, Hazel wasn't sure she had all that much fight in her—certainly not enough to be pursuing a career as a fighter pilot. Considering how she was standing up for her squadmate, however, that judgment of character was probably undeserved.

"This is a friendly exercise," Shiy continued. "We're on the same side here. You don't need to be so combative all the time."

"Careful who you go colluding with, Shiyana." Horatio jabbed a pudgy sausage of a finger into Hazel's shoulder; it took every ounce of restraint she had not to immediately snap it off.

"This one? She's a leech sympathizer. Just like her treacherous mother was."

He turned his head and made the fatal mistake of locking eyes with her.

"Maybe you and that waste-of-space brother of yours should pack your shit up and screw off to the Mouth just like she did. Leave defending the *Novara's* airspace to those of us who are loyal to the Union."

Now you've done it, Guzman . . .

Rage fulminated like magma in her stomach. She was sure when she opened her mouth it would spew like a molten geyser and liquefy the ignoramus where he stood. She stepped forward, halting almost nose to nose,

accentuating her height advantage and making sure he was acutely aware of
it.

"If you so much as mention my mother again or even think about questioning my loyalty, I will gun you the fuck down out there. I don't care if I get
court-martialed, stripped of my wings, and locked up for the rest of my life. It
will be more than worth it to watch you meet the void, dirtbag."

"Charlie! Delta!" The wing commander's strained voice struck with the
full force of a kinetic rail gun round. Hazel and Horatio immediately separated, standing at attention.

"Do we have a problem here?"

"No problem, sir," Horatio spluttered, as if the wind had been knocked out
of him. "Just discussing the plan of attack with Delta."

"There is to be no 'plan of attack.' If either of you lays a finger on your
trigger without my express say so, you will be swiftly ejected from the corps
for disobeying a direct order. Do not make me regret giving you both flight
leader."

Hazel gave Horatio a hearty slap on the shoulder, intended as a gesture of
cooperation but almost certainly taken as a preemptive strike.

"We won't, sir. You can count on us."

The Silo, as it was commonly known, was the NTSC's primary installation
for fighter deployment. Built just below the *Novara*'s dorsal hull, its unique
structure comprised six independent launch chutes, arranged concentrically around a three-hundred-and-sixty-degree observation tower. Hazel had
always likened its design to the cylinder of a revolver, which was especially
fitting considering the bullet-like acceleration with which it catapulted fighters into space.

The kestrels allocated for today's training exercise were suspended
upright, one per chute, rail-clamped to towering frameworks of red-painted
metal, reaching up to the fission field–protected aperture at the summit of
the facility.

Hazel sat cross-legged atop a munitions crate on her assigned boarding platform, beneath the dormant pulse engines of her slumbering steed.
Through an access hatch she could see into the neighboring launch chute,
where Horatio was clambering into his cockpit to begin final preflight checks.
He was bellowing something inane to the chief deck officer about the alignment of his lateral stabilizers. One of his wingmates hovered nearby, watching the scene unfold with the despondent gawk of someone standing in the
path of a hurricane. Charlie Team didn't appear to have a wealth of confidence in their flight leader. It would have brought Hazel no end of satisfaction

to see Guzman trip over at the starting line, but she knew any setbacks now would inevitably delay her own launch window, and she found herself in the peculiar position of actually rooting for him.

Zain Cantrell, Delta's third and final member, slid down the ladder from the observation tower and stylishly hopped onto Hazel's boarding platform. Tall, dark-skinned, and modestly handsome, his self-deprecating brand of humor had a tendency to both charm and infuriate, given he was easily the most intelligent, attractive, and supremely confident individual in any room he stood in. Hazel liked him a lot; she might have found herself falling into the lustrous viridescence of his eyes had her father not made such a fuss about him being "exactly the type of impressive young highflier she should make every effort to attract."

"Are you still stewing over that Neanderthal Guzman giving you shtick in the briefing room?" asked Zain, running his hand adoringly along the inboard aileron of her kestrel's left shoulder wing.

She let slip a rueful sigh. "Is it that obvious?"

"As plain on your face as the medals on Luscombe's lapel. Now, I've spent enough time with you, Edevane, to know you keep a cool head right up until someone brings your family into the equation. So, who was it he bad-mouthed: your little brother or the councilman?"

She wrinkled her nose, undecided on whether she was more piqued at the insinuation that she was *that* predictable or the fact that he'd pegged her down to a tee.

"Well, he *politely* suggested my political beliefs make me unfit for service in the NTSC and recommended my brother and I pick up where our 'treacherous mother' left off in the Mouth. The irony is that I don't think you could get Tobias beyond the blockade, even if you paid him my father's salary."

"Really? I woulda thought an aspiring politician like your li'l bro would jump at the chance to get a sternside sabbatical on his resume. You know: see the sights, get a taste for the culture, orchestrate a few narcissistic photo ops building shelters for the poor and needy."

"I think you just described his idea of hell." She smiled self-consciously. "I'm genuinely starting to worry about him, you know? Just this morning over the luma-caster he was regurgitating a load of extremist talking points he'd picked up at a Humanity First demonstration about 'separating from the *Devourer.*'"

Zain sneered. "Yeah, that guy Abernathy is a real snake-oil salesman, huh? Don't get me wrong: I'd like to see the resurgence of the pre-Collision glory days just as much as the next dedicated unionist. But, then again, I'm also quite fond of being able to breathe. They blather so much about the cohabitors being the root of all evil that they seem to conveniently forget the conduits are the only thing keeping our core systems up and running."

"Exactly! And Tobias is smart—Academy educated. He knows full well it's all insubstantial drivel, which makes it all the more disconcerting that he seems to be subscribing to it."

Zain gave a dejected shrug. "Prejudice can be a potent tonic. It distorts your vision, impairs your ability to think rationally. Sounds like your bro got downright drunk on it. But don't worry, I'm sure he'll sober up soon enough."

The hatches between chutes began to seal automatically, the shrill klaxon that warned of imminent launch sounding from the observation tower. Hazel sprang off the munitions crate and darted for the access ladder.

"You coming to watch Charlie launch?"

"The only reason you give a crap is cuz you think Horatio's gonna balls it up and want to be there to watch him do it," Zain replied, hot on her tail. She scoffed to save face but admitted quietly to herself that he was, aggravatingly, right again.

They arrived in the tower and saluted Wing Commander Luscombe, who stood like a pillar of diligence and authority by the operations station, overseeing the exercise.

Moving toward the forward-sloped window that overlooked Horatio's launch chute, Zain continued in hushed tones, "Trust me. You don't want any misfires now. Luscombe will cancel the whole exercise and then you'll never get out there."

"Thanks, Captain Obvious."

He gave a cocky shrug. "Hey, I'm just making sure you get a chance to throw up in your helmet, OK? It's nothing to be ashamed of. Happens to the very best of us . . . namely me."

She turned to him with a smile of playful disapproval, admiring the way the indigo light from Guzman's igniting pulse engines complemented the soft but graven angles of his face.

"Don't worry about Horatio," he said. "Everyone here knows you're gonna be a shit-hot pilot. That's why he gives you such a hard time—because he's threatened by you. Thing is, he thinks we're gonna be out there reliving the dogfighting days of the Antonelli expansion. Once he realizes he'll be spending the majority of his time issuing penalties for port speed and docking infractions, he'll burn out. Whereas you and me, we're in this for all the right reasons, and I know we're gonna go the distance."

A silver arrowhead propelled by two columns of brilliant blue fire, Hazel's kestrel blasted out of the Silo at breakneck velocity. She felt the air ripped from her lungs by a combination of the nine Gs bearing down on her chest and the sheer majesty and cold indifference of the star-spattered expanse draped beyond her nose cone. In less than a second, the circular aperture at the end of her launch track had expanded from a narrow porthole into an all-enveloping emptiness. After a lifetime spent imprisoned in the decaying confines of a marooned generation ship, she was finally free to stretch her wings.

"How we doin', Flight Leader?" Zain's voice rattled through speakers in her helmet. "You got zero-g chunks floating around beneath your visor yet?"

She turned her head to catch sight of his kestrel banking into formation on her starboard side, the yellow LEDs lining his flight suit reflecting chaotically in the glass of his canopy.

"Hate to disappoint you, Delta Two, but that's a negative."

"It's beautiful, isn't it?" said Shiyana, drifting into position on Hazel's nine o'clock. "I mean, I've seen stars before, but never like this. It's actually a little overwhelming."

"I'm right there with you, Delta Three," Hazel replied. "But let's not get distracted, we've got a job to do."

"Copy that, Flight Leader."

Hazel pulled back on the yoke and pitched upwards, leading Delta into a leisurely loop and bringing them about near the bridge of the *Novara*. Shiy and Zain both instinctively tightened their spacing as she accelerated down the ship's spine and vectored toward the perimeter of NTU airspace.

In spite of its vintage, her kestrel handled like a dream. Gentle manipulations of the flight controls translated into smooth, elegant movements while rapid bursts from the lateral stabilizers provided quick and nimble maneuverability. It didn't quite feel like the razor-sharp precision she had grown accustomed to in the simulator, but it was more fluid and organic. The fighter responded as though it was an extension of herself: body, mind, and machine melded into something far superior to each component alone. She felt the endless night calling, beckoning her deeper inside its bosom. She felt a sense of belonging the likes of which she'd never experienced before—a profound and incontrovertible understanding that she had found her place in the universe.

"Look! At our two o'clock. Is that the Debris Belt?" Shiy's excited voice broke Hazel's reverie.

"Affirmative," she replied, scanning the distant clouds of wreckage—streaks of burnt umber undulating incongruously with the stillness of the perfect black beyond. "I don't see any sign of Charlie."

"They're probably making their way to the CAP point already," Zain said.

"Do you think they found anything during their sweep?" asked Shiy.

"Nah. The docks are still locked down after what happened at the block-ade," he replied. "It's highly unlikely there's anyone out here other than us. This whole op is gonna be a walk in the park."

"That's no reason to let our guard down," Hazel added sternly. "Let's pro-ceed with our perimeter patrol then move to rendezvous with Charlie."

Stars wheeled overhead as Delta Team rolled into a low orbit around the *Novara*'s midsection. On their port side, a network of floating buoys with flashing beacons delineated the edge of NTU airspace. If at any point they were to cross that perimeter, they would be in breach of the terms laid out in the wake of the Antonelli expansion and trespassing in *Devourer* terri-tory. They would be completely at the mercy of cohabitor interceptors and, though there hadn't been any instances of hostilities in nearly thirty years, Hazel wasn't about to test the resolve of that ceasefire now.

Shiyana, on the other hand, seemed far less concerned about Delta's pre-carious proximity to restricted airspace . . .

"Watch your heading there, Delta Three. You're drifting off course—get-ting a little too close for comfort."

"Sorry, Hazel. Shit! I mean, Flight Leader. It's just . . ."

"What is it?"

"Well, I got a ping from a transponder when we were finishing up that last rotation. At first, I thought it was Charlie Team, but then I ran a sensor check and the readouts suggest it's a hauler—a balaener class."

Zain whistled sharply. "Balaener class? You don't see many of them nowa-days. Must be a relic!"

Sure enough, the thermal signature of the vessel now appeared on Hazel's scopes, its registration indicating that it was civilian and not part of one of the Administration's own salvage outfits.

"It's probably just welders—maybe a salvage crew."

"It could be glow runners," Zain posited. "I've seen pretty nifty cargo hold modifications that can make an old boat like that perfect for concealing con-traband. It would explain why they're out here when all the docks are sup-posed to be on lockdown. Could be worth investigating."

"But . . . wait . . . that doesn't make any sense," Shiy said, the girl's scattered communication becoming something of an annoyance.

"Talk to me, Delta Three. What's going on?"

"Well, it looks like it's coming from outside NTU airspace, way beyond the perimeter."

Hazel paused. "Then it's none of our concern. I don't doubt they're up to something nefarious out there, but remember what the wing commander said: we're here to observe and report—not to lay down the law. We're not breaking protocol or exceeding our remit, so let's just complete our assignment then mention it when we debrief."

"Copy that, Flight Leader."

The gargantuan form of the *Devourer* crept over the *Novara*'s horizon as they completed their final rotation. The sight of it latched on to the hull triggered a memory of something Hazel had seen in an old zoology textbook displayed in the archives on the Silk River Concourse: an artist's rendition of a colossal squid with its tentacles hooked around the thrashing body of a sperm whale—two extinct oceanic titans embroiled in a vicious battle for survival. It's forbidding appearance marked Delta's final waypoint, but before she could feel any kind of pride or elation over her team's perfect execution of their orders, Shiyana's panicked voice came clattering through her helmet speakers again.

"Hazel! I mean, Flight Leader! I just picked up weapons fire!"

Hazel jolted to attention, hands tightening around the yoke, darting eyes scanning the instruments on her dashboard.

"Delta Three. Report!"

"Heat spike at seven point zero. Declination thirty-eight point six—right near our CAP point. It was plasma discharge or maybe a particle burst of some kind. I . . . I'm not really sure; energy signature reads like nothing I've ever seen."

A frantic visual scan yielded no results; other than the buoys rhythmically drumming past on Hazel's port side, her field of view remained completely clear. There was no sign of Charlie Team nor the mystery hauler, and certainly no evidence of a supposed engagement.

"Are you absolutely sure about this, Delta Three?" Zain asked, apparently sharing some of Hazel's growing incredulity.

"You're welcome to come over here and check, Zain. But I'm telling you, I saw it!" Shiy's feral voice broke into a pitiful whimper. "Could it be interceptors? Did we cross the perimeter?"

The thought had crossed Hazel's mind. As confident as she was in her own team's ability to follow such a simple instruction, she couldn't say the same for Horatio Guzman . . . If *he* had picked up that transponder ping too, there was every chance that, despite the wing commander's strict orders, he had gone to investigate and gotten his whole team wiped out by interceptors.

"We don't know what the situation is yet, Delta. Let's just keep our heads on a swivel and continue to assess."

They approached the CAP point—an area of space about twelve kilometers above the *Novara*, positioned directly over the bridge. Glancing down, she spied the enormous glass dome that enclosed the Center of Horticultural Preservation, which, from this distance, was just a tiny bubble of light protruding from the dorsal hull. She felt a sudden pang of homesickness for the days spent mucking about in the gardens with Tobias, accentuated enormously by the perilousness of her current predicament.

Oh, Tobias. I do hope we haven't had our last argument . . .

She wanted to take control of the situation—to prove to herself and the others that she could effectively manage a crisis. But she had to acknowledge her own inexperience, as well as the reality that the lives of her two wingmates were currently her responsibility. With some reluctance, she hailed the wing commander.

"Command. This is Delta actual. We have successfully completed perimeter patrol and have advanced to the CAP point. However, we have no visual on Charlie and may have detected potential weapons fire. Please advise. Over."

The resounding radio silence was even louder than the thrum of her pulse engines.

"I think we're being jammed." The tremulous inflection of Zain's voice sent Hazel into a quiet panic. "I've checked every frequency, even the wideband; we aren't even receiving civilian chatter."

"That doesn't make any sense. I can hear you just fine!"

"Well then it's localized jamming. I don't know! All I can tell you is that we're on our own out here! We're not getting any backup!"

The proximity alarm sounded in her cockpit; a cacophony of crashing, scraping metal startled her as her kestrel blew through a fine cloud of debris, smoldering fragments ricocheting off her canopy like the pellets from a shotgun blast. She spotted a larger chunk of wreckage, spinning in the distance—a charred wedge of fuselage on which she could discern an incomplete portion of the NTSC's insignia.

"Lei-Ghannam . . . It's Charlie Team." The comms delay meant that by the time Shiyana's voice sounded in Hazel's helmet, the girl had already been atomized by a blinding salvo of hellfire.

The shockwave from the explosion of Delta Three's kestrel knocked Hazel off course, causing a near collision with Zain, who spiraled away to avoid her.

"Interceptors! Break formation!"

Performing a nearly blackout-inducing evasive maneuver, she whipped her head around in search of targets, catching a flash in her peripheral vision: two fighters of unknown origin and design, with, as far as she could tell, no thermal signature nor any recognizable flight characteristics. They were like nocturnal predators, striking from shadow, using the remains of their last kill as bait to lure Delta into a trap.

Shiyana is gone; these bastards murdered her in cold blood. Hazel knew it would do no good to dwell on that now. The attackers had gotten the drop on her team by exploiting their fear and confusion. If she were to have any hope of turning the situation around, it was time for swift and decisive action.

"Delta Two. We are weapons hot!"

"But the wing commander said—"

"I know what he said, Zain! Do you wanna get court-martialed or killed? Now shut up and prepare to engage! Sidewinders only!"

Her hard points thunked into position—two gatling-style rotary canons unfolding from compartments along the sides of her nose cone.

"We need cover, Hazel! We're fish in a barrel out here!"

She knew he was right; something felt inherently wrong about using the *Novara*—her only home—as a shield. But as she watched the enemy fighters swing around implausibly fast for a second run, she knew it was that or die.

"Dive! Dive! Dive!"

She nosed down and took the stick full burn, gritting her teeth to stave off the waves of assailing g-force. With Zain following closely behind, she leveled out sharply and proceeded to hug the *Novara*'s surface, swooping and slaloming through the cityscape of spires and structures extruding from the hull. Soon she had expended her entire knowledge of zero-atmo avionics in an unavailing attempt to shake the pursuers. No matter what she tried, they were always there—impossible apparitions skulking in the black, frequently exhibiting non-ballistic movement and, on occasion, disappearing from sight completely.

With their cover thinning, she knew a second attack run was imminent. Resigned to the fact there was almost certainly nobody listening, she hailed command a final, frenzied time.

"Command! This is Delta actual in the blind. We are being engaged. Repeat: we are engaged. Charlie Team and Delta Three are KIA. We have interceptors bearing down on us and need immediate assistance. Over!"

"They aren't interceptors," Zain said, his tone unnervingly subdued. "Check their wing profile."

Serendipitously, the enemy fighters performed a steep, banking turn, allowing a clearer view of their outlines and upper flight surfaces. He was right—they weren't interceptors at all; they were kestrels, heavily modified with what appeared to be reconfigured *Devourer* biotech. They looked as if they had been struck by some terrible skin affliction—coated in ink-black viscera, spewing volatile and discolored exhaust trails from their stripped-bare pulse engines. They moved with incomprehensible synchronicity, darting and strafing in perfect unison, almost as if somehow controlled by the same mind.

For the first time since the engagement began, Hazel briefly managed to acquire one of them in her sights. She squeezed the trigger on her yoke, sending a phosphoric volley into the black, which her target dodged with a maneuver that laughed in the face of everything she knew about physics. Zain followed suit, but his sidewinders may as well have been loaded with confetti for all the good they did.

Almost as if mocking them, the targets stopped dead, accelerated instantaneously, and lined up for a final pass.

"This is it, isn't it?" Zain said, his voice weighed by forlorn acceptance.

Feeling completely and utterly helpless, Hazel softly replied, "Yes, it is. I'm sorry."

THIRTEEN

Devruhkhar's workshop was hidden deep within an industrial area known as the Langrenus Harrow—a vast processing plant where the mountains of lunar ore churned up during the *Devourer's* excavation of the Mouth were reforged into building materials and other commodities. A ramshackle conglomeration of refineries and warehouses, the region was under stringent control of the Glow Syndicate. It was the wellspring from which Vidalia Drexen armed his Monarchs, fortified his installations, and essentially ran a monopoly on the only resource the district had an abundance of that was worth a damn.

Eamon parked up on the outskirts and headed in on foot, primarily because the gunsmith was—although a ruthless peddler of illicit firearms—easily spooked. He'd have the place shuttered and barricaded the second he caught wind of a DMED cruiser snooping around the neighborhood, making getting answers about the origins of the alien-augmented pistol a mite problematic.

Secondly, the marshal had begun to suspect that the Administrator's true motive for offering to replace his prowler was so she could keep tabs on his whereabouts. Madeline knew he had zero intention of stepping aside and letting Phalanx counterterrorism handle Harmony. The donated cruiser's Hypatia VIOS link had only been installed to keep him from sticking his nose into places it didn't belong. But Eamon's sense of smell was superhumanly attuned; something about this whole situation reeked worse than his ex-wife's home cooking, and it would take more than a tight leash to stop him sniffing it out.

Abraham scouted the way forward, down a desolate avenue, stopping occasionally and sitting down in stubborn protest of the doubly reinforced K-9 Kevlar he was being made to wear.

Sorry, boy. I know it chafes, but after that clusterfuck at the Phalanx compound, we're not taking any chances—Deputy Jyn Sato's orders.

Heavy cargo barges lumbered overhead. Chimney stacks belched foul obelisks of smoke into the sky, accented a sickly copper by the Höllengarten as it hung aloft like a canopy of glowing embers. Its ability to filter toxins from the atmosphere was fortuitous, considering without it, the Mouth would be more polluted than Earth had been in the long gone days of fossil fuel combustion. *And these folks have enough to worry about without adding lung rot to the list of miserable ways to die in the district.*

Chief on that list was getting executed in an alleyway by the Governor's Monarchs—a fate that famously befell the last poor bastard who wore the marshal's badge, and one Eamon had begun to suspect might be a very real and imminent possibility for him too. At some point since disembarking from the cruiser, he and Abe had picked up three tails: a cohabitor and two humans wearing urban-camouflage tracksuits; they were keeping their distance but were armed and in pursuit. DMED was generally granted amnesty as long as they stayed ignorant of syndicate affairs, but if Drexen had found out about the *Devourer*-spliced weaponry in Eamon's possession, it was possible that long-standing agreement had expired . . .

He whistled sharply to recall Abe and took a sudden left turn down a perpendicular alley. His followers would be nigh on impossible to lose while on their employer's turf, but perhaps they could at least be delayed by a few unexpected route alterations.

After a prolonged and suspenseful zigzag through the nexus of the Langrenus Harrow, the intrepid pair finally arrived at the gunsmith's workshop, which was situated in an unremarkable alleyway and fronted by a yellow-painted blast-proof hatch. Normally sealed tight with a paranoia-induced number of padlocks and latches, the hatch had, curiously, been left ajar. It wasn't like Devruhkhar to neglect security; on a previous inquiry it had taken a half hour of intense negotiations just to get the neurotic reprobate to even consider opening the door. Something was wrong.

Eamon unholstered his Chevesic MK2 and used the butt of it to apply force to the hatch. If someone had gotten to Devruhkhar first, it was possible they would still be on the premises. His hopes for a stealthy ingress were dashed when the slab of refined nanocarbon swung open with a grating screech, alerting anybody who might have been waiting inside. He winced, expecting his oafishness to be met by a hail of bullets. Instead, other than the fluctuating hum of fluorescent light tubes, all was quiet.

Abraham bounded into Devruhkhar's showroom: a circular space with a ring of gilded display cases and freestanding gun racks, centered around a rock garden water feature that stank of chlorine. The gaudy decor on show had the sense of belonging to a man with an excess of wealth but not an iota of style, completely at odds, aesthetically, with the formidable array of plasma and projectile weaponry on sale. It was all standard fare—nothing that bore any resemblance to the abomination stowed in Eamon's inside pocket. Then again, if there was any *speciality stock*, he imagined it was likely tucked away in the back, out of sight.

Machine pistol held low ready, he began a cautious sweep of the showroom's perimeter. Immediately signs of a struggle became apparent: documents scattered about the floor, a display case toppled over and shattered, a crimson handprint streaked across garish Persian wallpaper. At first glance there didn't appear to be any merchandise missing, meaning this wasn't the aftermath of a holdup but something potentially more insidious.

Abe whined from across the showroom, signaling impatience as he often did when he wanted to play but was being ignored. The macabre implications of the whine sent a chill down Eamon's spine: it meant the mutt had found Devruhkhar, or at least what remained of him . . .

The gunsmith sat against the wall behind the main desk, slumped unnaturally to the side. He was a balding rodent of a man, wearing an embroidered waistcoat with round, heavily magnified spectacles dangling askew from his nose. He looked more like the sweet old owner of an antiques store than the biggest supplier of armaments sternside of the blockade—a ploy to trick the more heedless of his clientele into mistaking him for a senile old codger, which would cause them to let their guard down, ultimately strengthening his bargaining position.

A fat lot of good it had done him in the end: the poor bastard's abdomen was honeycombed with a cluster of craterlike scorch wounds extending an inch or two into his chest cavity, the surrounding flesh and clothing seared to a blackened crisp. This was, no doubt, the work of the hybridized weaponry, although the projectile spread was more indicative of a point-blank shotgun blast, suggesting the Composer had more in her arsenal than the augmented XT-90s wielded by her acolytes at the compound.

The cause of death served only to reinforce the hypothesis that Devruhkhar had been supplying weapons to Harmony. It would explain why he had seemingly opened the door to his executioners. As to why their business relationship had soured, Eamon could only speculate that the Composer had caught wind of his own acquisition of her prototype tech and was making an effort to cover her tracks.

Couldn't even get one foot through the door and she's already a step ahead of you. Jyn was right: maybe you should have left this one to the professionals.

"Nasty way to go."

Eamon whipped his head around to face the owner of the surly voice that had come from behind him. Blocking the entrance like bouncers outside a nightclub stood the two human Monarchs from earlier—a man and a woman, prime examples of the Governor's finest: Mouth rats plucked off the street at an early age and set loose on the district with military-grade weapons and dangerous delusions of authority, undying fealty drilled into them by a megalomaniacal combination of cruelty and generosity.

Their nonhuman associate—the single most fearsome cohabitor Eamon had ever laid eyes upon—loomed behind them: a towering specimen with battle-worn chitin, the side of aer face marred by distinctive streaks of scar tissue running down the crest of aer neck to aer thorax. Dispatching a bug to handle grunt work like this wasn't exactly standard protocol, which made Eamon wonder if Drexen had determined bringing the *marshal* in necessitated a little more muscle than usual. He might have been flattered were he not busy making mental preparations for an uncomfortably close-quarters firefight.

With a restraining hand wrapped tightly around the collar of Abe's vest, he stood up slowly. "I thought I lost you guys back there. You had me worried sick."

The female Monarch stepped forward, chapped lips curled in disapproval. "You should know better than to go strolling through the Harrow without an escort, Marshal Wyatt. This is an active industrial area, you know? Accidents happen all the time."

"Well, you can tell the boss I appreciate the concern. Figured I was safe enough with you three kindly watching my back."

"You can tell him yourself." Grinning balefully, she turned to her male counterpart. "Get Naught to search this fool."

The male—a cipher—promptly attained resonance with the cohab apparently called Naught, silently but brightly relaying the instruction. Eamon raised his hands submissively as the menacing brute approached and felt Abraham nuzzle the back of his legs in fear. Hot, nauseatingly sweet breath doused his face as he was patted down with a pair of mighty four-digited paws. Naught disarmed him, then delicately removed the spliced pistol from his jacket pocket, inspecting it closely in what appeared to be recognition—and perplexment—of its unusual modifications.

"The Governor wants to meet with you," the cipher said gruffly.

Eamon gestured with a nod toward Devruhkhar's pocked corpse. "I've kind of got my hands full at the moment, guys. My friend here, he's not feeling so good."

The Monarchs trained their shoulder-strapped viperinae SMGs on him in unison, the weapons' heatsinks purring as they charged. They were plasma clipped—not capable of the damage sustained by the gunsmith but more than deadly enough to turn Eamon into ninety-five kilos of shredded white meat should he choose not to comply.

"Vidalia doesn't make requests, Marshal. You're coming with us."

While Abraham hopped in excitement, having mistaken their captors for new friends, Eamon was led at gunpoint back out into the alleyway and shoved into a rapid aerial personnel transport (or raptor for short): a Humvee with matte-black armor, hovering on heavy-duty repulsor pads with a riot shield mounted to the windscreen.

Eamon half expected the boss man himself to be waiting inside but was surprised, and perhaps a little disappointed, to find the passenger cabin empty. He wondered briefly if they planned to take him to their hidden HQ, but the fact that he was bundled in without a blindfold suggested otherwise. As the raptor began to ascend, an alternative possibility took root in his mind: maybe the plan *was* to zero him after all . . . *Seize the spliced tech then fly the meddling marshal and his flea-bitten mutt a kilometer above ground, toss them both out, and let the fall do the rest—quick, clean, and impossible to trace.*

Before any further consideration could be given to the harrowing notion, something peculiar happened. The raptor decelerated and the surrounding atmosphere appeared to swirl and garble, almost as if the vehicle had punctured a hole in reality itself. Eamon realized the disorienting effect was caused by traversal through a luma-cast veil—cutting-edge stealth tech in the form of a spherical projection, two hundred feet or so in diameter, that mimicked its surroundings and subsequently rendered anything within its illusionary perimeter completely invisible. The originating point of this ingenious concealment then came into view of the windscreen. A lavish pleasure yacht hung daintily above the district—a beautifully modern aerial vessel flourishing a chrome-clad exterior, as well as an immaculate outdoor terrace with authentic wooden decking.

Eamon had to scoop his jaw up from out of the footwell. All this time he'd thought the Governor had been running his empire from some hidden compound, when in fact he had been stalking unseen high above the district, lording over his domain from a luxurious mobile base of operations. It was hard not to admire the genius of it.

The raptor pulled up alongside a boarding point where Vidalia Drexen stood awaiting their arrival. Wearing a tan suit, he had the demeanor of a man whose greatest machinations had finally come into fruition, the harsh geometry of his dark face etching a look of predatory glee. Their long game of cat and mouse had finally come to its conclusion; the Governor had yet another unwitting marshal ensnared in his web and held completely at his mercy.

Eamon was ushered out of the passenger cabin and forced onto the terrace, where Drexen's entourage of half-cut, scantily clad sycophants were bathing and schmoozing beneath the vitamin-giving radiance of the Höllengarten. Eyeing the crowds of self-absorbed airheads, it dawned on him that the yacht was like an oasis: bobbing along in a moral vacuum, its lazy amble unswayed by the bloodshed and the turmoil raging in the slums below. Harmony, Humanity First, the grenadiers—it all felt like it was a million miles away; he almost envied their capacity for such callous obliviousness. *Oh, how easy life would be if I too could just simply not give a shit.*

"Your companion will be staying with my associates for the duration of our liaison," Vidalia said while leading Eamon into the main deck, flouncing his arms as if giving a grand tour. "I hope that is acceptable. I'm afraid I have something of a nervous disposition when it comes to toothed animals."

Eamon followed in step, thrown by the Governor's affable tone—as though the years spent thinking they were sworn nemeses had been a complete misreading of their relationship on his part and that, in truth, they were old friends or esteemed business partners. It would have been convincing could he not still feel the muzzle of the cipher's viperinae pressed into his spine.

"That's fine by me, Gov," he replied, playing up to the charade. "But you should know, your guys might end up developing a similar *disposition* if they lay a finger on him. Abe won't take too kindly to getting roughed up by strangers."

"He will be treated with the utmost respect. I assure you."

Curiously, the sumptuous extravagance of the yacht's furnishings was limited to the outdoor terrace area; inside, the decor was brutally stark. The walls of Vidalia's study were fashioned from hexagonal tiles of unplastered concrete, dimly lit by evenly spaced wall fixtures. His desk was a rustic stone slab levitating on a single repulsor pad and positioned in front of a panoramic wall aquarium. Eamon didn't know all that much about aquatic wildlife, but he doubted the shadowy invertebrates gliding through the murk were from Earth—more likely they were of *Devourer* ecology. Interestingly, they were not the only animals present in the study. As Vidalia dismissed his Monarchs and busied himself with the pane on his desk, Eamon was left free to mosey over to the cylindrical vivarium that stood on a pedestal in the center of the room. Encasing a pillar of dense foliage, the enclosure was home to a mesmerizing collection of orange-and-black insects. He marveled at their disproportionately massive yet paper-thin wings that allowed them to dance and flutter through the air as if wholly unconcerned by the laws of aerodynamics.

"Danaus plexippus," said Vidalia, rising from his desk and starting toward the vivarium. Hands clasped behind his back and a reverent quality to his voice, he seemed more like a mild-mannered museum curator than a bloodthirsty kingpin.

"They are a species of Rhopalocera, from the order Lepidoptera. Monarch butterfly, or Hú Dié in common tongue."

Funny. I always thought the whole Monarch thing came from some insane delusion of royalty, Eamon thought to say, but instead replied, "Pretty little critters, ain't they?"

"Indeed. A testament to the boundless creativity and meticulous efficiency of Mother Nature."

Vidalia brought himself shoulder to shoulder with Eamon, leaning in to admire his kaleidoscopic congregation. How surreal it felt in that moment, standing so close to the single most ruthless criminal to have ever plagued the district. How many people would be better off if Eamon were to wrap his hand around the back of the narcissist's neck, ram his temple into the corner of his ostentatious desk, and spill his brains out on the travertine floor tiles? The Monarchs waiting outside would come bursting through the door guns blazing, of course, but part of him couldn't help but wonder if it might be well worth the cost . . .

Unaware that his brutal murder was being given serious contemplation, Vidalia continued with scholarly enthusiasm.

"By way of metamorphosis, these fascinating creatures undergo several distinct stages throughout the course of their life cycle." With neatly trimmed fingernails, he tapped on the glass, indicating a tiny, grub-like organism dangling from the end of a thin branch.

"They begin their lives as simple larvae. They then gorge on their surroundings to fatten and grow their strength. When the time is right, they form a hardened chrysalis around themselves—a protective shell called a cocoon in which they secrete an enzyme to, in effect, digest their own corporeal matter. Then begins reconstruction; painstakingly, they resculpt their physiology into its adult form. When fully developed—once they've reached their fullest potential—they can finally emerge, remade anew into the transcendent beauties you see before you. The animals in the aquarium behind my desk undergo a similar process."

"That is a mite interesting." Eamon cast a sideways glance in disbelief that the gentle soul standing beside him could be responsible for so much pain and suffering. There was an unexpected charisma and sophistication about the man that, instead of putting him at ease, gave him cause to be even warier.

"Is this why you brought me here, Governor? Show and tell?"

Vidalia briskly returned to his throne and sat back with steepled fingers.

"I imagine that, given our history, you may be harboring some concern over your well-being right now, Marshal. Perhaps you believe I plan to execute you."

"The thought had crossed my mind."

"Well, allow me to disabuse you of that notion. No harm will come to you while you are in my care. The truth is that you are here because I feel it is long overdue we pressed the proverbial reset button—turned over a new leaf, so to speak. It is something I have intended for some time, but the untimely and quite unfortunate demise of Devruhkhar—our mutual acquaintance—compelled me to expedite our meeting."

Eamon made a mental estimate of how many people had been killed with the gunsmith's merchandise in the last year alone. "Oh yeah. A real goddamn tragedy."

Vidalia took on a solemn bearing: one near impossible to gauge the veracity of. "Devruhkhar was a long-standing business partner of mine. I would even go as far as saying he was a close friend. His death has affected me on a deeply personal level. And, as you can imagine, it will cause no small amount of disruption to my operation. I trust that, given the circumstances in which my Monarchs found you today, his passing has hindered your current efforts too."

"I'll admit it is a little inconvenient."

The Governor gave a deliberative pause. "I am a businessman, Marshal—this you know. For the information I am about to disclose, I will require payment. I believe the extraordinary weapon my associates confiscated from you in the Harrow to be a suitable means of remuneration. Are these terms of trade acceptable to you?"

Eamon shrugged. *As if I have any choice in the matter.*

"Take it. Damn thing freaks me out anyway. All that sinew and cartilage on a peashooter—ain't natural."

Vidalia delicately tapped a combination of keys on his pane, triggering the lights in the study to dim. The butterfly vivarium then retracted into the floor, replaced by a luma-cast projection of none other than the gunsmith himself. Devruhkhar appeared in shimmering tones of copper and gold, the look of dread and panic on his rodent-like face rendered in striking detail.

"I received this message earlier today," Vidalia somberly explained. "Regrettably, I was indisposed and unable to take the call at the time. Perhaps had I made myself more available, then poor Devruhkhar might still be with us."

Eamon forced the mouthful of vomit sent up by the bogus show of sentimentality back down his throat. He stepped forward, putting his mind into analysis mode, determined to let not one detail of whatever he was about to see elude him.

"Vidalia. I beg you to answer!" Devruhkhar's panicked voice sounded from speakers in the ceiling, bouncing frenetically off the barren walls of the study. "Oh, your disappointment in me will be immeasurable. But there's no time for groveling. I need urgent protection! I'm afraid I have been involved in something of a . . . conflict of interest. In short, I sold a sizable weapons shipment to a representative of Harmony. I didn't really have any idea what they planned to do with them. You know my policy: I don't ask my customers questions as long as they've got the scrip. But the Composer—that leech-sympathizing bitch—now her deranged militants have gone and launched a suicidal assault on the blockade using my merchandise!" He produced a handkerchief from the breast pocket of his unhoneycombed waistcoat and used it to wipe the sweat from his glistening brow.

"It would appear they made some ghastly modifications to the iron, but I don't doubt Phalanx will have any trouble tracing it back to me. I expect they, or perhaps that bungling Marshal Wyatt, will be here to interrogate me any second now, and if they don't get to me first, the Composer will surely have me killed to make sure there are no loose ends."

So, he knew Harmony was out for blood but opened the door to them anyway, Eamon thought, recalling how there had been a distinct absence of any sign of forced entry to the workshop, meaning the gunsmith was potentially unaware of his killer's connection to the terrorists. *Still something missing here. Need more data.*

There was a knock at Devruhkhar's door. He broke into a piteous sob, acceptance of his imminent demise like an anchor on the back of his neck.

"They're here. Vidalia . . . I never meant to betray you. The offer was just too good to pass up. If you can find it within yourself to forgive me and deem me worthy of vengeance, then you might find those responsible at 2801 Tycho Block—I don't know if it's where the wretches are nesting, but it's where I delivered the shipment. Goodbye, old friend."

Devruhkhar's image evaporated. The study brightened and Vidalia's transcendent beauties ascended from the floor. Eamon stood in ruminative silence, eyes fixated on the space where the gunsmith had virtually stood. The sniveling weasel had done nothing in life but arm degenerates with the tools they needed to wreak havoc on the district. How ironic that his final act should have been one of great public service. He'd given Eamon a tangible lead: Tycho Block—the residential tower in the heart of the Copper Swathes; if it wasn't where the Composer was hiding, it was, at the very least, where he could pick up her scent. All he needed to do first was get off the Governor's yacht in one piece . . .

"I cannot get involved," Vidalia said, his back turned and the purple aquarium light casting a neon outline around his hairless scalp. "The Composer and I have so far stayed out of each other's way. If I challenge her now, it will be open war in the streets. It must be DMED's responsibility to respond to this savagery. It is the only way the situation can be resolved without triggering an escalation that will get many people killed."

Eamon clicked his tongue in the corner of his mouth. "I get it now. You didn't bring me here to parley; it was so you could hire me as a hitman. You want the Composer taken out of the equation but don't wanna get your hands dirty."

Vidalia spun around to face him, arms wide and welcoming.

"Marshal. I know you and I have shared our differences over the years. But I have revealed myself to you. And I have shared this critical information. I had hoped you would accept these endowments as an act of good faith—a peace offering, if you will. We are both exceptionally astute men. I know you see the looming shadow as I do—the conflict that will soon envelop all who lie sternside of the blockade. There *must* be far greater cohesion between our two organizations if we are to have any hope of providing prosperity and security for our constituents."

He stood up, fingertips spread wide on his desk.

"There is an order here—an order that, whether you are willing to accept it or not, is the only thing keeping the Mouth from descending into a lawless Gomorrah. Harmony threatens that order, and it is for that reason they must be silenced. We will find no triumph over them as enemies; only if we work together can we prevail."

Eamon meandered toward the glass-curtain wall at the entrance to the study, where, over the starboard gunwale, the District of the Mouth stretched on as far as the eye could see. It was whiplash-inducing—hearing the Governor speak so compassionately about his "constituents" while gazing upon the squalor below—a ruination that his "business ventures" were largely the cause of. The marshal had held his tongue for long enough; the time for civility was over.

"With all due respect, Governor, it's you and your band of cutthroats the people here need protection from, your extortion and glow peddling that keep them in a perpetual state of destitution and dependency. Now, I won't argue that Harmony is a blight on this community that needed eradicating yesterday, but you . . . you're a rutting plague, and folks around here don't have any kind of future to look forward to while you've got 'em in a stranglehold. I appreciate you giving me a leg up with this investigation, but there will be no allegiance between us. As soon as the Composer is taken care of, it's back to business for you and me."

Vidalia paused to brush something off his desk, his countenance as unchanged as it was unreadable but the tension in his neck betraying a flaring temper.

"Glow peddling?" he repeated coldly. "Is that really all you think I hope to accomplish, Marshal? To profit off the poor and pitiless like they're cattle for milking?"

Eamon grimaced. "Mighta gone with a less graphic metaphor myself, but yeah, that about sums it up."

Vidalia straightened his posture, then clapped once, loudly. Eamon felt a ripple of apprehension as Naught entered the study, guessing he was about to receive a bludgeoning for telling the Governor what for. Thankfully, the scar-faced golem stopped by aer master's side.

"A question for you, Marshal. What are the cohabitors?"

"I don't follow."

"What are they, I ask you. Harmony thinks them victims; the Administration thinks them a threat; Humanity First and their followers think them a pestilence. They are many things to many different people, but I want to know what they are to you."

Eamon shrugged. "They're just folk, Vidalia. That's all. Folk tryna make the best out of a bad situation like the rest of us."

"No, Marshal, they are so much more. Personally, I believe they are tools—tools yearning for a craftsman to give them purpose. The upper echelons of their leadership were decimated in the Collision—then again in the Antonelli expansion. Now they are lost souls, wandering the *Novara*'s carcass without guidance or cause. The Divine Abyss has seen fit to bestow upon us these powerful contrivances; it is our duty to give them their purpose."

"Far as I'm concerned, that's just a pretty way of saying you mean to enslave them."

"No, Marshal. I mean to empower them." Vidalia gestured toward the vivarium. "I believe that, like Danaus plexippus, we are in a state of metamorphosis. Our current circumstances are not the eternal damnation most think; we are merely in a period of transformation. This colossal metal husk is our chrysalis. The cohabitors are the enzyme that will break us down and rebuild us anew. We must learn to wield their power if we are to grow our wings and break free from our cocoon."

He reached into his breast pocket and produced something Eamon was all too familiar with from his time in the GEA: a disposable inhaler containing a small amount of vaporized glow, commonly referred to as a cap.

"Glow is the secret to comprehending and harnessing the cohabitors' power," Vidalia declared, pinching the object with a finger and thumb before his nose, studying the swirling luminescence inside. "It must be consumed by as many people and as often as possible. Only then can we attain what is meant for us: transcendence."

He clapped again, signaling for Naught to strong-arm the marshal and start him back toward the study entrance, their "liaison" apparently now concluded.

"So you see, Marshal, I am no petty glow peddler—my business is the betterment of humanity. I know you do not see it that way now, but if you successfully eliminate the Composer, then perhaps I might let you live long enough to edify yourself."

FOURTEEN

The crew was recovering from the debilitating neurological effects triggered by traversal through the *Devourer*'s core. The *Assurance*, on the other hand, was still taking a severe punishing. Elusive forces dragged the careening hauler deeper into the intestinal recesses of the cohabitor dreadnaught, like a piece of driftwood tumbling in the ravenous current of a river, smashing and scraping against the mechorganic walls of the enclosing passageway, her fuselage howling and shuddering from the strain.

Each of Kahu's fraught attempts to regain control proved more futile than the last. His eyes wild, reddened by spools of burst blood vessels, he wrestled with the throttle as if it were the head of an attacking cobra, bulging biceps testing the elasticity of his flight suit.

"Structural integrity at eighty-six percent and falling fast! She wasn't built for rough terrain like this, Skip. Dunno how much more the old gal can take before she rips herself apart."

Perhaps one of the more stressful aspects of taking on a crew was the expectation that a captain couldn't lose composure in a crisis. The others looked to Delilah to keep a cool head when the chips were down—to have a solution to every problem and to never let fear or emotion get the better of her. So, although she wanted nothing more than to curl up into the fetal position and scream for the calamity to end, outwardly she had to stay poised to keep the crew focused and firing on all cylinders.

Bracing herself behind the pilot's seat, fingernails digging fervidly into the syn-leather of the headrest, she calmly replied, "She can handle it, Heperi. Can't exactly turn around, can we? Just press on and we'll get clear of this turbulence soon enough."

If there was one thing keeping her from falling apart completely, it was that Null and Mercy seemed relatively unfazed by the current pandemonium. Pendant clutched in hand, the young cipher stood by the windshield, half the size of the poncho-clad juggernaut beside her but just as trans-fixed by the aurora-like phenomenon dancing beyond the nose cone—a violescent whirlpool that seemed to be the culprit behind the *Assurance*'s noncompliance.

Delilah only wished the girl would turn around and offer an affirming nod, an encouraging smile—anything that might provide some reassurance that this was all expected behavior, part of the plan. She hated to be critical, but if Null was, in fact, responsible for directing whatever arcane mechanism had the ship fettered, then ae wasn't doing a very good job of it . . .

"This doesn't make any sense," Isaac proclaimed, sitting shotgun, hunched over the systems panel like a mad scientist whose creation had suddenly sprung to life and was now rebelling against its master.

"We're at full reverse burn. Whatever's got a hold on us is strong enough to negate fifty combined kilotons of force from the impulse thrusters."

"Are you done number crunchin' over there, glow worm?" Kahu snarled. "Cuz it's gonna take more than grease monkey mumbo jumbo to get us outta this mess—we need solutions!"

Isaac huffed in annoyance. "Don't call me a glow worm, you washed-up juicer. I'm thinking! OK . . . the impulse thrusters get a seven percent power boost when they're oriented vertically. We could nose up and start the land-ing cycle—wouldn't be much but could be enough to slow us down."

"Hate to break it to you, kid, but there isn't enough room to swing a cat in here let alone pull off a maneuver like that."

Delilah leaned in toward Kahu's ear, her scolding voice tremulous in the vibrations of the floor grating. "I assume, since you're hell-bent on shooting down everyone else's ideas, you've got your own to bring to the table?"

"Matter of fact, I do. That jump ship Bug and Bug-Eyed used to board with is still docked to the cargo bay, right?"

Bug and Bug-Eyed? She thought to lambast the unflattering choices of nicknames, but ultimately knew it was a sign the old grouch was warming up to them.

He continued, "I say we jettison it without cycling the airlock first. The sudden depressurization will give us a kick that just might be strong enough to kill our momentum. Tried something similar once when I was flyin' a bus back in 95 AC. Clunker lost its inertial dampeners, and it was the only way I could think to slow it down."

"Did it work?"

"Hell no . . . but it might this time."

Teo had been uncharacteristically silent since the harrowing plunge into oblivion began—caught at the intersection between paralyzing fear and wonderment. That was until Kahu's unfathomably stupid suggestion wrenched her out of her stupor. She leapt into the fold like a frog hopping out of a frying pan.

"Whoa, whoa! Are you serious? You want a three-ton skiff bouncin' around in here with us? We don't even know if there's atmosphere in this tunnel. If that thing cracks the windshield we're toast. Plus, wouldn't be fair to decomish such a nice jumper without consultin' Null first. That's just plain mean!"

A violent quake rocked the fuselage—the worst one yet. The *Assurance* screamed in agony, her buckling foundations succumbing to unyielding torment.

"I don't give a bug's ass what we do, as long as we do it fast," Kahu spat. "Me and this old gal got up to some real freaky shit over the years, and I ain't never heard her moan like that before."

Teo recoiled in disgust. "Thanks for blessing us with that delightful mental image—exact thing I wanted to be picturin' in my last few seconds of life."

"Don't thank me, Mouth rat." He nodded abrasively at the two standing forward of the helm. "Thank the Governor's mutes up there. They're the ones that got us into this scrape."

Just then, Mercy spun around, eyes burning bright like binary suns.

"Captain Holloway! Your pilot must relinquish control of this vessel!"

Kahu chortled mockingly. "Girl. Have you lost your damn mind? The second I let go of this flight stick we'll be pulverized, kaput! Nothin' but a skid mark on the wall of whatever the crud this is we're hurtlin' down right now."

A gullet, Delilah thought. *That's exactly what it looks like.* She had long suspected the *Devourer* of being an enormous living organism. Maybe what they were "hurtlin' down" was, in fact, its food pipe—soon to arrive in a cavernous stomach chamber, where they would be digested by a lake of metal-eating gastric acid. Thankfully, Mercy's growing agitation distracted her from having to dwell on that possibility any further.

"The Savior has granted us safe passage and is shepherding us through its core. The more Mr. Heperi resists its influence, the more damage we do to ourselves. We must relinquish control!"

Delilah turned her gaze from the girl's pleading expression to Kahu's one of withering skepticism.

Injecting gravity into her voice, she ordered him to do as Mercy had advised. Naturally, the resounding objections were loud and emphatic, but then a weariness came over him. He looked tired—mainly from the endless headbutting with his crewmates, but also physically exhausted from grappling with the *Assurance*'s unruly flight controls.

"You'd better hope there's not an afterlife, Delilah. Cuz we'll be having fisticuffs at the gates to Pasture if this doesn't work."

Wincing, he released the flight stick and exaggeratedly threw his hands in the air. However, the obliteration he was anticipating never arrived. Instead, the incessant howling of tortured metal was immediately silenced, the sudden absence of bone-rattling vibrations like being spat out of a tumble dryer. As if possessed by some benign spirit, the *Assurance* began to guide herself autonomously along the dismal tunnel, rolling and strafing to clear her extremities of the sinister environment at narrow points. The furious rapids they had been caught in for what seemed like an eternity now felt more like a tranquil stream, pulling the ship along gently and steering her clear of its jagged banks.

Both Delilah's pilot and her engineer saw fit to abandon their stations, drawn to the windshield like moths to the flame. In true fashion, Isaac began reeling off potential explanations, tugging absentmindedly at the goggles slung around his neck, his analytical mind desperately seeking to understand what his clouded eyes could not make sense of. "A gravitational slipstream, perhaps? No . . . the adjustments are too finite, too precise. Maybe we aren't so much being physically dragged as we're being guided. It could be a firmware daemon that's overridin' the guidance systems—commandeering the flight controls."

"Why does it have to be any of that?" Teo asked dreamily. "Why can't it just be magic?"

Arm outstretched, Kahu placed a hand against the windshield, playfully mimicking Null. "Pretty good at that. Ay, Bug? Is this how you tell me I'm fired, Skip? Doesn't look like you need me anymore."

Delilah gave a chuckle tinged by a sigh of relief. "If only that were true."

Teo gasped in amazement. "This tunnel goes on forever! The *Devourer* . . ." She paused, glanced at Mercy. "Sorry . . . the Savior—it's so much bigger than I originally thought it was."

"It's a monster," affirmed Kahu. "About a third the size of the *Novara*. Got pretty close to the surface a couple times during the expansion—didn't think I'd ever be flying *inside* the darn thing. If only Tala could see me now." He ripped his hand away from the aluminosilicate like it was scalding hot to the touch and gave Null an anxious look before hurrying back to his station.

That name, Tala—it wasn't the first time he had uttered it. Occasionally it slipped out in a half-drunken mumble or could be heard as a tortured howl through the walls of Delilah's quarters, the old dog often plagued by distressingly vivid night terrors. Never once had he expounded upon who this Tala was or what she meant to him—perhaps an old flame or a close friend killed in the line of duty. Whichever it was, her memory haunted him, and if allowed to fester in his mind would trigger days-long bouts of excessive drinking and self-loathing that were notoriously difficult to pull him out of. Delilah had never pressed him on the subject for fear it might open Pandora's box and put him out of action indefinitely. It didn't mean she wasn't curious to find out the truth but rather knew the man would in all likelihood take it with him to the grave . . .

A deluge of muted gold light flooded the bridge as the tunnel's terminus neared—a triangular opening comprising three membranous flaps that retracted upon approach like the valves of a coronary artery. The *Assurance* blew through the opening and sheared into the yawning expanse of the Mouth, the scraptropolis rolling out below like lava fields punctuated by spires of ice and rock.

It was fortunate Kahu had already returned to the helm, as the ship dropped like a lead balloon the second the *Devourer*'s intangible shackles released their hold. He swiftly engaged the landing cycle and set her down gently in a barren patch just beyond the outskirts of the Cohabitor Ghetto. As the moon dust settled, Delilah took pause to contemplate how strange it felt to see the conglomeration of pods and domes that formed the alien settlement beyond the nose cone—to have landed a two-hundred-fifty-foot hauler in a region of the Coalescence that had been hitherto inaccessible via spacecraft. She found it hard not to lament the time and effort wasted smuggling goods through Antaeus Gateway when the *Devourer* had been keeping a direct route into the Mouth hidden through its innards all along. The secret to gaining access: having a cohabitor aboard. Null and Mercy had yet to divulge how long they intended to stay after the job was done. But with the prospect of unlimited exo-tech salvage on the horizon paired with this new means of entering the district, Delilah hoped the agreement could be an indefinite one.

Without so much as a nod of acknowledgment, Null lumbered to the auxiliary system's console and remotely initiated aer jump ship's homing pigeon protocols. The craft detached from the cargo bay and rocketed off toward the empty space over the Copper Swathes before vanishing into the luma-cast stealth bubble that concealed Vidalia's luxurious pleasure yacht—something Delilah only knew about thanks to a tip-off from an acquaintance who had once been fortunate enough to get invited aboard.

Lucky bastard.

With Isaac topside taking a rough damage assessment, she headed down to the cargo bay to oversee the preparation of the hydro-ionizers for delivery. Great plumes of excess heat vented from underside exhaust ports as the boarding ramp extended. Teo and Kahu sped down on a burro, a four-wheel heavy-duty cargo transport, with the merchandise on a trailer in tow before unloading at the second set of coordinates provided by Mercy's locket.

The cargo bay and everything inside it shook as Null bounded down the boarding ramp, kicking aer legs and braying excitedly. Aer behavior was the least difficult to interpret that ae had exhibited since coming aboard: aer stay on the *Assurance* had been, understandably, distressing, and ae was happy to finally be home. Ae galloped on all fours past Teo and Kahu toward a clumsily arranged huddle of domiciles at the edge of the clearing, where residents were emerging in droves to investigate the sudden appearance of a human ship on their doorstep. Crowds of cohabitors gathered wearing tattered rags over cracked and discolored chitin, all emaciated and suffering from various ailments, some hunched over with missing limbs replaced by splints or makeshift prosthetics. The degree of poverty here made life in the slums look like pure luxury and life beyond the blockade an impossible utopia. Casting troubled eyes over the lineup of glum starvelings, Delilah gasped—so loudly, in fact, that Mercy heard and was compelled to ask whether everything was OK.

"Yes. Of course! Well . . . I suppose it's a little shocking to see just how bad things have gotten. The situation appears to have deteriorated quite rapidly since the last time I was this side of the Çorak."

Sadness pulled at the young cipher's gaunt face. "This is what existence looks like for most cohabitors, Captain. Now you understand why our mission is so critical."

She shook her head in disbelief. "But what about the conduits, the water, and the protein they take? I don't get how poverty on this scale is possible when they're siphoning so much of our resources?"

"The Savior provides what little sustenance it can by way of the Höllengarten, but the majority of its intake must be used for fuel so that it can, in turn, power the *Novara*'s hydroponics. It is a delicate balance: the Savior exists to give life and protection to the Prey, but it must be able to breathe in order to do this."

Delilah followed as the girl started down the boarding ramp, eyebrows pinched in deep thought. "So, this plan to tap a conduit and create an artificial river along the Çorak . . . " She paused, wrangling with Mercy's alternative terminology. "The Savior hasn't necessarily given its blessing for the Prey to do this—taking from its supply could, in actuality, be putting it in jeopardy."

Mercy gave a forlorn nod, gesturing delicately at the impoverished gaggle still keeping their distance. "The Prey feel great shame at this, but as you can see, things have become very desperate. If we do not act soon, then a great many may not survive this drought."

The onlookers were suddenly scattered by what sounded like the menacing thrum of an approaching hornet swarm. A convoy of raptors descended from the heavens and circled once overhead before setting down in a tight arc formation around the *Assurance*'s landing zone. A cavalry of Monarchs kitted out in signature urban camouflage streamed from the armored transports, setting up a perimeter with blistering speed and proficiency.

"Best hope the Governor don't plan on fleecing us right now," Kahu said, leaning nonchalantly on the hood of the burro and sizing up Vidalia's forces with a measuring stare. "Ain't nothin' we can do if he decides to take the booty and leave us in the muck."

"You're being paranoid." Delilah felt her hand inch instinctively from her gun-belt to the repeater strapped to her thigh. "It's gonna go smooth . . . *has* to go smooth."

Vidalia disembarked from the nearest raptor wearing a bulletproof vest over a fine Ulster coat. He moved across the clearing with the unrelenting pace of a sandstorm, halting suddenly at a cautious distance, his enigmatic austerity filling the space between them. Mercy moved to greet the man, head bowed subserviently, looking more in that moment like an indented servant than a cherished associate. She took her master aside to convene briefly—hopefully, Delilah thought, sparing him some of the *finer* details regarding the ins and outs of the expedition. From the way Vidalia turned to greet the captain (arms wide with a beaming smile) it was clear Mercy had done just that.

"I must tell you, Captain Holloway: rarely do I find myself in a debt of gratitude with those whom I take on contract. But yours was a perilous task—one with many uncertain variables—and yet you have delivered as promised without complication or delay. And what's more, returned my companions happy and unharmed—quite exemplary work."

Mercy gave a knowing smirk over Vidalia's shoulder; a number of truths had almost certainly been tactically omitted.

These two must really be desperate to escape the Governor if they're prepared to lie to his face just to secure permanent residence on a weld and salvage ship, Delilah mused. *Especially one piloted by a drunken lunatic like Kahu.*

"Job was as routine as they come," she said, chest puffed up like a robin's. "Null and Mercy were instrumental in helping us deliver the quarry safely; it was a pleasure having them both aboard."

"That word—routine," Vidalia said, pensively stroking his chin. "There are some who take it to mean mundane or run of the mill—it is a word used by the unimaginative to describe an uneventful or boring situation." He approached slowly, ran a hand cladded in a syn-leather glove across the top surface of one of the ionizers, brushing away a layer of crystallized space dust. "But with the monumental importance of what these ancient contraptions will empower us to do, an uneventful retrieval was precisely what I had hoped for. You have proven yourself reliable, Captain, and reliability is something I hold in high regard and reward handsomely." He nodded to the nearest Monarch, who swiftly returned to one of the raptors, presumably to retrieve payment. It was then Delilah realized that at no point in the run-up to the job had they negotiated a fee for her services. She cursed under her breath.

Amateur.

"As for Null and Mercy," Vidalia continued, "it would seem you left quite the impression on them. Mercy just notified me of their shared desire to remain on the *Assurance* for the foreseeable future. I have no doubt they will be invaluable assets to your crew—if, of course, it is your wish for them to stay. It would mean my keeping a closer eye on the *Assurance* going forward but would come with the promise of regular contracts."

She straightened her face, hiding the fact that inside she was jumping for joy. "That works for us. As you know, most salvage outfits turn their nose up at the *Devourer* wreckage scattered throughout the Debris Belt. With Null at our disposal, we'll be the only crew in operation bringing in all that valuable exo-tech—we'll corner the market! Naturally, you'll get a generous percentage of the take, given the contribution you're making."

A grin that was as devious as it was strangely affable swept across Vidalia's sculptured face. "Just as I always say, Delilah: if there are nunits to be made, then we *must* endeavor to make them."

The Monarch who had gone to retrieve payment returned carrying a metal flight case, painted red and emblazoned with Vidalia's initials in golden calligraphy. He placed it at her feet, bowing cordially before hastening back to his post. Another of the Governor's lackeys—a herculean cohabitor with a face that looked like it had lost a fight with a knife rack—trudged over to the burro and began unloading the ionizers. Feeling a palpable rush of relief and accomplishment at the transaction's completion, Delilah turned to Kahu and whispered, "Told you: smooth."

Vidalia narrowed his stare. "I know we never agreed upon a fee, but I trust the amount will be satisfactory. I leave you now with an invitation."

"An invitation?" she echoed. *Aboard your fancy yacht, I hope.*

"Yes, to a ceremony of sorts—one to commemorate the installation of the hydro-ionizers. I would like for you to witness firsthand the lifeblood you have helped inject into this forsaken place. And for the people here to know the faces of those who would come from beyond the blockade to assist in their plight—to bask in the glow of heroes."

Delilah felt a sharp catch of unease. "That sounds nebula. But unfortunately, we need to be returning dockside. We're long overdue now, and I imagine the harbormaster will be getting fairly suspicious regarding our whereabouts."

Vidalia's amicable manner soured suddenly. "It was not a request, Delilah. Consider it mandatory. The ceremony will not be for a few days, giving you plenty of time to check in and make any preparations you need for your return via the *Devourer*'s core. Know that failure to attend will put you all in breach of contract, and that would greatly affect the future of our business relationship."

Kahu cleared his throat, took a step forward with what looked like a clumsy, half-assed curtsy. "Just one question, if you please, Gov. Is there gonna be grub at this shindig?"

Delilah sat at the island countertop in the galley, counting her riches. She had opened the flight case to find it overflowing with stacks of translucent notes: twenty-five thousand nunits in total—double the highest amount she had been paid for any job previously and then some. Although she couldn't deny the Governor's insistence on attending the "installation ceremony" was a little disconcerting, she simply chalked it down to his eclectic personality. After all, her faith in him had otherwise been vindicated: the compensation was more than generous and, despite Marshal Eamon Wyatt's warnings, she now had every confidence the hydro-ionizers were being put to good use. With Null and Mercy sticking around, she was growing increasingly optimistic about the future of her operation. Finally, all seemed right with the world, which made it all the more terrifying when the world suddenly flipped upside down. The return journey through the *Devourer*'s core had, so far, been considerably calmer than the way in. They had made it to the surface without issue and were now on the ordinarily humdrum last leg to the Lower Amidships Docks. Clearly, though, something had gone awry: the *Assurance* was rolling sporadically, pitching up and down like a rodeo bull bucking off its rider.

"What in the stars is going on up there?" she rasped, scrambling to make her way to the bridge, loose nunits falling like scattered leaves in the air. She sprinted up the helm access corridor, the sounds of a commotion exploding from up ahead, and arrived to find Kahu at the helm, wailing on Null's carapace with one hand and furiously trying to wrestle the flight stick out of aer paw with the other. The cohabitor bleated loudly in distress, hell-bent on taking control of the helm and changing course. Where to, exactly, not even aer cipher could ascertain. Taking a less tactile approach to getting Null's attention, Mercy stood forward of the helm, waving her arms frantically with her irises aglow.

"What is it? Tell me what's wrong!" But not even their strong empathic connection could sway the pertinacious alien.

Delilah braced herself in the bridge entrance, curls of black hair strewn about her enraged face. "Anybody gonna tell me what the hell is going on?"

"Damn bug's tryna hijack us, Skip! Wants to kamikaze the *Assurance* into the *Novara!*"

"Let aer go, you big lug!" Teo pleaded, fruitlessly attempting to separate the grappling pair. "Obviously ae's not tryna crash the *Assurance*. Just let aer steer and let's see where ae wants to go!"

Kahu didn't get the opportunity to concede before Null forcibly removed him from the helm with a powerful shove. The old pilot floundered backward and careened into a storage locker with an almighty crash. Then, free to steer, Null vectored the ship away from the *Novara* and out into the endless night, filling the windshield with a bleak and crushing nothingness. Hyperventilating through gasping breathing holes, ae pointed into the black with a single trembling digit. Mercy tried once more to glean the alien's intent, this time managing to pry out an answer.

"There's somebody out there, Captain!"

"That's impossible," Kahu spluttered, brushing himself off. "We're way too far out. Ain't nothing yonder but dust."

But Mercy was right. Against the boundless cloak of stars there was a distant point of light, yellow in hue and winking rhythmically. As Null accelerated, the object's humanoid shape gradually came into view. The light was in fact coming from beneath the visor of a helmet, its blinking pattern due to its wearer's uncontrolled rotation.

"It's a pilot!" Kahu yelped excitedly, recognizing the NTSC-issue flight suit the strandee appeared to be wearing. "They must have had to eject. We gotta help him, Skip!"

Teo—the only crewmember with any medical training—darted for the biometrics console. "Linkin' up to their suit now. Female, late twenties—she's alive but not for long. Scans suggest severe cranial trauma, and her life support's at two percent. I'll prep for EVA."

"No!" Delilah snapped back. "We don't have time. We'll have to reel her in. Isaac, gear up on the grapple, and be careful! Teo, report to the cargo bay with a medkit and get ready to assist."

She stared out through the windshield, fearless resolve flooding her chest. "Whoever you are, just sit tight. Help is on the way."

FIFTEEN

It wasn't long after meeting Humanity First's director, Bhaltair Abernathy, that Caleb and Tobias found themselves becoming an integral part of his campaign strategy. They were the new blood—living proof the organization didn't just represent disenfranchised laborers and stuffy aristocrats, but that it was also gaining traction with a more youthful, energized demographic—those who would eventually stand under the shade of trees grown from seeds planted today, Tobias's father had once said.

On Bhaltair's campaign barge they were ferried up and down the *Novara* in a dizzying ballet of meetings with various dignitaries and community figures. Their task: to convince the good citizens of the NTU that Humanity First strived to abolish its disreputable name, and that their cause was one worthy of the public's support (and generous donations).

It had become readily apparent, though, that not only was this to be the extent of their engagement in Bhaltair's movement, but that it was all he really aspired to achieve: amassing a horde of devotees and systematically relieving them of their hard-earned nunits. Bhaltair had, on multiple occasions, reassured them that his plans necessitated extensive fundraising. But continuous failure to elaborate on what those plans actually entailed had left Tobias feeling uncertain. After expending all the smooth talk in his repertoire, he was struggling to persuade people of that which he himself was unconvinced: that separating from the *Devourer* was even remotely achievable, let alone humanity's last hope for survival, as his father continuously insisted.

Even the irrepressible Caleb had begun to lose steam—not from a lack of belief in the message but from growing dissatisfaction with the level of tangible activism in which the group was actually involved. That first rally in Xìngyùn Square had sparked a fire in her belly that nothing short of personally storming the council chambers in Chennai Plaza and demanding the immediate expulsion of the leeches would extinguish. More and more,

Tobias sensed her growing disillusion with Bhaltair's methods, and he suspected it would only be a matter of time before she regressed to wanting to violently take matters into her own hands, just as she had threatened to in the Conservatory.

Things, it seemed, were about to reach boiling point, but any discussion about potentially absconding was suddenly derailed when news about Hazel arrived.

The call came in from Admiral Coombs himself, which under normal circumstances might have had Tobias starstruck—to be speaking with such a titan of political and military mastery. But the grave and strangely unauthoritative quality to the man's voice immediately gave him pause.

Something terrible has happened . . .

In no uncertain terms, the admiral apprised them of how a swarm of leech interceptors had violated *Novara* airspace and attacked an NTSC training exercise. Hazel was assigned flight leader to one of the two squadrons completely wiped out in the onslaught—"fledglings viciously picked out of the nest by despicable opportunists."

Though the rest of her wingmates were killed, miraculously, she had survived. Tobias figured it was those same sharp reflexes that made her such a terror with the long rifle in their favorite childhood virtu-sim, *Insecticide 3*, that had allowed her to eject before her fighter was obliterated. Still, she had not come out of the ordeal completely unscathed. A preliminary investigation revealed that a failure had occurred with her kestrel's canopy, and that it had not fully opened as she rocketed away to safety. Upon striking the glass, her helmet had absorbed most of the impact but failed to protect her completely.

She had been cast adrift for some time with dwindling life support when a salvage crew, who were starside despite the ship-wide lockdown, snatched her out of the black and delivered her to Aegis Infirmary. Coombs was hesitant to go into any further detail regarding her present condition and would only disclose that she was unconscious but stabilizing. It was only when Tobias and his father went to Aegis themselves that they learned the gut-wrenching truth: Hazel had suffered serious cranial trauma; she was in a coma, her prospects of waking up were minimal, and her neck injury was so severe that if she *were* to recover, she would probably never walk unassisted again.

She lay inclined on her gurney, a mass of monitoring cables sprouting from her upper body like conduits, heavy bruises covering her neatly shaved crown in brushstrokes of purple and black. A repulsor-suspended halo brace kept her head firmly in position, its intricate framework of plates and rods screwed into her shattered skull like some barbaric medieval torture device.

While his father trod the warpath, interrogating medical personnel with the same belligerence as someone complaining about their food at a restaurant, Tobias sat by his sister's bedside, her icy-blue hand limp in his. To see her in this way took a far greater toll than he feared he could stand. She had always been the more resilient, the more independent of the two of them, and he took nothing but pride in acknowledging that fact. Yet here she was, clinging on to her final, tenuous strands of life, his pillar of strength reduced to an enfeebled husk, barely held together by her metal exoskeleton.

"What have they done to you?" he whispered, breaking into a half sob, feeling at this point like the leeches were specifically targeting those he cared for. Clearly, they had a vendetta—a score they intended to settle by constructing a suffocating prison of grief around him, bolstering it with more death and destruction every time he dared hope he might break free. The sorrow he harbored was so raw and so palpable that it was physically painful to bear. Caleb's burning desire for retribution—he understood it perfectly now.

The ambush had not yet been made public knowledge, but the second it was, Administrator Vargos and her useless gaggle of corruptocrats would be out on the feeds, verbally condemning the atrocity and giving their hollow sympathies to the loved ones of those lost. But *again*, there would be no serious repercussions to this blatant act of war. Like the siege at the Phalanx compound, the diabolical ghouls responsible would emerge entirely unpunished, free to retreat into their grotesque fortress to plot and scheme their next egregious slaughter.

"Not this time," Tobias said, unintentionally squeezing Hazel's hand so tightly that he feared he may have added to the long list of broken bones in her body.

He had come to realize that parading among Bhaltair's flock, spewing endless verbal diarrhea in the name of a cause he didn't fully believe in, would suffice no longer. Caleb was right: they needed to take action, *real* action, for the fate of the *Novara* and all those he held dear now hung in the balance.

First, he had to get out of this place—this sterile maze of waiting rooms that reeked of death and disinfectant. It was haunted by the specter of his mother, whose memory he'd kept incarcerated here since the day she was lost so as not to bedevil his otherwise blithe existence. Feeling as though he could stomach it no more, and that nothing helpful could come from further pining by Hazel's side, he summoned a swoop and left to meet with Caleb for a much-needed drink.

His first inclination was to go somewhere familiar: a bar on Capella Promenade, perhaps, or one of the many syn-breweries cropping up in Halvorsen Commons. He decided instead that it should be somewhere dingier, rougher around the edges—somewhere down in the nether decks that might complement his dour mood. The lowest one could descend before straying into the abandoned and infamously treacherous Vestiges was a region called Cendre Vale—a grimy, humid industrial strip that ran along the Canyon floor, so far down that even the simulated daylight draped above struggled to reach it.

Comprising a miscellany of fabrication plants and swoop factories interconnected by a network of low-income neighborhoods, it was inhabited mainly by the working class, rife with transients and hooligans—a far cry from the mutinous scum occupying the slums in the Mouth but definitely a caste worth watching one's step around.

On a rundown precinct there was a popular dive bar called the Smith's Anvil, notorious for its cheap, high-percentage syn-beer—the kind of sordid place you go looking for either a fix or a fight. Tobias and Caleb had once been on a misguided and pitifully unsuccessful quest to score a few glow caps, back in their more rebellious pre-Academy days. Now, of course, the thought of ingesting even a wisp of that hallucinogenic poison engendered pure repugnance. Accordingly, he and Caleb usually made a concerted effort to stay away from such places, but today, it was where they decided to wallow—to set the world to rights by drinking until they were numb enough to forget their woes—easier said than done, especially given their arrival coincided with the beginning of what would surely be another tumultuous news cycle. There were numerous widescreen panels positioned throughout the Anvil, usually reserved for bootleg casterblade streams but now tuned to the NTNN broadcast. All eyes in the establishment were glued to the images on-screen: some jaded with a tipsy thousand-yard stare, others scintillating with unadulterated bloodlust.

The panels displayed the live feed coming in from the emergency meeting taking place in the council chambers, where the leech emissary was facing Administrative inquiry regarding the NTU perimeter violation and subsequent attack. Its brainwashed translator stood nearby, spouting lies and excuses on its behalf, even going so far as to propose the insulting notion that the instigating fighters were, in fact, human in origin and design. The vile creature's refusal to accept responsibility, paired with its apparent lack of remorse, spurred the other patrons into a ranting, howling rage. Tobias recognized the burly man who had clambered atop a barstool to begin conducting the wrathful choir as Jonah Sinclair—a loutish freighter captain who, as far as he understood it, had no official role or title in regard to his position in Humanity First but was indisputably affiliated with Mr. Abernathy. Tobias suspected him of being something of an off-the-books handyman: someone who could discreetly take care of more *delicate* matters without necessarily being tied to the organization.

Jonah spotted them through the drunken rabble. He peered with excited eyes over the rim of his pint glass as he chugged the dregs of his syn-beer before hurling it at the ground with an almighty smash to rambunctious applause.

The intention had been to come to the Smith's Anvil to find some somber peace and quiet, but only minutes after arriving they found themselves sharing a booth with perhaps the loudest man on the *Novara*.

Their table adjoined a catwalk on which a luma-cast exotic dancer spun and contorted around a neon pole. The projection had been hacked, replacing the virtual performer's head with that of Administrator Vargos, who gyrated seductively with a stone-faced expression. Tobias might once have found it in poor taste, but in these dire times, he would take any reason to laugh he could get.

Whatever Jonah was taking out of the Humanity First honeypot was enough to keep him flush; the rounds were coming thick and fast—not just for the three of them in the booth but for everyone in the Anvil, the evening's uproarious revelry being funded entirely out of his pocket.

Naturally, the conversation centered mainly around the ambush, becoming uncomfortably personal upon the revelation that Tobias's sister was the lone surviving pilot. They drank to the dead, then to her swift recovery—futilely, Tobias feared.

Jonah spoke at great length about his ship, *The Segregator*, which, as he put it, was the largest grub-runner in the Novarian fleet—used to transport massive shipments of hydroponic produce from the docks of Lower Amidships all the way up to Quarterdeck. He even joked that, as students of ACS, any greens they'd eaten at the Academy would have at some point been stored in his cargo hold.

Adopting a solemn tone, he went on to speak of how his business was being negatively impacted by the constant lockdowns triggered by leech aggressions near the blockade, citing the exorbitant cost of filling the fuel tank of a pugnator-class freighter and that going even one day without recovering that cost immediately put him in the red—just one of the many factors that had driven his interest in Humanity First.

Caleb and Tobias expressed similar sentiments, revealing their own personal reasons for joining up with Bhaltair, Caleb tearfully recounting the terrible fate of her betrothed. Jonah, undoubtedly already aware, sat in tentative silence, just listening. Tobias was put at ease by the man's blunt yet earnest manner and, feeling a little loose-lipped after that last round of firewater, went on to mention their growing despondence with the way Bhaltair was running things as well as their desire for a more hands-on brand of activism.

"Yep. Bhaltair's keepin' stuff a whole lot closer to his chest nowadays," said Jonah, applying his thumb to the payment terminal embedded in their table, casually authorizing another round for everyone in the Anvil. "There was a real shitstorm last year when we gave those leech-sympathizing students a thrashin' in Halvorsen Commons. After that he wanted to give Humanity First a face-lift—make us look more respectable so politicians like your father could feel better about makin' their support public. Rest assured, though, the old guard are still out there, fightin' the good fight."

He sat back with a look of gleeful surprise. "So, you two uptown sprites are lookin' to get your hands mucky, huh? Think I got somethin' comin' up that just might pique your interest."

The following day was showtime. Wearing their ACS uniforms, Caleb and Tobias awaited Jonah's arrival on a Canyon landing platform. The blockade towered before them, a mosaic of repurposed heat shielding like the scaly pelt of some colossal reptile, its sheer enormity dizzying at such close proximity. Ahead lay the tunnel entrance to the transfer checkpoint, the surrounding area now a busy construction site with engineers and laborers carrying out repairs to the wrecked facility. Jonah's plan was to weasel their way through and sneak into the Mouth under the pretense they were on official Administration business, but with the amount of personnel in the area, Tobias was skeptical of how successful the ruse would be. That changed, however, when Jonah, posing as their armed escort, finally rocked up having procured authentic Phalanx enforcer gear, from combat boots to a tactical Kevlar vest with matching helmet—the whole kit and caboodle. To complete the ensemble, he wore a bandolier stacked with 12-gauge rounds for the semiautomatic shotgun slung around his shoulders, its fierce outline triggering a nervous flutter in Tobias's stomach. He had only agreed to participate in today's *excursion* beyond the blockade with the stipulation that nobody was physically hurt by their actions. Although the weapon was only for show, it served as a stark reminder of the seriousness of what they were about to do . . .

"Smuggle ourselves through the blockade and use nonlethal tactics to disrupt an agricultural supply chain," Jonah had said, which was a wonderfully sanitized way of describing what could potentially be considered an act of domestic terrorism. It was perfectly justifiable in Tobias's eyes, given what had happened to Jade and Hazel and every other life decimated by the leeches in the course of their murderous crusade. Those insect devils deserved far worse, but having never committed even so much as a misdemeanor in his admittedly mollycoddled life, for him, even this was way beyond the pale.

"Well, look at you two," Jonah said, his fearsome appearance tempered by the comical way his beard parted around his helmet chinstrap. "All spick 'n' span, like a dog's dinner."

"I guess we at least look the part," Caleb replied. "I just hope this bluff of yours works."

"It'll work. Worst-case scenario, we name-drop Tobias's old man and then sail on through."

Tobias ardently shook his head. "No. We can't risk it getting back to him that Caleb and I were involved. This must be kept between us. Understand?"

Jonah shrugged acceptance. "A damn shame; I bet a true Novarian patriot like the councilman would be real proud to see his own son personally takin' a stand against the enemy. But don't worry, I hear ya loud and clear. We'll think of something."

Projecting Quarterdeck superiority, they marched beneath scaffolding towers to the bombarding racket of construction machinery. The tunnel entrance to the transfer checkpoint was preceded by brand-new security scanners manned by a lone enforcer kitted out in the same gear as Jonah.

"Are you three lost?" the enforcer asked as they approached. "You gotta be. There's nothing this way but glow dens and big puddles of leech piss."

Caleb stepped forward, head held high. "We're on assignment—here to oversee a grenadier firmware update as part of vocational experience."

The enforcer rolled her eyes, glanced down at her data pad. "Great, a school trip. Huh—that's weird, I don't have anything listed for today. I might just need to clear this with my superior."

"That really won't be necessary, Sergeant. We're officers in training, which means this directive comes from the very top."

"Be that as it may, I still need approval before I can let you through."

Tobias felt a flush of confidence. He waved a hand abrasively. "We don't have time for that. This is a critical update with fixes for several recently identified vulnerabilities. Or would you like to personally explain to Administrator Vargos why, when the leeches attacked, our infantry stood around like a bunch of brainless test dummies?"

The enforcer placed a hand warningly on the grip of her sidearm. "Watch it, kid. You might be officers in training, but you aren't officers yet."

Evidently, it was Jonah's turn to try and appease the woman. He moved in close before rolling up the sleeve of his khaki under-armor, revealing a tattoo on his wrist depicting the interlocking rings that represented Humanity First. "We're here on behalf of Bhaltair Abernathy. He sends his regards."

A toothy grin of comprehension slithered across the enforcer's face. "Don't cause too much trouble. Can't promise it will be as easy getting back through," she said with a coy smile, stepping aside and ushering them past.

"How did you know?" Caleb whispered, hurrying the other two through the deactivated scanners.

"I didn't," Jonah replied. "It was just a hunch. But you often find the closer these leathernecks are stationed to the Mouth, the more likely they are to sympathize with Bhaltair's cause."

"You sound like you've done this before," remarked Tobias.

"Yep. I've been bowside a fair few times now. Usually make sure not to come back without blood on my knuckles. Happy to take it nice 'n' easy for you greenhorns, though."

An oppressive darkness filled the passageway through the blockade, lifted intermittently by yellow work lights on tripods that illuminated the extensive burn damage tarnishing the walls. It felt like a tomb, the weight of those killed in the siege bearing down like a sudden change in air pressure. Tobias knew from her melancholy silence that Caleb's thoughts were on Jade—likely envisioning her, as he was, trapped here in between a ravenous inferno and an alien execution squad. He reached out and touched her hand. "We'll get them, you know. We'll make them pay."

She returned a bittersweet smile. "I know. We have to."

Tobias found stepping out into the Mouth for the first time to be an overwhelming and disorienting experience. The cavity the *Devourer* had gouged out of the superstructure was far bigger than he ever could have thought possible; a third of the *Novara* had essentially been hollowed out, all that lunametal reappropriated into the construction of a sprawling settlement. He gazed in a stupor at the rust-enameled skyline, suspecting he would need a tetanus shot from even just looking at it. The *Devourer* loomed beyond like a spiraling cyclone of fangs veiled by thick copper haze. Certainly, the last thing he had expected was to be awestruck by this place, but gawking at its sheer immensity, its haphazard yet undeniable beauty, he found it difficult to be anything but.

As had been the case sternside, the Phalanx compound hummed with construction workers. Nevertheless, they made it through without garnering any unwanted attention, the grenadiers guarding the perimeter paying no mind as they skulked past and headed out into the slums.

Before pressing on any farther, they darted into a secluded alley to convene. While Caleb and Tobias began wrapping themselves in drab tunics and cowls to blend in with the crowd, Jonah reached into his duffel bag and retrieved two spherical metallic objects with blinking blue lights on opposite poles.

"Concussion charges," he explained. "*The Segregator* is a beaut but not exactly the most maneuverable hunk in her class. I use these bad boys to clear debris from her path instead of tryna swerve it. Should make a pretty nice kaboom in atmos."

Caleb took the devices and stowed them in her satchel. "So, you break us into this leech agricultural facility and keep the locals distracted while we plant the charges on the target?"

"Yep. Then we find ourselves a nice perch where we can stoop and watch the fireworks."

"Shouldn't we wait until *after* we've crossed back through the blockade?" Tobias asked, hating to be the nagging voice of reason but feeling the need regardless. "Seems like an unnecessary risk to pull the trigger while we're still sternside. What if Phalanx lock down the checkpoint?"

Jonah produced a second device from his duffel bag—a radio transmitter with a stubby antenna and a red illuminated thumb switch.

"This detonator has a limited range. Need to make sure we're still in the vicinity when we blow the charges or this is gonna be a real anticlimax."

Taking point, Jonah led the way through a dense region he called the Copper Swathes, snaking through back alleys to strategically avoid the crowded high streets. Occasionally Tobias would catch glimpses of the strange frontier that lay beyond: tumbledown residential complexes, marketplaces, and bazaars buzzing with activity—not quite the plague-stricken shantytown he had envisioned all his life but considerably more established. From the foreign stench that filled his nostrils to the dark rhythms pulsing in the distance, there was not one of his senses left unassailed by this staggering new horizon. With every turn he felt the limits of his understanding growing exponentially, soon coming to realize that his narrow, dogmatic view of the world had left him wholly unprepared for the reality of life in the Mouth.

Traversing deeper, he began to spot tall, nonhuman forms lurking amid the throng, their indiscernible physiology obscured by the tattered rags they were draped in. Electricity cascaded down his body when his eyes met those of another—four pairs, to be precise: cold, black, and lifeless, not unlike those of a shark. It was as though, despite all the evidence suggesting otherwise, he hadn't really believed the leeches existed up until now, as if they were nothing more than an urban myth—the bogeyman hiding under his bed. But in that moment, the reality of being marooned with them in this tiny oasis in an endless, unforgiving desert became all too real; it terrified him to the very core.

Before long they had transitioned into an industrial area called the Langrenus Harrow, named after the Langrenus refinery on Luna, where a great deal of Novarian metal was originally mined, Tobias presumed.

Veering off a desolate avenue, Jonah brought them to the mesh-wire fence encompassing his targeted facility—a rundown warehouse that at first glance seemed relatively unremarkable but upon closer inspection was far stranger. From a ventilation funnel on the roof snaked a pillar of tangerine smoke, lucent from within as if enshrouding a sepia-toned lightning storm. In the courtyard outside stood an intricate installation comprising various pumps, tubes, and turbines centered around a large chemical vat containing an orange, bubbling substance. The technology the unusual equipment had been constructed from was ostensibly human, but the way it was arranged, anything but.

An automated cargo barge hovered low over the vat, outfitted with a sinister assemblage of gnashing, gnawing metal teeth on its bow.

"Is that the target?" Tobias asked.

Jonah nodded. "Locals call it a harvester."

"And what, precisely, is it meant to be harvesting?"

The burly freighter captain turned his eyes upwards, indicating something that Tobias had noticed already but was so utterly bizarre that his mind had all but banished it from his awareness. The ceiling of the Mouth was alive—completely overgrown with a heavy blanket of alien foliage igniting the upper atmosphere with its fiery radiance.

"They call it the hell garden. Not hard to see why, eh?"

"Do the leeches eat it?" Caleb asked, grimacing in unbridled disgust.

Jonah shook his head. "Beats the shit outta me, but I know it's important to them, which is why wiping this facility off the map is really gonna chap their ugly asses."

Just then, the harvester unleashed a blaring noise that sounded like a mixture between a warning klaxon and the howl of a wounded animal. Its several repulsor pads fired up, propelling it toward the hell garden at lightning speed.

"That's our cue," Jonah said, dropping his duffel bag on the floor and retrieving a pair of heavy-duty wire cutters.

"That thing just goes up and down at regular intervals all day. It'll be back in a minute or two with a fresh batch of that nasty orange shit to unload. You two get in position before it comes back, then stick the charges to the undercarriage and hotfoot it outta there. This whole gig is completely automated, so we should be clear of any prying eyes, but I'll stay put and keep watch just in case."

He cut a hole in the fence wide enough for them to clamber through. They scuttled across a dangerously exposed stretch of land before slamming their backs against the side of the vat, the noxious miasma of its spuming contents stinging the back of their throats.

As predicted, the harvester returned soon after with another load of putrid hell slop to deposit, coming to a stop with its undercarriage just out of reach. Grinning wildly, chest heaving from the sheer thrill, Caleb climbed onto Tobias's shoulders and began attaching the charges. It was something they had done countless times growing up together, but never before had he been so invigorated by the feeling of the warmth of her thighs around his neck . . .

Stay focused.

The charges began a steady, metronomic beeping, indicating they were primed and ready to fire.

"OK! I think they're secure," she squawked over the drone of the repulsor pads, her fiery locks a furious scribble in the idle propulsion. He lowered her to the ground, she took his hand, and they scrambled back to where they had left Jonah by the fence.

Minutes later they were standing on the dilapidated rooftop of a nearby building—as close as they could get to the Phalanx compound while staying in range of the concussion charges. Caleb and Tobias had now removed their disguises and were all set for a frantic sprint back to NTU sovereignty.

"Better off waitin' for the harvester to reach maximum elevation before we get this party started," Jonah advised, staring into the chaotic vista with his brutish features drawn in childlike enthusiasm. "Seems like you two have got the knack for this stuff. If it just so happens you got a taste for it too, there's plenty more sites like this refinery we could hit. Or if you're lookin' for somethin' a little spicier, there's this 'sanctuary' out in the Warrens—basically a damn spawning ground. With the leech population spiralin' out of control, places like that are dangerous—just beggin' to get put outta action."

Tobias was only half listening, focusing instead on just how utterly radiant Caleb looked in that instant. She took his hands, clasping them in her own so they were both holding the detonator. Staring into her yearning, wistful eyes, his lifelong bitterness at having never been able to watch a real sunset vanished, for he was certain now that he had seen something far more beautiful.

In the distance the harvester sounded its electronic shriek, telegraphing the beginning of its ascent toward the hell garden. He positioned his thumb over the trigger switch, waiting, as instructed, for it to fly as high as possible for maximum damage and spectacle.

"For Jade."

Caleb smiled in response and tightened her grip around his hands.

"For us."

Like candles extinguished by the crack of a whip, a soundless detonation snuffed out the harvester's repulsor pads. Spluttering bronze mist from its churning mandibles, it plummeted toward the industrial wasteland below. The subsequent explosion engulfed the facility; Tobias could feel the heat lapping at his cheeks even from this distance.

Pumping his fist, Jonah leapt into the air. "Take that, you scum-suckin' leech bastards! That's whatcha get for messing with the greatest goddamned species in the galaxy!"

Beaming from ear to ear, Caleb pulled Tobias toward her body and enveloped him in a tight embrace, his heart pounding so rapidly in his chest he feared it might explode from his rib cage. Even to be reciprocating just a sliver of the pain and suffering the leeches had inflicted—it was electrifying; he knew then that for the both of them, it would probably just be the start . . .

With little time to retake the scenic route, they made their way down the main drag, barging through swarms of locals transfixed in morbid fascination by the smoke rising from the Langrenus Harrow. Ahead, Tobias could make out the perimeter of the Phalanx compound, the grenadiers there watching dutifully but not so concerned by the scenes of destruction that they had yet initiated lockdown protocols.

He could hardly believe it: soon they would have made it back through the checkpoint without a hitch. Just as he allowed a prolonged sigh of relief to leave his lips, he heard the hair-raising sound of a dog barking.

"DMED! Freeze!" The voice belonged to a man, who they turned to find sprinting full pelt toward them as his snapping, snarling beast quickly gained ground.

"Get to the perimeter!" screamed Caleb. "They lose jurisdiction as soon as we cross that line! We just gotta make it past the grennies and we're clear!"

Adrenaline flooded Tobias's system. Legs exploding into action, he sprinted harder and faster than ever before, lungs screaming as they were stretched to their very limits. But for all the physical exertion he could manage, it was not enough; searing pain shot up his leg as rows of tiny daggers sank into the skin of his calf. He tripped and slammed shoulder first into the ground, the dog's jaws tightening like a vise as the pair rolled together in an avalanche of fur and dust.

Sliding to a painful stop, he lifted his head just in time to see Caleb turning to come back for him before Jonah seized her by the arm and dragged her reluctantly through the perimeter. Then, they were gone.

The stranger—a lawman wearing a fur-collar jacket, came to a stop over him, his weathered features like whittled oak.

"Alright, boy. C'mon, let him go." The dog released its hold and returned to its master's side. The man crouched down, holding in a leathery hand the concussion charge detonator that Tobias had lost at some point during the tumble.

"Think you dropped something, Mr. . . . " He pointed a finger at the name-tag on Tobias's uniform, raising a thick eyebrow in an unsettling show of surprise and recognition. "Edevane, huh? Well, I'll be damned . . . Looks like your pals have skipped town, Tobias. Guess that means I got you all to myself."

SIXTEEN

Eamon thought it best to leave the kid stewing in a holding cell until he could figure out what to do with him. A repair team was already on site and would have the Höllengarten pulp refinery that Tobias Cole Edevane had targeted for unsanctioned demolition up and running within a day or two. But in no way did that mean he was off the hook; this was the first time DMED had apprehended someone for human supremacist–related terror offences. How the proceedings were handled would set a precedent for any future arrests, and so could be nothing short of unimpeachable.

With Humanity First gathering so much steam bowside, Eamon wondered if perhaps an opportunity had arisen to send Bhaltair Abernathy and his band of sycophantic cohorts a strong and unambiguous message: that spiteful, reckless behavior like this would not be tolerated in the District of the Mouth; that anyone engaged in wanton destruction of public property would incur the full force of the law, which, unfortunately for the councilman's son, meant a metaphorical but very public execution.

Make an example of the kid—that was certainly the marshal's first inclination. But then, as satisfying as it might have been to see the Quarterdeck elite meltdown over one of their prized specimens getting slapped with charges for domestic terrorism, there were other things at play that bore consideration: nominally, the fact that there was still a fair amount of hearsay and confusion regarding the incident in the Harrow, the general consensus among mouthians being that the harvester had fallen out of the sky due to a simple repulsor pad failure. Eamon was undecided on whether it was better to keep it that way . . .

Mouth folks won't go down without a fight. The second they get wise to the truth that the refinery was wrecked by some Upperdecks brat with a grudge and a superiority complex, there'll be hell to pay. Inevitably there will be retaliation, escalation—an eye for an eye until the Novara eats itself from the inside out.

Tobias's sentence had to be severe—there was no question about that. But it couldn't cause a media circus. In the interest of keeping the peace, it had to be as discreet as possible too . . .

The kid isn't going anywhere, he told himself, catching a glimpse of his haggard reflection in the rearview mirror. *There'll be plenty of time to figure out exactly how screwed he is later.*

Right now, navigating the Warrens required the marshal's full attention. Hovering at ground level, the width of his new cruiser made it wholly unsuitable for the grime-ridden trellis of alleys and passageways that ran like mineral veins through the heart of the Copper Swathes, inhabited by the scummiest caste of crooks and glow addicts the district had to offer. He had learned his lesson about traveling alone on foot through neighborhoods as treacherous as this one and was quite happy to risk scuffing the pristine paintwork if it meant making it to the rendezvous without getting kidnapped again.

He flicked on the wipers to clear away the droplets of red liquid that had begun to collect and form trails on the windscreen. It was perhaps one of the stranger aspects of living and working in the Mouth: the presence of a climate. At regular intervals, the Höllengarten produced a concentrated vapor, presumably something to do with purifying and oxygenating the atmosphere. It would mix with the rising current of warm air and condense, resulting in a sudden and often torrential deluge of bright red precipitation. Residents of the district called the phenomenon blood fall, which, considering how harmless it was, Eamon had always thought sounded a little too apocalyptic.

Some believed blood fall to be a sign of good fortune; others, an omen of coming tribulation. For him, it was a simple fact of life—a nuisance in almost all respects. The downpours left behind a red, chalky residue, which, incidentally, was what gave the Copper Swathes its rusted appearance. The evaporite stank like rotten wood and, after years of exposure, had stained the rich brown of his beloved jacket an ugly mottled sienna. The low visibility caused by the liquid's opacity also made for perilously hazardous flying conditions; even the cruiser's high beams could do little to cleave the crimson veil asunder, instead reflecting it in a prismatic haze as if the air itself were laced with diamonds.

He slowed to a stop at the maw of an underpass. Beneath it, Dr. Faye Lucero sheltered from the vermillion downpour. Wearing a black anorak, she looked quite literally like a deer caught in the headlights. She was Phalanx's resident forensic pathologist for the District of the Mouth—like Eamon, another wayward soul, banished from beyond the blockade as penance for transgressing against the Union. He'd never thought to look into what exactly she was doing time in the Mouth for; it was plainly obvious from her severe cataracts, gaunt physique, and pallid complexion that it was related to serious and ongoing glow abuse.

What a way to help someone recover from an addiction: exile to the one place on the Novara *where a glow cap comes easier than a glass of clean water.*

Setting Hypatia to sentry mode, he climbed out of the cruiser, warm cherryade dousing the back of his hand as he cupped it protectively over his newly lit cigarette.

"Helluva nice spot you picked to meet, Faye," he said, unfolding the fur collar of his jacket to cover his neck. "We couldn't have done this at the morgue, or that place near the precinct house that does the ramen, maybe?"

Faye ran bony fingers over her shaved scalp—not a stylistic choice, given she was hardly one for fashion. Nor was baldness a known side effect of substance abuse as severe as hers. More than likely, it was a sign of mental and emotional instability—a mild form of self-punishment or a desperate attempt to regain some control over her patently out-of-control life.

"I had to make sure it wasn't somewhere I could be followed," she replied skittishly. "You have no idea how much I'm risking coming to meet with you, Wyatt. I don't have a lot left to lose, but you better believe there's people out there that won't think twice about stripping it from me if they find out."

He tutted, joining her beneath the underpass. "Who'd you piss off this time? It's not Drexen, is it? I'm sorry, but I've got my own Governor-related problems to worry about right now."

"Trouble with the Governor I can handle. I'm afraid it's far worse than that."

"Pfft . . . worse than the Governor? I'll believe that when I see it."

She plucked the cigarette from his mouth, took a long drag, and exhaled smoke through pursed lips. "Feels like the district's going up in flames, Marshal. Terrorist attacks at the blockade, harvesters dropping out of the Höllengarten. I hope you're managing to stay on top of it all."

"Yeah, the thing out in the Harrow," he groused, pinching the bridge of his nose. "Keep this to yourself, but I've got a kid in custody at the precinct house—the son of a big shot politician from the Upperdecks. Stars know what I'm supposed to do with him."

She took a calculated pause. "And what about Anaya Lahiri? Last I heard, you'd run into something of a brick wall. I don't suppose you've made any more progress?"

"Is that who this is about? You already submitted your report, Faye. Don't tell me you've been holding out on us." He took the cigarette from her hand and finished it off before extinguishing it beneath his bootheel. "I had my finest on it for a week and she turned up nada—precisely zilch. So, if you've got some information that, for whatever reason, you neglected to include in your report, you'd better cough it up fast."

She glanced nervously over her shoulder. "Well, as you know, Phalanx would only let me do a preliminary investigation—I got to take surface scans of the lacerations to her neck and torso, which they basically forced me to profile as fission shank–inflicted, as per my report. But that was the extent of exploratory testing they would permit. The whole thing was just a formality, really; I've never seen them so eager to repatriate a body before."

Her vacant expression collapsed into a look of contempt: a woman scorned, barely able to repress the hatred she felt toward the orchestrators of her situation.

"Evidently they still don't credit me with an abundance of intellect. I might have made some mistakes in my time, but I'm not an idiot. It would have taken someone far sloppier than me to miss this."

"Faye, please. Nobody's doubtin' your powers of perception here; I just wish I knew what the hell you're talking about."

She sighed. "Those lacerations were inflicted postmortem, Wyatt. Anaya wasn't killed by some deranged leech with a shank, although somebody went to a hell of a lot of trouble to make it look that way. The scans to her torso showed severe internal bruising around her rib cage, suggesting catastrophic rupture of the lungs and subsequent death by asphyxiation."

"Rupture of the lungs?" he repeated, grimacing. "Any idea what could have caused that?"

"Remember what they used to tell us in school: the worst thing you can do if you ever get caught in a hull breach is to hold your breath—this is why. Anaya suffered rapid decompression and prolonged exposure to a vacuum. My hypothesis: someone airlocked her."

Airlocked . . . Eamon went cold at the mere thought of it: the idea of restraining someone in a pressure chamber and exposing them to the empty black. There were only two groups sadistic enough to utilize such a barbaric practice: those crazed fanatics in the Church of the Abyss and, of course, the Governor and his bloodthirsty Monarchs. The latter were known for using it as an interrogation technique—letting the cosmos in on some unfortunate bastard at brief intervals until they crumbled and spilled their guts—like repeatedly dunking someone's head in a bathtub full of ice water, only much worse.

Looks like poor Anaya got dunked one too many times.

"So, what?" he said, staring apprehensively into her eyes, which were like tiny moons fashioned from honed marble. "Someone airlocked her, diced her up with a fission shank, and then dumped her on the outskirts of the Cohabitor Ghetto to make it look like interspecies homicide?"

Faye shrugged. "After all that dirt she dug up about tracing government funds back to the Glow Syndicate here in the district, you really think the Administration is gonna just let her walk around freely?"

"Lei-Ghannam, Faye! This is sounding a lot like a conspiracy to me. So not only do you think someone staged the murder, but you believe the Administration was in on it too?"

"Don't tell me you haven't already considered it, because I don't buy that for a second. You and I know better than most how cruel and ruthless Madeline Vargos can be with anyone who jeopardizes her position. We were the lucky ones. Anaya, not so much . . ."

Eamon rubbed his eyes with the heels of his hands in disbelief that he was really giving any credence to the notion.

"Why come forward with this now, Faye? Why didn't you include any of this in the report you submitted?"

"Because I'm not like you!" she rasped impatiently. "I haven't settled into exile in the Mouth like it was a nice new pair of shoes. I despise this place and will do anything I have to to get back home. So when something like this comes along that the higher-ups clearly don't want any attention drawn to, the best thing I can do is be a good little pathologist and pretend like I didn't see anything."

He nodded. "Guess your conscience got the better of you then, or we wouldn't be standing here."

"It did . . . I had to give it some time to make sure I wasn't being watched, but you needed to know . . . because there's something else."

She reached into the pocket of her coverack coat and fished out what appeared to be a small thumb drive. Initially, Eamon assumed the reddish-brown substance staining the inside of the plastic bag it was contained in to be dried blood fall, but upon closer inspection, it was clearly blood itself.

"In the biz we call this an endo-chit," explained Faye. "It's a simple storage device, usually inserted surgically under the skin—a last line of defense for those who fear they're being hunted for the knowledge they possess. They can be programmed to mass transmit their entire packet upon the user's death, but that didn't appear to be the case with this one. I found it buried in Anaya's forearm and managed to remove it without my Phalanx chaperones noticing."

Eamon took the plastic bag and held it in his palm. "Have you tried plugging it into a terminal to see what's on it?"

Faye nodded. "I did, but I couldn't crack its encryption. It looks like it's encoded to a specific terminal, one in her office or her condo, perhaps—I don't know, but I guessed you'd have a better shot at figuring that out."

"Thanks, Faye. This could be a game changer." But as he pulled his arm away, she grabbed his sleeve, gripping the syn-leather with chipped fingernails and clinging on like a feral animal.

"You have to get me out of here, Wyatt. You're much closer to the Administrator than I am. Tell her it's not safe for me here. Surely, I must have finished my sentence by now. If she doesn't transfer me back soon—when there's all this shit with Harmony and the Governor going on—she's condemning me to death. Both of us, in fact!"

He pried his arm free before placing it supportively around her shoulders.

"Faye, I know us exiles have to look out for one another, but she won't listen to me! You don't think if I had that kind of influence, I wouldn't have done it for myself already?"

She inhaled sharply through quivering lips, trying and failing to stifle tears.

"Who are you kidding, Marshal? You'd sooner hand in your resignation than get transferred bowside again. You're right at home in this cesspool. You always have been . . ."

With Anaya's endo-chit burning a hole in his pocket and the late gunsmith's tip-off concerning Harmony's alleged residence within Tycho Block weighing on his mind, the very last place Eamon wanted to be was back in his office, staring into the luma-cast but no less fearsome eyes of Councilman Atherton Edevane. Not even the relatively low resolution and muted colors of the comms projection could mask the furious red in the man's expression. He stood rigidly against a backdrop of obscene wealth like a Renaissance portrait come to life, his voice a barrage of cannons rumbling vociferously through the console speakers.

"You've gone too far this time, Wyatt! I know you and I have our history, but that doesn't mean you need to take your frustrations with me out on my son!"

Frustrations—that's putting it lightly.

Of the few council sessions Eamon had been granted participation in, there hadn't been *one* in which the pair didn't end up in a screaming match. Atherton was a relentless, morally bankrupt, walking, talking embodiment of some of the worst values held by citizens of the NTU—completely intolerable at the best of times, and now Eamon had his son . . .

"For the last time, Ath, Tobias isn't being detained for petty thievery or minor glow possession. This isn't a misdemeanor we're talkin' about. Your boy destroyed a pulp refinery that a whole lot of folks in the district depend on. And because of your and his affiliation with Bhaltair Abernathy—a known political extremist and agitator—I've got no choice but to classify this as an act of domestic terrorism. This ain't something DMED can just overlook; there *must* be due process."

Atherton swatted a hand dismissively. "Oh, please. You expect me to believe there is anything remotely worthy of being called due process in that blighted scumhole? No! A vendetta is precisely what this is. You won't rest until you have successfully decimated the careers of every unfortunate soul who just so happens to disagree with your juvenile ideology. It wasn't enough to bring down your partner with those absurd allegations; now you're out to desecrate my family's reputation as well!"

"If reputation is all you're worried about, Councilman, I'd maybe think about finding some other cause to pour your nunits into. Humanity First don't exactly represent the epitome of decency and respectability, ya know?"

"My affiliations are my business alone, Marshal Wyatt—as is how and where I choose to spend my money."

Eamon swung his boots off his desk and sat forward in his seat.

"You can't expect me to believe you were completely oblivious to what your son and his accomplices were up to. You both signed up for this as soon as you got involved with that snake, Abernathy."

"Oh, please. Had I known, I would not be standing here having this ridiculous conversation. I sincerely doubt Tobias fully understood what he had gotten himself into either. Obviously, he was goaded or coerced into this by some ringleader. I have yet to find out who the responsible party might be, but I can tell you they were most definitely *not* acting on behalf of Humanity First."

"Sure. I bet His Royal Highness is just torn up over this."

Atherton met Eamon's sardonic sneer with an exaggerated eye roll.

"I would not expect someone as dogmatic and single-minded as *you* to comprehend Bhaltair's aspirations, but your ignorance in the matter is duly noted."

"Keep talking, Councilman." He shrugged blithely. "Every time you take a jab at me, I add another month to the boy's sentence."

"And I suppose that's your idea of *due process*, is it? Rest assured, Tobias will receive the best legal representation available on the *Novara*; I hope you're ready for a fight."

"Nebula. I was counting on one." But then, in the moment of quiet tension that followed, Eamon felt the impudent grin that had been plastered across his face throughout the call begin to melt as something occurred to him . . . It had been all over the NTNN for a full cycle now—the purported ambush that had left five NTSC pilots dead and Atherton's eldest battling for her life in

Aegis Infirmary. Anyone could be forgiven for thinking the councilman had not yet been made aware, the way he had hardly deviated from his haughty, belligerent self. If he *was* harboring any grief or despair regarding his daughter's situation, he was hiding it remarkably well.

Mentally kicking himself for only just putting two and two together, Eamon stood up and approached the bay windows of his office in quiet introspection. He knew carrying on berating and provoking the councilman would achieve nothing but a sudden and unsatisfactory end to the conversation.

Time for a different approach.

"Your girl," he said after a moment, turning back to the councilman. "Hazel, is it? How's she doing?"

Atherton was taken aback: both disarmed and visibly wary of the marshal's sudden candor. "Her prognosis is . . . ongoing."

"I'm glad she's still with us in the realm of the living. Sincerely, I mean it."

"That remains to be seen. But . . . your concern is appreciated."

Eamon studied the frail, defeated husk that now stood in place of the imposing magnate with whom he had been feuding not seconds ago.

"I know your family has been through a lot over the years. And it sure doesn't look like you're getting a break anytime soon, but I'm afraid I can't show your boy the leniency you're asking for."

Atherton's lips tightened into a thin line. "I do not need your pity, Marshal. And I am not asking for leniency; I am merely requesting that Tobias be handed over to the appropriate authorities so this can be handled discreetly."

Eamon shook his head vehemently. "He needs to pay, Ath. And when I say that I don't just mean pay for the damage he did to the refinery, because I know that'd be no skin off your nose. There needs to be repercussions."

"Wyatt! I implore you to reconsider. The boy has been punished enough; you need not take away his future as well!"

"That's not my intention, Councilman. You want discretion—I get that. It just so happens keepin' this hush-hush suits my needs too. So, Tobias is staying with me; he's serving his time, but we don't need to make a big song and dance out of it. You have my word."

Eamon left his office and headed downstairs, having realized in the suffocating silence that came after ending the call that Abraham was nowhere to be seen or heard. Given how difficult it was to get five minutes alone in a room without him, it was a minor cause for concern.

"Anybody know where the mutt got to?"

"Think he's keepin' an eye on our guest," Deputy Keller hollered over the hubbub of the bullpen. Sure enough, Eamon found him in the custody suite, sitting just beyond the fission field of Tobias's holding cell, tail wagging with his head tilted inquisitively at the disheveled young man slumped forward on the bunk inside.

"Should take that as a good sign, kid," he said, pulling up a chair by the inmate processing desk. "Doesn't mean you're off the hook by any stretch, but it definitely helps your case."

"Seems like a different animal from the one that was gnawing on my leg earlier," Tobias ruefully replied, his ACS uniform dirtied and torn as a result of his forceful canine takedown.

"Yep. Big idiot never was any good at holding grudges." Eamon lit a cigarette, took a long drag, and exhaled a plume of smoke into the air above him with an exhausted sigh. "Just got off the caster with your old man. What a piece of work that guy is. Honestly, if I had to grow up answerin' to an asinine gasbag like that, I'd probably want to blow shit up with concussion charges too."

"Did he say anything about her?" Tobias asked hurriedly, brow peaked in concern.

"About who?"

"My sister—Hazel. Did he say if she'd woken up yet? Is she alright?"

Eamon turned his palms up apologetically. "Sorry, kid. Sounds like her situation is . . . unchanged. You'll know the second I hear otherwise, though."

Tobias let his head slump back down below his shoulders, the very last of the fight left within him finally snuffed out. Eamon wanted so much to be furious at the boy, but the pieces of the puzzle were beginning to fit together.

"Is *that* what this was about? Revenge for what happened to your sister? Because I've gotta tell ya, I'm a little mystified as to how a good kid from an affluent background such as yourself goes from straight A Academy student to human supremacist vigilante seemingly overnight. I guess that'd explain it, though—you think the cohabitors are responsible for what happened to your sis, and your little stunt out in the Langrenus Harrow was a means of getting back at them."

Tobias's face crumpled in irritation. "What do you mean *think* they were responsible? Of course they were!"

Eamon pursed his lips, shaking his head. "I've got friends who have it on good authority that, despite what you probably heard on the NTNN, at no point were interceptor heat sigs detected in breach of the NTU perimeter. The marauding fighters—whoever they were—left standard pulse engine exhaust trails. I know you think you know everything, Tobias, but clearly you don't."

The boy went rigid, sitting straight with his spine like someone had shoved a one-meter ruler up his ass, staring unwaveringly at the opposite wall of the holding cell.

"I don't think I should be speaking to you until I have legal representation present."

Eamon shrugged apathetically. "Nebula, cuz I got no need for you to talk, just listen. Whether it was revenge or a dare or some other stupid shit, it's got you in some hot water—I'm talkin' boiling point. Now, my first thought was to string you up by the neck for the whole *Novara* to see—make an example outta you so the next idiot who wants to come here and make people's lives a misery thinks twice. But after that pleasant little chat with your pops, I've had, let's say, a change of heart."

Tobias relaxed slightly, as if Eamon's next words were about to be something to the tune of "you're free to go, don't do it again."

Naive punk.

"Don't get me wrong—what you did was downright reprehensible. Had you gotten anybody killed, this conversation'd be going a whole 'nother way right now."

The councilman's son turned pale, steady eyes focusing on a distant point, as if witnessing through a window in reality the grim alternate universe where such had been the case, quailing at the fate that could have been.

"Everybody's got their rock bottom," Eamon began. "The lows we don't think we have it in us to ever surpass. But the truth is there's always circumstances that can push us to dig that little bit deeper. There was another time I picked up some down-and-out whelp who'd recently found out what his circumstances were. Kid's name was Isaac Verhoeven, and instead of throwing him into a hole and makin' sure he never saw the light of the Canyon sky again, I put him to work on a weld and salvage ship—had him contribute something useful to society. It did wonders for him; I'm thinkin' it might do some good for you too."

SEVENTEEN

Suffice to say, Captain Holloway was less than enthused about the prospect of having Tobias see out his community service on her ship.

"C'mon, Lilah," Eamon had urged her over the luma-caster earlier in the day. "Your whole damn crew is made up of strays who couldn't get a second chance anywhere else. What makes this kid any different?"

"Because I know his type all too well," she replied in that austere but strangely endearing tone. Her main grievance with the proposal was what it would mean for her newest crewmember—a cohab exo-tech specialist named Null. Taking into account the destructive and discriminatory nature of the boy's crimes, she feared having Tobias join her ranks would pose a threat to aer safety, which, given aer affiliation with Vidalia Drexen, was absolutely paramount.

"Tobias isn't dangerous," Eamon reassured her. "He's just a product of his environment—another malleable, overprivileged idiot, chewed up and spat out by an institution that thrives off people's ignorance. Spendin' a little time cuttin' his teeth in weld and salvage, living and working close quarters with Null? It'll be good for him—might help him see the cohabs for the docile giants they really are, instead'a the savages he's obviously been programmed to perceive them as."

"You know I can always use an extra pair of hands on the *Assurance*," Delilah replied, the caster rendering those mesmerizing eyes in such arresting detail that the memory of them chilled him to the bone even now. "But this is a bad idea. Recruiting someone with such close ties to Humanity First when I've got a cohab on my damned crew? A recipe for disaster."

"This isn't your average human supremacist thug we're talkin' about," Eamon countered. "This is the son of Councilman Edevane. Like I said, he ain't violent, just got mixed in with a bad crowd is all. If somethin' drastic isn't done to change the course of this kid's life, you can bet he'll be claimin' his father's mantle within the decade. Unless we want a repeat of the last hundred-odd years since the Collision, it's sproutin' politicians like Tobias we need on our side. And if there's *anyone* on the *Novara* who can drill a little sense into him, it's you, Lilah. Just think about it: if all goes to plan, then you get some real respectability on that old scrap trawler of yours—consider the leverage having the son of a nobleman at your disposal will give you in negotiating your fees. And, more importantly, the people in the district will have gained a powerful ally beyond the blockade. This could do wonders for the human-cohabitor relationship going forward."

Never one to turn her nose up at sound reasoning, Delilah ultimately agreed. So, at the earliest opportunity, Eamon bundled Tobias into the back of a cruiser and tasked Jyn with taking him home to pack, before ferrying him to the Lower Amidships Docks. The deputy bemoaned with all manner of colorful language the marshal's decision to delegate babysitting duties to her. But unfortunately, she was the only staffer in the department with the stones to go toe to toe with Atherton, who would undoubtedly be awaiting his son's return, foaming at the mouth for another round of verbal fisticuffs.

Jyn won't be nearly as reserved as I was with that bigoted stuffed shirt. He'll be sorry he even opened his damn mouth. Kinda wish I could be there to see it.

With Tobias out of the picture, Eamon was finally free to resume normal duties, which, in reality, meant completely abandoning them and redirecting all his efforts toward pursuing the Composer. Ideally, he could have had the whole department rallied and descending on Tycho Block like flaming chariots from the heavens, triumphant fanfare blaring. But by continuing this line of inquiry, he was acting in direct contradiction to the Administrator's explicit orders—to involve anyone else at this juncture, with so little intel, would be to implicate them too. So, as furious as Jyn would inevitably be at him for diving in headfirst once again, this time, he had no choice.

You're just here to do a little recon, he told himself, pushing the throttle and accelerating toward Tycho Block. *Track down Devruhkhar's weapon shipment and scope the place out. If you can confirm this is where the Composer is hiding, then maybe think about launching the full-blown assault.*

Tycho Block was the largest of the residential towers in the district. Resembling the rock sentinels that once stood tall in the now-frozen desert planes of Earth, it comprised a massive, relatively intact pillar of superstructure, eroded not by wind but meticulously whittled into shape by the *Devourer* in the aftermath of the Collision. Eamon guessed it played some vital role in the Mouth's ecosystem—structural, environmental, or otherwise.

As far as he was concerned, it was nothing more than a headache, its hyper-dense architecture providing a safe haven for criminals and degenerates—the types who apparently had something to gain from justifying every prejudice and stereotype bowsiders held against them.

Keeping one hand on the flight wheel, he unclipped his marshal's badge and stuffed it into his jacket pocket. DMED's authority counted for very little in this den of thieves; drawing any attention to himself could result in a tumble down a garbage chute into a disposal furnace—somewhat counterproductive to the task at hand.

Scanning the structure's haphazard cladding for signs of activity, he circled around once, dipping and swerving to avoid the tangle of exposed power cables running like jungle vines from balconies to the slums below.

Are you in there, Composer? If you are, you'd best make peace with the Void, cuz there ain't a thing on the Coalescence that can stop me from hunting you down and bringing you to justice.

He brought the cruiser to a low hover over the rooftop landing pad and disembarked, using his VIOS-link wristwatch to direct Hypatia to execute an aerial patrol. Entering the main stairwell, he heard the whine of repulsor pads swell as the vehicle lifted off, silenced abruptly by the door slamming shut behind him.

Soon he was subsumed in a disorienting labyrinth of poorly lit hallways and vandalized communal hubs, the air permeated by a nauseating mixture of glow, dried urine, and unappetizing home cooking. Passing residences, contemptuous eyes peered at him through apartment doors held ajar. Marshal badge or no, the residents of Tycho Block knew precisely who he was and word of his arrival seemed to ripple down the building's many levels faster than he could descend them.

Best keep your head on a swivel; only thing worse than kickin' the bucket now would be giving Jyn the satisfaction of being right.

Even if Devruhkhar ended up being wrong about the Composer's presence in Tycho Block, her influence was stronger here than anywhere else in the district. Gradually, the wall graffiti began to morph from elaborate gang tags and barely comprehensible profanity to colorful murals dedicated to Harmony's incognito leader. At a T-intersection, Eamon paused to observe what could only be described as a shrine—an almost messianic depiction of a veiled woman leading a pilgrimage of impoverished humans and cohabs through darkness toward a bright light, the words "Quell the Dissonance" scrawled in red above. The floor here was awash with bundles of fine cloth marked by blobs of dried candle wax that glowed like bloodstains under ultraviolet light. A myriad of trinkets and small treasures had been left in tribute, giving him cause to ponder what exactly this woman had done to earn so much reverence from her adherents. *Massacred a few dozen innocents, sent the district into raging conflict, obliterated the already fractious relationship between mouthians and the NTU?*

It was mystifying how anyone could think her capable of bringing salvation, when all she had wrought so far was bloodshed and chaos. Burrowing like a parasitic worm into the hearts of the oppressed and persecuted, she had amassed an army of deranged militants, their minds twisted by the vindictive tenets of her doctrine. Seeing now the way in which people had begun to worship her, it was clear how dangerous she had really become. The Mouth would be in turmoil as long as she was breathing, and it could never begin to heal unless she was eradicated once and for all. Even if it got him kicked off the force, imprisoned for disobeying direct orders, or assassinated by her vengeful acolytes, he knew there and then that he had to kill her . . .

According to the gunsmith, the shipment of prespliced weapons had been delivered to apartment 2801. Eamon was now on the right floor, skulking down the right hallway, but something was clearly wrong. So far, he had been under the constant scrutiny of the tower's occupants, but now the good folks of Tycho Block had seemingly retreated into their residences, apartment doors shut tight. It was dead silent—no muffled voices, no loud music thumping through the walls.

Something's got these folks spooked, he thought, trembling hand inching closer to his holstered machine pistol. *Do they know something I don't? Are they taking cover in anticipation of a firefight?*

Finally, he arrived at 2801. The other apartments on this floor had standard sliding doors with magnetic locks—easily disintegrated with the metal-melting cinderkey he had "borrowed" from contraband storage—but the door to 2801 had been replaced with a blast-proof hatch, secured with a rugged external locking mechanism that the cinderkey could do nothing to bypass.

With bated breath, he cautiously pressed his ear to the hatch, listening for hushed voices or stifled movement. He was relieved, if perhaps a little disappointed, to find the apartment beyond completely silent.

Looks like nobody's home.

Taking a step back to assess his next move, he noticed the door to the next residence had been left ajar, allowing a thin slat of bronze Höllengarten light to breach the gap and filter into the hallway. He carefully pushed the door aside, revealing a squalid apartment with a stained mattress and a floor carpeted by used glow caps. Fortunately, it was unoccupied, but the presence of a warm stench suggested someone had made use of it fairly recently.

Have to be fast.

He stormed across the apartment and headed out onto the balcony, then clambered atop the rendered wall on the left-hand side. Foolishly, he took a nervous glance at the mosaic of rusted rooftops beneath him, realizing perhaps a little too late in life that he was, in fact, afraid of heights. Pounding his chest to rebolster his constitution, he took a deep breath, then leapt across the two-meter gap to the adjacent balcony, landing with about as much grace as an elephant on repulsor blades. He hastened to his feet and slid into cover, hugging the wall cladding beside the screen door of 2801. Leaning over to peer through smeared glass, he confirmed that the apartment was vacant as he had suspected, although, unlike that of the malodorous glow den next door, the security latch was locked. He removed his jacket and wrapped it tightly around his clenched fist, unwilling to let a meager pane of glass impede him when he had come so far. Wincing in anticipation of triggering an alarm, he hurled his improvised wrecking ball through the glass, punching a hole just wide enough to reach through and disengage the latch from the inside.

So far, so good . . . maybe a little too good.

Until now, he had managed to repress it—that gnawing suspicion that this was all too convenient, that he was almost certainly walking into a trap. But driven by an insatiable hunger for truth and justice—an irrepressible desire to make the Composer answer for her crimes come hell or high water—he swatted away his aversions and continued.

Upon entering the premises, his first thought was that in the manic haste of the moment he had accidentally jumped to the wrong balcony; 2801 was not only devoid of life but completely lacking in any furniture or equipment. Certainly, there was no sign of Devruhkhar's weapons shipment, nor any evidence that insurgents had been operating in the space at all, for that matter. That was until he moved farther inside and caught sight of a tall, imposing figure lurking in his peripheral vision. He spun around, instinctively unholstering his machine pistol, expecting to come face to face with another of the Composer's crazed cohabitor fanatics. Instead, a lone grenadier stood quiet and still in the corner of the room, the status lights beneath its chest and faceplate pulsing standby blue. He could only surmise that Harmony had somehow incapacitated one of the units from the garrison currently holding the Phalanx compound before bringing it here to Tycho Block. For what purpose, though, he couldn't say.

A portable pane sat on the floor by the android's hydraulically driven feet, reams of indecipherable code cascading down its screen like blood fall on a windshield. A data-transfer cable ran from an outlet on the device's chassis up to the installation port on the back of the grenadier's neck, only one that looked as though it had been encased in a length of decomposing small intestine. Were Eamon not already familiar with this kind of hideous hybridized biotech from his encounter with the spliced pistol, he might have been utterly revolted by the sight of it. But instead, it filled him with resolve, serving as confirmation that he was indeed on the right track.

He moved in closer with the intention of ascertaining the foul contraption's purpose. But then, something struck him . . . There were two very distinct smells present in the room, only one of which he could put his finger on. He recognized the rich, creamy odor suffusing the air as a pheromone given off by cohabitor chitin—a bug had definitely been present recently. But then, in contrast to the starkness of the apartment, there lingered a sweet and citrusy aroma that was intensely pleasing—familiar but impossible to place. On the cusp of revelation, with the answer of where he recognized it from on the tip of his tongue, the grenadier suddenly reactivated and shattered his focus. The machine jolted to life as if startled from deep slumber, status lights switching to a disconcerting yellow, head turning slowly as it surveyed its environment. It then took several thumping steps toward him, dragging the pane across the floor by the grotesque appendage attached to its neck, twitching sporadically as if possessed by some malignant spirit. Just as he thought it might barrel straight into him, it stopped abruptly, close enough that he could hear the whirring of its neural cortex going into overdrive behind its faceplate.

"*IDENTIFY,*" its synthesized voice blared from the speaker in its abdomen.

Eamon reached into his jacket pocket and coolly presented his badge.

"Easy, metal man. Marshal Eamon Wyatt of the District of the Mouth Enforcement Department. Got no beef with you."

After a moment of suspenseful deliberation, it replied, "*CREDENTIALS ACKNOWLEDGED. THREAT STATUS RECOGNIZED. MOVING TO NEUTRALIZE.*"

The lights beneath its faceplate switched to an alarming electric red. Then, before Eamon had a chance to react, it grabbed him by the throat and slammed his limp body against the wall. The force of the impact tore the air from his lungs, turning what should have been a scream of shock and surprise into a guttural, gurgling whimper. He wrapped shaking hands around its mighty mechanical fingers, desperately trying to pry them away from his neck. But all his strength was no match for the configuration of actuating servomotors crushing his windpipe.

The world began to darken, consciousness slipping away from him like the final grains of sand in an hourglass. He didn't feel fear or sadness in that moment, just annoyance at having been bested, ashamed by his own ineptitude and the complete and utter totality of his failure. Staring with bulging eyes into that cold, emotionless death mask, he felt himself gradually beginning to let go. But before his vision could blur completely, he glanced at the spliced cable still attached to his adversary's armored neck. It wasn't so much plugged in as it was clumsily fused with the nanocarbon of the bot's spine. Gritting his teeth as he let his jaw support the full weight of his body, he summoned the very last of his strength, gripped the cable in his hand and yanked as hard as he could. The organic material ripped with ease. The cable fell away, spewing arcs of golden energy as it coiled tightly around his arm like a beheaded constrictor.

Staggering backward, the grenadier immediately released its hold, temporarily immobilized by the abrasive disconnection.

Clutching his searing neck, Eamon fell to his knees, his addled brain flooding with a potent rush of oxygen. He had only seconds to catch his breath, as the grenadier was already recovering from its stunned state. He darted across the room to safety, raising his wristwatch and frantically hailing Hypatia for a rapid evac.

"Unable to comply. User inaccessible," she replied in a placid tone wholly inappropriate for the peril of the situation.

"Emergency override, dammit! I need a pickup now!"

"Confirmed."

The grenadier started toward him, arms outstretched like a child asking to be picked up, only far more menacing. Back against the wall, he drew his pistol and fired three panicked shots into its chestplate. The stopping power of the armor-piercing rounds marginally slowed its approach but did little else to deter it. Moments before it came within reach of him, the silhouette of a cruiser appeared outside, just beyond the balcony. Hypatia had brought the vehicle to a stationary hover and preemptively opened the driver's-side door. Eamon immediately caught on to what she was suggesting; it was insane but his only option.

He fired a point-blank shot directly into the grenny's faceplate then ran for the balcony, using the balustraded wall to vault through the open air into the cruiser.

"Get us the hell out of here!" he shouted, pulling himself out of the footwell and buckling himself in. Hypatia complied. Banking sharply, she spun the cruiser round and prepared to accelerate. But before the maneuver could take apartment 2801 out of sight completely, Eamon spied his relentless pursuer crouched on the balcony, poised to continue its attack. Demonstrating the immense, inhuman strength of its legs, it sprang like a frog through the air and landed on the hood, its heavy frame sending the cruiser into a steep descent.

"Danger! Maximum load exceeded. Unable to maintain altitude," Hypatia warned, repulsor pads spluttering and terrain alarms blaring.

"Heavy son of a bitch!" Eamon rasped, eyes transfixed on the grenadier as it crawled its way toward the windscreen. He grabbed the flight wheel and turned it hard right, rolling the cruiser upside down and casting the mechanical bastard off with powerful centrifugal force. Leveling out, he craned his neck to watch as it plummeted toward the slums below before impacting the ground in an abandoned construction site.

He landed the cruiser nearby and disembarked, pistol held low ready, determined to finish the job. With broken, twisted limbs, the grenadier crawled toward him through the dirt, unintelligible nonsense disgorging from beneath its buckled chestplate. It clawed at him like a rabid animal, unperturbed by its mangled lower half, hell-bent on fulfilling its murderous directives. Eamon crouched over it, placed the muzzle of his pistol against the weak point at the back of its head, and fired a single finishing shot directly into its neural cortex.

EIGHTEEN

With two days of community service under his belt, Tobias had begun to regret agreeing to forgo standard criminal proceedings. Marshal Wyatt's punitive measures had, so far, felt more like a cruel and unusual punishment than a preferable alternative to facing trial and conviction. Obviously, he hadn't expected it to be a pleasant experience, but neither did he think the labor would be quite so grueling, nor his work environment—a stuffy cargo bay in which he was essentially being kept prisoner—so hazardous and filthy.

The ship's crew of rapscallions and rejects had, despite his being perfectly cordial, shown him nothing but disdain. Of course, he was no stranger to being judged or disliked given the position of power and privilege tied to his family name. And at the end of the day, he wasn't on the *Assurance* to make friends, and he was quite happy to keep his head down and focus on getting the work done.

One thing he could not so easily overlook, however, was the small matter of the leech . . .

At no point had the marshal elected to warn him that this "community service" would entail breaking bread with an enemy of the NTU. For reasons that completely evaded him, Captain Holloway had granted the creature free rein of her ship; it roamed the claustrophobic interior like a predator stalking its territory, poisoning the recycled atmosphere with its fetid, alien stench. Tobias had done everything he could to keep his distance, which was becoming increasingly difficult due to the alarming fact that it seemed to have developed something of a fascination with him. Wherever he was, whatever he was doing, the leech was there: skulking around corners and lurking in the shadows, never properly engaging him but never far away. It was difficult to understand—harder to explain—but even when separated by two decks and on opposite ends of the *Assurance*, he could still feel it watching him, its

soulless obsidian eyes boring into the back of his skull, conveying unquestionable but devious intelligence.

He began to wonder if, perhaps, it had learned about his involvement
with the events in the Langrenus Harrow . . .

Maybe it's looking for a little payback, he hypothesized. *Hoping to catch
me alone and off guard, waiting for an opportunity to viciously exact revenge
for destroying that slop refinery.*

With every passing hour he grew more suspicious about the creature's
intent and had all but abandoned his duties to mentally and physically prepare for eventually needing to defend himself. After all, he wasn't hopeful the
crew would come running to his aid should the beast choose to attack.

In fact, they're probably counting on it, he thought, sitting forward on his
fold-away bunk in the scruffy secondhand coveralls he had been given to
wear.

*They'll let it happen, jettison my mutilated body into the endless night, and
report my death as a workplace accident. Maybe this was the marshal's plan
all along—a very elaborate, but very discreet, execution.*

He took a calming breath, realizing his thinking was bordering on paranoid delusion and suddenly acutely aware of the daunting amount of work
he had to get through. He glanced despondently across the cargo bay at the
jagged mounds of assorted scrap metal reeled in by the *Assurance's* debris
net during the last salvage run. His job: to sort through it with a handheld
composition scanner and feed appropriate material into the magma cannon's
slag furnace. Naturally, his perspective was that the Administration's commissioning of a ship to maintain the hull around the Mouth—a place that, as
far as he was concerned, should be hastily demolished—was a gross misal-
location of funding and resources. But refusing to fulfill his assignment on
the basis of those beliefs was hardly any way to gain favor with the captain.
And, unfortunately, impressing that screw-faced harpy was his only means
of expediting his departure from her depressing junker and returning to his
rightful place in the Upperdecks.

Resolving to clear the entire pile by the end of second shift, he plunged his
arms into the yield and began sifting through the ancient detritus of the Collision. Hands blackened by the crystalline-powder residue that seemed to coat
all scrap recovered from the Debris Belt, he used the composition scanner to
discern the welding suitability of each piece, casting appropriate metals into
the furnace and the rest into a storage crate labeled "sellable scrap."

As he toiled away, he allowed his thoughts to amble to the dear ones he
had left behind. Caleb, Hazel—those who needed him now more than ever
but whom fate was cruelly keeping him separated from. After he'd vowed

never to leave her side again, Caleb's grief was now hers alone to bear and the guilt he felt at no longer being able to help alleviate that burden churned his insides.

The harder you work, the sooner you can get back to her.

He gritted his teeth and pushed on for a while longer, until his flow was broken by the sounds of a ruckus coming from the opposite side of the cargo bay. *Something* knocked an empty power cell off the storage rack near engineering, and it rolled across the floor toward him. He instinctively reached into the pile of scrap and fished out the longest, sturdiest piece of metal he could find, brandishing it overhead like a casterblade saber.

He scanned the shadows for the leech's forbidding silhouette, knowing instinctively that the hapless monster was scurrying about behind the parked burro, from where it had been silently observing him. Wondering if it intended to finally make its move, he struck the cargo bay door control column with his improvised bludgeoning device.

"Come out! I know you're there," he blurted in a faltering voice, trying his hand at intimidation but failing miserably. "You don't scare me, you rotten insect. So either stop wasting my time and show yourself or leave me the fuck alone!"

His rigid fighting stance withered as the gloomy cargo bay responded with only crushing silence. He couldn't see the leech, but every fiber of his trembling being screamed at him that it was there, assessing him with cold and calculated indifference.

Focused so intently on the shadows, he nearly jumped clean out of his skin when Captain Holloway's galling voice rattled through the ship-wide intercom.

"Mr. Edevane, would you be so kind as to grace us with your prodigious presence on the bridge? There's a matter we need to discuss."

He reeled his arm back and hurled the baton into the darkness, hopefully buying himself enough time to dart for the access ladder without getting ensnared.

"Captain Holloway," Tobias exclaimed as he exploded onto the bridge, probably looking and sounding more like his father than he cared to admit. "I understand I'm in no position to be making demands of you and your crew, but could you please make at least *some* effort to keep that abominable nightmare away from me!"

The captain stood just beyond the helm, busying herself with the overhead instrumentation panel, seeming to make a point of not greeting or addressing him as he entered. She was a tall, brown-skinned woman who certainly dressed the part of brigandish plunderer but spoke and carried herself with all the grace and eloquence of somebody from the Upperdecks. Tobias even suspected her of being ACS educated, but how an officer in training could have ended up captaining a Debris Belt trawler was nothing short of utterly mystifying.

"Abominable nightmare?" she repeated mockingly. "Kahu! Have you been terrorizing the passengers again?"

"Not sure what you're insinuating by that, Skip," Kahu Heperi jibed. Slumped sideways in the pilot's seat with his boots hanging over the armrest, the disgraced NTSC veteran was shelling and devouring nuts from a crumpled ration bag and offhandedly dropping their husks on the floor.

"I didn't mean Mr. Heperi," Tobias impatiently clarified. "I meant the lee—"

"I know who you meant," the captain snapped, her nonchalant demeanor immediately soured. "We don't use that word on this ship, Mr. Edevane. I'll ask that you think with more care about how you address and speak of my crew."

"I use that word all the time," Kahu murmured, earning himself a thump on the shoulder from his captain.

Tobias cleared his throat. "Apologies. The . . . co-ha-bit-tor. It's just that I have a lot of work to get through and would appreciate being left alone to do it without distraction. I don't think it's fair the *cohabitor* should be allowed to come and go through my quarters as it pleases."

"But you don't have quarters. I'll kindly remind you that where you're staying is still an active cargo bay." The captain turned to face him, piercing eyes matching the deep brown of her well-worn duster coat. "I think you should be grateful we could even spare you a bunk. As my exo-tech specialist, Null needs around-the-clock access to the lower deck, which includes the cargo bay. So I think it'd be best that you two just learn to get along with each another. I'm sure, being the son of a big-time politician, you'll have no problem with a little diplomacy."

"Is that why you summoned me to the bridge, Captain, to insult me and my father?"

"As satisfying as that would be—no."

She directed his attention through the windshield, where, before the unsightly backdrop of the Lower Amidships Docks, he spotted an automated vehicle parked in the *Assurance*'s docking bay. It was a hazardous waste disposal caddy of some kind—a cylindrical tank on all-terrain wheels with a long, heat-shielded trunk plugged into an outlet on the ship's underbelly.

"You see that? We have to purge about two hundred gallons of partially processed welding slag. Now I know you're working hard down there, but I need a little more due diligence from you regarding what materials you're feeding into the furnace."

Watching the trunk bulge and swell as it siphoned molten metal into the caddy, Tobias swept his untidy bangs back in a show of defiance. "I don't see why such precision is necessary. It all gets melted down anyway, doesn't it? Seems a little excessive to be dumping an entire load."

"You've mixed about fifty kilos of tungsten into the alloy. And now I find myself in the *frustrating* position of having to tell you a second time that the melting point of tungsten is too high for the slag furnace to break down effectively. If we tried to seal a rupture with the current mixture, the hold would be too weak. That'd leave the Mouth vulnerable to a serious breach, and there are people depending on us with their lives to do a good job."

"Sorry, but you'll have to forgive me for not fretting quite as much about the well-being of a bunch of glow-thirsty mutineers." Tobias attempted to swallow the words before they left his mouth but was too late. They were far too cruel—out of character. He could tell he'd crossed the line by the furious expression that appeared on the captain's face—one that, strangely, she appeared to make a conscious effort to suppress.

"I get that you're angry," she said, voice rippling as she fought to temper it—an undeservedly lenient response, given his discourteous behavior. "But you will *not* take that anger out on us. Don't forget the kindness I'm doing by even letting you set foot on the *Assurance*."

"Captain. I spoke out of turn. Please accept—"

She silenced him with a glare that felt like needles on the skin of his forehead. "Doesn't make a lick of sense to me why Eamon decided to go so easy on you. If it were my decision, you'd be staring at the same four walls of a brig cell for the rest of your days. Seeing as this is the hand he's chosen to deal you, I'm willing to cooperate. But you *will* start taking your responsibilities seriously, and you *will* treat my crew with the respect they deserve."

Tobias dropped his stare to his feet, feeling not like he had been taken down a rung but knocked clean off the ladder. He began another futile apology, but before he could get the words out, she was halfway down helm access, voluminous curls bouncing in the motion of heavy footsteps.

He lingered in the bridge entrance in pensive, defeated silence, arriving at the stark realization that failing to improve his attitude would result in a swift ejection from the *Assurance*. And whatever the alternative to the marshal's community service was, he sincerely doubted it would be anything favorable.

Buck your ideas up, he chided himself. *If you have any hope of preserving your career and reputation when this is over, you need to stop being so obnoxious to these people.*

Oblivious to his quiet self-enmity, Kahu thrust the ration bag toward him. "You want a peanut?"

Choosing not to point out that they were, in fact, cashews, Tobias politely declined and started for the cargo bay.

"Your sister's got chops, kid," Kahu said, stopping Tobias immediately in his tracks. "There's only one other pilot in the history of the NTSC who could have survived a bushwhacking like that."

Tobias approached the helm and lowered himself into the copilot's seat, surprised and humbled that anybody aboard the *Assurance* even knew who Hazel was, let alone her present situation.

"Who?" he asked.

Kahu set the ration bag down and pulled his gray, matted dreadlocks over his shoulder, revealing scar tissue that ran down his face and neck like the meandering path of a desiccated riverbed cutting through parched terrain.

"You're lookin' at him. When you next get a chance to speak to her, you tell her she has the respect of Wing Commander Heperi—if she's half the pilot I think she is, then she'll know exactly who that is."

Although the chances of ever getting the opportunity to do so were discouragingly slim, the thought alone was enough to cause Tobias's heart to swell with appreciation.

"Thank you, Mr. Heperi. That means a lot; I will be sure to tell her."

Shoveling another fistful of Abyss-knows-how-old cashews into his mouth, Kahu went on to ask, "How is she doin', anyway? Looked pretty banged up when we saw her last; wasn't sure she was gonna make it."

Tobias stood up suddenly, betraying confusion with his stupefied expression. "Excuse me? You saw my sister? When?"

"Didn't the marshal clue you in?" Kahu asked, chewing noisily. "We were the ones that rescued her. We were headed back out of the *Devou* . . . Erm . . . I mean, from runnin' salvage when we spotted her free-floatin' in the black. Scooped her up with the grapple and dropped her off at Aegis Infirmary. I thought you knew already?"

Troublingly, he did not . . . and as a result, he had allowed himself to behave like a petulant ingrate to a group of individuals to whom he, in fact, owed an incalculable debt.

Why the marshal had chosen to deny him this critical information was a mystery: to humiliate him, perhaps? Or to teach him some self-righteous lesson about not judging a book by its cover? Either way, he hoped it was not too late to atone.

Leaving Kahu looking bemused on the bridge, he hastened to the galley, where the rest of the crew was currently assembled. They regarded him with about as much interest as they had since coming aboard—absolutely zero. The only one who acknowledged him at all was, ironically, the leech, who watched him intently from where it stood in the lounge—a ghoulish apparition making itself visible to his eyes alone, for surely if the others could see it, they would be fleeing in terror.

"Captain Holloway!" he uttered breathlessly.

"Mr. Edevane," the captain replied, stirring a loose leaf tea strainer into a mug of hot water, once again refusing to make eye contact. "Haven't you incited enough drama for one day?"

"Please, Captain. I'm not here to start an argument."

Sitting at the island countertop, Miss Brižan briefly met his eyes before exaggeratedly turning her head, flicking her metallic-blue plait over her shoulder.

"I'll believe that when I see it," she muttered under her breath, making no secret of her utter contempt for him; given she was a native of the Mouth, he supposed he didn't blame her.

"At first I thought Marshal Wyatt assigned me to this particular ship as a means of punishment," said Tobias. "But now I understand it was to give me an opportunity to repay my debt to you."

The captain scoffed. "Don't be ridiculous. You don't owe us a damned thing."

"You're wrong, Captain. You saved my sister from certain death. I'm not stupid; I know what you must think of me: callous, narrow-minded, self-obsessed—maybe some of those things are true. But rest assured, little on the *Novara* matters more to me than family, and you have done mine a great service—one that I'm not sure I can ever properly reimburse you for . . . although I would certainly like the opportunity to try."

The captain sighed, rubbing the bridge of her nose. "Fine. Well, if you *have* to thank us, then I suppose you can start with Isaac. If it wasn't for his proficiency with the pneumatic grapple, we would have wasted a lot of valuable time going EVA to fetch her."

Isaac Verhoeven, the *Assurance*'s glow-addicted engineer, accepted Tobias's offering of a hearty handshake with the same hesitance as someone forced to grab a cactus.

"We did what anybody else would do," he said, averting his gaze either in animosity or in embarrassment over how clouded the lenses of his eyes were.

"And then, of course, there's Null," said the captain, seeming to take a sadistic pleasure from Tobias's immediate apprehension, a devious smile etching its way across on her face. "If it weren't for aer, we never would have known Hazel was out there. Ae practically hijacked the helm in order to get us within range to intercept. If there's *anyone* you should thank, it's aer."

Tobias cast a nervous glance at the creature, then back at the expectant look on the captain's face.

This is punishment, he thought. *For the tungsten debacle, and probably for my general impertinence too. Well . . . if this is what it will take to make amends, so be it.*

The leech, which hadn't taken its eyes off him since he entered the galley, huffed from its large neck orifices as he approached, dousing his face in its hot, repugnant breath. Illuminated from below by Holloway's peculiar collection of antique lamps, its chirping, nattering mandibles revealed themselves in frightening detail; he feared that at any moment it might snatch him off the ground and use them to tear his upper body to bloody ribbons. Fighting the compulsion to flee, he offered his trembling hand, completely ignorant as to whether it even knew what a handshake was.

"Thank you," he said, his throat as dry as when he had been breathing the arid air of the Mouth. Ignoring his hand, the leech bowed its head toward him, bringing the tip of its snout centimeters from his nose. Then, something strange happened . . . Initially, he suspected a power surge, as the light from the encircling lamps seemed to brighten and intensify. But moments later, aural opalescence consumed the entire galley—brilliant shades of orange and violet cascading over his vision like a phantasmal sheet. He closed his eyes tightly in an attempt to block out the bombardment, but it persisted beneath his eyelids, seeming to emanate from somewhere behind his retinas.

The crew, the galley, and everything in it vanished in the swelling tide of light, and all that remained discernible to him was the leech, still staring down with its eight unblinking eyes.

Shapes emerged in his peripheral vision—dark, imperceptible forms, expanding and dividing like bubbles of wax in the convection current of a lava lamp. The shapes congealed into a central mass that then began morphing into recognizable imagery. Soon he was presented with a vision of a horizon—an unfamiliar landscape resembling neither Earth nor the computer-generated approximations of the surface of Pasture seared into the minds of every Novarian. It was a rocky world of desolation and ruin, distant cities burning beneath a turbulent magenta sky. Surveying the dramatic hellscape, he was visited by a sudden and inexplicable terror—as though pursued by a predator, a cruel and merciless entity that would not relent until it had hunted down and consumed him.

Feeling fear and hopelessness, he watched as millions of tiny beings flocked together below the gigantic mass that was now descending from the raging heavens. It was the *Devourer*, and as it touched down on the swathes of scorched terrain, his implacable sense of dread transmuted into overwhelming relief—the palpable feeling of being given refuge from the storm by something ancient and benevolent.

As though someone had shaken the Etch A Sketch of his consciousness, the vision evaporated before reforming into something slightly more familiar. He saw the *Novara* in all its pre-Collision glory, unleashing a devastating salvo from her main battery as the assailing *Devourer* sank its teeth into her hull, responding in turn with a crippling barrage of plasma fire. Watching the fateful battle unfold, he fell prey to a gnawing hunger, a thirst for water the likes of which he had seldom experienced before, exacerbated by an agonizing burning sensation in his chest. He couldn't speak from experience, but he likened it to what he imagined it might feel like to suffocate . . .

The visions became faster and more chaotic, each harder to interpret than the one preceding it. He saw the roots of a plant anchored in soil, but then the roots became conduits, and he was imbued with an innate understanding that the *Devourer* was the beating heart of an enormous circulatory system. From its core emerged the figure of a woman cradling an infant leech in her arms. There were no identifying features that he could discern, but he knew inherently that it was his mother. Despite all the anger and resentment usually whipped up by her memory, he found her presence intensely soothing. A weighted blanket of nurturing warmth and maternal tenderness enveloped him—attributes that he had never personally associated with the woman but now rendered his understanding of her in new and exquisite shades like paint poured over a lifeless black-and-white outline.

Then, just as soon as she had appeared, she was gone. The visions receded into the shallow waters of his awareness; he was returned to the galley of the *Assurance*, and although it felt like he had been ricocheting around space and time like a pinball for an eternity, it dawned on him that in reality, it had only been a few seconds. He held on to consciousness just long enough to see the concerned faces of the crew, then fell to his knees and let go.

⋂ I ⋂ ⋿ T ⋿ ⋿ ⋂

Probably for the best the kid is out cold," Kahu remarked, buttoning up his threadbare blazer with one hand and combing his unruly mustache with the other. With the crew en route to Vidalia's "installation ceremony," the old pilot had apparently deemed it prudent to smarten up for the occasion. "He couldn't even manage a damn handshake with the bug . . . I doubt he'd have the stomach for crazy shit like this." He motioned toward the *Assurance*'s nonhuman crewmember, who stood meditatively by the windshield, masterfully guiding the ship through the *Devourer*'s core. Although the harrowing journey had come to feel like second nature to Delilah and the crew, Kahu was right: it would have been a baptism of fire for somebody as mollycoddled as Tobias Cole Edevane.

Busying herself with the comms terminal, she replied, "True. He'd probably have an aneurysm if he found out how we get around these days."

"So, what's the plan? Are we really bringing him along to the Governor's ceremony? Aren't you afraid he'll make a scene?"

"Not in front of Vidalia. He'll probably be on his best behavior. I imagine he'll want to make a good impression."

The old pilot eyed her with a look of skepticism, buckling himself in and beginning landing preparations.

"You really think that uppity spit is the type to wanna rubberneck with a crook like the Governor?"

"Vidalia has a much better reputation in the Upperdecks than he does sternside of the blockade. He's got powerful connections, not to mention the hefty donations he makes in order to keep his enterprise running without Phalanx interference. Back home he's seen as a wealthy tycoon philanthropist. I wouldn't be surprised if his influence went all the way to the top—we'd do well to remember that."

Kahu half snorted, half laughed. "Yep. Guess even the bureaucrats gotta get their glow from somewhere, huh?"

She took a cautious glance down helm access to make sure Isaac wasn't lingering within earshot. The mere mention of the source of his addiction had, at times, been the trigger for bouts of self-destructive behavior that could, at worst, lead to a relapse. Fortunately, he was elsewhere. She blew a sigh of relief.

"Tobias obviously doesn't think very much of us or what we do for a living. Maybe seeing the impact these ionizers have in the community will help him reevaluate a few things."

"You got a soft spot for him or something, Skip?" Kahu jibed, smirking. "I've seen you reduce a man to tears for bein' half as stupid before. Surprised you didn't chuck him out the airlock already."

Delilah shook her head ruefully. "Wouldn't call it a soft spot . . . but pity? Maybe . . . Don't forget: if he hasn't lost his sister yet then he's damned close. A loss like that—family—it can make people do crazy things. You know it, same as me."

Kahu nodded in humble acceptance, firing up the *Assurance*'s vertical stabilizers as she exited the *Devourer*'s core and barreled into the Mouth's expanse.

"And it might sound crazy," she solemnly continued, the disorganized architecture of the Cohabitor Ghetto now filling the windshield, "but I see a little bit of myself in him too."

"Lilah, please. You're nothin' like that self-entitled brat." There was a surprising note of admiration in the old pilot's voice.

"How I used to be, then," she corrected herself. "Ignorant, stubborn, narcissistic . . . Someone helped me pull my head out of the sand a long time ago—I kinda feel like I have a responsibility to pay it forward."

Leaving Kahu on the bridge, she headed toward the galley, followed by the irregular thumps of Null's plodding footsteps as ae lumbered behind her. Ae had seemed fairly on edge since the incident with Tobias in the galley, as if concerned he'd been injured during their startling first encounter and feeling partially responsible. What exactly had happened between the pair wasn't yet clear: something amazing and unexpected for certain, but not something she was about to start blaming the guileless alien for.

Entering the communal hub connecting the *Assurance*'s several living quarters, she found the rest of the crew crammed into the med cubby—a small room reserved for medical emergencies with a gurney and a few cursory first aid supplies.

Isaac and Mercy looked on as Teo begrudgingly tended to Tobias. Nobody had been more displeased about the boarding of a Humanity First activist than Delilah's mouthian salvage specialist, which made it all the more ironic that, since *she* was the only one with any clinical skills aboard, she had to care for him.

"It's so unfair, Captain! What a waste!" the girl proclaimed, fastening a monitor strap around Tobias's forearm. The boy moaned, steadily regaining consciousness but still groggier than Kahu after a heavy night of syn-rum.

"Of all the good folks out there who the Divine Abyss could'a blessed with the gift, it's *this* ignoramus!"

"The gift?" Isaac echoed, retying the sleeves of his jumpsuit around his waist as he leaned against the supply cabinet, seeming a little fidgetier than usual. "You think this guy is a reader?"

Mercy stepped forward and placed fingertips against Tobias's temple.

"Not yet. But his resonance is undeniable. With training and meditation, Mr. Edevane could become a powerful cipher."

Teo rolled her head back and unleashed an indignant guffaw. "A cipher? You gotta be kidding me!"

Choosing to ignore the colorful show of disdain, Delilah asked, "Can you elaborate any further on that? I mean to say, why so powerful? What is it that differentiates *his* abilities from your own?"

Mercy contemplated her words for a moment, pendant clutched in hand. "His emissions—the light from his eyes—they were the brightest I have ever seen. And as I previously mentioned, not *every* cipher can attain resonance with *every* cohabitor—they must share a level of compatibility. So, there is the matter of the statistical improbability of making such a strong bond with who I assume is the first cohabitor he has ever met."

"Spent his whole life in the Upperdecks," Delilah concurred. "I doubt he's ever come within a kilometer of one before."

"Interesting . . . It would suggest a heightened level of compatibility with Mr. Edevane—perhaps even hyper-resonance!'"

Isaac twitched as though an insect had landed on the back of his neck; the conversation wasn't centered around glow, per se, but Delilah could tell it was getting under his skin.

"Hyper-resonance. What does that mean?"

Teo answered by loudly ripping the seal off a coolant pad and slapping it against the bruise on Tobias's cheek, which he had sustained when collapsing. "Means this intolerant blockhead could waltz right into Tinji Marketplace and speak to any cohabitor he damn well pleases. Course, chances of him actually having anything *nice* to say are pretty much nonexistent."

"Is it common?" Delilah asked. Mercy shook her head, sunken eyes rendering a look of revenant awe.

"In over a century of cohabitation, there have been very few instances. To my knowledge, there is just one other known hyper-resonant on the Coalescence at present: a DMED deputy by the name of Jyn Sato. It is incredibly rare, to say the least."

Jyn—Eamon had mentioned her before: his relatively green but exceedingly talented translator, who was helping the department make tremendous strides in building outreach with the nonhuman community. What wasn't obvious was whether the marshal had known about Tobias's condition prior to their arrangement. If his true intentions were to train up another "bilingual" deputy, then surely it would have made more sense to disclose that little detail before dumping him on Delilah's ship—the *only* ship in the *Novara* fleet with a cohabitor serving aboard.

Choosing to ignore the reciprocating eye roll, she ordered Teo to administer a stim shot in hope of speeding up Tobias's recovery. The girl stomped across the cubby, practically shoving Isaac out of the way to retrieve a glass vial from the supply cabinet that contained a substance the same shade of sparkling blue as her hair. She zipped down her patient's coveralls and stabbed the vial's needle directly into his chest; as the stimulant suffused his nervous system, he bolted upright, taking a strenuous breath like someone resurfacing from water, panicked eyes darting between the faces of the others as though surrounded by his hostage takers.

"Am I dead?"

Teo angrily but dutifully applied a synthetic cotton swab to the puncture wound. "Unfortunately for us—no. But just stay put while that stim shot wears off or else you'll be bouncin' off the walls."

"Mr. Edevane!" exclaimed an uncharacteristically animated Mercy. "You must tell me, have you ever attained resonance before? How vivid were your emissions? What imagery did you glean; what emotions did you feel? Was it monochrome or in full color? Were there any auditory components to what you were presented with?"

The boy was unable to answer any of her questions, of course, shooting a petrified glance at the cohabitor lingering in the entrance to the med cubby. He sent the captain a look of pleading desperation, wordlessly begging for her to remove Null from his vicinity.

"Teo," Delilah said softly. "You've done stellar work as always, but why don't you take Null into the galley and keep aer entertained for a little while."

In true fashion, the girl protested about the unfairness of such a request when ae had been "as sweet as a peach," but ultimately complied.

She took aer gently by the paw and led aer away, allowing Tobias to finally settle down. Although, when probed further about his experience, he grew increasingly reluctant to acknowledge that anything unusual had happened at all.

"You must have seen or felt something, Mr. Edevane," Mercy insisted, brushing strands of ghost-white hair away from her face. "Ideas, visions, emotions. They may have been scrambled—difficult to decipher."

He rubbed his forehead in deep focus, working hard to piece together the events leading up to his collapse. Then his face became a picture book of disparate responses to whatever details he had managed to recollect: shock, disbelief, fear, and remorse, all eventually swept away by a painfully unconvincing look of nonchalance.

"Visions? I don't know about that. No, I think the simple truth is that I overexerted myself. The temperature is sweltering down in that cargo bay, and I've been working in it nonstop! The shock of having to come face to face with the leech must have tipped me over the edge."

"Don't bullshit us!" Isaac spat, looking like the final few millimeters of fuse on a stick of dynamite. "You were completely entranced. Your eyes were lighting up like afterburners. We all saw you make a connection with Null, so stop feigning ignorance and tell us what you saw."

"I really think you people ought to lay off the glow. I passed out and hit my head on the floor. Sorry, but that's all there is to it."

Demonstrating more patience than Delilah and Isaac put together, Mercy said calmly, "That isn't an adequate explanation for what we all witnessed."

"If it's an explanation you want, might I suggest using your little mind trick to coax one out of that ghastly pet of yours, since it was the one who decided to knock me out in the first place."

Isaac spun around and slammed his fist into the side of the supply cabinet. Delilah caught him by the arm as he angrily headed for the exit.

"Hey! What's gotten into you?"

He turned to her with eyes like scintillating pools of fury. "I know you wanna do right by the marshal, Captain. Abyss knows I haven't forgotten the debt I owe to that man. But how much more of this are we gonna take? I'm sorry, but if you don't kick this arrogant son of a bitch off the *Assurance*, then so help me, I'll do it myself!"

He shook his arm free before storming out, leaving the cubby and everyone in it in glum reticence. Tobias retreated into his shell, probably realizing too late that he had stepped over the line. Delilah stared at the boy with as much vehemence as she could summon, saying nothing, for what was there to say that she had not said a thousand times already?

All it takes to stay out of prison is for you to treat us with a little respect. Was it so much to ask? Evidently, yes.

This spate of impertinence more than warranted early termination of his service aboard the *Assurance*, but the revelation regarding his supposed hyper-resonance meant things were not so cut and dry. She didn't fully understand the implications yet—only that it was something that had to be nurtured if Eamon was to gain his "ally to the Mouth." The boy would never receive the support he needed to hone his abilities should she choose to send him packing back home to Emeral Heights. And in his current mindset, there was probably little he would regard with more disinterest than learning to communicate with cohabitors.

If we're gonna get him on our side, it's time for an intervention, she thought. *Something that might drill a little humility and empathy into that thick skull.*

If there was anything that might potentially sway his mind, it would be to see the Çorak with his own two eyes; there'd been another wayward ACS student many years ago for whom it had done just the same . . .

She ripped the monitor strap off his arm, not letting on that she wasn't absolutely furious, which, judging by his skittish reaction, he was completely convinced of.

"You've got twenty minutes to change into your civvies and get your head straight. We're going for a ride."

Raptors piloted by surly-faced Monarchs descended on the *Assurance's* LZ like a kettle of vultures, dispatched to retrieve Delilah's crew and ferry them to the site of the installation ceremony. The strip of uninhabited land where the proceedings were to take place was known by locals as the Çorak: a desolate waste acting as a buffer between the Cohabitor Ghetto and the Copper Swathes, seen as little more than a dumping ground by those residing on either side of it. Soon, with the strategic placement of the three hydro-ionizers retrieved from the Debris Belt, it would be transformed into an artificial river, bringing revitalizing infrastructure to the single most neglected region of the *Novara*.

This, knowing Vidalia, was undoubtedly all part of some larger scheme meticulously orchestrated to reaffirm his status and result in massive financial gain. But fundamentally, it involved providing critical aid to the severely disadvantaged—all the justification Delilah needed to overlook any additional potential benefits he might reap.

Wearing a pastel-blue shirt beneath a stylish trench coat that was wholly unsuitable for the arid climate, Tobias occupied a rear-facing seat, watching in ruminative silence as the poverty-stricken surroundings raced by. Delilah hoped—maybe naively—that he was seeing the district through a different lens than when last he was here, afforded some new understanding after inadvertently communing with Null.

Naturally, he would deny experiencing any such clairvoyance to his dying breath, but try as he might to conceal it, the incident had clearly left him rattled. The layers of obstinance and temerity that, up until now, he had worn like a suit of armor had been stripped away, laying bare the timid cub that had always been encased beneath.

She didn't proclaim to know exactly what he was going through, but she could attest from firsthand experience that for those who had known nought but privilege, comprehending the scale of destitution in the Mouth could be a daunting reality check—that paired with the consternation he undoubtedly felt regarding his *affliction* meant Tobias was well and truly being put through the wringer. While still quietly simmering about his mistreatment of her crew, it was becoming harder and harder *not* to feel sorry for him.

A crowd had assembled at the edge of the Copper Swathes around a low scaffolding stage erected at the foot of a massive conduit—easily three meters in diameter. Erupting from a fissure in the ground like the breaching tentacle of a leviathan, the behemoth cut perpendicularly across the Çorak before snaking off in the direction of the blockade and plunging back below the surface. Delilah pondered where in the *Novara* it had burrowed its way to: a reservoir in hydroponics, or the massive protein stores in the Statera Basin, perhaps—only the folks working in exo-cartography could know for certain. Presumably it was this mighty specimen that Vidalia had selected for water siphoning; looking at the immense size of the thing, it wasn't hard to understand why.

The raptors circled once before touching down, providing a sweeping view of the PVC-lined channel excavated to guide and distribute purified water from the ionizers along the length of the Çorak—a simple but tried and tested method of irrigation as old as civilization itself.

The crew alighted and were directed to follow a sumptuous red carpet, which cleaved asunder the increasingly animated crowd, leading to the stage from which Vidalia and his retinue eagerly beckoned them. Garbed in a depressing motley of grays and browns with pails gripped feverishly in emaciated hands, the ceremony attendees were like sepia-toned stills from periods of early-twentieth-century recession, varying in species, race, and age but sharing the same degree of severe impoverishment. The humans cheered and blew kisses while the cohabitors waved their arms and trumpeted in excitement, welcoming the crew with a warm and almost messianic zeal.

"Wish you'd told me this was gonna be a fancy thing, Captain," Teo mumbled, pulling loose threads from her knitted sweater as she kept pace.

Clearly enjoying the attention, Kahu chuckled to himself, heartily shaking hands as they were thrust toward him. "They're really rolling out the red carpet for us, huh? Haven't had this kind of welcome since back in the glory days. And to think all we did was hand over a bit of salvage!"

"Might just be inconsequential scrap to us," the girl countered, "but for some, those ionizers will be a lifeline. Gotta hand it to the Governor: he's doing more for folks here than the Administration has in nearly a century."

Delilah suspected the remark was bait—expressly tailored to provoke some kind of a response from Tobias. However, eyes scanning the gaunt faces of the enveloping throng, the boy was far too engrossed to care. He went rigid as an elderly cohabitor outstretched aer arm and gently touched his shoulder; the old woman standing beside aer—presumably aer cipher—smiled wistfully, clasping hands to her heart with tearful eyes.

"You OK there, champ?" Delilah asked. "Lookin' a little pale. Not gonna pass out again, are you?"

He shook his head, trying and failing to bury his utter disbelief.

"What is this place? And why in the Abyss is it even inhabited? For what reason would anybody in their right mind choose to live this way?"

Delilah nodded toward the blockade, which from this distance was almost completely masked by the sludgy, luminous haze radiating from the Höllengarten.

"That hulking eyesore over there ensures *choice* is the last thing mouthians have in the matter. If you're unlucky enough to get born on the wrong side of it, this is what life probably looks like for you. Course, conditions are a mite improved deeper into the swathes; Tycho Block—the residential tower over there—even has running water and power, if I'm not mistaken. But just like any overpopulated, underpoliced urban center, it can be a treacherous place to put down roots: there's street gangs, terrorism, organized crime—it's a real cesspool. For folks out here and in the Cohabitor Ghetto who're just tryna get by, this is their lot in life."

He hurriedly hopped onto the stage and cordially offered a hand to assist her up, probably in lieu of any kind of poignant response. *I'll be damned, a bona fide gentleman.*

"I'm confused, Tobias. You're a bright kid—what exactly did you expect to find coming here?"

"I'm not entirely sure, Captain," he replied, surveying the surging tide of malnourished people like a mournful shepherd watching over his plague-stricken flock. "But it definitely wasn't this."

Vidalia greeted the crew as one might champions returning victorious. He showered them with a bouquet of flowery and extravagant language, only to butter them up, it turned out, for the revealing of some disappointing news: that, following delivery, two of the hydro-ionizers were found to be in an irrevocable state of degradation and disrepair. Unless more could be located in the Vestiges or the Debris Belt, the predicted water output for his artificial river would be drastically reduced.

The seeds of doubt initially planted by Eamon Wyatt that Delilah had since managed to quell sprouted once again. She couldn't know for certain whether the Governor was being completely forthright; it wasn't beyond the realm of possibility that he would withhold two perfectly functional hydro-ionizers for one of any number of insidious purposes. Ultimately, she had no choice but to take him at his word and count her blessings: Null was already in the process of splicing the one remaining ionizer into the conduit. The crowd watched aer work in fervid anticipation, cracked lips burning for that first touch of crystalline elixir. Unfortunately, they would have to wait a little while longer, as the event's host would have never wasted so much time and effort putting on this gratuitous spectacle without taking the opportunity to grandstand for twenty minutes first. With the crew standing shoulder to shoulder behind him like a comically mismatched identity parade, he began a speech that was as self-serving as it was cringe-inducingly gushing. It wasn't that Delilah felt undeserving of such praise, but still, being hailed as "selfless heroes" and the "saviors of the Mouth" when the job had been fairly mundane and the payment so very handsome was hard to swallow. She realized, though, that it was more for the benefit of those in the audience than it was for her—to know, as Vidalia so eloquently put it, "that the citizens of the New Terra Union have not completely forgotten about us in the District of the Mouth. That there are still those who know our plight and would travel great distances risking incarceration and death to come to our aid in these most trying of times."

She glanced up and down at the ragtag bunch standing beside her, swelling with pride and admiration as Micah's voice reached out to her through time and space.

"No matter what you do, just promise you'll try and make things better for people."

Cutting through all the doubt and uncertainty, she could rest assured that they had accomplished just that.

Then, something caught her eye: a peculiar shimmer drifting across the stage, bending and distorting the air like a mirage. It floated past her seemingly oblivious crew, coming to a stop just short of where Vidalia stood before suddenly disintegrating. In its place appeared a raw-boned man wrapped in brown robes, previously veiled by a mobile iteration of the same reality-refracting stealth tech that Vidalia used to conceal his yacht. Undoubtedly a Harmony insurgent, the intruder produced an augmented firearm from beneath his garments and pressed its grotesque muzzle against Vidalia's temple.

The crowd was thrown into a frenzy; they shoved and trampled one another like stampeding animals as they clamored for cover. A similar outburst of movement erupted on-stage as Kahu instinctively wrenched Teo out of harm's way while Naught lunged protectively toward Vidalia, who raised a glove-cladded hand to halt the brute in aer tracks; he must have known, as Delilah did, that any further advances might cause the situation to deteriorate very quickly.

"Choose your next move wisely," he calmly advised. "Whether or not it will be your last is entirely up to you."

But hell-bent on fulfilling a very specific task, the assassin was impervious to the Governor's silken tongue.

"Quell the Dissonance!" he shrieked, his fraught voice laced with a note of insanity. Gritting a set of rotten teeth, he tightened his posture and pulled the trigger. But the weapon misfired. Disgorging a grimy plume of smoke from its chamber, it showered its unwitting operator with a presumably unintentional volley of sparks. He cast the weapon aside and recoiled his smoldering arm, his bloodcurdling howls of agony turning into a strained splutter as Naught seized his neck with a viselike paw. Ae brought him before Vidalia like a hound presenting a fresh kill to its huntsman while aer cipher stood by with eyes aglow, ready to relay the execution order.

Vidalia stood over the assailant, looking down with narrowed eyes completely devoid of compassion and mercy.

"No," he said, straightening his tie. "Not here. We'll deal with this one on the yacht."

With a flick of his hand, he signaled for his security detail to take the would-be assassin away.

"You fools!" the man screamed, bare feet dragging in the dirt. "You must join Harmony! The Governor seeks to lead you all astray! Submit to the will of the Composer or face annihilation!"

Delilah and her crew watched on as Naught stuffed him into the back of a raptor. She knew, as his pleas were silenced by the slamming of the passenger-side door, that he would never be seen or heard from again.

The ceremony finally resumed following a tense intermission, the atmosphere somewhat less jubilant now than it had been prior to the attempt on the Governor's life. Though Harmony's effort to assassinate him had been thwarted, the obvious truth that it was only thanks to a fortunate weapons malfunction clearly weighed on his mind. With the bearing of a fallen deity suddenly made aware of his own encroaching mortality, Vidalia hurried through the rest of his speech, eager to wrap things up and deal with the unfinished business waiting for him on his yacht.

Null powered on the lone hydro-ionizer, sending what seemed more like a dribbling brook than an artificial river ambling along the Çorak. It soon disappeared beneath the thrashing horde of water-lusting mouthians, which Tobias sat watching from the edge of the stage in solicitous fixation. Delilah could tell there were a million questions resting on his tongue, all vying to be the first to leave his lips. But the one he ultimately decided on was not one she had been anticipating, nor one she was sure she knew how to answer.

"Captain Holloway. Who . . . or *what* is Harmony?"

She would have thought, given his close ties with the Administration, that he would have been intimately familiar, but his apparent ignorance on the matter served as proof of something Eamon had previously warned about regarding the boy.

"*The Upperdecks has done a real number on this kid,*" the marshal had told her. "*He couldn't be more disconnected from the way things are around these parts—doesn't have the first clue about the situation beyond the block-ade. Thinks if you've got two eyes you can only be a glow worm. Eight, then you must be a terrorist. He's gonna have a tough time coming around to the reality that there's humans in the Composer's posse too, especially when the NTNN has made every effort to convince him otherwise.*"

Clearly there was considerable work to be done in bringing Tobias up to speed, but it would have to be put on the back burner for the time being—as the ceremony came to a close and the Governor prepared to take his leave, Delilah realized when accounting for her crew that in the fray, Isaac had gone AWOL. Considering the volatile mood the boy had been in prior to depart-ing the *Assurance*, that he was now nowhere to be found was a point of grave concern.

She'd seen this pattern of behavior before: the fidgetiness, the impatience, the lashing out. Frustratingly, she had failed to recognize the obvious signs that the recent turmoil had pushed him to the point of needing an urgent fix, and that he would take the first opportunity he could find to slip away unnoticed.

TWENTY

With Abe in tow, Eamon and Jyn made their way to a place on the edge of the Warrens called the Drunken Shovel. Part of the *Novara's* original fleet of terraforming engines, this particular watering hole was an old six-wheel excavator, flipped on its side with its undercarriage scooped out and refitted with barstools, syn-beer taps, and occasionally functional hover hockey tables.

Eamon had only been once before, making inquiries into a trafficker named Montserrat Volk, who was smuggling cohabs through the blockade for forced labor in his Cendre Vale warehouse. Long story short, Phalanx shut the operation down but ended up charging the scumbag with some inane crap like a shipping permit violation.

No goddamn justice on the Novara...

Although loath to admit it, the reason Eamon generally avoided the establishment was the poignant sense of kinship he felt with the place: a once mighty machine fueled by high-octane fission energy, built to move mountains and shape the earth, now reduced to a decaying, obsolete husk, stranded belly-up on a lonely hill, stained by years of blood fall and filled with nothing but pisswater and regret.

Cuts a little too close to home for my taste.

Naturally, Jyn was suspicious as to why, of the plethora of dive bars dotted throughout the district, he'd chosen this "depressing slimehole" for their usual debrief. He had his reasons but up until now hadn't been ready to disclose them. The deputy didn't know about his brush with death at the hands of the reprogrammed murder-bot in Tycho Block, mainly because of how utterly furious he suspected she would be with him for walking into such an obvious trap.

He couldn't keep her in the dark for much longer, though. His urgent need for her talents now outweighed his reluctance to implicate anyone else in his rogue escapades, as what had become harrowingly clear was that Harmony had found a way to use *Devourer* biotech to bypass the grenadier's encryptions and install a core directive–overriding subroutine. Eamon had barely made it out alive going up against just one of Vargos's metal men; there was no telling what havoc the Composer could sow with the entire garrison—the most formidable fighting force in human history—at her beck and call.

Fortunately, the installation cable recovered from apartment 2801 was still coiled up in his jacket pocket like some hideous cyborg centipede. It was now imperative he uncover the source of the spliced technology before Harmony used it to start a war—something he couldn't do without Jyn's help.

The Drunken Shovel was a breeding ground for notorious types. Its owners, the Hades sisters, stayed just clean enough to skulk under DMED's radar but surrounded themselves with a protective shield of dangerous outlaws to maintain their "untouchable" repute. One such individual was an illicit tech peddler who went under the alias Nada—a cipher-less cohab, and one of the few nonhuman vendors in the district who would deal directly with humans. Making a transaction was fairly straightforward, as Eamon understood it: keep piling nunits into aer lap until ae handed over the goods; complain about the price tag and get thrown out on your ass.

He wasn't looking for stolen fission cells or counterfeit identity chits, however—what he wanted was information, which he doubted he could attain without Jyn's linguistic acumen.

Approaching the establishment, he unclipped his badge, intending to flash it at the snarling bouncer guarding the bead curtained entrance. Before he could, the woman gave Jyn a knowing nod and stepped aside, cracking an unintended smile at Abraham as he happily trotted past.

Evidently the deputy was not so much of a stranger to the Shovel as he was. There were still a number of blank spots in regard to Jyn's preservice history, but clearly she'd traveled in some unsavory circles prior to her recruitment. The ease with which they had gotten inside might once have given him cause for concern regarding potential corruption. But these days, if it helped him get through doors that might otherwise have been shut, it didn't concern him in the slightest.

"Pretty sure Nada's been hawking junk here since before either of us was born," Jyn said, taking point down a narrow corridor, her ponytail glowing an eerie purple under the decorative black light strips on the low ceiling.

"You gonna fill me in on why we're takin' an interest all of a sudden? Don't honestly see aer connecting to any of our current investigations."

Eamon cleared his throat, offering a pathetically lackadaisical response: "Need to source some tech I picked up on a recent inquiry in Tycho Block. Hoping ae might be able to point us in the right direction."

"I presume this 'tech' is alien, then? Wouldn't need to speak to Nada otherwise."

Eamon shrugged and assumed a lopsided smile. "Put it this way: it sure as hell ain't somethin' I could haggle for in Tinji Marketplace."

He reached for the door leading to the main bar area before Jyn jammed it shut with her boot. She turned to face him, her piercing eyes picking apart his dumbfounded expression like scavengers on carrion.

"This trip to Tycho Block you neglected to mention until now. Wouldn't have something to do with that pearl necklace you've been tryna hide from me, would it?"

She pulled aside the fur collar of his jacket and brushed fingertips against the ring of bruises encircling his neck—a tender memento from his perilous run-in with the grenadier.

She made a face that was difficult to decipher: anger, obviously, but then there was unequivocal sadness too—a regret, perhaps, that she hadn't been there to back him up.

"I told you to be careful."

He gently moved her hand away from his neck. "You should see the other guy."

"Don't joke, Wyatt. You can't keep leavin' me outta the loop like this—I grew up in the Mouth, you know? Might as well have blood fall runnin' through my damned veins. And you venturing into Tycho Block alone without consulting me first, when you've got my knowledge and experience at your disposal, is a surefire way of gettin' yourself zeroed. Don't you trust me anymore?"

"Of course I trust you, Jyn, but this matter is beyond sensitive. Had to make sure all my pieces were in place before involving anybody else. Just knowing what I know puts you at risk."

She clucked her tongue in vexation. "Don't talk to me like that—like I'm Keller or one of the other clueless bozos back at the precinct house. You and me are supposed to have each other's backs. I don't care if it puts a big red target on mine, you need to start telling me this stuff."

He sighed, rubbing his forehead. "I'm sorry. You're right. I just didn't want your neck on the chopping block beside mine unless it absolutely had to be . . . Turns out, it does."

He placed his hand on the small of her back just below the edge of her Kevlar vest, gently ushering her forward. "Let's go see what we can squeeze out of Nada. Then we'll grab a beer and I'll give you the full rundown—warts 'n' all. Nebula?"

Inside, the Drunken Shovel was about as inviting as a den of alligators. The air was pervaded by the overwhelming stench of body odor and cigar smoke. Faded posters featuring local troupes had been used as wallpaper in a fruitless effort to conceal the cold, industrial aesthetic of the defunct excavator's cave-like interior. Patrons sat hunched over their drinks like bundles of sodden rags, turning to glare over their shoulders at the entering trio with contemptuous eyes. Jyn may have had the cred necessary to gain them access, but by no means did that mean they were welcome . . .

Eamon spied a twentieth-century jukebox that had been disemboweled and hooked up to a set of speakers occupying the far corner. A VI modulator had been installed to add post-Collision sensibilities to the archaic music, which basically meant distorting the melodies beyond recognition and adding dark, chest-pounding rhythms. The pulsing sound waves caused ripples in the fluctuating layer of glow hanging in the air overhead, like treading water just below the surface of a turbulent sea of shimmering gold. Jyn, who was a keen musician at heart despite having never played an instrument, described the noise as an "unholy goddamn desecration"; Eamon dared not admit how innovative he considered it and how catchy he found the beats.

Nada stewed behind the bar in a shadowy alcove that was laminated by a thick coat of obsidian-like resin. Thousands of logic board fragments embedded in the hardened substance glinted like an embarrassment of sapphires, reminiscent of the old myth regarding crows and their propensity for stealing shiny trinkets to decorate their nests.

Eamon reassuringly ruffled Abraham's hackles as the mutt began a nervous growl at the aged cohabitor standing to greet them. It was not known what the maximum lifespan of Nada's kind was, but the cracked and discolored condition of aer chitin suggested ae was old—so old, in fact, it was entirely possible ae had witnessed the events of the Collision with aer own eight eyes.

The conversation began as they always did: a wordless exchange of pleasantries in the form of a mesmerizing display of effulgent retinal light. Eamon had always been curious to know what those initial moments of resonance entailed . . .

After all, what exactly constitutes empathic small talk? "Nice to feel you today . . . Hope you enjoy scouring the deepest recesses of my consciousness . . . Try not to overload my squishy primate brain with the entire compendium of cohabitor understanding and experience."

After a moment of silent deliberation, Jyn turned to him and cautiously suggested, "Ae's feeling pretty nervous. Think ae might have had a few bad experiences with DMED over the decades."

"Well, we ain't here to interrogate aer, Deputy. All we're after is a little intel."

She nodded, then relayed the message, to which Nada made a subdued grunt of acknowledgment.

"I'm getting . . . relief, gratitude," Jyn explained. "The concepts of exchange . . . commerce. Alright, alright . . . cheeky bastard . . . Looks like Nada wants payment—ae's prepared to help if ae can, but ae isn't doin' it for free."

Eamon took a sideways glance at the shelf beside him, stroking his rugged chin in contemplation. He began sifting through disorganized piles of miscellaneous tech before picking out a used Sinegex field resonator—one branded with the unmistakable signet of the NTU.

"Got some real big-ticket stuff in your inventory, Nada," he said, throwing the component in the air and catching it centimeters before aer snout, oriented in his fingers so ae could plainly see the mark.

"Shame some of it's been tagged by the Administration. I'm afraid that means it's technically stolen. I'd hate to have to confiscate all this valuable stock as contraband, but if you don't tell me what I wanna hear today then you may leave me with no choice."

Obviously, the words meant nothing to aer, but Eamon's demeanor was surely intimidating enough to transcend any language barrier.

Jyn crumpled her face in disapproval, going on to reluctantly convey the marshal's vague threat. Nada issued a sharp whine from aer breathing holes, raising aer paws in an unmistakably defensive gesture.

"Alright," she grumbled, the words *so much for this not being an interrogation* practically plastered across her face. "Ae's sufficiently spooked. What's this all about?"

Eamon whipped out the installation cable and dropped it on the table before Nada. Jyn stiffened, the surrounding air seeming to plummet in temperature as though she had been replaced by an astoundingly lifelike ice-carved sculpture of herself. There were few on the *Novara* as astute as the deputy; her extrasensory abilities came paired with unparalleled powers of discernment. She knew the profound ramifications of the cable's existence: the lines between human and alien culture and technology beginning to blur. This went far beyond a few clumsily augmented firearms; someone, somewhere, had learned to harness the ancient celestial power of the *Devourer* and integrate it with modern computer engineering—a technological breakthrough with the potential to alter the course of history, or depending on who was wielding it, spell certain doom for all on the Coalescence . . .

"Oh, Marshal . . . where in the Abyss do you keep finding this stuff?"

Eamon took a deep breath, feeling as though he were about to off-load a mountainous weight from his shoulders. "Before Devruhkhar met his unfortunate end, he managed to send the Governor a communiqué—it mentioned an apartment in Tycho Block where he supposedly delivered a weapons shipment. Safe to say, I didn't find any weapons, but what I did find was an incapacitated grenadier. It was hooked up to a pane with this here cable, which I presume was being used to brute-force its encryption and overwrite its friend or foe identification—ruttin' thing tried to zero me as soon as I set foot in the room. I suspect what I encountered was just a prototype—a field test doubling as a trap for whichever poor sap the Governor sent to investigate. The Composer probably knew Dev would spill the beans and took the opportunity to put a few unwitting Monarchs on ice . . . Doubt she expected the marshal to come rocking up instead."

Jyn managed to break free from the shackles of her stunned silence, reticently muttering, "I'd wager you're right about that."

Nada collected the cable and began scrutinizing it, purring in low, oscillating tones from somewhere beneath aer thorax. Abraham mistook the noise for fightin' words and, naturally, responded in turn.

In a stirring moment of mutual understanding, the merchant stared at Eamon with luminous eyes clearly communicating recognition and comprehension, running a digit along the unusual artifact's gruesome anatomy. Just as he thought ae might open up aer mandibles and start speaking Union standard, Jyn's emissions flared, and she said, "Nothing."

He turned to her with a puzzled expression that she reciprocated with a perfunctory shrug.

"Sorry . . . I got nothing: no memories, no emotional associations, no ideas or concepts. Ae's had no prior experiences in relation to this object."

"Are you certain?" Eamon asked. "Might not be the best at reading alien body language, but for a moment there it kinda seemed like otherwise. How can you be sure ae isn't holdin' out on us?"

Jyn snatched the cable out of Nada's paws and shoved it back inside Eamon's jacket pocket.

"Cohabitors can't lie, and it's hard to keep secrets when someone's inside your head. Ae's intrigued—that much goes without sayin'—but I'm afraid ae's just as clueless as we are in terms of where it came from or who made it. I'm sorry, but there's no answers to be found here, Marshal."

It was an interesting notion, that the cohabitor method of communication meant that since they lived wearing their heart on their sleeves, every nuance of experience and emotion playing like a film on the cinema screen of their cognizance, deception wasn't a concept they were familiar with. He guessed it was why they were naturally such unconfrontational beings—when your only means of hashing it out with an adversary is to literally feel what they feel, to see and understand their perspective, standing your ground in an argument is probably easier said than done. Still, the fact that Nada *couldn't* lie wasn't exactly conducive to the matter at hand.

Jyn slapped him on the shoulder, snickering at the sheer perplexed expression on his face.

"C'mon. You wanna carry on harassin' the locals, or you wanna sink a pint of that Hades sisters home brew?"

"You know that stuff can turn you blind, Deputy."

"Maybe just a schooner then . . ."

They hunkered down as far away from the blaring noise of the frankenspeaker as they could to set the *Novara* to rights. Sitting beside Eamon in a grimy booth, Jyn had slipped out of her boots and was resting her bare feet on the opposite side, where Abraham was curled up, affectionately licking her soles.

Kinky bastard.

Although speaking to Nada had amounted to a dead end, Eamon agreed to uphold his side of the bargain and spent the next hour going into the nitty-gritty of his recent efforts, regaling her with everything from his meeting with Dr. Faye Lucero to being held captive aboard the Governor's yacht to the death-defying leap from the balcony of apartment 2801. Jyn alternated between nodding and shaking her head, making snide vocalizations that suggested he was merely confirming things she already knew or had suspected. She seemed awfully well-informed for someone he'd strategically kept in the dark, but then again, she wasn't his head deputy for nothing . . .

"You're gettin' sloppy, dude," she warned, pressing her thumb against the glass payment panel embedded in their table to order another round. "Just blind luck you're breathing right now. I dunno how many times you gotta escape death by the skin of your teeth to know there's no shame in calling for backup."

"Pfft . . . and let someone else take all the glory? Not my style."

"It ain't funny." Her playful manner flatlined. "I know you like actin' up to the whole depressed, washed-up twentieth-century film noir cop thing, but there's so much more at stake here than just your sorry hide. The district *finally* has a marshal that actually gives a shit about us, one who's willing to do what's necessary to make a difference. You may not think your life's worth two shits, but it is—to a whole mess of people, including me. Just wish like hell you'd start takin' that seriously."

"I guess I never looked at it that way," he replied absently, knocking back the dregs of his Hades sisters home brew, his vision still, thankfully, intact.

Jyn gave a solemn shrug. "Maybe it's time you started. Cuz if you think after you go and get your throat slit that the next Phalanx reject Vargos hands stewardship of the Mouth to will be anywhere near as sympathetic toward the plight of its inhabitants, you can think again."

He turned to her, head tilted to signal incredulity. "It sounds like what you're asking here is for me to take a back seat when there's folks gettin' slaughtered by the dozens, just so I can save my own skin. You know I can't do that, Jyn. I don't rest until Harmony is eradicated, until the streets are free from the Composer's poisonous influence."

"I'm not telling you to quit, just to be careful." The gentle curves of the deputy's face sculpted a crestfallen expression. "The way you carry the fire for me and mine is downright admirable. But at the end of the day, you're a bow-sider, and you're throwin' yourself headfirst *again* into shit that's way above your pay grade. All I'm sayin' is, in order to protect and serve these people like you're so hell-bent on doin', you need to, ya know, be alive."

He could see her eyes looming in his peripheral vision—two softly lucent marbles exuding genuine concern for his well-being like he wasn't sure anyone had previously held for him—certainly not the ex-wife, at least.

"You have my word," he said earnestly. "I'll involve you in everything going forward. And I promise there'll be no more one-man-army antics, but we aren't done until the job's finished."

She smiled. "That's all I was fishin' for. And I know: we're just gettin' started."

There was a commotion near the bar—the nonhuman server heading over with their second round collided with a patron who was standing up, having loudly announced his intention to "take a slash." The cohab dropped aer serving tray, sending two schooners of home brew crashing to their rightful place on the filthy floor.

"Eight goddamn eyes and you good-for-nothin' leeches *still* can't watch where you're going!"

Jyn clenched her fist, looking ready to jump out of her seat to intervene, but settled instead for glaring at the doltish loudmouth with the heat of a thousand suns. Eamon subconsciously took the opportunity to gaze admiringly at her neck, which was as supple and slender as the rest of her, of course. What his attention was drawn to, however, was the prominent veins climbing from her clavicle to her temples like the branches of a withering tree, seared beneath her golden skin. Evidently, the booze had affected his reactions, as she spun around and caught him ogling before he could clumsily rip away his gaze. The fury she had been directing at the disruptive patron morphed into an elfin grin.

"Why is it after nearly four years of me being here tidyin' up after you that you've never asked me how I got them?"

"I may be just a 'dumb bowsider,' Jyn, but that doesn't mean I haven't picked up a thing or two during my time in the Mouth. I know exactly how you got 'em, but seein' as how you never mentioned religion before, I wasn't sure whether you gettin' 'baptized in the endless night' was by choice or not. Didn't figure it a particularly polite topic of conversation."

She tapped her empty glass with her fingernails, carefully contemplating her next words.

"Might surprise you to learn that, in fact, yeah: it was completely by choice. My mom and dad raised my two brothers and me as ardent devotees to the Church of the Abyss. My dad was kind of like a pastor, and we lived, worked, and worshipped in the convent surrounding the decommissioned starboard-side vehicular airlock."

"That thing's massive," Eamon interjected. "Big enough for engines like this old excavator to disembark, right?"

She nodded. "Mhmm, biggest on the *Novara*. So, naturally it's a pretty sacred place to COTA—practically a cathedral. I was very young at the time, of course, but old enough to know I was part of something really special. It's hard to describe what it felt like, ya know? That feeling of oneness with something so vast, profound, and magnanimous—like a warm embrace or an interconnectedness with the entire universe that made you feel intrinsically bound to all life and all things, but also so incredibly insignificant and alone."

"Sounds like you were a true believer . . . I'm guessing somethin' happened that means that's no longer the case?"

She turned introspective for a moment, staring through steel and nano-carbon to a nonexistent horizon.

"Well . . . with faith as blind and unquestioning as that, fear inevitably follows. COTA don't just worship the endless night: they're terrified of it. As time went on, with the gradual deterioration of the *Novara*'s hull, they began interpreting every catastrophic rupture as a sign that the Divine Abyss had become angered with the human remnant and that it needed to be appeased with . . . offerings."

Eamon sat back in his seat, dropping his shoulders in abrasive realization. "Human sacrifices? Lei-Ghannam! I thought that was just an urban myth."

"Not just any human—that would never satiate the desires of the Divine Abyss in their eyes. It had to be something far rarer—more . . . precious."

"Ciphers?"

She placed an open palm against her chest. "When I found out I was resonant, I confided in my parents, thinking they'd protect me—that they'd find some way to convince the elders to spare my life, or that we'd collectively renounce our faith as a family and find a new life somewhere in the slums. Didn't exactly pan out that way, though . . . My parents were so devout in their beliefs they were prepared to sacrifice their own daughter in the name of the Divine Abyss, just to conciliate the demands of an increasingly fanatical community. Absolutely fucked, right?"

"Unconscionably."

"On the night before my offering, my uncle—a man called Hiroki Sato— managed to free me from captivity and smuggle me out of the convent. He had been keeping his wife, Yua's, resonance a secret for years and, fortunately for me, couldn't very well stand by and watch as his niece got spaced. We all escaped together and lay low in the Copper Swathes for a while. I haven't seen or spoken to any of my immediate family ever since."

Eamon leaned closer to touch her shoulder with his in support. "Unbelievable . . . I never knew you went through such trauma, Jyn. I can't imagine what it must have been like—to have everyone you know and love suddenly turn against you. Lucky this Hiroki guy was watching out for you. What ever happened to him?"

"He and Yua ended up helping this wealthy bowsider with a guilty conscience set up an interspecies sanctuary for orphaned kids—a place in the Warrens called Juniper. I stuck around to help out for a while, but it was a tumultuous time for me. I was angry, bitter—ended up clashin' with them quite a bit. Eventually it all came to a head and we decided it would be in everyone's best interest for me to leave and go it alone."

Eamon went to take a swig from his glass and realized for perhaps the fifth time that it was, in fact, empty. "Jeez . . . It was daunting enough gettin' dumped in the Mouth as a grown-ass man. Must have been a shock to experience that as just a wee girl."

"It was . . . I remember heading into Tinji Marketplace looking for work. Figured my hyper-resonance was rare enough that it'd come in handy to someone, somewhere. I met a cohab called Absence who had a spare parts stall. Ae was in need of a translator so ae could deal with humans who weren't in a ciphered pair, so ae took me on. It turned into quite the friendship; we were as thick as thieves for a long time. Most of the Prey I meet show little interest in human culture and society, but Absence was fascinated by it— especially art and music. Ae had an old vinyl player in aer stall and we'd spend all day listening to classical music and sharing the emotions it made us feel through resonance."

"Absence," Eamon repeated. "Sounds like an eccentric character. Can't say as you've ever mentioned aer before . . . Is ae still around?"

Jyn was consumed by remorse. "I wasn't strong enough," she mumbled hoarsely. "It might not look like it on the surface, but cohabitors are incredibly emotional beings. They feel joy and compassion to a euphoric degree—there isn't anything remotely comparable in the human experience."

Eamon glanced across the Shovel at the nonhuman server, who was presently repouring their second round, as stoic and expressionless as every alien he'd encountered prior.

"Now there's a depressing thought."

"Thing is," Jyn continued, "that means they're also capable of fear and sadness so profound, so overwhelming, that it just dwarfs anything on the human emotional spectrum. When you attain resonance, your experience is theirs, and vice versa. But our brains aren't equipped to feel what they feel, so what for them might be emotional turmoil manifests itself for us as brutal, physical agony. And believe me: the cohabs in this place have a whole lot to feel miserable about."

"You're preachin' to the converted, Deputy. Sounds difficult. But if I know you, you stuck it out for as long as you were physically able."

She rubbed her temples, recalling the excruciating sensation.

"I honestly believed it would kill me if I stayed . . . Problem was, this was after the Antonelli expansion, when all cohabs were deemed enemies of the NTU and the Administration was cracking down on *any* nonhuman criminal activity in the district. Like Nada over there, Absence's stock wasn't strictly legal. Couple weeks after I left, ae was arrested and taken in for questioning. I never saw aer again, so presumably ae was executed."

"But you don't know that for certain. Ae could still be alive."

She shook her head as a lonely tear rolled down her cheek.

"Ae's gone . . . gone because I wasn't there to speak on aer behalf. Like so many others, ae was persecuted for not having a voice, for being unable to defend aerself . . . I don't know how I can ever forgive myself."

Eamon wrapped his arm around her shoulder in a gesture that felt distinctly reminiscent of his old man.

"There's no sense beatin' yourself up over it, darlin'. What happened was obviously terrible, but look at where you are now. Before, you were using that magic brain of yours to help just one bug—now you're helping literally thousands. When all this shit with Harmony is over, I promise: you and me, we're gonna give the cohabitors their voice. If Absence *is* dead, then ae didn't die in vain."

She used the fur collar of his jacket to wipe away the tears on her face. "Thank you, Wyatt. I know we're doing everything we can. It's just that, sometimes, I wish we could do more . . ."

The server finally returned, and as ae set two chalices of carbonated paint stripper down on the table, Eamon clandestinely slipped a twenty-nunit tip into aer paw. Ae hastily stuffed the translucent bill into aer apron pouch, bowing aer head in something like gratitude. Jyn wriggled closer into his side in response, roosting her head into his shoulder and swaddling him in the zesty scent of her perfume. His emotionally stunted brain was basically incapable of deciphering any meaning behind the action; all he knew was that he never wanted that moment to end.

"Why do they all have funny names like that?" he asked, watching as the server returned to aer post behind the bar. "Nada, Null, Absence, Naught—they're all variations of the same concept: nothing."

"Cuz nothin' is exactly what you'll find," Jyn replied, her voice resonating in his chest cavity, her warm breath caressing his neck. "The Prey don't have names. Names predicate the existence of language, which is a completely foreign concept to them. Whatever you end up callin' them is usually just an interpretation of the nothingness you're confronted with when you go inside their head looking for one. That's just the way it's always been."

"That doesn't make any sense . . . They must have some way of referring to or distinguishing from one another."

"Let me ask you this," Jyn said, eyes resplendent with mischief, her intention to torment him abundantly clear. "How do you feel about me?"

"Like you're tryna get me in trouble," he replied with surprising bravado.

She chuckled. "You don't need to answer . . . Whatever those feelings are, they're unique to me, right? You don't feel the same way about anyone else?"

He swallowed the embarrassingly large lump in his throat.

"No, Deputy. I can't say as I do."

She lifted her head and pecked him on the cheek with velvet-soft lips, sending an exhilarating wave of electricity coursing through his body.

Smiling, she said, "Well, then there's your answer."

Flown by their VI driver, Hypatia, the pleasantly tipsy pair headed back to the precinct house. Once stationary, they tumbled out of the cruiser and headed across the rooftop landing pad with Abe bounding excitedly ahead. Arriving at the main stairwell entrance, Eamon clumsily slammed shoulder first into the door's steel cladding as he habitually scanned his ID card, throwing his entire weight forward. Oddly, the door's locking mechanism failed to disengage, resulting in a painful but admittedly hilarious collision.

"Damn, dude," the deputy jeered. "You really can't handle your booze anymore, can you?"

With a rueful smirk, he swiped his card again, this time triggering the reader to display the words "ACCESS REVOKED" in angry red text.

"Is there a single piece of equipment in this building that isn't busted?" Jyn asked, using her own card to successfully unlock the door.

She's right: probably just a hiccup. Damn place is falling apart.

While Abe hurtled downstairs to greet his fellow compadres working in the bullpen, Jyn followed Eamon to his office, the plan being to go over the evidence he had gathered so far with a fine-tooth comb to see if there was any further insight she could offer. The plan changed abruptly, however, when he swung his door open and came face to faceplate with yet another grenadier.

Rasping a profanity, he fumbled out his machine pistol, taking aim at the android and readying to squeeze off a few preemptive shots.

Not catchin' me off guard this time, you son of a bitch.

"Ease down, Marshal," Jyn said, pulling on his bicep, forcing him to lower his firearm. "Check the status lights. It ain't hostile."

As usual, the deputy was right: unlike the grenny he'd encountered in Tycho Block, this one's armor pulsated zero-threat-condition green. He didn't have the foggiest idea what it was doing standing alone in his office, but he could be sure at least that it wasn't there to kill him.

It took two thumping steps forward, coming in range of the slivers of light cutting through the partially open window blinds that raked its head and torso in diagonal streaks of glowing bronze. A compartment opened on its shoulder, revealing a compact luma-caster that began projecting the life-sized image of Madeline Vargos.

"Marshal Wyatt. Deputy Sato," the woman said dryly. The projection was monochrome, but Eamon could tell even through the glimmering golden tones that she was wearing the same suit she had worn to the meeting at the letterbox—the garish red two-piece she usually donned when planning a ruthless scolding . . .

"Administrator!" he announced, hiding his pistol behind his back so as not to reveal how rattled the appearance of the grenny had had him. "To what do we owe the displeasure?"

His routine display of roguery was not met by the usual exasperated sigh. Instead, a cruel and insidious grin swept across the Administrator's wrinkled face—one he found deeply and inexorably discomforting. It gradually dawned on him that there may have been a potential connection between his ID card not working and this impromptu and highly unorthodox meeting . . .

What are you up to, Vargos?

"This isn't a social call, I'm afraid."

Eamon glanced in feigned befuddlement at the fearsome machine relaying the Administrator's call. "Is that so?"

"Yes. The truth is that I've heard some troubling things about you, Marshal." Her cunning smile collapsed into a dour expression. "I gave you a very simple task—one I expected completion of days ago. And yet, I've heard tell that you've been running rampant throughout the district, getting up to all manner of mischief: secretive meetings with members of the Glow Syndicate, breaking and entering private premises without a warrant, and seemingly endless drinking while on duty."

Ruminating on how his suspicions that the cruiser's VIOS link was being used to spy on him were seemingly confirmed, he curtly replied, "You know I like to stay busy."

She tutted condescendingly. "Really, Eamon. You used to be such an obedient, well-mannered young man. What in the stars has gotten into you recently?"

"I'll admit I may have gone a little off-piste. Thing is, I'm not sure if you're aware, Administrator, but we're having a few problems over on this side of the blockade—problems that are only gettin' exacerbated by the complete lack of support from Phalanx and your Administration. We're hanging on by a thread, here. So yeah: I guess you could say I've been a little disgruntled as of late."

"Disgruntled?" Vargos took a calculated pause. "Is that what you call it?"

She tapped a few keys on her wristwatch, triggering the projection of a rectangular 2D screen, which hovered beside her own image. It showed time-stamped security footage overlooking what, at first, was a seemingly nondescript construction site in the Langrenus Harrow, but Eamon soon recognized it when he spotted the crippled grenadier crawling into frame, its lower half broken and contorted as a result of the fall from apartment 2801. He then saw himself enter the scene, limping through the dirt before crouching down over the grenny and firing a point-blank shot into the back of its head. Without the appropriate context, the footage resembled a callous execution.

"You decommissioned invaluable Administration assets without prior authorization. Feeling 'disgruntled,' as you put it, scarcely justifies the destruction of an irreplaceable neural cortex."

Eamon hung his head, feeling Jyn angrily squeezing his wrist from behind. The deputy was right—he *was* getting sloppy—and now Vargos had him caught like a rat in a trap.

"Ma'am . . . you have to believe me. That thing was trying to kill me."

"Ridiculous," the Administrator spat, arms interlocked rigidly behind her back. "In nigh on a century of impeccable service aboard the *Novara*, there has not been a single incidence of errant target acquisition. Their fail-safe programming is totally infallible."

"This wasn't just some isolated software error, though—it'd been hacked! Someone's found a vulnerability in their programming, you have to believe me. I don't really know the scale of it yet, but you *need* to recall the garrison from the compound immediately or we could have a massacre on our hands!"

"I will not waste another second of my time listening to this absurd notion. You and I both know grenadier encryption is absolutely airtight—they cannot be 'hacked.' And if you think I would *ever* consider leaving the blockade defenseless, when hordes of vindictive savages wait to strike in its shadow, then I sincerely doubt your capacity for critical thinking."

Eamon's temper flared. He gritted his teeth and clenched his fists, knowing she would only use any emotional outbursts to her advantage—better to bite his tongue.

"Enough of this." She flicked a hand dismissively. "Marshal Wyatt, in light of recent events, I'm afraid I have no choice but to suspend you from active DMED duties pending an investigation into potential criminal conduct. You are hereby recalled to New Terra Union sovereignty, where you will remain until the council decides on an appropriate course of action. The unit currently relaying this call will escort you back through the blockade, so make whatever arrangements you need to and return bowside."

The council, he thought. *If Atherton Edevane is the one to be deciding your fate, then truly this could be the end of the line . . .*

The situation had become painfully evident: his recent endeavors had brought him far too close to the truth. The Administrator had wanted him out of the picture for some time, and now he had given her all the justification she needed to make it so. Staring into those devious, pixelated eyes, something Jyn had said back at the noodle joint in the Amaali Bazaar repeated in his mind: about the investigation into Anaya Lahiri's murder being dead in the water unless they picked the trail up bowside.

For all the intel Vargos had collected on him, there was *one* thing she didn't know about: the endo-chit that Faye Lucero had dug out of Anaya's arm. The good doctor had suggested whatever secrets it held were only accessible via the specific terminal that it was biometrically encoded to—one likely in either Miss Lahiri's workplace or personal residence.

Vargos's plan for his extradition was really a ploy to sequester him somewhere he could cause no further trouble, when, in fact, she was essentially delivering him to the very place he needed to be to unravel the entire conspiracy.

"Understood," he said, injecting ample submissiveness into his voice so as to seem defeated—for this to work, Vargos needed to believe she had his full compliance.

"Deputy Sato," Madeline said, staring over his shoulder at Jyn as she stepped forward and stood to attention.

"Ma'am?"

"I am promoting you to marshal effective immediately. Congratulations."

Jyn shot Eamon a trepidatious look, searching his face for approval and reassurance. He nodded, mouthing, "It's OK."

There was no telling how long he'd be gone; perhaps he'd never return. But at least he could leave with the confidence that the district and its inhabitants were in safe hands.

Time to go blow the lid off this thing . . .

TWENTY-ONE

Alone on the bridge, Tobias crouched low by the helm with his eyes fixed on the outbound call screen pulsating on the comms console. He flicked a hurried glance down helm access, wary of anybody who might be approaching from behind. Captain Holloway's "house rules" were many, but she'd been especially adamant that the bridge was off-limits without escort. He'd already done enough to incur the captain's wrath—another misstep would surely result in expulsion from the *Assurance*.

A discordant chime sounded as the words ***CALL FAILURE*** flashed on-screen in obnoxious bold text. He bit his lip and slammed his fist against the console's paneling, taking only a second to temper himself before furtively redialing Caleb's ident number.

The first call attempt rang indefinitely; the second failed to connect altogether. Bitter indignation crept in at the prospect that she may be actively ignoring him but was soon negated by just how desperately he yearned to hear the intoxicating cadence of her voice. Recent developments had left him feeling as though he were treading water, barely able to keep his head above the voracious spume, adrift in an ocean of the unknown. She was the only person on the *Novara* who could toss him a lifeline—who could help make sense of things: from the bizarre and utterly terrifying torrent of hallucinations plaguing him when in close proximity to the leech to the paradigm-shattering degree of poverty he had witnessed at the so-called Çorak, there was so much he needed to discuss with her.

The call failed again, but before he could make another frantic attempt, footsteps came pounding down the helm access corridor like surging war drums. He jostled to shut down the console and maneuver himself into a less conspicuous position as Captain Holloway stormed onto the bridge, her heavily degraded concussion repeater resting on her shoulder. She had been on high alert since the assassination attempt at the Governor's ceremony, sent into a fluster by the disappearance of her engineer, Isaac Verhoeven. By the looks of it, she was gearing up for an operation—a rescue mission, most likely. Evidently there was little time for pleasantries . . .

"You know you're not supposed to be in here," she seethed, making a beeline for the storage lockers. Tobias hastily sidestepped to get out of her way, feeling as though he were jumping out of the path of a runaway train.

"Sorry, Captain. I was just—"

"You were fiddling with the comms console again," she interrupted. "Something I recall explicitly telling you was not for personal use." She pulled open the locker and retrieved an acetyl box containing stacks of cylindrical concussion rounds, which she began loading into the empty slots on her gun-belt.

"Remember, you're here on probation, Tobias. I don't think Wyatt would be pleased to hear you've been trying to contact someone. Who is it you're tryna reach, anyway?"

"Nobody," he murmured, making little effort to conceal his utter despondency. In truth, he wouldn't know how to begin adequately describing his and Caleb's relationship, even if he wanted to. Delilah waited a beat, then shrugged off his reticence.

"Well, when you get done talking to *nobody*, join the rest of us in the galley. We need to talk shop."

She cracked open her break-action repeater and began sliding rounds into the chamber. Strangely captivated by her dexterity with the weapon, he asked, "Are we expecting trouble, Captain?"

"Trouble's a commodity folks have an unfortunate excess of around these parts. But don't fret—I won't be putting you in harm's way anytime soon. Wyatt would never forgive me for getting the son of a councilman killed—far too much paperwork."

"I'd hate to inconvenience the marshal so." He offered a mirthless smile, understanding that such a jibe was an attempt at comradery. "I appreciate the reassurance . . . Although I must ask: that lunatic who almost killed Vidalia Drexen—you said he belonged to a band of similarly deranged insurgents. How can we be sure they don't pose a threat?"

"They pose a threat to everyone, Tobias. Harmony is sweeping across the district like a plague of locusts. I'd wager it won't be long before they're very much a *bowside* problem too. Although, I suppose, after what happened at the Phalanx compound, that's already the case."

Tobias nodded in agreement, even if still quietly dubious of the suggestion that there were humans among the perpetrators of the blockade bombing.

Surely if that was the case it would have been major news—the top story on the NTNN for two days straight?

He, like everyone he knew bowside of the blockade, had credited the rising aggressions to the leeches and the leeches alone. But if Delilah was right, the situation in the Mouth was far more complicated than he had been led to believe. These were not simply acts of war but the work of a growing interspecies movement in which leech and man stood arm in arm, rallying together *against* the NTU. The implications were unsettling to say the least. Perhaps even more so was the inevitable conclusion that the Administration was using the network to purposefully censor this critical information. What their agenda could be for doing such a thing remained unknown. If there was anyone who could shed some light on the matter, it was his father. But with the man seemingly quite content with the way things had panned out—as in, *not* having had to suffer the career-ending embarrassment of seeing his son imprisoned for domestic terrorism—Atherton had so far been disinclined to offer any assistance whatsoever . . .

Reaching into the locker, Delilah produced a second firearm—an ancient, fixed-cylinder revolver that would have looked right at home in his father's collection of coveted historical artifacts. Tobias didn't need to be an enthusiast to surmise it was a damn sight more lethal than the concussion repeater slung around her shoulders. Recalling the signs that Isaac Verhoeven was likely a recovering glow addict, paired with the caliber of firepower the captain had apparently deemed necessary to retrieve him, he realized the mortal danger the wayward engineer was potentially in.

"Is there really no way I can help?" he asked, having to put an embarrassing amount of effort in to sound sincere. "I understand you don't want to put me in danger, but there's nothing I dislike more than feeling useless."

She cast him a skeptical glance, but after a moment of intense scrutiny, seemed to accept there was no malicious undercurrent to the offer. "There's plenty of ways you can be useful, Tobias—you don't have to be a spare part—but I can't let you help with this. Isaac might have gotten himself mixed up in something pretty nasty. If it's as bad as I think it could be, we may be going to some of the most dangerous places in the district, perhaps even underneath it. I appreciate you wanting to help, but I need you to stay put."

He watched as the captain spun around and stormed back toward the galley, surprised to find himself filled with reverence and admiration where once there had been only contempt. It dawned on him that the qualities of compassion and selflessness Delilah had already demonstrated on multiple occasions suggested she could be more to him than just a prison warden. With every revelation, every new challenge to his narrow perspective, he found himself craving guidance—the very same guidance she and Marshal Wyatt had both been ready to offer but which he, being his arrogant, petulant self, had been unwilling to accept.

That changes now, he decided. Evidently, the *Novara* was far larger and stranger than his bubble-wrapped existence had ever allowed him to perceive. If empathy and understanding were what he sought, then the time had come to sweep aside his prejudices and finally start listening.

Save for Isaac, the crew was assembled in the galley, perched on stools around the island countertop, eagerly awaiting Captain Holloway's briefing. The NTNN broadcast played with the volume muted on a panel in the lounge area, the images only just managing to breach through the fingerprint-riddled reflections of the surrounding lamps.

On-screen, Administrator Vargos addressed the public from her immaculate office in Chennai Plaza, the subtitles below transcribing her pledge for a *"safe and secure future for the NTU."*

Tobias had once admired her impassioned approach to public speaking—commanding allegiance and respect by way of forceful hand gestures and intense stares into the camera. But armed with the knowledge that the Administration was tailoring the facts about the conflict in the Mouth to manipulate public opinion, her frenzied gesticulations suddenly seemed unnervingly authoritarian.

He cringed to think of how captivated he had been in the days following the blockade bombing, sifting through repetitive headlines, feverishly hunting for any modicum of new data that would further enrage him. Only now, having been disconnected from it all, could he see what an unhealthy obsession it had become. Since boarding the *Assurance*, his appetite for political discourse had dissipated drastically. Free from its toxic influence, the fog benighting his vision had begun to clear, and for the first time in weeks, he was finally able to think straight.

Giving Captain Holloway an acknowledging nod, he pulled up a stool on the opposite side of the countertop to the leech. Though gradually becoming more at ease with at least being in the same room as the creature, whenever he strayed too close, his mind was impregnated by a flood of incoherent thoughts and feelings: emotions completely incongruent with his own mood; ideas and imagery that had no relevance or basis in his own train of thought. It was as if something had commandeered his mind and shuffled the deck of cards of his consciousness, casting psychological aberrations that were, admittedly, less intense than that first encounter but disturbing nonetheless.

Most harrowing among them were the incessant manifestations of his mother, her ghost like the leech's shadow, following wherever it roamed as if their two souls were inextricably bound. He had done his best to ignore her so far, maintaining to the crew that there was nothing out of the ordinary regarding his mental state—a fabrication that, of course, *none* of them were buying. Most insistent was the leech's translator, Mercy, to whom sooner or later he would *have* to disclose the details of his affliction. But, guessing that he shared some of her own exo-communicative abilities, he dreaded what that conversation might entail.

The captain hoisted a supply case onto the countertop and flicked open its latches with her thumbs. She swung open the lid, revealing stacks of nunits in various denominations. Tobias kept his mouth shut but sincerely doubted it was legitimately acquired tender—the nylon fiber bands binding the stacks together suggested they could only have been the earnings of criminal enterprise. Evidently, Holloway was using her ship for more than just weld and salvage . . .

"OK, I'll keep this brief," she said, transferring several stacks from the case onto the countertop. "We've got a man overboard. I don't know where Isaac's ended up, but it can't be anywhere nice. Every minute he's AWOL is worse than the last, so me and Kahu are gonna head out into the Copper Swathes to try and find him."

"You sure we got time for this, Skip?" Mr. Heperi asked, compressing the ends of his ungroomed mustache between finger and thumb. "We're already way overdue. Harbormaster's gonna be gettin' mighty suspicious if we don't check in soon."

"We're gettin' our engineer back, harbormaster be damned." Holloway slid the ancient revolver across the countertop. The old pilot caught it then popped open the cylinder to check whether it was loaded.

"Got rounds for this?"

"It's just for intimidation, big guy. Not planning on shooting up the neighborhood. I just need you to scare anybody that needs the fear put into them."

Kahu chuckled to himself. "That, I can do."

The captain pushed the piles of translucent bills across the countertop to Miss Brižan. Wearing a vibrant knitted sweater over an engineer's bodysuit, with her back turned and her arms folded rigidly, the girl was making it clear she had yet to change her mind about Tobias. Reflecting on his own behavior over the course of the past week, he couldn't say he blamed her.

"Teo," Holloway said. "Take the burro into Tinji Marketplace and get us some supplies. We need rations, spare parts. Let's restock the medical cubby while we're at it. And treat yourself to anything you could have used during the ionizer extraction but didn't have at the time."

"I will, Captain," Miss Brižan replied. "If you're gonna be out for some time, then would you mind if I took some rations back to Juniper Sanctuary? It's been a while since I visited."

With a winsome smile, Holloway reached into the supply case and added another stack to the girl's pile.

"Keep your feather handy. Don't wanna have to launch a search party for you too."

Just then, the leech, who had so far been sitting in silence, suddenly became agitated. Breathing erratically from the gaping orifices in its neck, it turned its head toward Mercy, who sat beside it with skin and hair as white as the peace lilies in Jade Tanaka's garden. The pair flooded the galley with what Tobias had overheard Mercy call their "emissions," making the antique lamps in the lounge seem dim by comparison. As he watched them commune, a thought crept into the back of his mind like a meandering stream of water, finding its way through a crack in his subconscious. A piece of their private conversation had inadvertently broken free, fluttering across the table in range of whatever extrasensory perception he was now burdened with.

The Savior is sick . . . The Savior is dying.

The words were his own but were only a rough interpretation of a concept he barely understood. They echoed in his psyche, repeating like a supernova shockwave in his gray matter. He had no idea what they meant, only that they were accompanied by a feeling of impending doom and a sense that time was running out.

"Captain!" Mercy announced. "There is an urgent matter we must attend to. May we request shore leave?"

"Of course—you know you're both free to come and go as you please. Still, I wouldn't be much of a host if I didn't ask if it's something we can't help you out with?"

Mercy shook her head, staring distantly. "No, it is not . . . We are needed in the Magnanimous Hollow, a chamber deep within the heart of the Savior. It is a sacred place; only cohabitors and their ciphers are permitted to enter. We appreciate your offer but must be allowed to go alone."

Holloway nodded. "Understood. Well . . . seems like we're all goin' our separate ways. I want everyone to stay in communication and to be back aboard the *Assurance* for oh one hundred hours." She flicked an accusatory glower at Miss Brižan—one suggesting the girl had a habit for tardiness. "That includes you too, Teo. Kahu's right—at some point we'll have to show our faces at the docks if we wanna avoid suspicion."

The Savior is sick. The Savior is dying.

There it was again—Tobias's own voice whispering behind his eyes in a tongue he understood about something he did not. Although this time, he was able to comprehend that "Savior" was just another word for the *Devourer*. He had always assumed the leeches had constructed their monstrous warship just as humankind did the *Novara*, but he was beginning to realize that it wasn't a vessel—not in the traditional sense, anyway. It was, in fact, alive: sentient, benevolent—an entity that he need not fear but one deserving of reverence and devotion.

A cold shiver ran down his spine—such considerations were utterly alien to him, and he wondered if these profound internalizations were his own or if they had been instilled in him by the leech.

His mind had been compromised—violated, in a sense. The lines were blurring rapidly, and he could no longer be certain of which thoughts were his own and which were Null's.

He returned to the conversation, readying to ask Captain Holloway what his role was to be in all of this disorganization. But then the imagery displayed on the panel in the lounge drew his attention. Chest sinking in mortification, he spied familiar plumes of feculent smoke rising from a fire in the Langrenus Harrow . . .

"Hey, look!" Kahu called. "The kid's handiwork's on the broadcast!"

Tobias dismounted from his stool and moved into the lounge to confirm. The pilot was right: the footage was indeed of the refinery that he, Caleb, and Jonah had destroyed. What he couldn't figure out was *why* the NTNN had waited until now to cover it. The incident had barely even caused a ripple, and he had resigned himself to the fact that it would probably never hit the headlines. Yet here it was: the worst mistake of his life, disseminated ship-wide for all to see.

Ignominy washed over him. He felt the eyes of his crew members digging into the back of his skull; they already knew the broad strokes of his despicable behavior, but now they could see for themselves.

Much to his dismay, Captain Holloway unmuted the panel with a sharp voice command. The nasally voice of a reporter then accompanied the images on-screen.

"More reports of unrest beyond the blockade today as cohabitor extremists detonate an improvised explosive device, destroying a pivotal NTU-controlled agricultural facility. The attack comes in the wake of the ambush in which five NTSC pilots were killed, as well as the devastating attack on the Phalanx compound, marking the third instance of interspecies aggression in the past two weeks."

"Lei-Ghannam!" Tobias exclaimed. "Wha . . . what is this? Cohabitor extremists, NTU facility? That's not what happened at all!"

"You never get the full picture when it comes to the network," Holloway explained. "They always put a spin on things, usually making links between completely unrelated events to create a false narrative to fit their agenda." She gestured toward the panel. "This? This is nothing new."

"What's your problem, kid?" Kahu interjected from the galley. "Woulda thought you'd be relieved. At least they ain't showin' your mug shot. Looks to me like you're off the hook."

"I . . . I am. But that's hardly the point. There's putting a spin on things and then there's broadcasting egregious, outright fabrications as fact. I cannot fathom what motivation they would have to lie about this."

The captain stood up from the countertop and joined him in the galley. "Suits the Administration much better for people to believe the cohabitors are solely responsible for what's going on in the Mouth. Vargos doesn't want to have to deal with the ugly truth that she's got an interspecies insurgency on her hands." She sidestepped into his line of sight to steal his gaze away from the panel. "The Administration wants one thing, Tobias: control. In order for it to keep it, the blockade *must* remain in place. It needs the support of the public, so it'll take any opportunity it can to demonize the cohabs in the media. Ironically, that includes the actions of a human supremacist organization like Humanity First."

Tobias felt the ground beneath his feet crumbling, the very bedrock of his understanding eroding like sediment. This was dangerous propagation of disinformation that, frankly, bordered on tyranny—expertly tailored to weaponize the fear and ignorance of gullible idiots like himself. How much of what he knew about the Mouth was truth and how much was reckless propaganda? Whatever the answer, he had been lapping it up for years . . .

The feed transitioned from the smoldering ruins in the Harrow back to the newsroom, where an anchor by the name of Damaris Ilna sat behind a news desk.

"Welcome back. We're joined in the studio today by Mr. Bhaltair Abernathy, the founding member of Humanity First—a self-proclaimed group of 'human enthusiasts' advocating for the Novara's separation from the Devourer."

Tobias made a tight fist as the feed cut to a shot of Abernathy. Decked in the same ridiculous Earth-map suit he'd proudly worn to the rally in Xìngyùn Square, he sat with his hands clasped on the desk, a detestable smirk stretched across his clean-shaved face.

"Oh, turn him off, Captain. I hate this guy," Miss Brižan heckled; Tobias found himself in stark agreement with her.

"Tell me, Mr. Abernathy," Damaris continued, *"with the relationship between our two species steadily deteriorating, what do you think incidents*

*like this mean for the 'safe and secure future' the Administrator alluded to in
her address?"*

"Well—what can I say?" Bhaltair replied, giving a blasé shrug. "*Another
beautiful day aboard the* Novara, *another heinous demonstration of antihu-
manism by our neighbors from across the blockade. No . . . as long as we're
kept stranded in dark space by our parasitic captors, with their ever-increasing
intake of power and resources, it's a preposterous notion that there could be
any kind of future for the human remnant at all."*

Miss Brižan signaled her disdain once again, catechizing from the galley,
"They don't *take* power, you backward troglodyte—they give it to us!"

Abernathy ran fingers through pompadoured peroxide-blond hair. "*The
so-called cohabitors are simply too violent, too hateful for the human remnant
to ever form an allegiance with.*"

The feed cut back to Damaris. "*You often use words like 'violent' and 'hateful' to describe them. But surely you're aware that up until very recently, there
were those who would use similar terminology to paint the actions of Humanity First—your own organization?*"

Bhaltair gave a contrite and sickeningly rehearsed nod. "*Damaris, I believe
wholeheartedly that people should take ownership for their mistakes, so I'll be
the first to put my hands up and admit that some of the methods we utilized in
the past were not the most constructive. But now we're pushing forward with
a renewed focus on peacefully and effectively communicating our message.*"

"*And tell me, what is your message?*"

"*Simply this: that we* can *free ourselves from the clutches of the* Devourer.
We can *restore the* Novara's *ripple-space functionality. Not only does the human
remnant have a fighting chance at survival, but I believe we can once again
become the proud, spacefaring civilization we once were. With hard work and
determination, we* will *reach the Grasslands of Pasture.*" Abernathy rapped the
news desk with the gaudy rings on his knuckles to emphasize his point.

Tobias found himself falling for the man's rhetoric again and had to gently
remind himself exactly where following the rambling megalomaniac had gotten him.

"*That's very inspiring,*" Damaris replied, sporting a jaded smile. "*But what
would you say to the naysayers who posit that what you're talking about is
impossible? That we simply do not have the resources, nor the manpower, to
repair the* Novara? *That with the damage done to her superstructure in the
Collision, she could never be made ripple space worthy again? And that, with
the alien conduits still providing the massive power requirements necessary to
keep life support and hydroponics in operation, separation from the* Devourer
would mean certain extinction for the human remnant?"

Using expert media training to dodge what were, in fact, very salient points, Abernathy leaned forward and said, *"To those naysayers, I would say that future generations will remember how little faith they had in mankind's innovation and dedication. These things are not impossible. Daunting, perhaps, but not impossible. The problem is that we don't currently have the right leadership. The Administration is paralyzed by bureaucracy; it's incapable of making the necessary tough decisions if these feats are to be achieved. The Union needs strong, ruthless governance, and I believe Humanity First can provide that strength. That's exactly why my focus is on transforming this organization from a group of concerned citizens into a viable political party. With the help of seasoned veterans such as Councilman Atherton Edevane and young voices such as Miss Caleb Callaghan of ACS acclaim, we can—kzzt."*

The image of Bhaltair's face dissolved into nothingness as Tobias angrily flicked his hand by the panel's on/off sensor. He had listened to about as much as he could tolerate, and the gloating mention of Caleb had tipped him over the edge. The only thing left to contemplate: what her level of complicity and involvement in this farce was. Using the destruction of the pulp refinery as a platform to launch this new political campaign was a smart move—one necessitating far more resourcefulness than he would *ever* credit Bhaltair with.

No . . . this was Caleb's idea; it had to be.

The reason why he'd had such difficulty contacting her became suddenly apparent. While his own discontentment with Humanity First stemmed from the doubtful feasibility of Bhaltair's plans for separation, Caleb's was in response to the lack of organized, effective activism taking place. This new push to reform the organization into a "viable political party" had her prints all over it. It was the perfect marriage between her Academy training, her fierce aptitude for debate and diplomacy, and, of course, her ambition to exact justice for Jade.

Evidently, there was little room in her plans for a carping cynic like Tobias, so she and Bhaltair had callously hung him out to dry, allowing them to kick off this deceitful press junket without his bemoaning interference.

And to think you were so enamoured with her, he told himself. *You would have followed her through hell and back. But she has become so twisted by grief that she would trample anyone who dared come between her and avenging her beloved . . . Nothing else matters now: not you, not Bhaltair, not the future of the human remnant—only that the leeches are made to pay . . .*

He spun around to find that the crew had already begun preparing to depart on their respective objectives, some giving him a look of genuine concern as he met their gaze. He realized they might just have been the only people on the *Novara* who actually gave a crap about him, and he wasn't sure if that was a depressing or humbling conclusion to come to.

Even Null—the *cohabitor*—seemed to be regarding him with a certain solicitude, standing motionless in the galley as the others bustled around it. As hesitant as he was to admit it, the two of them were connected. He didn't understand the nature of that connection but knew that in some way it involved his mother, which was something he *had* to better understand.

It . . . or *ae*, bowed aer head; he bowed back, vowing in that instant to wipe the slate clean, to not let how he behaved toward aer be tainted by the vitriolic lies of the NTNN but to spend time forming his own opinion instead. His "hyper-resonance," as Mercy had called it, didn't need to be considered a curse: it was an opportunity to broaden his perspective. The veil of reality had been pulled aside, allowing him to glimpse something profound and mysterious that lay hidden in the space beneath. He had only scratched the surface of what was possible, but by making peace with Null, he fully intended to learn all there was to learn and to master his powerful new abilities.

Teodora Brižan marched barefoot across the galley with the keys for the burro in hand, stopping by the entrance to the cargo hold stairwell and slipping her feet into a pair of psychedelically painted work boots. Her convictions concerning his character would prove the most difficult to reverse, but he had never been one to turn down a challenge.

Clearly her connection to this Juniper place ran deep, and if it was anything like the sanctuary Jonah Sinclair had spoken of—where infant cohabitors were sheltered and raised—it was somewhere Tobias desired to see for himself.

The face the girl made when he asked whether he could accompany her to the marketplace was one of caricature-esque cynicism, her pixie features drawn in angry impatience. She likely would have declined the offer had Captain Holloway not insisted she "take him along to see the sights."

"Fine," she grumbled, staring him up and down with eyes like pools of crystal blue. "But you'll stick out like a sore thumb dressed up all fancy like that. Go and get scuffed up a little, then we can head on out."

TWENTY-TWO

From the darkest alleyway in the Warrens to the most secluded corner of the Cohabitor Ghetto, Delilah and Kahu left no stone unturned as they scoured the district in search of Isaac. During her time dabbling in the *Novara*'s criminal underworld, Delilah had accrued a lengthy list of contacts attributed with a certain notoriety. Before long, they had crossed off every name on that list, bartering with a sordid welter of ruffians and racketeers for any snippet of information relevant to the boy's disappearance. With every passing hour he became more of a danger to himself, and she feared that if they didn't find him soon, they never would.

Eventually, growing desperation forced the pair underground into the sprawling subterranean labyrinth of the Vestiges. It was somewhere on these abandoned engineering decks that Micah had been lost over a decade ago, and Delilah had no reason to suspect they were any less dangerous now than they were back then. As emotionally distressing as it was utterly panic inducing to find herself traversing them once again, she couldn't help but revel in the sadistic sense of irony of it being in the interest of yet another unruly Verhoeven boy.

"Not far now," she said, quietly repelling a conflagration of memories from her last foray into this hellish place, her grip on the concussion repeater slipping in the sweat of her trembling hands.

"You sure?" Kahu replied, his grizzly voice inflected with a note of uncertainty as he kept pace beside her. "Kinda feels like we're going back on ourselves. Don't know how you can tell any of these maintenance passageways apart—all look the same to me."

Delilah raised the locator strapped to her wrist up to eye level, checking the steadily quickening frequency of its pulses.

"We're less than a hundred meters out—still on track."

She knew the old pilot was hoping for a little more reassurance but wanted to keep the chatter to a minimum. Traveling in silence, she found it far easier to listen for that tormented screech of rotting metal, the thunderous crash of disintegrating superstructure—she knew all too well the cacophony that would announce a hull rupture. Expecting a breach at any moment, she'd taken a few detours, ensuring they were never more than a short sprint away from a closing bulkhead should they be caught out by decompression countermeasures. The route wasn't particularly efficient, but at least it was safe . . .

They cut through the remnants of a communal laundry room, where, among rows of long-dormant washing machines, there were signs that the facility had been more recently occupied: sleeping bags, syn-beer bottles, and empty ration packets scattered around a heat generator aglow like the embers of a dying fire.

"Can't believe people really choose to live down here," Kahu said, stopping over the deserted hovel.

Delilah joined him. "Even with the Vestiges being as treacherous as they are, doesn't stop people coming down here seeking refuge."

"I don't see how life could get any better in this dump than it is up in the district."

She shrugged despairingly. "Desperation drives people underground; necessity forces them to stay. I guess for some, a life lived in fear of a rupture is a fair trade-off for leaving behind the hardships of the Mouth. With tensions between Harmony, Phalanx, and the Governor's Monarchs reaching critical mass, it wouldn't surprise me if even more start resorting to vagrancy down here."

Kahu nodded his understanding; she gave a doleful sigh.

"Just imagine how bad things must be gettin' up there if *this* seems like a preferable alternative."

Pressing on down another dismal passageway lit by lengths of tangled light rope coiled beneath the floor grating, the pulsing of her locator quickened its pace again. "Fifty meters out. Stay frosty."

"So, you used to run with the cat who's in charge of this joint," Kahu clarified. "They call her the Bookmaker, right?"

Delilah released a labored exhalation—for someone so cagey about his own personal demons, the old pilot certainly took pleasure in acquainting himself with those of others.

"Once upon a time, yeah. But she didn't go by the Bookmaker back then."

"Damn, Skip. Is there a crook in this town you aren't personally affiliated with?"

Delilah simpered. "I came to the Mouth with nothin' but the clothes on my back and my dad's nunit chit, which he summarily canceled, of course. I had no plan, and certainly no street smarts, which is good for one thing this side of the blockade: gettin' yourself mugged or taken advantage of. Greta Hox, as she was known then, found me looking like a lost lamb in the Warrens. She took me under her wing, showed me the ropes. The Copper Swathes are hardly any kind of place for a naive ACS girl pretendin' to be some kinda missionary. I doubt I would have survived long if it weren't for her protection and the lessons she taught me."

"And now she's the boss lady down here?"

Delilah pointed the muzzle of her repeater up to the ceiling. "Up there is the Governor's domain; here in the Vestiges, however, Greta rules the roost. We might not be in as high standing with her as we are with Vidalia, so we need to watch our step."

"How comes you two aren't pals no more? Trouble in paradise?"

"Guess you could say that," she answered, surprised to find a wistful smile touching her lips. "Greta's a pertinacious woman. She'll take any opportunity she can to get to the next payday. There's no venture too small, no scheme beneath her, if it earns big fat stacks of nunits. All she ever wanted was to pull herself and those she cared about out of the muck—that drive eventually got her embroiled in some stuff that I couldn't reconcile with, morally speaking. I tried to leave, she tried to stop me . . . That was the end of it."

"Pertinacious," Kahu repeated, twiddling the ends of his mustache. "Sounds like my kinda gal!"

"You better stow that talk, pilot. She will eat you alive—that's not a joke."

"Well, what's this 'morally unreconcilable' stuff she got you wound up in then? We're smugglers, Skip—it can't be that bad."

Delilah sighed. "There's vulnerable folks in the Vestiges—more so every day. Wherever you find vulnerable folks, you can count on criminal entrepreneurs making it their bread and butter to prey upon them. Greta built an empire down here doing just that—feeding off the misery and misfortune of the down and out like a . . . well, like a leech—an *actual* leech."

"What's her business, though?" Kahu whined, discontent with the fragmented information he was receiving. "Gambling, glow running? You haven't told me what actually goes down in this place where we're headed."

She shuddered. "You'll see soon enough. For the time being, just try and look tough, and keep your damn mouth shut."

"Got no need to try, Skip," Kahu retorted, flexing the muscles in his neck as he swaggered beside her. Wearing a black tactical jacket in lieu of his decades-old military blazer, he did look relatively thuggish. Hopefully rough enough to distract Greta from the soft, creamy center buried beneath his rugged exterior. She was renowned for preying upon fragile men, having no patience whatsoever for weakness and insecurity. If Kahu let slip his nervous disposition, she wouldn't relent until he was reduced to a weeping, fetal heap on the floor.

The locator sounded a steady beep as they arrived at the entrance to a dark, descending stairwell—from the bottom of which came the pounding rhythm of heavy music and the roar of a voracious crowd, accompanied by the assaulting odors of sweat, cigarette smoke, and potent cleaning chemicals.

We're definitely in the right place . . .

At the bottom of the stairs, a narrow hallway led to the establishment's main space: a vast maintenance shaft that might once have cut its circular profile up through the entire two-kilometer height of the *Novara*—before a third of her internal superstructure was devoured.

The altitudinous nature of this expanse meant the space twenty to thirty feet above ground fell out of range of the subdeck gravity emitters, creating a zero-g field accessible via two opposing scaffolding towers. The interspecies crowd responsible for the ruckus was huddled between the structures: gamblers and addicts alike, taunting and hollering with crumpled betting slips clutched in pumped fists, heads turned upwards at the scenes of carnage transpiring above them. In the zero-g field overhead, two adversaries battled in free-floating hand-to-hand combat. They twisted and tumbled in the weightlessness, grappling and striking one another, embroiled in a beautiful but violent ballet. The nauseating cracks and grunts of the fight reverberated around the shaft, every successful blow sending the mob into further hysteria.

What made this brutal competition so enticing to those below was that it pitted two gladiators of vastly disparate physiology against each other—one an obscenely muscular man and the other an equally burly cohabitor, locked in a deadly struggle for physical superiority.

Scanning the crowd, Delilah saw countless hopeless souls, driven to the Vestiges in sheer desperation, squandering their final nunits on glow caps and gambling on blood sport. It was precisely the type of grimy, illicit enterprise she'd expect to find Greta running and a striking reminder of exactly why she'd been forced to flee so long ago.

She glanced over her shoulder to find Kahu gawking at the savagery, his face a mask of morbid fascination.

"We gonna stay and watch the fight, Skip?"

The resounding death stare mitigated the need for any kind of verbal response.

Tucking her nose under the collar of her blouse, careful not to inhale any of the glow suffusing the air, she barged her way through the bloodthirsty horde with Kahu in tow. Ahead, a group of armed guards stood around the edges of a raised platform where Greta Hox sat leg over leg on a throne fashioned from precious metals and swathed in sumptuous fabric. With long, thinning silver hair resting on skeletal shoulders and pallid skin marred by deep wrinkles, age had caught up with the woman considerably since Delilah saw her last. But even her frail physique could do little to diminish her guileful, imposing presence.

Spotting their approach, she rose to her feet with the help of a cane sporting an ornate brass handle. Wearing an emerald gown encrusted with sparkling sequins, she moved gracefully to the edge of the platform, almost as if gliding on air. Delilah knew a time when Greta had garbed herself in the dreariest of blacks and browns—a means of camouflage that allowed her to blend into the scenery so as not to draw unwanted attention: a style which, consequently, she had herself adopted. But here was a woman who had acquired significant wealth in her advancing years and apparently felt no shame in flourishing it.

With all eyes transfixed on her, Greta raised a hand, silencing the crowd and immediately halting the airborne carnage. The two contenders hung awkwardly above, beaten, bruised, and panting heavily, awaiting permission to resume, with chains tied around their waists preventing them from drifting too far up the shaft.

The Bookmaker opened her arms wide as a sinister grin carved itself across her aging face.

"My dearest Lilah . . . Finally, you have returned."

"You're looking well," Delilah said while a robed assistant poured a measure of dark brown liquor from a crystal decanter into her glass. It was undoubtedly synthesized but warmed her belly up just right.

"Don't be ridiculous," Greta snapped, glaring at her garments as she flattened out a crease with the palm of her hand. "I look like a Winter Solstice ornament. But it *does* keep the riffraff in check. People are far more receptive to being ruled when you inject a little regality into your persona. You should try it."

"I'll keep that in mind."

As Delilah had predicted, Greta set eyes upon Kahu, approaching the old pilot spindle-limbed, like a feline stalking her prey, and taking his chin firmly in hand.

"This one's quite a specimen, Lilah," she said, scrutinizing his brawny physique as a cattle rearer might once have inspected livestock. "You should let him fight for me. People would wager handsomely to see this brute go toe to toe with one of my gladiators."

Wing Commander Heperi had commanded squadrons, faced down swarms of interceptors, suffered terrible defeat, and lived to overembellish it, yet here he was: out of his depth in every conceivable way. His thuggish facade began to falter; his eyes betrayed disquiet as they looked to his captain for assistance, but she couldn't help him. Greta would only see the bond Delilah held with her crew as a sign of weakness. She would expect a ship captain to treat the people under their employ with the same callous indifference she demonstrated to her own underlings, and only by speaking the Bookmaker's vernacular were they getting the information they needed.

"I'm sure they would," Delilah concurred, shaking her head in feigned disappointment. "And while I have no doubt it would be quite a spectacle, I'm afraid Mr. Heperi is far too useful behind the helm to risk losing in a game of chance."

Greta released the old pilot and flicked a hand dismissively, her Machiavellian smile melting into a look of mild disdain. "A stick jockey—how very tiresome."

Kahu stumbled backward, rubbing the scratch marks inflicted by Greta's needle-sharp fingernails with coarse hands. Rattled, he hurriedly took his already empty glass to the assistant and demanded a refill.

"He's terribly clumsy as well," Delilah continued. "Handy in a bar fight, but hardly blessed with the agility and dexterity I imagine are required to win a free-floating fight."

"I didn't say he needed to *win*," Greta said, pale eyes peering over her glass as she held it coyly before her face.

"And as I said, his skills are indispensable to me. I couldn't risk losing them."

The woman smiled insincerely, gesturing with her cane to the weapon slung around Delilah's shoulder.

"Well, at least you didn't come back to me completely empty-handed. I see you were kind enough to return my beloved heirloom."

"And here I was under the impression it was a parting gift." Delilah replied, placing a protective hand on the stock, recalling the moment she swiped the weapon amidst the chaos of her frantic escape from Greta's old safehouse.

The woman's countenance turned severe. "Permitting you to leave with your life, my dear Lilah—*that* was my parting gift to you."

Behind her back, she inched her hand closer toward the trigger guard of the repeater—five nonlethal rounds loaded in the chamber, hardly enough to blow their way out should the situation deteriorate, but it would have to do. Some abiding resentment over her impromptu departure was to be expected, but apparently Greta was far more capable of holding a grudge than she had anticipated.

By now the gladiators had resumed their scrimmage, the thick tension atop the platform accentuated by the awful din of the battle raging overhead. The nonhuman contestant swung aer body around in an incredible feat of aero-gymnastics and hooked aer reversed knee joint around the neck of aer opponent, locking him in an unbreakable chokehold. The human spectators below were whipped into a rumpus by the move; the alien using aer unique anatomy to gain the upper hand was apparently considered illegal in the context of the game. The punters howled and gestured angrily at the Bookmaker, goading her to disallow the play. A mediator as much as she was a facilitator to this circus of brutality, Greta stepped forward and afforded a thumbs down, instructing the cohabitor to release aer adversary and continue the fight.

She turned back to Delilah, giving an enervated exhalation.

"My time is valuable, Lilah. I assume this isn't just a social call, and frankly, I'm not in the business of entertaining guests, so why don't you get to the point and tell me exactly what it is you need."

"We're looking for somebody," Delilah explained, moving her hand away from her repeater. "A young engineer by the name of Isaac Verhoeven. Boy's got a terrible weakness when it comes to glow. He's been clean for a while now, but we suspect he may have suffered a relapse and gone looking for a vent."

"I see. And I'll hazard a guess this insipid whelp is *indispensable* to you also?" Greta posited, flicking a disdainful look at Kahu, whose attention had been stolen once again by the fight.

"Very much so. We've checked every den in the Mouth, spoken to every major player from Nass Jovia to the Hades sisters. Problem is, they all know he's affiliated with me, so anywhere he went looking for a fix, he got turned away. We figure he must have come to the Vestiges as a last resort . . . hence the reason we're standing here before you."

Greta began pacing contemplatively around the platform. "Really, Delilah. I thought I taught you better than this—dragging yourself through the muck, risking your life coming to the most dangerous place on the Coalescence, just to retrieve some pathetic wretch with a substance abuse problem."

"You taught me to surround myself with the strengths of others. There aren't many engineers left with the knowledge to keep an old balaener class like mine in the air. Isaac knows the *Assurance* better than anybody. Without him, my operation is dead in the water. So, finding that boy is of the utmost importance—well worth any trouble the Vestiges can throw our way."

"Do not speak to me of worth," Greta hissed, clutching her cane tightly. "There isn't a soul eking out a sad existence on this decrepit wreck worth jeopardizing your position over, worth losing what you've earned—what's rightfully yours. You've allowed yourself to become attached to the people who serve you, exposing yourself to emotional coercion and exploitation. You've made yourself weak."

"And I suppose you'd know a thing or two about exploiting people," Delilah rebutted, indicating the ravenous throng below with a suggestive glance. Greta's acrimonious manner thawed. She displayed a surprising look of tenderness, hampered somewhat by her supercilious attitude. "There's that bright spark I saw years ago. A young girl—fierce and precocious—poised for greatness, were she not so prone to sentimentality. I told you to *wield* the strength of others. Give only what you must to garner people's allegiance, then take from them everything. That's the only way to elevate yourself above the rest—it's the only way to survive."

Delilah resolutely shook her head. "I survive by having people I can rely on at my side. Doesn't matter how hot things get, I can always count on my crew having my back." As if on cue, she felt Kahu maneuvering into position behind her, ready to intervene. Were she not presently engaged in an intense staring match, she would have turned around and covered his mug in kisses. "And it's not *just* because they're on my payroll."

"How revoltingly poignant," Greta remarked. "I don't know where you learned to be so very sanctimonious, but it certainly wasn't from me." The woman released a sardonic chuckle, but then her eyes glazed over. Knees buckling, she collapsed into her throne, beginning a hacking, spluttering cough. She reached over her arm rest and retrieved an oxygen mask, pressing it to her face and breathing deep from the air supply. Alarmingly, neither the woman's assistant nor her security detail seemed even remotely concerned by their master's violent convulsions. Delilah instinctively moved to assist, but Greta waved her away, taking a final, strenuous breath, the fluid in her lungs rattling like loose bolts in an engine turbine.

"Leave me be," she rasped as she pulled the mask away, leaving a single strand of saliva dangling from her lips.

"Is it serious?" Delilah asked, dismayed at finding herself struck by genuine remorse that the woman's health had seemingly deteriorated so severely.

Greta wiped her mouth with the sleeve of her gown. "There are many benefits to keeping an operation such as mine running beneath ground. A decade spent breathing this wretchedly thin atmosphere is not among them. Ventilation is severely limited down here; the air is polluted by toxins, gases, and stars know what else that seeps through the superstructure. It wreaks havoc on the respiratory system, especially one as decrepit as mine."

"Is there anything we can do to help?"

Greta shook her head, still struggling to regulate her breathing. "You can go back to where you came from. You and I parted ways for good reason, Lilah. I see no cause for a reunion now. I implore you to leave the Vestiges while you still have the choice."

"We plan on doing just that. But not without finding Isaac first."

Greta rolled her eyes. "Oh, you are relentless, aren't you? Well, needless to say, I don't know where your missing engineer is. I control most of the vents beneath ground; if he wound up at any one of mine, I would have been made aware." She paused, dull eyes brought back to life by a flicker of cunning intent. "Having said that, I do have an idea where he *might* be."

She summoned her assistant—a young boy, gaunt-faced with vacant eyes—who brought to her a small keepsake box, bowing his head submissively as he approached. Dismissing him, Greta retrieved a glow cap from the box and passed it to Delilah, who studied the object in the palm of her hand— a small pill-shaped canister with a protrusion for inhalation and a clear plastic cap revealing the swirling luminescence stored within. On its casing was a set of initials engraved in gold.

"VD," she read aloud. "The Governor?"

Greta nodded. "For years now there's been an unspoken understanding between me and that narcissist about the boundaries of our two operations. Above ground belongs to him, below to me. It would appear, however, that this agreement no longer suits, as he has elected to establish his own capping plant right down here in the Vestiges. Now, caps like the one in your hand have started showing up all over my territory."

"Capping plant?" Delilah echoed, betraying her naivety in the matter.

"A barbaric practice, even by my standards. They'll sweep hopeless addicts like your missing engineer off the street and exploit them for free labor— shove them shoulder-deep inside a vent to let them get their fill while forcing them to collect concentrated glow in caps such as this one to be sold on the street to other, equally hopeless addicts."

"Horrible," Delilah muttered, turning ice-cold at the thought of Isaac being caught up in such a place.

"Indeed . . . Perhaps your unannounced arrival doesn't have to be such a burden to me after all. I believe we may have an opportunity on our hands that could be mutually beneficial."

"I'm listening," Delilah said, leaning on Kahu's shoulder, making it abundantly clear that the hulking man was under her command and she under his ward.

Greta sat forward in her throne. "I'll provide the location of the Governor's capping plant so you can find your stray pet. In exchange, you cause as much of a disturbance to the operation as you can in the process. I'm sure this blunt instrument of yours is capable of a great deal of havoc, allowed off the leash." Greta prodded Kahu's gut with the end of her cane. "Let him tear the place down. Make Vidalia think twice about ever moving in on my patch again."

"We ain't mercenaries," Kahu rebuked, batting the end of her cane away with a muscular hand. "Aren't exactly kitted up to mount a full-blown offensive against the Governor, are we?"

Greta threw her hands in the air. "Rejoice! It speaks! Ah, but fear not, my articulate friend, for this is a small operation. I have it on good authority the plant has minimal security—two or three Monarchs at the very most. I don't imagine they will cause too much trouble for you."

Delilah took a moment to consider the proposal. Meanwhile, the fight raged on above the platform. The human contender unleashed a volley of punches into his adversary's thorax, futilely pounding on aer impenetrable carapace with bloodied and broken hands, faltering more with every failed blow. He relented to catch his breath, foolishly giving aer an opportunity to counterattack. Pivoting backward, ae swung aer sharpened elbow with blinding speed, viciously striking the man in his temple. Rendered instantly unconscious, his limp body spun in zero-g like a rag doll in a tumble dryer. To the thrum of the crowd below, the cohab wrapped aer paw around the man's throat, sending him back in range of the gravity emitters with a gentle push. Delilah watched in consternation as his limp body plummeted toward the ground and was consumed by the mob of fervid gamblers, discarded betting slips dancing like confetti in the air.

Finalizing her decision, she said, "Ping us the location," catching a look of uncertainty from Kahu.

"Excellent," Greta declared gleefully, tapping a combination of keys on her data pad to transmit the coordinates in question to Delilah's locator. "With your help, the Vestiges will soon be rid of that wretched man's interference, and the natural order of things can be restored."

Delilah raised a halting finger. "We aren't agreeing to help. I need to see this place for myself, *then* we'll decide on an appropriate course of action."

"Very well," Greta spat impatiently. "Do what you must, but I trust that when you witness the true extent of Vidalia's cruelty, you'll have no choice but to intervene, being the anointed saint you are."

The woman waved a frail hand to see them off. "Come back to me with news of the plant's destruction or not at all, my dear. I cannot promise I shall react as favorably should you return empty-handed once again."

TWENTY-THREE

Tobias rode pillion behind Teodora Brižan as she piloted the cumbersome four-wheel burro down the confined alleyways of Tinji Marketplace.

He estimated it to be sometime in the afternoon, although in the absence of an artificial sky, like the one projected along the Canyon ceiling, *and* with his feather still confiscated, it was hard to be precise. In truth, there was something quite liberating about not being quite so bound by punctuality—a quality one could ill afford to neglect living in Quarterdeck but one of little importance to the denizens of the Mouth.

Heeding Teo's advice concerning his attire, he had ditched the expensive trench coat for a yellow canvas jacket, which he had found buried in a storage locker in the cargo bay. Since none of the crew had claimed the garment, he suspected it predated perhaps even Mr. Heperi's ownership of the *Assurance*. Even though it was stained and frayed and exuded quite an unpleasant musk, he was relieved to finally feel like he blended in with the crowd.

He sat in ruminative silence, watching as the frontier raced by, intent on absorbing every facet of his surroundings through the new lens afforded by recent experiences. This place, which had long been the object of such fear and resentment on his part, was now opening up to him in an exhilarating bombardment of the senses. The lambent glow of the Höllengarten dappled through holes in a dense patchwork of material awnings, drenching the marketplace in a soothing tangerine fog. Beneath the growl of the burro's archaic engine, he heard the babel of a hundred languages while exotic music thumped from somewhere in the distance. The air was redolent of cultivated meat seared on the grill, punctuated by a melange of unfamiliar herbs and spices. He wasn't sure where they were headed but hoped it was in the direction of the delectable aroma filling his nostrils.

Surprisingly, the buildings in this area were an amalgamation of repurposed superstructure as well as the prefabricated domiciles originally meant for use by the first settlers on Pasture. He couldn't help but laugh inwardly at the thought of how enraged his past self would be to see NTSC commodities, which it might once have been *his* responsibility to allocate and distribute, used by squatters. Now, he felt genuine contentment that they were being put to good use.

Scanning the faces of residents and traders as they sped by, he was overcome by shame and regret, for they were definitely *not* the faces of "mutineers" and "terrorists," as he had once expected to find. They were people—some humans, others not, cohabiting in relative peace and harmony. The turmoil at the blockade seemed a million miles away from here, and he now saw a clear divide between those instigating the violence and those trapped on the wrong side of it. How foolish and how single-minded he had been to confuse the two . . .

Teo took his hands and placed them firmly on her waist.

"Makes it a whole lot easier luggin' you about if you just hold on to me," she instructed for a second time. "I'd sure hate for you to fall off and get caught under the wheels; you'd probably bust the axle, and Divine Abyss knows where I'd find a replacement for this old crate."

His sense of chivalry screamed at him to keep his profusely sweating hands to himself, but the more polite and reserved he behaved around the stalwart salvage specialist, the more exasperated with him she became. Repressing a flush of embarrassment, he tightened his grip on the belt loops of her bodysuit and pulled himself closer, catching the scent of her unruly plait of cerulean hair as it bobbed up and down before his nose: an oddly alluring mixture of tropical fruits and engine fumes.

She tore around a sharp corner and clipped the stall of a clothing vendor who hollered profanities as she accelerated away, flashing a mischievous grin back over her shoulder. Then, splayed out beneath a cluttered canopy of exposed power lines and neon signage, they arrived in an open clearing with an amphitheater at its center where street performers frolicked before crowds of riveted onlookers. As if caught between two dimensions, this bustling square comprised a violent melding of disparate architectural styles, with buildings that were obviously human in design practically smashed together with the misshapen domes and spires of what he presumed were cohabitor construction. Truly, it was the intersecting point between human and alien culture—the very nexus of the Collision itself.

They disembarked, setting the burro into sentry mode and directing it to trundle along beside them. Teo took point on their mission to restock the

Assurance. Tobias followed, occasionally struggling to keep up as she whirled ritualistically from stall to stall, collecting fresh produce, tools, and ammunition as if performing dizzying interpretive dance. She was well-known among the locals, each vendor greeting her with more fondness than the last, many lighting up at the sight of her face and offering discounted or complimentary goods without thought or hesitation. The foul-tempered sprig who had regarded him with such disdain back on the ship soon blossomed into what he realized was her default, exuberant self; she was like a bird held captive for a lifetime, released from her cage and finally allowed to spread her wings in familiar skies.

"Hold on to this for me, will ya," she chirped, stacking several cans of dehydrated protein onto the already precarious pile of assorted items he had offered to carry.

"I think I'm getting a sense for why you agreed to bring me along," he joked, straining under the weight of the load.

"No sense coming with me if you ain't gonna make yourself useful."

The owner of the produce stall they were presently shopping at leaned over the counter—a squat woman with wild auburn hair accented by streaks of gray. Inquiring whether they were headed to Juniper Sanctuary, she handed over a clear plastic bag containing balls of candy wrapped in different-colored foil, going on to caution them not to let the "cohab littl'uns" eat the blue ones, "else you'll give 'em a terrible thorax infection."

"Oh, you spoil 'em too much, Mauve," Teo replied, shoveling the bag and a handful of silver ration pouches into her satchel.

"Make sure you watch out for Harmony too," Mauve continued, warily surveying the crowd. "They're out in full force today—dragging the streets, lookin' for more gullible fools to recruit. That Composer is a nasty piece of work, I tell ya. Can't believe a word she says, nice as it might sound."

The Composer. Captain Holloway had mentioned how the leader of the interspecies insurgency wreaking havoc across the District of the Mouth remained anonymous. All that was known about her was that she was a cipher . . . just like him. A shudder rattled down his spine as he contemplated whether a future spent as a violent pro-cohabitor freedom fighter was predestined for all who were born resonant. How far would the pendulum swing in his case? After all, it wasn't so long ago that he professed an uncompromising hatred of the creatures. Would his new ability to comprehend and empathize with their struggle drive him to commit atrocities on their behalf too? He didn't think so, but then again, he didn't know *what* was possible anymore.

"I was on board when they were fighting for an end to the oppression, but they lost me as soon as they started targeting innocent civilians. Ain't no kind of utopia gonna come from that."

Teo reached out and gave the woman's shoulder a reassuring squeeze. "We'll head straight back to the *Assurance* when we're done at Juniper—I promise. Harmony won't even know we were here."

With a tender farewell, she set them off in the direction of the final stall on her list, but it wasn't long before Mauve's stark warning about the prevalence of insurgents in the area bore fruit. Two humans wearing the same mottled-brown robes as the failed assassin at the Governor's ceremony approached, the crowd parting around them like a school of fish dividing around a prowling shark.

"Quell the Dissonance!" one of them wailed in a bell-like voice as the other rang a set of metal chimes for attention. "Submit to the will of the Composer or face annihilation!"

Teo grabbed Tobias by the hand and abruptly diverted her route to skirt around the crowd instead of cutting through it, the autonomous burro only just managing to track the sudden change in speed and direction.

"Brazen zealots are gettin' more fanatical by the day," she said. "Don't see any weapons on 'em, but who knows what they could be packin' beneath all those rags. Best stay clear."

"I can't believe they're allowed to wander around freely spewing radical fundamentalism like that," said Tobias, immediately realizing the hypocrisy of such a statement when he had basically done the same in the name of Humanity First. He had only been concerned with the potential dangers separation from the *Devourer* posed to the human remnant. Now, he had to consider what it would mean for the cohabitors too.

Genocide.

"Where are Phalanx, or DMED?" he asked. "Doesn't Marshal Wyatt have something to say about it?"

"DMED can't do jack about this," Teo retorted. "They're underfunded, understaffed—hardly equipped to fight a terrorist cell. Anyhow, I heard that Administrator Vargos gave Eamon Wyatt the boot for drinkin' on the job. I dunno who's runnin' the show now, but they don't seem the least bit concerned about the Composer's thugs harassing folks."

Tobias stopped dead in his tracks, glancing over jumbled, ramshackle rooftops at the colossal shape of the blockade.

I could make a run for it, he thought. *This "community service" is nothing more than a gentleman's agreement between my father and the marshal. With Wyatt out of the picture, there's no paper trail, no court order—no legal obligation for me to stay aboard* the Assurance *whatsoever. The Phalanx compound isn't far. I could sprint for it, declare my NTU citizenship, sail through the transfer checkpoint, and go home.*

Teo stopped, turning to face him with a hand on her hip and an eyebrow raised inquisitively. "Don't you go disappearin' on us now, Tobias," she warned, decrypting his thought process as effortlessly as though it were printed across his forehead in bold text. "Just cuz the marshal got the axe, it don't mean you get a free pass. Besides, it'd upset the captain if you left now after all she's done. And I don't take kindly to folks who upset the captain . . ."

He fiddled nervously with the zipper of his jacket, trying not to betray with his expression that she had him pegged entirely. She was a few years younger than him but remarkably astute for her age. Ultimately, she was right: there may have been no legal obligation keeping him, but after his actions in the Langrenus Harrow, he owed her and every other mouthian an insurmountable debt. And, of course, there was the consideration that without Null and Captain Holloway's decisive actions, Hazel would still be adrift in the endless night—he owed them a great deal too.

He smiled, shrugged off the insinuation. "Thought never crossed my mind."

"Of course it didn't." Teo nodded over her shoulder to usher him forward. "C'mon. We just need to pick up some pulp for Null and then we're all done."

"Pulp?" he repeated. "That's that stuff up there, isn't it?" Teo followed his gaze up to the glowing carpet of alien vegetation covering the ceiling of the Mouth.

"Mhmm. They fly up there and harvest it with . . . well, you already know that part." She flicked him a fleeting but suitably accusatory glower. "They refine it down into that orange slop and store it in canisters. Cohabs go crazy for the stuff."

"It sounds almost sacred."

Teo nodded. "They call the *Devourer* the Savior, ya know? This is just one of the many ways it provides for and protects them."

"I wouldn't have thought humans would be allowed to purchase something so coveted."

"Normally we ain't. Pulp is highly toxic to the likes of you and me. Plus, it's a finite resource; can't afford to go selling it to folks who aren't gonna use it for its intended purpose."

"So how come they're gonna sell it to us today?"

Teo assumed a devious grin. "Because we have you."

Needless to say, Tobias felt some apprehension about Teo's proposal of using his abilities to haggle with a cohabitor vendor for goods. He couldn't be sure he even knew how to initiate his resonance, let alone how to have a full-blown conversation with it.

"What if it knocks me out again?"

Teo met the panicked query with an artlessly pragmatic answer. "Then I'll get Nimic to hoist you onto the burro, drive your unconscious ass back to the *Assurance*, and give you another stim shot."

Nimic was the name of the vendor in question. Swaying gently from side to side, which Teo explained was a behavior cohabitors exhibited when they were feeling relaxed and content, ae sat among aer wares beneath a tepee tent stitched together from recycled kestrel ejection seat parachutes. A food chiller lay on its side behind aer with its doors ripped off, dousing the ground in a fluctuating layer of ice-cold water vapor. Inside, Tobias spied the canisters Teo had spoken of—expended fission cells containing a viscous substance that looked like fire somehow distilled into liquid form.

Nimic greeted them with a gentle bow of the head as the pair entered. Tobias returned the gesture, meeting four pairs of vertically arranged eyes, which were not the pits of bottomless black that he had once perceived them as but colored a deep navy blue pervaded by sparkling flecks of violet. A soul stared back: warm and welcoming, emanating intelligence and understanding, aer amiable personality shining through.

Teo reminded him that hyper-resonance like his was rare, and that at first, Nimic might be surprised to be attaining such an intense and immediate connection with a stranger.

"Just go easy on aer is all."

"Go easy?" he mimicked. "I have no idea where to even begin."

"Sure you do . . . Just picture two canisters in your mind and think about buying 'em."

He glanced up to see Nimic stepping forward, seemingly already aware of the empathic bridge fizzling into existence between them, cocking aer head to the side in intrigue.

"I doubt it's that straightforward."

"The whole point is that you shouldn't have to think too hard about it—it should just come natural." Teo positioned herself directly behind him, bringing her chin to rest on his shoulder and placing fingertips against his temples. "I knew a cipher who once told me he used to 'paint' what he wanted to convey on a canvas in his brain. Maybe you should try that."

Locking eyes with Nimic, Tobias's surroundings were drenched in the golden light erupting from behind his retinas. His emissions, as Mercy called them, were considerably less intense now than that blinding first instance in the galley. They didn't smother his other senses like they had then but were soothing—accompanied by a comforting sensation.

As per Teo's suggestion, he sketched the outline of two pulp canisters on the canvas in his mind, going on to fill in the color and detail with the same methodical approach as if physically painting them with a brush. He envisioned himself plucking the canisters out of the air and offering a palm full of nunits. Alarmingly, he could feel Nimic lurking in his psyche, watching the scene play out from somewhere deep within his conscience.

There was a moment of confusion, uncertainty. He wasn't sure he'd managed to convey anything at all, but then came Nimic's response in the form of an arresting salvo of colorful flashes: electric greens and yellows, bright blue, hot orange; he was overcome by feelings of nausea, fear, and a sudden compulsion to recoil away from something hazardous.

"You gettin' anything?" Teo asked.

"Nothing obvious. Just concepts really: death, poison, danger. I feel like I'm looking at a venomous snake or . . . a bug that might give me a deadly bite."

"It's a warning. Nimic's tryna tell you pulp is toxic to humans. Ae's warding you off from buying it."

He shuddered. "Ae's definitely achieved that . . . I feel like my skin is crawling."

"Let's try something a little more complex." Teo moved her chin to his other shoulder, seeming more comfortable touching and being around him than he ever thought she would be. "Draw Null on your canvas and picture aer holding the canisters. Think about the *Assurance* and focus on how ae's serving as a fellow crew member."

Tobias complied, using metallic shades of purple and green to detail the iridescent qualities of Null's beetle-like exoskeleton, not forgetting to include aer signature hooded poncho in the depiction.

Nimic threw aer head back and brayed jubilantly—either ae was already acquainted with Null and recognized aer or was simply enthralled by the prospect of a cohabitor serving aboard a human vessel. Ae lumbered to the chiller and retrieved two canisters, placing them delicately at Tobias's feet. After a brief lull, his emissions flared as an image cemented itself in the forefront of his awareness: eighteen sporadically arranged ovals, as clear and as vivid as if they were floating before his very eyes. The words "balance" and "fairness" arrived on his tongue, and he instantly understood that he was being given a price for the goods.

"Eighteen nunits for the pair."

Teo scoffed, folding her arms snuggly. "What a rip-off. You tell aer we ain't paying more than six per can, and that ae can take it or leave it."

The heavens opened up. Without warning, the Höllengarten unleashed a heavy deluge, draping the District of the Mouth in a blanket of vermillion precipitation. Tobias's horror was short-lived, courtesy of a speedy explanation from Teo about the mundanity of the phenomenon.

"We call it blood fall," she said, removing a tarpaulin sheet from a pouch on the burro's undercarriage and using it to protect the stowed goods from the downpour. "Makes it sound a lot more sinister than it really is. Folks around here think it means good fortune—personally, I think it's a pain in the ass."

He reflected on how interesting it was that people had now inhabited the Mouth for long enough to develop superstitions about its bizarre ecosystem. Sensing that vocalizing such an observation would be uncouth, he instead opted to simply ask, "What is it?"

"Not sure exactly. I know it helps purify the air. What with the amount of crap that gets pumped into the atmosphere by the refineries in the Harrow, we'd be keeling over, clutchin' our necks right now if it weren't for the Savior."

"Amazing," Tobias mumbled, completely engrossed. Teo took him by the hand and led him beneath the overhang of a nearby structure to take shelter. He reached out to catch the red liquid in his hand, scrutinizing the droplets as they collected on his palm. "When I first attained resonance with Null, I saw a map of the conduits . . . hundreds of them, riddling the *Novara*'s superstructure. Intentional or not, I got the sense I was being shown the roots of a plant or the veins and arteries of a circulatory system. In a way, this kind of confirms that for me; it's almost as if the Savior acts as the lungs of the Coalescence."

"That's a real nice way of putting it," Teo said, eyes brightening as they searched for his. He drew his brow together, forming a sullen expression.

"People beyond the blockade—myself included—they have no idea what it really is. They don't even try to see past its fearsome appearance. They focus their anger so intently on what it takes from us that they completely ignore what it gives in return. I understand now that it's part of the *Novara*—just as much as any other part of the ship. The problem is, not everybody has the luxury of being able to see things as I do now; I just don't know how we get people to see the light."

Teo licked the sleeve of her sweater then took his hand to wipe the blood fall off his skin. "The residue stains somethin' awful when it dries—takes a lot of scrubbing to get it out." Dropping his hand and taking on a solemn bearing, she continued, "Doesn't make a lick of sense to me, Tobias—just how many misconceptions you had about the way things are, considering who you're the son of, I mean."

His eyebrows shot up. "Is that a joke? My father gave me every misconception I have. I *never* would have gotten involved with Humanity First if it weren't for having his political rhetoric drilled into my head for the past twenty years."

"I'm not talkin' about the councilman, doofus. I mean Tabitha Edevane—your mother."

In a secluded courtyard somewhere in the Warrens, Tobias found himself staring longingly into the eyes of his mother, her image luma-cast by an emitter onto a standing glass plate erected atop a commemorative plaque in the middle of an overgrown garden.

Her image played on a loop of around seven seconds: she blinked, then smiled, tilting her head slightly before the sequence started over again. The fidelity wasn't quite up to scratch with modern projection tech, but it was decent enough that if he squinted, he could pretend she was really there, standing before him looking strikingly like Hazel: slim build with shoulder-length brown hair, her facial features soft but stern, her demeanor caring but determined.

The memorial stood near the trunk of a pear tree, its pale green leaves filling the courtyard and stretching up and beyond the four weathered walls of the enclosing buildings. The sweet smell of its produce perfumed the air, while the rotting husks of its yield lay strewn about the ground in ruby-red puddles left over by the now subsided blood fall.

Tobias reached up and plucked a plump specimen from the tangled branches, bringing it to his nose for closer inspection. "I didn't think anything grew outside of the Conservatory."

"Don't normally," Teo replied, taking a seat on a bench at the edge of the garden. "The Höllengarten gives off something close to sunlight, but it's the lack of good soil that's the problem." She kicked the ground with the heel of her boot. "I guess somebody imported this stuff from bowside of the block-ade. It's been here as long as I can remember."

Tobias's eyes fell to the text emblazoned in bronze on the cast-iron plaque. "In loving memory of Tabitha Edevane—a bridge between two worlds, two peoples lost together in the void."

Teo stood and joined him. He kept his eyes fixated on his mother's projection but felt the girl's concerned stare boring into his cheek.

"What did you know about her?" she asked in a plaintive voice.

Tobias crouched to his knees to wipe away the chalky rind of blood fall residue that had collected along the upper edge of the plaque. "Well . . . she died when I was very young—before you were born, I guess. I knew she had ties to the Mouth—doing charity work or providing some kind of humanitar-ian aid—but seeing as the people she was helping were considered enemies of the NTU, it was always a point of contention with my father. To us, it was treason; she was an embarrassment to the family name. After she passed away, I don't think we spoke about it again. I didn't know she was doing anything *this* significant—something she would be remembered or revered for."

In a surprising show of affection, Teo folded her arms on his hunched shoulders and brought her chin to rest on the back of his head, her musical voice vibrating in his molars as she spoke. "I only know what the housefather at Juniper taught us about it, but things got pretty rough after the Antonelli expansion. The human-cohab relationship was at an all-time low, and cuz of that, the Administration cut the Mouth off entirely. There was famine, disease, and a massive surge in organized crime. The situation was dire, but then Tabitha showed up. She brought enough wealth and influence to pull the district back from the brink. She helped heal some of the wounds left lingering since the Collision and managed to bring security and infrastructure to what was essentially a lawless land. Facilities like Juniper Sanctuary wouldn't have been possible without her. I and many others who grew up as Mouth rats have Tabitha to thank for . . . well, just about everything."

Transfixed by his mother's luma-cast image, he was reminded of the vision Null had presented to him in which the woman smiled, tenderly cradling an infant cohabitor. Knowing now just how widespread her influence was, and how present in the district she had been, he wondered if it had been aer intention to convey that the infant cohabitor was, in fact, ae. If so, then Null had shared aer experience of physically being in her presence, in a way, acting as a conduit for Tobias to vicariously be with her too.

Eyes tearing slightly, his voice choked, he said, "I can't believe I wasted so much time thinking of her as a traitor; I was ashamed of her, and she was a saint." He stood up and turned to face Teo, awkwardly holding her gaze. "Is that why you hated me so much when I first arrived? Not because of my involvement with Humanity First but because you expected me to be like her?"

Teo laughed. "I think it was a healthy dose of both."

"How about now?"

She shrugged. "Captain always says, 'If you judge people by their worst actions, then you'll never get a chance to see them at their best.'"

Smiling wistfully, Tobias gave a nod of acceptance. "You were right to be disappointed in me, Teo: I'm nothing like my mother. But that doesn't mean I can't try."

"You have to—for all our sakes. What you got inside that noggin' of yours, it's not a gift: it's a responsibility." She took his hand, spoke in a gentle tone. "The Divine Abyss works in mysterious ways. I'm not sure why it chose you of all people for hyper-resonance, but all I know is that you got a duty to make good use of it. Just like Tabitha, you gotta be a bridge—help unite us all and put a stop to the hatred and the violence." A somber look overcame her. "The way things are going now with Harmony and Humanity First gearing up for war, the Coalescence don't have much of a future, not if you don't play your part."

TWENTY-FOUR

Descending farther into the Vestiges, the effects of exposure to the attenuated atmosphere were beginning to take hold. Delilah felt lightheaded, her respiration labored and irregular. She contemplated retreating to the *Assurance* to then return with the appropriate breathing apparatus, but she grew more reluctant to do so as they drew closer to Greta's coordinates.

Kahu removed his jacket and tied it around his waist, revealing muscular biceps covered in faded tattoos and glistening with sweat.

"Feels like we just did the Canyon Marathon," he huffed. "I haven't been this knackered since boot camp."

Delilah tried to laugh, but sheer exhaustion turned it into a snort. "The Vestiges are rampant with conduits," she breathlessly explained. "I'm surprised they haven't been sucked completely dry. We're lucky we can breathe at all."

Kahu eyed his surroundings with a look of contempt. "Yeah . . . I consider myself very fortunate."

The passage widened into an open concourse as they transitioned from the lower maintenance block into the *Novara*'s aftmost defense sector. A century ago, these labyrinthian depths were bustling with military personnel. Now, they were completely abandoned, petrified by time, left untouched since the day the ill-fated expedition to Pasture went awry.

Kahu nodded in the direction of a shimmering blue rectangle floating upright in the air ahead. Projected from a thin slit in the floor paneling, it was a luma-cast map detailing the local area. Delilah approached to inspect the directory as it flickered intermittently, likely powered by a nearby conduit spliced into the grid.

"Point defense, main battery ingress, ordinance storage. Damn, we're really down in the nethers now."

"You think anybody's ever made it this deep before?" Kahu asked, squinting at the intricate array of corridors and chambers floating before him.

"I imagine only very few," she replied, keeping to herself the truth that she was among those who had. "Bar Vidalia's Monarchs, of course. Apparently, he's got no qualm putting people to work this close to the void."

Kahu turned to her, narrowing his eyes. "You sure we're going about this the best way, Skip? Why don't we just get the guy on the caster? I bet he'd personally bring Isaac back to the *Assurance* wrapped in a pretty pink bow if he knew the boy was one of ours. He'd probably give us another big crate of nunits too."

"I don't doubt it." She gave a dispirited shrug. "But you heard what Greta said about what he might be forcing people to do in this place."

"I get it, the boss man's got some real horrific shit going on down here. But what I don't get is how any of it's our responsibility. We worked hard to cozy up to the Governor. Now we finally got in his good books and you wanna interfere with his business? Let's just ask him to free the boy, then we can get back to work." A look of sincerity appeared on the old pilot's hoary grill. "It's not so bad having Bug and Bug-Eyed aboard, and we haven't been paid this good in months. We've got a cushy gig here—doesn't make sense wrecking it all now."

Delilah twisted her lips in deliberation—she hadn't considered the potential implications of disrupting Vidalia's operation when it came to Null and Mercy. Would they stay aboard a ship whose captain had so flagrantly crossed their master? It was unclear whether the choice was theirs to make . . .

"I haven't decided anything yet. Let's get into this capping plant, *then* we can figure out our play. If there's an alternative solution available, I promise we'll take it. But I won't stand idly by while innocent people are being trafficked and exploited. And I know you won't stand for it either, Heperi—you're a good man, as much as you might want folks to think otherwise."

"Hit the nail on the head as usual, Skip," Kahu said, giving a lopsided smile. Beneath mounds of unkempt facial hair, she imagined he might have been blushing.

Much to the old pilot's delight, their route took them into a derelict NTSC installation called the Ventral Launch Facility, or VLF. It was one of the *Novara*'s primary installations for fighter deployment, which Kahu expressed surprise at finding intact, given it was assumed destroyed during the events of the Collision. Vaulting over a set of defunct security scanners, he took point, leading the way through a lattice of dark hallways. It soon became apparent that others had come before them, as numerous hatches had been forced open, some sliced through with a fission cutter, creating a direct route through the facility toward Greta's coordinates.

From the main vestibule, they cut through the barracks—a time capsule of pre-Collision history. Delilah could almost see the specters of those who lived and worked in the facility over a century ago, carrying out their duties, happily oblivious to the devastating circumstances humanity would soon find itself in . . .

She wiped her hand on a glass briefing board, clearing away ancient scrawlings depicting various maneuvers and flight formations. "How come we thought the VLF was lost? Place looks pristine."

Kahu picked up a small sculpture of a kestrel from a bedside cabinet and began fondling it in his hand. "Well . . . just like everything else about first contact, details are a bit hazy. We know command scrambled the fleet when the *Devourer* yanked us out of ripple space, but it's said the five squadrons who were stationed down at the VLF never even made it out of the hangar. Nobody knows why. The rest is history, I guess." He went to set the model back down but opted to pocket it instead—another useless decorative trinket to stick atop the helm console.

While the barracks were a perfect snapshot of their pre-Collision state, other areas of the installation had not been left quite so preserved. The armory, for example, had been pillaged, stripped of all ammunition and fire-arms, almost certainly at the behest of the Governor. His Monarchs were skulking somewhere nearby, and by the looks of things, they would be armed to the teeth . . .

Kahu led them through the VLF's repair bay, where a fighter was suspended from the ceiling with its belly opened up and its entrails spilling into the maintenance trench below. Running his hand along its aerodynamic flight surfaces, he began a giddy explanation about how one of his wingmates flew a condor just like it back in 97 AC.

Delilah was about to tell him to cut the chatter when the loud crack of a gunshot silenced the babbling pilot midsentence.

The pair dove for cover, slamming their backs to either side of a set of partially opened blast doors, beyond which the gunfire had emanated. Delilah cursed under her breath—they'd been too loud on their approach. Vidalia's Monarchs had been alerted to their presence, and any element of surprise had now gone out the airlock. She flicked the finger lever of her repeater to charge a round, hating having to improvise but now left with no choice.

There came another shot, although this one was preceded by muffled laughter. Focusing, she detected the faint sound of music as well as a second voice, this one unmistakably female. As a third shot rang out, it dawned on her that they may not have been spotted as she had presumed. The rounds were ricocheting off metal at what sounded like relatively close range, and the voices she could hear were calm and jovial. It was either target practice or Vidalia's thugs messing around with the stock they had looted from the armory.

She peeked around the edge of the blast door to survey the terrain beyond. The repair bay connected to a vast hangar, with rows of docking bays housing a murmuration of slumbering fighters—a graveyard overflowing with the carcasses of a long-extinct avian species.

From each docking bay, launch rails extended to a wide rectangular aperture, although the shroud of night normally visible through such an opening was blocked by the sinister exterior of the *Devourer*, its engineered physiology spilling into the hangar like swollen organs bursting forth from a gaping surgical incision.

"Guess that explains why the squadrons stationed here never joined the fight," Kahu whispered. "The *Devourer* must have plugged the VLF up as soon as it grabbed the *Novara* . . . We never stood a chance out there."

The fission field that once would have protected the hangar from the vacuum of space had long since stopped receiving power. Now, the ebony mass of flesh and hull breaching through from outside was the only thing keeping the hangar airtight. Delilah traced the path of a conduit as it meandered along the flight deck, snaking between fighters and in one instance crushing the wing of a kestrel under its hulking weight. Eventually her gaze arrived at something horribly familiar: an arrangement of glow-spewing gills known as a vent; Vidalia's capping plant had been established around it. Two human Monarchs stood near a mountain of red storage crates, encircled by a perimeter of halogen work lights. One—a male—stood wearing urban camo gear with an arm outstretched, taking potshots with an NTSC-issue sidearm at a syn-beer bottle placed atop the pulse engine of the nearest kestrel. His associate—a woman with short platinum-blond hair—stood behind him, laughing and jeering in ridicule at his abysmal aim.

"Hey, Skip. Don't we know that bug?" Kahu nodded toward the third and final Monarch: a cohabitor who towered a good two feet above aer accomplices with distinctive scarring running down the side of aer face.

"That's Naught," Delilah confirmed, watching as the juggernaut loaded storage crates, presumably containing glow caps, onto a ZT-LL, short for zero-terrain load lifter—a quad bike suspended in the air via repulsor pads with a levitating flatbed in tow.

"This must be an important operation if the Governor's got his right-hand leech overseeing it," suggested Kahu.

Delilah tutted at the slur—"bug" she found endearing, but "leech" was crossing the line. "Could be. Or this is punishment for failing to stop that zealot from getting onstage at the installation ceremony."

Kahu pointed at the vent with the barrel of his unloaded Onema-77. "Hey, look! That old crone was right. Isaac *is* here."

Horrifyingly, every word of what Greta Hox had said concerning Vidalia's operations in the Vestiges had been accurate. Delilah spied the orange of Isaac's jumpsuit. On his knees with his head and shoulders completely immersed inside the conduit, the boy was reaching through the vent, making sweeping, manic motions with his arms, collecting concentrated glow in capsules before dispensing them into a storage crate. There were two others toiling beside him, similarly engrossed by the cosmic hallucinogen disgorging from their work stations but markedly more enfeebled. Delilah suspected the gaunt gray figures had been capping for a while longer than Isaac, and they served as a stark reminder of the grim fate that awaited him should she be unsuccessful.

She turned to Kahu, eyes alight with conviction. "We're putting an end to this—right now."

"I'm with ya, Skip. We got a plan, though, or you just wanna wing it?"

She dove across the blast door gap and shimmied up beside him. From her pocket she produced a silk pouch containing two wireless earbud communicators. "We're splittin' up," she said, pushing one of the devices into her ear and hearing the static purr of it powering up as Kahu followed suit. "I want you to head over to the other side of the hangar and make a distraction."

"How much of a distraction?" he asked, showing an impish grin.

"Medium stupid. Nothing too crazy. I just need you to get their attention and lead them away from the vent. Buy me enough time to get Isaac to safety."

"Gotcha. Then what about putting this place out of action for good? Any ideas?"

"None. But I'm open to suggestions."

Kahu scanned the hangar, twiddling the end of his mustache as he formulated a plan. "Think I might have something. Leave it with me."

She gave him a gentle thump on the shoulder—one of trust and appreciation. "Thank you for being here. You didn't have to see all this through with me, but it means a lot that you did."

He leaned into her, assuming a winsome smile. "The *Assurance* is everything to me, Skip. And there ain't no one else on the *Novara* I'd rather have in command of her than you. I know what the boy means to you, so helpin' get him back is the least I can do for giving me and that old hauler a new lease of life."

* * *

While Kahu headed off on his quest to cause mischief, Delilah began edging her way toward the staging area, using a succession of metal racks stocked with ordnance for cover. Eventually she came within range of the conversation taking place between the two human Monarchs.

"How much longer do you think the Governor will have us down here?" the male asked, lining up the beer bottle in his sights for another attempt.

"Wouldn't get your hopes up," the woman replied in a grating voice. "As long as this vent is spittin' out the good stuff, he'll want someone guarding it."

"Well, you'd better tell him we'll need another delivery of glow worms, stat; a couple of our cappers aren't lookin' so hot."

"They'll last us another cycle or two. No need to pester him about it just yet."

Delilah glanced at the aforementioned cappers—a middle-aged man and an elderly woman, just as feverishly enslaved to the vent as Isaac. Getting him out was obviously her priority, but hearing the other two spoken about like nothing more than empty fission cells to be discarded only strengthened her resolve—she *had* to get them out, and make sure nobody could fall prey to such unspeakable exploitation ever again. *The Governor has a lot to answer for . . .*

Pressing on, she soon ran out of cover and realized the only way forward while remaining undetected was to creep along the conduit, hiding in its shadow. Pressing her back against the alien contrivance, she felt the whorls and ridges of its irregular surface pressing into her spine. It expanded and contracted rhythmically, emitting the same ominous thrum of breathing that she had spent twelve years trying to forget . . .

She tucked her nose under the collar of her duster jacket in a pointless attempt to avoid inhaling the luminous particles now heavy in the air. She could already feel it, though: her heartbeat racing out of control, every nuance of emotion amplifying tenfold as colorful aberrations crept in around her peripheral vision. She couldn't deny it was a pleasant sensation, but that only made her detest it even more.

Focusing her attention on staying compos mentis, she didn't notice the machine obstructing her path until she kicked it with the toecap of her boot. Running her hand along its flat upper surface, she immediately recognized what it was: a hydro-ionizer—one of the very ones Vidalia had described as inoperable following their delivery. Like the one supplying his artificial river at the Çorak, it had been spliced into the conduit and was siphoning purified water. A plastic hose connected to its main outlet, looped and wreathed across the floor toward the vent where the elderly woman, kneeling beside Isaac, was using a dispenser tap to inject bursts of fluid into each cap, presumably enabling the vaporization and subsequent inhalation of the glow stored inside.

That lying snake, Delilah thought, clenching her teeth so tightly that an extra ounce of pressure might have cracked a molar. She'd been played for a fool; Vidalia knew all along she never would have gone through with the hydro-ionizer extraction had she known his true intentions. After all his platitudes about providing a lifeline to those in need, he only wanted them to serve his reprehensible enterprise. The artificial river, the installation ceremony—it had all been a ploy meticulously designed to coerce her into doing his bidding. And now, blinded by generous paydays and promises of work, she had unwittingly made a condemnable contribution to the already spiraling out of control glow crisis.

This is no longer just a rescue op. This is asset denial and repossession. Even if it means going to war with the Governor, we're taking back the hydro-ionizers and making sure they end up in the hands of those who really need them.

She lowered to a crouch, pressing her finger against her communicator to activate it. "Kahu. Are you in position?"

Kzzt. "Just about. Ready to give these goons a wake-up call?"

She drew a deep, steadying breath. "Green light."

"Alright, Skip . . . Just promise you won't be too mad, OK?"

Delilah's heart sank in her chest, which was subsequently rattled violently by the raucous sound of thruster ignition booming from across the hangar. The Monarchs were catapulted into instant panic. Naught spun around, knocking a storage crate off the ZT-LL and spilling mounds of caps onto the flight deck. Meanwhile, aer human associates scrambled to identify the source of the noise, gawking at one another with looks of pure stupefaction. With their attention elsewhere, Delilah dove out of cover and scurried around to the far side of the staging area. She slammed her back against a thrust-dispersal barricade just in time to catch sight of a kestrel clearing its docking bay and rising over the shape of the conduit.

"Heperi!" she whispered forcefully. "I said *medium* stupid! What in the name of Lei-Ghannam do you think you're doing?"

The kestrel dipped its nose and began drifting forward, kicking up a century's worth of dust with its vertical thrusters as it hovered lazily over the flight deck. The pillars of fiery propulsion from its vertical stabilizers keeping it aloft refracted into bright, prismatic geometry in the air, the glow now seriously impeding her ability to perceive reality. Even so, she could make out the old pilot's face of unbridled glee beneath the fighter's glass canopy.

Kzzt. "You wanted a distraction!" he replied, his voice smothered by the loud hum of cockpit instrumentation. "They look pretty distracted to me."

As if on cue, the gangsters abandoned their post and bolted off in Kahu's direction, leaving Isaac and the other captives completely unsupervised.

"Dammit, you old fool," Delilah hissed, seizing her opportunity and starting toward the vent. "This isn't exactly what I had in mind!"

Kzzt. "I'm sorry, Skipper. I saw this vintage birdie with her keys still in the ignition and I just couldn't help myself!"

The Monarchs halted below the hovering kestrel, shielding their faces from the downward thrust. There was a moment of shared deliberation before they simultaneously decided to open fire. A sustained hail of bullets ricocheted off the fighter's armored skin, revealing the walls and ceiling of the hangar in coruscating white light.

Kzzt. "Don't think they're too happy about my little impromptu air show, Skip," Kahu said, responding to the enemy fire with an offensive hand gesture. "You'd better pull Isaac out quick while I've got 'em in a fluster!"

But Delilah was way ahead of him. She stood behind the boy's hunched figure, readying herself to wrap her arms around his abdomen and tear him away from the conduit. She remembered how futile her attempts to pry Micah away had been—how immovable he was, how viciously he'd fought to remain in place. But she was stronger now—physically and mentally. If she had to crack this hopeless boy over the head with the stock of her repeater in order to save his life, then she was prepared to do just that.

She peered over his shoulder into the opaline abyss surging from the vent, struck by a wave of terror as she envisioned the walls of the hangar disintegrating around her. The glow was continuing to work its wicked magic, heightening her emotions to a level tantamount to neurosis. Mentally batting away her apprehensions, she lunged forward and dragged him out of the vent. Arms flailing, he whipped his head around and stared into her eyes, his face a tortured mask of despair.

Delilah, he mouthed, only air escaping from his vocal cords. He couldn't have weighed more than sixty-four kilos, but enervated by the thin atmosphere, pulling him to safety proved an exhausting task.

"What is it with you Verhoeven boys and this awful stuff?" she spluttered. "All it's good for is giving you a headache and turning you blind!"

Flinching with every gunshot, Isaac's dolorous expression transmuted into one of fear as he gradually woke up to the surrounding pandemonium.

"Ignore all that. You're safe," she cooed, doing her best to prevent him from succumbing to outright panic.

"Lei-Ghannam! I'm still in the Vestiges, aren't I? Captain . . . you have to get me out of here!"

"Stay calm. We're gettin' you home."

"I tried to leave; I promise I tried." He broke into tears. "They wouldn't let me . . . The vent—it wouldn't let me. I couldn't . . ." He trailed off, his attention stolen by Kahu's airborne antics.

"Don't get me started," Delilah groused. "For some reason that old fool thought now'd be the perfect time to take one of these ancient crates for a joyride." She produced a bandage from a utility pouch on her gun-belt and wrapped it snuggly around Isaac's hands, his palms dry and bloodied from prolonged exposure to the noxious substances inside the conduit. "At least he's keeping those Monarchs occupied."

"I wouldn't be so sure about that," cautioned Isaac. Before Delilah could decrypt what he meant, she felt the cold muzzle of a pistol pressed into the back of her neck.

"To your feet!" the female gangster ordered from behind her, having apparently returned to the staging area. "Drop that repeater and back away from the boy."

Delilah turned slowly. "OK, OK. We're just here to get our man. We didn't come looking for trouble."

"I don't give a leech's ass what you were looking for—what you found is a fight with the Governor. You know what he does to folks that try and steal from him?"

"I suspect something horrible," she countered, placing the concussion repeater at her feet, careful to position the trigger guard in reach of Isaac's shaking hands. She gave him a subtle wink; he shook his head, knowing precisely what she was proposing but stunted by hesitation. Leaving her faith in him, she stood to face the impatient Monarch, who growled, "Now tell your idiot pilot to land that fighter and walk over here with his hands up."

Delilah shrugged. "You're making a big mistake. We're on good terms with Vidalia. He won't be best pleased if anything happens to us."

"Quit yammering or else I'll blow this whelp's head clean off his shoulders." The Monarch turned her aim to Isaac. Then, her baleful expression yielded to a look of shock, the color draining instantly from her ratlike features. She was catapulted off her feet by a plume of shimmering blue energy, the time it took for her to hit the deck suggesting she'd been hurled a good ten feet or so into the air. Delilah turned to find Isaac slumped to the side with the repeater held awkwardly under his arm, its muzzle still aglow from the concussion discharge.

"Great shot, Verhoeven. I'll take it from here." She held out her hands, catching the repeater as he tossed it with a wince.

Kahu's agitated voice came squawking over the communicator again, warning that the remaining Monarchs were on their way. She didn't have time to respond. Flicking the finger lever, she charged another round, turning just in time to catch the male gangster materializing in the halogen glow of the work lights. She pulled the trigger, dispersing a focused cone of distorted reality directly into his chest. He unleashed a bloodcurdling shriek as he was sent barreling limp-bodied into the mountain of supply crates.

Kzzt. "Skip! The bug's coming your way, and it looks pissed. I've got no ordnance! There's nothing I can do!"

As if summoned from the pages of Lovecraftian horror, Naught emerged from the gloom, bobbing aer head in a birdlike motion as ae approached, aer pace steady and unrelenting. Delilah raised her repeater with another round charged and ready to fire, but before she could pull the trigger, she noticed a dull ache fulminating in the back of her skull. The unusual sensation rapidly developed into excruciating pain, like a red-hot coal searing the gray matter behind her eyes. Completely paralyzed, she watched as Naught came to a stop before her, tilting aer head and assessing her with cruel eyes devoid of emotion. This was why Kahu feared them so: their ability to incapacitate humans by way of psychic torture. As Teo had explained, it was no more than the biological by-product of resonant incompatibility. But understanding the cause of the onslaught made it no less painful to endure.

Feeling as though she could withstand no more, the world began to darken around her. Beneath the pounding of her own heartbeat, she heard Kahu's panic-stricken voice once more. "Captain! What should I do?"

Through gritted teeth, she managed a two-word response. "Maximum stupid."

Kahu swung the kestrel round, bringing its starboard side adjacent to the staging area. Naught's attention was momentarily taken by the sudden maneuver, causing the pain in Delilah's head to briefly subside. She didn't know what the old pilot was planning but readied herself for something spectacularly dangerous. Sensing Isaac behind her, she kicked him with the heel of her boot, impelling him to back away from the distracted alien. The kestrel's lateral thrusters growled as Kahu rolled the fighter on its side, scraping metal on metal as its wingtips collided with the ceiling and flight deck of the hangar. As the canopy swung open, she saw him holding himself in position with one arm while he used the other to pull a lever on the instrumentation panel. There was a sudden expulsion of smoke and fire as the kestrel's rear seat was ejected from the cockpit. Propelled by compact thrusters, it rocketed sideways across the flight deck and struck Naught with the lethal velocity of a ballistic missile. Delilah dove backward, twisting in the air to shield Isaac from the incoming projectile with her body. Burying her face into the boy's neck, she heard the roar of thruster ignition swell as Kahu clumsily realigned the kestrel's belly to the ground.

She glanced over her shoulder as the smoke cleared, finding only a fine purple mist lingering in the air where Naught had been stood, as well as a dismembered paw twitching sporadically on the floor.

"Wha . . . what happened?" Isaac mumbled as Delilah pulled the boy to his feet.

"I think we just started a war with the Governor."

Kahu arrived, out of breath and drenched in sweat. He cast his eye on the body part squirming on the ground. "Can't say I ever tried that during the expansion."

Delilah grabbed him by the neck and kissed him forcefully on the cheek.

"You incredible, ridiculous man. That was the single most amazing and idiotic thing I have *ever* seen. The Governor's gonna come at us with everything in his arsenal now, but I'll be damned if it wasn't all worth it just to see that."

"You said maximum stupid, Skip," Kahu said, throwing his hands in the air defensively. "The bug had you pinned; I didn't know what else to do."

"You did the only thing you could, and we're alive because of it. But we need to get back to the *Assurance* before Vidalia catches wind of this. She's parked right in his backyard, and he'll unleash hellfire on her the second he finds out."

There was no time to revel in their success. Kahu loaded the two hydro-ionizers onto the ZT-LL while Isaac helped Delilah pry the other addicts away from the vent. She told him to rest, but not even captain's orders could stop him from emphatically offering assistance.

Standing by a terminal, Kahu gleefully presented a lanyard with a rectangular ident pass attached.

"Swiped this when we were back in the barracks. It belonged to a pre-Collision flight commander." He raised the key card to inspect the faded image of a young woman in uniform, her rank and operating number printed beneath. "Couldn't have cracked that birdie open without it. I'm hopin' it'll give us control over the hangar's emergency decompression countermeasures too."

He swiped the pass by a nearby console to gain access. A discordant symphony of screeching metal filled the hangar as hidden machinery, dormant for over a century, groaned to life. Two immense bulkheads began closing in, sealing the launch aperture shut as they would have done automatically in the event of a fission field failure. The conduit writhed and contorted like an animal desperately trying to free itself from the closing jaws of a predator. The bulkheads slammed together, cleaving the massive alien tentacle asunder. It went still, and the glow billowing from the vent began to dissipate. Isaac was safe, and Vidalia's capping plant was no more.

TWENTY-FIVE

Sequestered on a quiet side street in the Warrens, Juniper Sanctuary was a narrow townhouse fronted by shuttered windows that looked as though they hadn't been opened in decades. Drainpipes scaled the height of the building, showing similar signs of neglect, the metal oxidized and corroded after so many years of blood fall. On the roof stood a tall pylon erected from the parts of a dismantled comms array, acting as a receiver to the strange network of undulating light that seemed to be distributing itself throughout the Mouth. Emanating from the spiraling entrance to the *Devourer*, a single luminous strand could be traced leading to the top of the residential tower known as Tycho Block, which then dispersed like a web across the district, drifting in the form of ethereal tendrils to the many other roof pylons throughout the area. Was it a power source? A means of communication? Tobias was unsure but eager to get inside and find out.

Looking ostensibly abandoned, the only indication Juniper was occupied at all was the fresh slew of chalk scribbles adorning the walls on either side of the entrance: vibrant renditions of flowers and animals long extinct and human and alien stick figures with smiling faces gallivanting beneath a cartoon starfield.

While the exterior of the building may not have looked like somewhere suitable for sheltering children, inside it earned its name as a sanctuary. It was a cozy, dimly lit refuge, every wall draped in swaths of terra-cotta fabric, every square inch of the floor covered in shag carpet and mounds of sumptuous pillows. Large glass containers filled with bundles of warm light ropes hung like lanterns from hooks in the ceiling, painting every room in a soothing luster and accentuating the ghostly wisps of incense smoke hanging in the air.

Tobias stood at Teodora's side, relishing the feelings of safety and tranquillity imbued in him by the rustic decor. It sparked a memory of building pillow forts with Hazel when they were kids, much to the annoyance of their father, of course, who had always been particularly anal about the upkeep of the furniture.

The calming atmosphere was mitigated somewhat by the presence of an interspecies gaggle of screaming children—twenty or so in number—running rampant through the halls, thrown into an excited frenzy by the arrival of guests . . .

Not just any guest, but Teodora Brižan, an ex-resident, who had apparently been given celebrity status by the current occupants. The little ones jumped and frolicked at her feet. Those capable of language chanted her name, while others squealed and brayed in delight as they took turns greeting her.

Tobias had never seen infant cohabitors before and was struck by just how ridiculously adorable they were, especially those young enough to have not yet developed their chitin exoskeletons. One tugged at the buckle strap of his canvas jacket with four grub-like digits, gazing up with inquisitive eyes that were disproportionately massive relative to the small size of aer tapering head. As he placed his hand on the nape of aer neck, it dawned on him that it was the first time he'd ever made physical contact with a nonhuman. He felt a rush of excitement as his fingertips touched soft, leathery flesh. He marveled at the cosmic strangeness of touching organic matter originating from some far-flung corner of the galaxy. The infant squinted aer eyes, emitting a purring sound in a clear show of affection.

"It would appear you have gained an admirer," Hiroki Sato postulated jovially—a man who, up until now, had been referred to by Teo only as "the housefather." He was an elderly chap of fairly short stature, sporting a knitted fleece not dissimilar in color and style to the one Teo wore, which gave Tobias cause to wonder if the garment was a handcrafted gift from the man who raised her.

Tufts of white hair perched on either side of Hiroki's otherwise bald head framed the once handsome features of his face—now tarnished by deep wrinkles and sagging skin. He suffered from an unusual vascular condition that caused the veins in his arms and face to appear strikingly prominent. Tobias knew after taking a lecture on the inevitable rise of religious sects in nascent societies that it was a sign of the man's belonging to the so-called Church of the Abyss—a group who had taken to deifying the endless night and saw Pasture as a divine afterlife accessible only by undergoing a lifetime's penance. There were a million things he wanted to ask, but bombarding the man with questions was hardly any way to make a good first impression.

"Tobias, was it?"

He looked up to meet the man's scrutinizing stare, careful not to betray that he had been studying the marks of his faith so intently.

"Yes, sir. Tobias Cole Edevane."

Hiroki shot Teo an astounded look, leaving the hand Tobias had offered to shake hanging limp in the air. "Edevane?"

Teo smiled. "That's right, this is Tabitha's son," she said softly. "He's been working aboard the *Assurance* for a while now. Came to us all the way from Quarterdeck. He's doing his part in the community, just like his ma did. In't that something?"

Tobias side-eyed the girl, surprised at her reservedness in explaining the reason for his presence. From the jubilation that consumed Hiroki, he realized the more tactful approach was really for *his* benefit rather than his own.

"Oh, Teo," the man exclaimed, clasping arthritic hands against his belly in adoration. "I just knew when you shipped off with that nice Captain Holloway that you'd be destined for great things. Look at you now: zipping up and down the *Novara*, side by side with dignitaries no less, keeping us all safe from the endless night and helping people in desperate need of it."

"Oh, tosh, it ain't all that," Teo said, pulling the sleeves of her sweater over the heels of her hands, abashed.

"Nonsense! I heard about what you did for those poor people near the Çorak, young lady. Folks around here are calling you heroes!"

"I didn't do all that much," she mumbled. "It was a cohab called Null who did most of the heavy liftin.' And if it weren't for that old flyboy Kahu, we never would have found those ionizers out in the Debris Belt."

"Regardless, ain't no bad thing getting on the Governor's good side, Teodora. You keep it up and just maybe he'll think about waiving some of that protection money we owe."

At that moment, an adult cohabitor entered the room through a set of saloon doors from what looked to be a kitchen, wearing a green pin-striped apron and dwarfing Hiroki in height twice over. Ae halted upon spotting the blue-haired salvage specialist, turning aer snout to the ceiling and trumpeting a loud whine of excitement.

"Yeah, that's right, you great big lummox," Hiroki said, rolling his eyes and waving aer over. "Look who decided to pay us a visit."

"Nanimonai!" Teo exclaimed, spreading her arms wide as the cohabitor bounded across the room toward her. Ae plucked her off the ground and brought her into an impassioned embrace, the young girl all but disappearing into aer large biceps.

Hiroki exhaled in a show of impatience. "Come now, put her down or you'll suffocate the poor thing." He turned his attention to the children. "Isn't this wonderful? Our beloved Teodora has returned to our humble sanctum, bringing with her the son of a saint, no less. I'd say this calls for a celebration, wouldn't you agree?"

"Way ahead of you," Teo said, handing over her keys. "The burro is stocked up and parked out front. Take whatever you need." A wide smile appeared on her heart-shaped face. "Let's feast."

While Hiroki and Nanimonai busied themselves in the kitchen, Tobias joined Teo on a deep-seated sofa in the playroom. They sank almost fully reclined into the threadbare fabric, watching the little ones prance and gambol at their feet in appreciative silence. A human girl and a young cohabitor had scaled the backrest behind them and were in the process of undoing Teo's untidy plait and tentatively reorganizing it into an intricate crown braid. Staying statuesquely still so as not to complicate the delicate procedure, she directed Tobias to retrieve the plastic bag of confectionery given to them by Mauve in the markets from her satchel and hand it out to the kids. A tremendous crash arrived from the kitchen—the clangor of plates and cutlery falling to the white-tiled floor, followed by Hiroki's muffled shouts of irritation.

"In the name of the Divine Abyss! Will you watch what you're doing, you insufferable oaf! I told you to be careful with the good porcelain!"

Teo rolled her eyes and gave a stifled chuckle, careful not to move her head too much. Tobias turned to her. "Go on then. What's their story?"

"Hiroki and Nanimonai? They're partners."

"Partners?" he echoed with a look of feigned revulsion.

"Not like that, sicko! They run the place together; they have done since way before I was born."

"So . . . is Hiroki a cipher then?"

Teo shook her head gently. "No. His wife, Yua, she was the resonant one. Problem was, they used to live together in a Church of the Abyss commune, and COTA have some pretty scary beliefs when it comes to ciphers. They had managed to keep it a secret for a long time when Hiroki's niece, who was also resonant, got found out. They all escaped together and settled here in the Warrens. Eventually, Yua got ciphered up with Nanimonai. Much to Hiroki's annoyance, ae basically moved in—one big happy family! It was then, I guess, that they met your mother. Hiroki expressed his interest in creating a sanctuary for others like Yua and his niece seeking refuge from COTA. Obviously, it ended up becoming so much more than that."

"So, where is Yua now?" Tobias asked.

Teo's delicate features were weighed by sadness. "I never got a chance to meet her . . . She got sick during that alien flu outbreak, back in 107 AC— same as your mother, I guess."

Tobias felt a sinking feeling in his chest—the devastating realization that he had never truly mourned his mother's loss. Feeling two decades of missed grief condensed into a single heart-wrenching instant, he could attest that he certainly mourned her now.

"She passed away," Teo continued. "Leaving these two with the joint responsibility of keeping the doors open. They can't stand each other most of the time; you'd definitely be forgiven for thinking they were a married couple."

"I don't understand," Tobias admitted, running a hand through his hair to physically dispel the agonizing thoughts of his mother. "How is it they manage to work and live together if they can't communicate? I thought cohabitors were incapable of language?"

Teo tutted loudly. "It's not that they're *incapable*—their brains just aren't wired that way. There's no need for language when you already know what's in everybody's head all the time. And anyway"—she shrugged—"you don't *need* to understand what someone's saying in order to treat 'em with dignity or respect, do you? What about all my cohabitor siblings? You don't think we couldn't manage to live harmoniously just cuz we couldn't talk to one another?" She reached over her head and gave the infant cohabitor straddling the backrest behind her a gentle squeeze on the arm. "Besides, these kids need looking after—I'd say that transcends any language barrier Hiroki and Nanimonai might have between 'em."

Tobias lowered his stare, allowing Teo's ever-pertinent insights to mull in his mind.

Evidently, sentient life—no matter how anatomically disparate—requires very similar basic emotional needs. Acceptance, compassion, a sense of place—sentiments that once felt distinctly human but really are essential for any creature with the capacity for self-awareness to feel fulfillment of any kind. The physical traits that make the Prey so fearsome in appearance are purely superficial—cosmetic evolutionary responses to the hostile environment they developed in. But what they carry inside of them—their soul—it's no different from the sense of presence we feel behind our eyes and in our chest. Whether your skeleton is on the inside or the outside of your body, sentient life is bound by consciousness—it's the filament holding the universe together.

The infant cohabitor who had taken an interest in him earlier reappeared, jolting him from his reverie. Ae dropped a toy gingerly in his lap—an antique action figure sculpted in the shape of a twenty-first-century astronaut, its paint chipped and faded. The little one pointed at the bag of sweets sitting on the sofa's armrest, thrusting aer other paw forward with digits splayed out expectantly. He didn't know what their mental capacity was at such a young age, but he could be sure at least that this one understood the basic concept of trade. Faint emissions began to gather in his peripheral vision, but the bond wasn't strong enough for anything to be ascertained or conveyed. He got the sense that just as he was still learning how to control his resonance, so too was the juvenile cohab standing at his feet.

"I can't imagine what it must have been like growing up here," he said, fingering out a green ball from the bag and handing it to the patient child. Ae snatched it hungrily and scurried off, likely in search of some other trinket with which to barter.

"Weren't all bad," Teo chirped. "Growin' up as a Mouth rat, I mean. Sure— it was a big responsibility, all of us having to chip in to make ends meet. Anybody with decent enough skills was encouraged to use 'em in order to put dinner on the table. Personally, I always had a knack for sniffing out valuable tech and just knowing how to take it apart. There's an emergency trapdoor in the dining room over there that'll take you down to the Vestiges. I used to use it to sneak down from time to time, as you could always count on there being good, sellable junk deep in the nethers."

Tobias nodded his acknowledgment, recoiling inwardly at the horrific notion of a young girl forced underground to dig for scrap out of pure necessity.

"I ended up getting pretty handy with salvage," Teo continued. "As it turned out, it was somebody handy with salvage that Captain Holloway wanted on her ship. So, I guess I'm grateful in a way. The *Assurance* is home now, and if it weren't for all that grafting, I may never have found my place on Delilah's crew."

She glanced sideways into the kitchen. "Hiroki and Nanimonai made this place as much of a home as they could with what little they had, which was a whole heap of love but not much else."

"What about the aid my mother provided? Surely that must have helped?" Tobias felt woefully ill-informed to be making such an inquiry but far too curious to hold his tongue.

"Well, yeah . . . I'm sure it did help, once upon a time," Teo rebutted. "Housefather says Tabitha helped build a network of support centers like this one throughout the Mouth, but when she died the financial support stopped. The centers that didn't close down had to be kept runnin' by the folks she left in charge. Hiroki and Nanimonai have been maintaining this place out of pocket ever since. The rest of them were either shut down or are run by the Governor now. I got no idea what a crook like Drexen wants with food banks and homeless shelters, but I doubt it's anything good."

Tobias felt his face twist into a poorly repressed scowl, coming to the realization that if the monetary aid *did* cease after his mother succumbed to infection, leaving the humanitarian centers she had worked so hard to establish destitute and fending for themselves, then there was only one man who could be responsible . . . Atherton Edevane was a megalomaniac when it came to his finances; he would have been acutely aware of where the money was going, which made it all the more abhorrent that he'd seemingly elected to cut funding after her death. Whatever it cost to run Juniper Sanctuary for a week would have been loose change to him, but instead of carrying on the good work she started, he chose to demolish her legacy, ensuring that a generation of children who could have known the same privileges and advantages Tobias and Hazel had were left knowing only hunger and deprivation.

He felt sick to his stomach, angry, and ashamed. He didn't know if he would ever return to the Upperdecks, but if he did, he would have a few choice words for his father . . .

"You OK over there?" Teo asked. "Look like you're about to burst a blood vessel."

"I'm fine," he mumbled, knowing the words were in stark contrast to his crestfallen expression. "It just doesn't make any sense—how I could have grown up in such abundance while there's people like yourself on the same ship barely managing to survive? It's that damned blockade! My whole life I thought it was there to keep us safe, but all it really does is create ignorance. It lets oblivious idiots like me bury our heads in the rubble, so we can swan about on Capella Promenade wearing tuxedos and drinking expensive cocktails, playing blind to anything that makes us feel remotely guilty or the slightest bit uncomfortable."

Teo nodded. "It's always represented a symbol of oppression to us. Used to think long and hard about how I'd go about bringing it down—storming the Upperdecks and liberating all my fellow mouthians. But I ain't stupid—Harmony wants the same thing, and all they've managed to do is get people killed . . . Mutiny ain't the right way to go about it."

"No . . . I fear it's not that simple."

"How do you mean?"

"Well, we abolished the role of captain some years after the Collision to stem the tide of tyrants abusing their powers for personal and political gain. After seeing how the NTNN is bending the truth about the Mouth and its inhabitants—spreading disinformation en masse, it's become clear to me that a dictatorship is exactly what we've ended up with. Although, I fear Administrator Vargos has become something far worse than just a ruthless despot. History tells of how the most dangerous tyrants were not those who ruled with an iron fist but those who wielded and manipulated the red tape to their advantage. Tyranny by way of meticulous bureaucracy is much harder to eradicate than a simple force to be reckoned with."

"So you're saying it's hopeless, then?" Teo said, plaintive and sorrowful. "Lei-Ghannam! I don't know where you learned to be so negative all the time, but you definitely *didn't* get it from Tabitha."

"No . . . not hopeless," he clarified. "It's just very difficult to bring reform to a system that's been in place for so long when those in power still have so much to benefit from it." Thinking about how aghast his father would be to hear his own son uttering such anti-Union sentiments, he continued, "If something is to be done, then it won't be a straight-up fight. I know the Administration inside out; it's built to withstand an attack on any and all fronts. Vargos's power is the unquestioning and unwavering support of the citizens of the NTU; only if she loses their support does she lose her power."

"How, though? How do we get so many to change their minds?"

"I don't know if we can."

"Ugh! So negative!" Teo repeated, the lines of her face drawn in deep understanding, as if she'd known him for a lifetime already: his flaws, his follies—she saw them all. And yet, there was acceptance in her expression—a comprehension of his character that he wasn't sure even *he* possessed.

Thankfully, the infant cohabitor returned with new goods to trade, affording him a swift escape from her penetrating stare. The child dropped aer new offering in his lap—this one a small ceramic globe attached to a brass stand.

"Is that Pasture?" Teo asked.

"No. Earth," he answered abruptly, thinking it unconscionable to not immediately recognize the blue and green splodges delineating the landmasses of home.

The little cohab thrust aer paw forward impatiently, incensed by the long delay in receiving payment for the exchange. Tobias fished out another tiny ball of alien-friendly chocolate, which the fledgling merchant seized before scurrying away once more.

He walked his fingers across the sphere from one continent to another. "My dad has one just like it in his parlor—a lot bigger, mind you. I used to like spinning it when I was a kid and then dropping my finger at random. I'd try to imagine what it used to look like wherever I landed: Was it cold, warm? Grassy, sandy? Could you see the horizon? Could you smell the ocean?"

"Huh . . . Why would you wanna go and keep a map of a dead planet?"

He turned to her, furrowing his brow. "It's not just a dead planet! Earth was the cradle of humanity. I think it deserves a little more reverence than that." He held the globe up before his face. "This is our history, our heritage . . . where we came from and where we've been—we have to keep these things in our memory so they can help guide our way into the future. Lost out here in the black, it's easy to forget who we used to be. Keeping mementos like this close to our hearts can help remind us."

Teo rolled her eyes. "Sorry, but I don't need some dusty old relic to tell me what it means to be human. I know exactly who I am."

He shook his head ardently. "The great nations of this world came together to build the *Novara*. Our ancestors worked tirelessly through a system-wide cataclysm so that we could survive. Don't they deserve to be remembered for the fresh start they died to give us?"

"Of course they do. But if we spend all our time pining for the past when no one today even lived it, we're liable to miss what's right here in front of our noses." She waved her arm, gesturing around the room at the exuberant mass of human and alien children at play. "I don't care about where we've been— where we're headed, Tobias, that's what matters."

TWENTY-SIX

Uargos's metal messenger marched Eamon through the blockade at gunpoint and abandoned him unceremoniously on the main landing platform. Other than an acerbic order to surrender his firearm, he was given no further instructions—only informed in a monotone voice that his council status had been revoked and any attempts to contact the top brass would be suitably ignored.

Vargos had alluded to an upcoming council summit in which the severity of his crimes would be determined and his fate decided, but the complete indifference with which the grenadier left him to rejoin its mechanical brethren gave him cause to suspect that no such summit would ever take place. He no longer worked for DMED, and his Phalanx status had been officially withdrawn; it was as though he had never been employed by the Administration, as though his twenty-plus years of service to the Union had been nothing more than an incredibly lucid fever dream. To Vargos, he was little more than a fly in the ointment, and she had plucked him out and discarded him accordingly.

Like the other commuters boarding the bow-bound Canyon tram from Zharady Station, he was now just a civilian—one with the dead-eyed zombies, faces buried in their feathers, content in being force-fed an unrelenting stream of partisan hyperbole curated by social media algorithms written expressly to divide and galvanize them.

These folks have no hope, he groused, turning his attention to the tram's info screen, which was currently displaying an NTNN live feed of a Humanity First presentation taking place in the main lecture hall at ACS. That suited charlatan, Bhaltair Abernathy, was onstage, the stench of cheap aftershave somehow managing to breach through the glass of the panel and assault his nostrils. Uncharacteristically, the man was keeping his mouth shut, instead allowing his tenacious new protégé, Miss Caleb Callaghan, to lead the discussion. Eamon had reason to suspect her of being one of Tobias's accomplices during Humanity First's guerrilla assault on the pulp refinery in the Langrenus Harrow, recognizing the tumble of fiery ringlets resting on her shoulders as the same he'd seen fleeing past the garrison and disappearing into the Phalanx compound. Out of some misguided sense of loyalty, Tobias had refused to give her up during Eamon's initial interview—not that a disgraced ex-marshal was in any kind of position to do anything about it had he complied.

"*So, believe me when I say that, perhaps like some of you, I used to be a skeptic myself,*" Miss Callaghan said, holding a microphone with one hand and offering the other pleadingly to the audience, white luma-cast vine leaves crawling up her arm. "*All I'm asking is that you give Mr. Abernathy a chance to prove to you, as he has done for me, that separation doesn't have to be science fiction. If we aspire for a day to come when our children's children can breathe fresh air and play beneath clear blue skies, if the human remnant has any hope of truly one day reaching the Grasslands of Pasture, then separation is not a choice; it is a necessity. Separation, or extinction.*"

The audience became a tempestuous ocean of forest-green uniforms as the countless young minds in attendance gave the utterly diabolical statement a standing ovation. Obviously, this spectacle was Bhaltair's latest ploy to target a younger demographic, and, dismayingly, it appeared to be working. Humanity First was no longer a fringe organization—the taboo surrounding them had been all but eradicated. There was, of course, no mention in Caleb's impassioned speech of Abernathy dispatching the more impressionable of his acolytes to commit acts of domestic terrorism in the District of the Mouth. That part of their manifesto, it would seem, remained omitted from the discourse. This constituted far tamer retheorizing than the group had demonstrated previously; it was no wonder a naive kid like Tobias Cole Edevane got swept up in it all—beguiled by pretty-sounding pseudo-philosophy and thinly veiled provincialism. With Harmony gathering strength in the Mouth and Humanity First winning the hearts and minds of the good people of the NTU, civil war seemed inevitable at this point. Infuriatingly, Eamon was the only poor idiot on the *Novara* who could apparently see the sunrise. He couldn't help but feel that someone or something elusive was pulling the strings on both sides, engineering the discord like somebody playing themself in a game of chess. To what end, he couldn't possibly fathom. All he knew was that if he didn't get to the bottom of it soon, the Coalescence would be engulfed in a lasting conflict that would make the Antonelli expansion look like a pissing match.

He turned his attention away from the panel to avail his tired mind of the troubling hypothesis. From his breast pocket, he fished out the plastic bag containing the endo-chit Faye Lucero had removed from beneath the skin on Anaya Lahiri's arm. If there *were* answers to be found, then he suspected he held them in the palm of his hand. He still had to find out which of Anaya's personal terminals it was encoded to before he could unlock its secrets, and he figured her residences would be as good a place to start looking as any. A cursory search on the Nov-Net revealed she had lived uptown before her death: Festa Heights, to be precise—an upper-class residential ward built into the starboard-side Canyon wall, nestled just below Capella Promenade—exactly the type of neighborhood where one would expect to find an ex-Administration official marinating in their accrued wealth after a lifetime of dedicated service to the Union. Unless, like Anaya, your last act was to blow the lid off some of the Administration's more scandalous dealings. In which case, the only thing you end up marinating in is your own body fluids, your corpse left maimed in a dismal alleyway to wrongfully imply cohabitor involvement.

I can't promise I'm in any position to bring those responsible for your death to justice, Anaya. But at least I can make damn sure people know the truth about what really happened to you.

The tram terminated at the Silk River Concourse, where he alighted and finished the remainder of the journey on foot. Before long, he had immersed himself in the cream-cladded hallways and flashy terraces of Festa Heights— as far removed from the dank, dingy confines of Tycho Block as one could hope to find themselves.

For privacy reasons, Anaya's Nov-Net listing didn't specify her exact address, but it didn't take him long to find it. The penthouse floor flourished several duplex condos—the door to one of which was covered in diagonal lengths of LCD crime scene tape. Its presence suggested there were likely no Phalanx personnel inside at present but also meant the forensic lab coats had already had their way with the place.

Hopefully there's somethin' left to find.

He pulled away the strips of translucent material, which flashed trespass warnings in electric blue and red, and checked over his shoulder for any sign of onlookers.

The door was locked, but the cinderkey stored in his wallet, which had failed to gain him access to apartment 2801, would have little trouble persuading it. The jerry-rigged key card slid through the door's locking mechanism like a hot knife through butter. He raised his jacket to stem the plume of metallic miasma erupting from the receptacle, wary of setting off any nearby smoke detectors. He pushed lightly on the door with fingers spread wide, causing it to swing open with ease.

*Second time breaking and entering in a week, Wyatt. You plannin' on
makin' a habit outta this?*

Cautiously, he entered a narrow landing that brought him into the main
living space: a capacious lounge with a sleek kitchenette situated in back,
facing a glass-curtain wall. What would have been a dazzling view of the
Canyon was obscured, somewhat, by a veil of cascading water falling from
above, which he soon realized was the result of the artificial beach that ran
the length of Capella Promenade. Rippling azure shapes danced across the
room as vehicles zipped by, their headlights refracted by the screen of falling
water.

"Shit," he rasped, the hushed expletive amplifying as it ricocheted off the
barren walls and varnished floor. He was exasperated, if a little unsurprised,
to find the spacious apartment completely empty. The stone-gray walls were
bare, each room totally devoid of possessions and furniture. The place had
been systematically and meticulously gutted, leaving no trace that it had ever
been inhabited in the first place.

Another empty apartment, he thought, bowing his head in defeat. As
always, whoever was pulling the strings behind all this was one step ahead
of him. Whichever device Anaya had encoded the endo-chit to had been
impounded, the information it contained likely destroyed. He took two
ponderous steps toward the glass curtain, turning his eyes up to frown at
his disheveled reflection, the bags under his eyes so heavy and swollen they
almost overtook his entire face.

Something caught his eye: a small rectangular indentation pressed into
the windowpane. It sat at the center of a nest of hair-thin geometric lines,
which fanned outwards like a pixelated spider's web. Closer examination
revealed tiny metal pins nestled at its base, suggesting it was, in fact, an electronic socket of some kind.

Trying not to get his hopes up, he fumbled the endo-chit from his pocket
and placed it in the palm of his hand. Evidently, there was some method of
magnetization afoot, because lining the chit up with the socket caused it to
jump clean out of his fingers. A chime sounded as it slotted itself in position,
the glass curtain turning opaque and enveloping the empty room in off-white
light. He stepped back as the logo for Sinegex Systems—the tech conglomer-
ate responsible for most modern computronics on the *Novara*—appeared.
The newly formed screen then displayed a high-fidelity mirror image of the
room he presently stood in. Except, as if he were gazing through a window
into an alternate reality, the space was cluttered with furniture and belong-
ings. Anaya's reflection stood in the exact same spot as him, her face distorted
in torment, her wavy black hair capitulating to streaks of gray, and her light

brown complexion succumbing to pallor. It was only a prerecorded message, but still there was something deeply unnerving about seeing her alive, as if finding himself confronted by her ghost.

The metal cart standing beside her housed a collection of surgical tools and medical supplies. His initial assessment was that she had paid some unscrupulous physician to illegitimately insert the endo-chit, but surprisingly, it looked as though she was preparing to do it to herself. Wiping a sterilizing swab on her arm, she glanced up and said, "Well . . . if you're watching this, then I guess I'm dead. Whether it was you, or whether it was somebody else, I just hope it was done clean."

Eamon mentally shook his head. *Sorry, Anaya. Those sadistic bastards let the empty black in on you then butchered you up with a fission shank. Wasn't anything clean about it.*

She exhaled slowly, the escaping air quivering as it left her throat, violent tremors coursing through her hunched body. Here was a woman burdened with knowledge that she knew forces greater than her would kill to keep concealed. And yet, she knew she had a duty to disclose it, even if it meant bringing about her own inevitable demise.

She turned her attention to the cart and picked up a surgical knife. Touching the metal to her arm, she paused. "If by some miracle whoever's watching this *isn't* on the Administration's payroll, you need to listen. I have critical information that *must* be distributed en masse."

Realizing this might be the only opportunity he'd get to hear the message, Eamon took out his feather and hit record. "Keep talking, Anaya. I'm all ears."

"This might be difficult to hear, but it's imperative people know the truth about the terrorist cell called Harmony gaining a foothold in the District of the Mouth. They're multispecies: cohabitors *and* humans. If that comes as a surprise to you, don't worry—I wouldn't expect to hear about this on the NTNN. It seems to suit the Administration much better if the general consensus is that it's the 'leeches' who are solely responsible for the mayhem going on over there."

Eamon took a heedful glance over his shoulder to ensure nobody had entered the premises after him. "You're singing my song, Anaya. Now let's pick up the tempo and get to the chorus."

Apparently unable to bring herself to make the first incision, she sighed, dropping the knife back in its place on the cart in visible frustration, her timorous demeanor tightening into one of contempt.

"The reason the higher-ups are so reluctant to publicly acknowledge the existence of this organization might be because they are secretly funding it. I have reason to believe the leader of this insurgency—a woman who goes by the alias of 'the Composer'—is actually a government agent. She has been planted in the District of the Mouth to sow destruction and chaos as a means of manipulating public opinion *against* the cohabitors—in effect strengthening the case for continued segregation. That way, the Administration can continue to reap the many financial and infrastructural benefits of symbiosis with the *Devourer* while keeping the cohabitor population under stringent regulation."

Eamon felt the weight of his jaw hanging slack below his face, his innards contorting in shock and anguish. Dr. Lucero was right—it wasn't a conspiracy theory after all. But she had barely even scratched the surface—silencing one whistleblower was, apparently, the very least of what Vargos was embroiled in. His chest swelled with indignation, his thoughts drawn to the men, women, and others killed in the attack at the Phalanx compound—countless innocents massacred, and for what? Power, political gain? This wasn't some government scandal Anaya had cottoned on to—it was totalitarianism, and there wasn't a doubt in his mind that the powers that be had executed her for her discovery.

Anaya drew a quick breath, picked up the knife once more, and hastily made a small cut just below her inner elbow. A meandering stream of thick blood made its way down to her wrist, trickling to the floor and forming a tiny puddle of dark crimson. Eamon looked down to find a mottled-brown stain on the wood next to his foot. A grim reminder that the terrified woman projected before him was perhaps hours away from a barbaric execution.

Wincing at the pain, she continued, "I've seen documents pointing to multiple meetings between this Composer and Administrator Vargos herself. There wasn't much in terms of identifying information that I could ascertain about the insurgent leader. I know that she's a cipher—I've seen correspondence mentioning the cohabitor she's in league with: serial number 241089RB."

Eyes widening in astonishment, Eamon rewound the recording on his feather by a second or two, making sure it had captured that last piece of intel. A serial number wasn't exactly a smoking gun—cohabs almost never stuck to the numeric identifiers given to them during processing. Only the ship's manifest could assist him in linking the code with the self-given moniker of the nonhuman person in question, which would be impossible to access while suspended from duty.

He put a mental pin in that thought, turning his attention again to Anaya, who, cleaning the incision with a sterilizing wipe, said, "Looks like they were known to law enforcement already—held in custody a few years back under contraband charges. Now the two of them are hybridizing human and *Devourer* tech to create weapons of mass destruction. Vargos is making sure that in the event of a genuine uprising, she has a powerful deterrent."

Eamon placed a hand on his breast pocket, feeling the shape of the spliced cable beneath the syn-leather of his jacket. The combined weaponry used in the blockade attack was like nothing he'd seen before: precise, vicious, and lethally efficient. It made perfect sense Vargos would be secretly funding research and development into this technological frontier to gain the upper hand. But there was something that didn't add up . . .

The Composer and 241089RB used this hybridized technology of theirs to override a grenadier's core directives. Why in the stars would the Administrator be subsidizing the illicit reprogramming of her own mechanical infantry? Anybody wielding that kind of technology would have instant command over an indomitable fighting force and could incite mass mutiny or a military coup at the press of a button.

Clearly there was something else at play here, something that perhaps even Vargos herself was not yet privy to. Only one thing was certain: he *had* to get into that manifest. Only then could he uncover the location of 241089RB and somehow get a warning out to Jyn.

Anaya glanced at the space behind him. "There's a wall safe over there. Inside you'll find a quantum drive containing invoices and correspondence that should corroborate all of this. I only hope *they* don't find it first . . . If they do, all you have is my word."

Eamon followed her despairing gaze to find a gaping hole in the wall behind him, as if an enormous fist had punched through the plaster and scooped out a perfectly square section. If there was a safe there before, it was gone now.

"Your word is as good as any," he whispered, unsure what the drive in question would have done to improve his situation. It would take a lot more than the releasing of a few redacted documents to expose Vargos. She would be well equipped to discount the veracity of any such leaking of information, and by playing his hand prematurely, he would only open himself up to further defamation.

The makings of a plan began to formulate in his mind. There were a number of government officials with whom he'd had dealings in the past who would have had access to the manifest, almost none of whom he could be certain wouldn't immediately shop him to the authorities. But then there was Delilah Holloway, captain of the *Assurance*. Since her hauler was commissioned for weld and salvage by the Administration, he suspected she would have access to a few low-clearance government directories—the ship's manifest being one of them. The location of the *Assurance* had become somewhat difficult to pin down in recent days, what with the captain inexplicably managing to move her ship through the blockade at will. She would still have to check in at the docks at some point if she hoped to keep her docking permit. Perhaps it was time to check in with the *Assurance*'s crew—*Maybe see how the Edevane kid is getting on.*

Eyes pleading for help, Anaya concluded the message with a heartfelt warning, advising that anybody armed with the knowledge she possessed was a target and likely in mortal danger. Eamon humbly accepted her advice. "You're a damned hero in my books, Anaya," he said somberly. "I wish like hell I'd known you in life."

The recording ended, and he was left in silence. As Anaya's specter disappeared and the window returned to its transparent state, something became visible that he hadn't been able to see through the images cast on the glass curtain. A scintillating green light, originating from the opposite side of the Canyon. It ignited the screen of falling water as it passed through, creating emerald aberrations that were almost blinding to look directly at. He felt a rush of adrenaline as it quickly dawned on him that it wasn't a light that had drawn his attention: it was a laser.

Not just any laser . . . a weapon's sight.

He'd already begun a frantic dive for cover by the time he saw the muzzle flash. A burst of light in the shape of a three-pronged star, emanating from the same distant point as the laser, momentarily illuminated the living room. Half a second later, the window disintegrated into a surging mass of fragmented glass and water vapor. Falling to his side, he slammed against the floor, feeling the air above him displaced by the passing of a high-caliber round, tiny splinters of glass striking his cheeks. There was an almighty crack as the sound of the shot arrived from across the Canyon, followed shortly by the sharp whistle of the round ricocheting off something solid. A guttural sound left his throat—an involuntary reaction to the concoction of shock and relief coursing through him. The dive had saved his life; a second later and he would have been as dead as Anaya. But while he had narrowly avoided getting skewered by a sniper round, lying on the floor, he was still dangerously exposed to the mystery marksman, and it was a safe bet they were already lining up a second shot.

He jumped to his feet and bolted for the door, feeling another projectile screaming past, missing his shoulder blades by an inch. The visceral pang of another gunshot rang out, then another, echoing throughout the Canyon and chasing him back down the landing.

He exploded out of the condo, slamming his back against the adjacent wall and stopping to catch his breath. As the adrenaline flooding his system began to subside, he noticed a dull ache to the right side of his midriff. Clutching the source of the rapidly intensifying pain, he glanced down to find his trembling hand soaked in blood.

TWENTY-SEVEN

T he dinner bell rang. Teo recruited a handful of the older kids to help herd the little ones together while Tobias assisted the two bickering chefs with transporting the grub into the dining room.

Carrying a stainless steel tub containing mounds of fragrant rice and pan-seared greens, he followed them into a space that resembled no dining room in which he'd previously eaten. In lieu of any chairs or tables, an elliptical ring of floor pillows lay arranged concentrically around a repurposed ventilation funnel. Hanging from the ceiling like an inverted chimney, it belched resplendent plumes of swirling orange and violet with ribbons of plasma orbiting like the magnetosphere of a planet. He was reminded of the pylon he'd spotted on the roof earlier in the day, as well as the spectral strands the structure appeared to be channeling into the building like a wave guide. Undoubtedly, the remarkable centerpiece before him was related in some way, but still its exact purpose evaded him.

The children—or the junies, as Teo had affectionately dubbed them— were remarkably well-behaved; they sat cross-legged, patiently waiting as Hiroki and Nanimonai ladled food onto their plates. The humans received generous helpings of cultivated meat, rice, and vegetables, while the infant cohabitors were given portions of steaming Höllengarten pulp directly from one of the canisters purchased from the markets.

It was a veritable feast, and Tobias felt a real sense of achievement knowing they would be far better nourished, thanks to their donation of foodstuffs. Those feelings of accomplishment were tainted somewhat by the nagging supposition that one hearty meal was barely enough to provide the drastic quality-of-life improvements they deserved. Atherton may not have deemed Juniper a worthy cause for charity, but Tobias had his own share of the Edevane family wealth, and he vowed in that moment that these children would receive every single nunit denied them by his father, and that his mother's support, which had since ceased, would resume effective immediately.

Finally sitting down to eat, he found himself sandwiched in between Hiroki and Nanimonai—almost certainly by the design of Teodora, who sat on the opposite side of the ring, telegraphing with a mischievous smile that he should expect imminent interrogation.

Hiroki appeared to wait right until he had a mouth full of rice before precipitating conversation. Leaning in close, the old man said, "That girl is a real treasure, you know?"

Caught off guard, Tobias hastily chewed his mouthful. "Oh, you don't have to tell me that."

Hiroki leaned toward him, bringing the tip of his bulbous nose uncomfortably close to his cheek. "If you *ever* do anything to hurt her," he whispered, "I will hunt you down, gut you like the cowardly slug you are, and hang you by your entrails."

Tobias turned his head to meet the man's dissecting glower. Evidently, the mild-mannered old man he'd shared pleasant conversation with in the playroom had been but a facade—the housefather was far savvier than he had initially let on.

"I assure you, that won't be necessary, Mr. Sato," he replied, choosing his words with great care.

Hiroki sharpened his gaze. "Oh, I'm not so sure . . . You see, I happen to know who you really are, my boy."

"Who I really am?"

"Indeed. You, Tobias Cole Edevane, are your father's son—an Edevane boy if ever I saw one." The man sneered, looking him up and down disparagingly. "I know your type, I know your associations and I know the *real* reason Marshal Wyatt dumped you on Captain Holloway, and it certainly wasn't because you came to the Mouth on the pretense of some phony humanitarian pilgrimage." He reached over toward Nanimonai and scooped up a handful of the orange sustenance from aer plate, bringing the repugnant goop before Tobias's nose.

"Refined pulp is difficult enough to come by as it is," he bitterly explained. "The last thing these kids need is some self-entitled swine from the Upperdecks dropping a harvester on one of the very few remaining places we can reliably source it. Now, I don't know what your intentions are, running about the district with little Teo, but you better believe I've had to crack a few skulls to keep my litter safe over the years. And let me tell you now, Mr. Edevane, I have *no* reservations about cracking one more. Not even one with a net worth such as your own."

He angrily returned his partner's dinner to aer plate. Nanimonai gave a perfunctory snort before continuing with aer meal.

Tobias dipped his head in shame, casting troubled eyes around the dining room at the innocent victims of his crimes.

"I'm not here to cause trouble," he said, pushing a chunk of broccoli around his plate. "There's nothing I can say to exonerate myself from what I have done. I know how wrong it was now, but I didn't then—I've learned so much since coming aboard the *Assurance*, since meeting Teo. I could never forgive myself, so I certainly don't expect those directly affected by my actions to forgive me either. All I'm asking for is an opportunity to prove that I can be better—a chance to pay restitution for the damages I've done."

Hiroki's hostile expression softened and his demeanor gradually returned to that of a kindly old man. Tobias waved a hand around the dining room. "And regarding this place, I promise I have every intention of picking up where my mother left off. I—"

Hiroki shook his head in fervid defiance. "No! Teo may have given you the benefit of the doubt, but you have a lot more to prove to me before I allow you to claim your mother's mantle so easily. Tabitha built this place from rubble out of the pureness of her heart while suffering vilification by everyone she knew as a traitor and a sympathizer. She quite literally worked herself to death in order to keep Juniper Sanctuary running. So if you came here hoping to fill her boots, then you should know they're about ten sizes too big for the likes of you."

"I know, Housefather. But if it's all the same to you, I'd still like to try."

Hiroki sighed, wearing a playful look of exasperation. "Well, my boy, I suppose for all the ways in which you fail to measure up to her, there's one thing you have that she did not."

"What's that?"

"Why, the gift, boy!" The old man tapped his temple. "You are a reader, are you not?"

Tobias gritted his teeth, no longer needing to wonder where Teo had learned to be so irksomely perceptive.

"Teodora told me to keep it quiet for the time being."

"Did she now?" Hiroki afforded Teo, who was presently helping the little boy sitting beside her cut up his meat, a rueful smile.

"How did you know?" Tobias asked.

"What? You think because your eyes aren't shining like swoop headlights right now that I can't tell? We have become quite adept at spotting the first signs of empathic compatibility. If there are children in our care fortunate enough to be born resonant, it is imperative we nurture it from an early age. The sooner we get them matched up in a ciphered pair, the better."

"Why is it so important?" Tobias asked, feeling a catch of concern.

Like melted wax, Hiroki's aged face became a visage of regret. "Resonance can be a blessing *and* a curse. There are many complications that can arise should an individual begin using it lacking proper guidance. Resonance enables a connection between two brains that have evolved with vastly differing mental, emotional, and sensory capabilities. Cohabitors manifest emotion as physical sensations: sadness, anger, fear, despair—for them, these feelings cause physical pain. By attaining resonance, a cipher willingly opens themselves up to that pain, and the dire situation the cohabitors find themselves in means it can be excruciating. In its rawest form, it can turn the human mind to madness."

"Strange," Tobias murmured, looking inwardly. "I haven't experienced anything like that."

"Ah! Then I imagine you have been very fortunate in that the cohabitor you bridged with was in relatively high spirits."

Tobias nodded. "Two cohabitors, so far. The first encounter was frightening, disorienting, the second more like polite conversation, but neither of them painful in any way."

Hiroki's bristly eyebrows jumped up in surprise. "Two? Divine Abyss! Then it would seem you are what we call a hyper-resonant—compatible with many, if not *all*, cohabitors . . . How remarkable. Coincidentally, the only other hyper-resonant known to currently exist happens to be my niece, Jyn—"

Tobias raised a hand to halt the increasingly animated housefather. "If you please, Mr. Sato. You said complications—as in, plural."

"Ah, yes. Well, on top of the *discomfort* attaining resonance with an emotionally distressed cohabitor can cause, there is also the issue of psychological trait transferral. You see, resonance is not just a window into another person's mind; it is a doorway. Things can be brought through—taken and left. For example, do you know what word best represents how the cohabitors think of themselves?"

Nobody had explicitly told Tobias the answer to that question, but somehow, after attaining resonance with Null, he knew. "The Prey," he said. "They call themselves the Prey."

Hiroki smiled. "Very good. They call themselves the Prey because it is precisely what they are. Where they came from, they did not sit comfortably at the top of the food chain as we had the luxury. They were hunted, and because of that, they do not know of the concept of preemptive attack. They know only how to flee and defend themselves. Unprovoked violence did not exist in their proverbial lexicon until they met us—the angry, destructive, savage little primates we are. And so, when resonance is attained, humans experience the agonizing despair the Prey feel about their circumstances, and the Prey, in turn, receive the concept of using violence not just to defend oneself but for achieving something—a goal or a purpose. They are, in a way, a reflection of their ciphers. So, this dangerous cocktail of trauma and new concepts can lead to disastrous consequences."

"You're talking about Harmony," Tobias professed.

"Precisely. The Composer's ranks are filled with lost, tortured souls who were never taught to wield the gift bestowed upon them by the Divine Abyss. So, you see, we must identify resonants as early as we can in order to give them the necessary guidance to prevent them from falling into the arms of Harmony."

Tobias's disquiet was apparently more visible than was his intent, as the housefather gave him a hearty slap on the shoulder in reassurance.

"You have nothing to fear, boy. Teodora used to give herself headaches trying to read her cohabitor siblings. She knows as much about the process as anybody can without being a cipher themselves. Everything you need to know to keep your brains from melting, that girl can teach you."

Tobias gave an appreciative nod, turning his head to find Teodora beaming back at him, glowing brighter than the brooding luminescence erupting from the ventilation funnel.

"Can I ask you one more question?" he said.

"Of course!" Hiroki replied, hungrily shoveling rice into his mouth. "As long as you promise to tuck in, my boy! I promise I'm done antagonizing you for the night, but I shan't be impressed if you let that go cold."

Tobias obliged and gratefully took another spoonful. "What is that?" he asked, grains of rice tumbling from his lips, gesturing at the ventilation funnel with his spork. "It's not glow, is it?"

Hiroki tightened his lips and furrowed his brow in concentration. "Well . . . I'm no cipher, Tobias. I can only relay to you what my beloved Yua told me before her passing, but in a way, yes, it is. Glow, emissions, the signal—whatever you prefer to call it—fundamentally, it's all the same thing. The light of the Savior."

"Isn't 'the Savior' what the Prey call the *Devourer*?"

"No." Hiroki shook his head. "What *you* call the *Devourer* is only its suit of armor, built as a gift of thanks by another civilization whom it chose to uplift, long before it rescued the Prey, a millennium before the Collision."

Tobias brought his forehead to rest on his fists, painfully aware of the embarrassing levels of befuddlement betrayed by the action. His head was spinning; it felt as though every time he managed to get a grip on reality, some new fragment of information would shatter his understanding and pull the ground out from beneath his feet. If Hiroki was to be believed, there were not *two* sentient species sharing the ruins of the *Novara* but three. The strange light he had been seeing in so many forms was, in fact, an ancient celestial entity, one composed of pure energy, which inevitably led to the startling realization that something, or *someone*, had been living inside his head, lurking behind his eyes, lying in wait for the moment it could enable that first connection with Null, perhaps even since birth.

Hiroki afforded a warm smile, chuckling softly at his visible consternation.

"Eat, my boy. Stay for tonight's dissemination, and I promise your mind will be put at ease."

With plates clean and tummies full, the children were huddled together on a pile of blankets, keenly awaiting the commencement of the so-called dissemination.

Nanimonai, who had been characterized by docile stoicism for the majority of the evening, suddenly sprang to life. Ae hopped about the room in an animated flurry, ensuring the children were warm, comfortable, and, most important, attentive to the show that was about to begin.

Teo provided a brief explanation about what to expect from the upcoming after-dinner entertainment while she and Tobias helped clear the pots away. According to her, this dissemination was some kind of educational transmission, broadcast by the Savior at daily intervals in an attempt to reach out and communicate with the inhabitants of the Mouth. Now that he understood the true nature of the incomprehensible swell of radiance bubbling from the ventilation funnel, there was an unusual sense of presence in the room. Staring into the light of the Savior, he couldn't help but wonder who, or what, might be staring back . . .

In eager anticipation, the little merchant from the playroom perched beside him, clinging amorously to his right arm. Teodora lay partially reclined with her back pressed into his side, holding his hand in her lap. It was truly humbling just how quickly she had seemingly warmed to him. He didn't consider himself deserving of such affection, but suffice to say, it was certainly *not* unwelcomed.

"OK, children," Hiroki announced, clapping his hands for attention. "Let us see what the Savior has in store for us tonight, shall we?" He joined Nanimonai on the opposite side of the hanging ventilation funnel. The otherworldly light spewing from its opening seemed to react to their proximity, bulging and pulsating, increasing in brightness and vibrancy. Nanimonai raised aer arms into the storm of glowing particles. In response, it focused and divided itself into individual ribbons, which began spiraling around aer great paws like water circling a drain.

"Let me see here," Hiroki mumbled, searching for recognizable patterns with a studious expression. "Ah-hah! We're in luck." Playful malevolence appeared on his face, his voice becoming deep and somber. "Children, it is time for the story of the Apex and the Prey!"

The junies squealed in a mixture of fear and delight. Teo tugged Tobias's arm excitedly. "Ooh, this is one of my favorites."

The surroundings seemed to darken. Then, the bands of illumination collecting around Nanimonai dispersed into thousands of individual points of light that hung still in the air. The children gasped as the light of the Savior focused itself into a model of the cosmos, filling the room with a teeming star field as dense and as bright as the expanse beyond the *Novara*'s hull.

"Incredible." The word slipped involuntarily from Tobias's mouth as the twinkling dots began drifting forward in unison, creating the dizzying illusion that the room was hurtling through the endless night at incalculable speeds.

"Journey back with me now, children," Hiroki whispered, gesticulating wildly with his arms for dramatic effect, "to a time long ago, when the ancestors of the eight-eyed among us knew only one great truth . . . *the hunt*."

The stars began condensing toward a focal point as though the depiction had a singularity at its center—a ravenous consumer of all matter unfortunate enough to exist within its gravitational pull.

The glimmering specks of light coalesced into an unshapely mass that, after a moment of calm, grew exponentially, gradually morphing into discernible and incredibly detailed shapes. Tall, moss-encrusted trees with bizarre, weblike branches sprung into existence, surrounded by rolling hills and ominous, billowing clouds looming above.

The light of the Savior became a diorama of a dense and verdant forest. It enveloped Hiroki's captivated audience like a lustrous blanket, transforming their drab surroundings into stunning scenery. Tobias marveled at what he immediately understood to be the cohabitor home world. It was alien but curiously familiar, like standing inside one of the biome exhibits up in the Center of Horticultural Preservation—this one far stranger than any he'd visited previously.

"Dark times were these," Hiroki growled, showing fangs. The children collectively held their breath in fearful anticipation. Obviously, the nonhuman among them lacked comprehension of the housefather's words but were enthralled by his animated delivery nonetheless. The tale was likely being regaled to them through some other, telepathic means, evidenced by Nanimonai's sudden head movements, aer gaze darting sporadically between the infant cohabs in the huddle.

"Existence for the Prey was a grave and everlasting struggle for survival. They were not the masters of their world but were succeeded on the food chain by a cruel and merciless intelligence."

Eerie figures manifested from thick foliage—towering creatures supporting their weight on muscular arms that were almost as broad as the trunks of the trees. Long, contrastingly elegant necks brought wide reptilian heads down to the ground. They slalomed side to side, gliding through the air as if completely independent of the hulking, cumbersome bodies they were connected to. The figures drudged forward with an unsettling mechanicality, prowling amidst the trees with unquestionable malice in their approach.

"The Apex reigned supreme," Hiroki said as the creatures drew closer. The little cohab sitting beside Tobias had all but buried aer face into the material of his jacket. He felt the vibrations of aer tiny, trembling body running up his arm.

"For aeons, they waged against the Prey an interminable campaign of torment and suffering. Their cruelty knew no bounds; nor did their hunger. Generation after generation, the Prey were subjected to industrial slaughter, brought to the precipice of extinction by an unrelenting enemy."

"How is he doing this?" Tobias whispered into Teo's ear. "I mean, how does he know what to say?"

Teo turned her head slightly. "Used to be that Yua was the storyteller. I think Hiroki sat through so many disseminations that he couldn't help but learn 'em all by heart. He was pretty reluctant to take over narration duty at first—I remember story time being dull as paper when I was just a squat. In his element now though, ain't he?" A frown appeared on her face. "Now hush up—you're gonna miss the best part."

The sea of luminous particles began to resculpt itself, this time into a scene strikingly familiar—Tobias recognized the burning hellscape that lay strewn out before him as identical to the one presented upon first attaining resonance with Null. The same aggregation of crumbling buildings sat perched upon the horizon, and the surging crowd of fleeing cohabitors present in the first vision could also be seen here in the throes of a desperate escape from the ruins of their settlements.

Nanimonai locked eyes with him. Emissions gathered at the forefront of his awareness, a multitude of confused emotions and ideas entrenching themselves in his mind: fear, desperation—a primordial impulse to flee a remorseless predator. It was a vertical slice of the trauma and tribulation imposed upon the ancient Prey, shared with him through space and time like a memory left in the ether, an emotional accompaniment to the Savior's visuals, contextualizing them in a far more visceral way.

This was nothing like reading about human history from the compendium on the Silk River Concourse—a famously dull affair. The empathic nature of cohabitor communication meant these events could be passed down through generations, transcribed in a medium that was far more tangible and tactile to experience. The cohabitors alive today endured the same pain and suffering their ancestors did with such lucidity it was almost as if they were living it themselves.

He looked down at his little cohabitor companion, conscious that ae too was experiencing firsthand what it felt like to be preyed upon—to be hunted. Ae stared back, gripping fiercely onto his arm in search of comfort. He ran his hand down the withers of aer neck.

"It's OK, li'l buddy. We're in this together," he cooed softly.

"The end was nigh," Hiroki rasped, gesturing to the ceiling in a dramatic sweeping motion. "But before the light could be extinguished completely, the Savior arrived."

A monstrous form punched a hole through the canopy of virtual clouds. The forbidding biomechanical husk, built to protect the light of the Savior— or the *Devourer*, as Tobias had known it all his life—fell from the heavens and touched down in a clearing.

The cohabitor junies bleated in glee. He watched with intense feelings of déjà vu as the vessel unfurled a colossal opening on its bow, allowing hundreds of thousands of tiny cohabitors to take refuge in its belly.

Hiroki's booming voice cut through the clamor of excitement. "In their gravest hour, a nearby voyager heard their collective cry for help and came to assist."

The war-torn landscape dissolved around him, the Savior reshaping itself once again into an endless cosmos.

"The Savior took pity on the Prey and uplifted them from ruination, providing safe harbor to the stars, seeking to deliver them to a new home where they could finally flourish and thrive."

The junies chirped noises of intrigue and surprise as the depiction of the Savior shrank into a tiny, glimmering arrowhead. A long comet tail delineated its trajectory as it hurtled through the simulated void, bouncing like a pinball from star system to star system with a prowling, menacing shadow following in its wake.

"But as the Prey took refuge in the beyond, the vengeful Apex, maddened by the escape of their subjugates, began a pursuit that would last centuries and span light-years. Their insatiable appetite took them across the galaxy, hell-bent on laying waste to every world the Savior touched down on, allowing the Prey little respite to catch their breath, unwilling to cease until the very last of them had been exterminated and consumed, their noble protector annihilated."

A chorus of pitiful whimpers rose from the huddle. A thirst overcame Tobias, paired with the feelings of defeat and hopelessness that had firmly taken root in his chest. Sadness roiled over the housefather's face as the arrowhead slowed to a steady stop. "Eventually, the Savior was left with no safe ground to go to and found itself stranded in dark space without air to breathe, nor water to drink. A great famine befell the Prey. Adrift for decades in a decaying sarcophagus, they began to wither, awaiting the reemergence of the dreaded Apex without any hope of salvation."

After a moment of solemnity, a jagged streak of light crept in from the outer edges of the projection. Racing toward the now stationary arrowhead, its brilliance illuminated the faces of the little ones, who leaned forward, effervescent with anticipation.

"But in the cold dark of the endless night, there was a glimmer of hope."

Nanimonai spread aer arms wide. The bright streak began to expand, its shape becoming clearer as the image magnified.

"Here we come," Teo said, squeezing Tobias's palm so fervently he thought it might bruise.

To vocalizations of unbridled amazement, a six-foot-long model of the *Novara* filled the dining room.

"A passing ark vessel, belonging to a species of busy little primates in transit to a new world to stake their claim, became an oasis in the desert. Through great fortune—or perhaps fate—the visitors came within range of the Savior, who in great reluctance, and in sheer desperation, had no choice but to intercept."

The Collision—the event that irrevocably altered the course of human history—played out before Tobias's eyes in stunning clarity. A lifetime spent visualizing and lamenting this fateful confrontation paled in comparison to the experience of witnessing it in conjunction with the sensory input provided by resonance with Nanimonai. He felt overwhelming guilt, shame, and remorse. Watching the *Devourer* tear into the *Novara*'s hull, he no longer perceived the alien warship as a vicious aggressor—it was more like watching a wounded animal trying to survive—a mother, perhaps, using the last of her life force to save herself and her cubs from certain death, no matter the cost.

Hiroki stepped forward, bringing his head and shoulders into the space between the projections of the two warring behemoths, the debris from their engagement spiraling like a maelstrom around his face. A calmness descended over him. "On the brink of suffocation, the Savior pulled the *Novara* out of ripple space so that it could breathe her atmosphere, nourish on her sustenance, and make use of her advanced aquaponics." The *Devourer* latched on to the now immobilized *Novara*, before reeling her in close and burying its bow into her stern, like an insect pulling its paralyzed victim with powerful mandibles. "And so began the great human sacrifice. The ancestors of the two-eyed among us relinquished their dreams of colonizing the stars so that the Prey and their protector could survive. Now, the Savior rebuilds and replenishes, readying itself for the eventual return of the Apex, growing its strength so that it might defend the two species cohabiting in its charge from those who would seek to destroy them."

The Savior's light flickered briefly. The image of the two incapacitated vessels, rotating aimlessly together like slow-dancing lovers, spluttered and waned, becoming more garbled and distorted by the second. As though the atmosphere in the room were being sucked out through a hull breach, the light of the Savior retreated back into the ventilation funnel, and in an instant, it was gone.

Nanimonai stared at aer paws, seeming perturbed by its unexpected disappearance. Incidentally, Tobias was reminded of an idea gleaned earlier in the day while unintentionally reading Null in the galley of the *Assurance*.

The Savior is sick; the Savior is dying.

He wondered if the light of the Savior's puzzling behavior was somehow related . . . Perhaps the pair were making progress in uncovering the root of the apparent ailment, or maybe this was a sign that something had gone wrong. Watching the increasingly bewildered Nanimonai, he began to suspect it may have been the latter.

Hiroki shrugged off his companion's disquietude, silencing the children murmuring among themselves by raising a finger to his lips.

"And so, the lesson is this: Although we may come from opposite sides of the galaxy, though our biology and our cultures may be vastly different, we, as dwellers of the Coalescence, are one people now. Whatever hardships the future might have in store for us, we will face together. It's incumbent on all of us to learn, understand, and appreciate one another, because if the Apex *do* return, we have a much better chance of surviving as a united people than we would were we divided."

TWENTY-EIGHT

With eyelids growing heavy and yawns spreading throughout the huddle of somnolent children, the time to retire had finally come. The housefather and his cohabitor counterpart readied the junies for bed, while Teo and Tobias began packing away the remaining produce in preparation of taking their leave.

"Don't wait too long before coming to visit us again, my boy," said Hiroki, carrying an impressive tower of dirty plates into the kitchen. "Nanimonai doesn't get out much; I'm sure ae enjoyed getting the chance to chew the fat, so to speak. I don't believe ae's bonded with a human since . . . well, since my Yua passed."

Tobias humbly accepted the invitation, already formulating a plan in his mind of how to go about restoring funding to Juniper Sanctuary. Undoubtedly, he would face all the same scrutiny and backlash his mother did, but for perhaps the first time in his life, how others perceived him sat at the very bottom of his list of priorities . . .

Teo snapped her fingers in front of his nose to rouse him from a daze. "You gonna stand there lookin' gormless or you gonna help me load everything onto the burro?"

"Sorry," he replied, hastening to relieve her of some of the items cradled in her arms. "My brain is absolutely frazzled. I think I could do with a little rack, to be honest."

She chuckled softly. "Learned a thing or two today, didn't ya? Don't worry; I know a lot of resonants who say it can really take it out of you at first. We'll be back aboard the *Assurance* soon. Then you can sleep it off to your heart's content."

He simpered, then allowed a troubled expression to take him.

"You know this Apex Hiroki spoke of during the dissemination—did they really exist? Could they ever return?"

Teo shook her head. "Naw . . . I mean, I don't doubt they really existed, but I don't think we'll ever see 'em. The housefather always said the reason they could never find the cohabs is cuz they're so well hidden out here in the empty black. General consensus is the Apex either gave up a long time ago or died off somewhere along the way . . . It's just a good story to get the kids playing nicely, ain't it? Like a metaphor."

"I'm just glad it was the Prey we collided with and not the predators. They sound nightmarish."

Swinging the keys to the burro around her finger, Teo reached out for the locking latch on the front door but lurched backward as a single metallic thud emanated from the far side. The pair mirrored a look of perplexment as further thuds arrived, each one louder and angrier than the last, as if the door's hardened plating were being struck repeatedly with a hammer.

Hiroki stormed toward the door, muttering to himself indignantly, standing on tiptoes to stare through the spyhole. "What kind of inconsiderate troglodyte is making such a racket at this late hour? If it's one of the Governor's debt collectors, I shall have Nanimonai string 'em upside down—see how they like getting hustled for once!"

Teo took a cautious step backward as the pummeling subsided. Behind her, Nanimonai was instinctively using aer tremendous size and strength to prevent the congregation of inquisitive junies in the dining room from getting any closer to the source of the disturbance.

Then, in the unnerving silence, Tobias heard a recognizable sound—a metronomic beeping steadily pitching up in frequency.

"Show yourself!" Hiroki's demand was tempered somewhat by the disconcerted inflection in his voice.

Realization hit Tobias with the full force of a concussion charge, which incidentally was exactly what he suspected to be responsible for the electronic chirping. He knew precisely what came next: a spherical detonation of impact energy that would likely blow a hole in the side of the building, as well as subjecting anybody standing in range to a lethal dose of blunt force trauma.

The next few seconds seemed to last an eternity, his perception of time warped by the adrenaline flooding his nervous system. He grabbed Teo by the shoulders and wrenched her away from the door. Concurrently, he reached out to Nanimonai with his consciousness, forming a canvas in his mind that he began frenziedly hurling buckets of paint at. Recalling the simplistic nature of the warnings conveyed to him by the cohabitor merchant in the markets, he made an effort to render only the most basic of concepts.

Danger . . . death . . . fire . . . warning.

The simpler they were, the easier they would be to interpret. The hope was that he'd given aer ample opportunity to get the kids to safety, but there was little time to check whether the penny had dropped.

"Hiroki! Get back!" He was certain the words left his mouth, but the warning was muted by the peculiar auditory effect the incoming shockwave had on the surrounding atmosphere—an all-enveloping silence that violently rattled his rib cage.

With Teo tucked firmly into his chest, the concussion blast carried them through the air as it tore like a tsunami through the playroom—an unstoppable bulwark of glass and debris. He struck the wall with his back, the impact sending a seismic wave of agony roiling down his spine, painfully expelling the air from his lungs. As their crumpled bodies slid to the floor, the unusual absence of sound gave way to the cacophony raised by the crumbling surroundings, undercut by Teo's increasingly hysterical whimpering. Strenuously lifting his head to survey the extent of the damage, he was horrified to find a gaping hole in the wall where Hiroki had been standing only moments ago, crooked beams of Höllengarten light spilling through and illuminating the dust hanging in the air. He glanced across to the dining room entrance, where, thankfully, Nanimonai and the junies were nowhere to be seen. Although eye contact had been broken, their empathic connection remained strong. He could feel the alien sentience lurking in the far reaches of his cognizance—ae was terrified, trepidatious, and keenly awaiting instruction. An image took shape in his mind of children huddled behind the ventilation funnel in the dining room, cowering under the protective shell ae had created with aer armored body. The warning had worked—for now, the little ones were safe.

Fighting to catch her breath, Teo lifted her head in the direction of a gurgling noise coming from beneath the staircase. Tobias followed her stare to find Hiroki pinned to the wall by a section of the front door, which had been blown clean off its hinges and sheared down the middle by the blast. A stream of blood so thick it was almost black poured from the abdominal puncture wound where the twisted shard of metal had impaled him. He pawed at it apathetically, head hung low, his sagging face a picture of defeat.

Teo began a panicked clamber to her feet. "Oh no . . . please no."

With an outstretched arm, Tobias forced her struggling body back down and restrained her, directing her attention with a firm stare to the three figures who had just entered through the blast hole, silhouetted by the bronze twilight seeping in from outside.

Immediately recognizing the threat, Teodora went deathly still. Though Hiroki needed urgent medical attention, she knew as Tobias did that until they could gauge the strangers' intentions, it was better to stay where they were, lying in the shadows, covered in a blanket of rubble and dust.

The tallest of the figures took point. Broad-shouldered and barrel-chested, wearing the same Phalanx enforcer gear as before, Tobias knew it was Jonah Sinclair even before he saw the man's wiry beard and round, hardened face. The brute led his equally intimidating accomplices through the ruined playroom with an almost jovial demeanor, showing blithe disregard to the scenes of decimation around him.

Tobias tightened his grip around Teodora, recalling Jonah's plan to stem the "out-of-control" cohabitor population in the Mouth by putting a sanctuary he had described as a spawning ground out of action. It had seemed like just talk at the time, no more harebrained or insubstantial than any of Bhaltair Abernathy's aspirations. Evidently, Jonah had been deadly serious. Assuming the viperinae submachine guns he and the other two wielded were as authentic as their uniforms, they had come to Juniper Sanctuary for a very specific purpose.

There was little time to get a warning out to Nanimonai. Fortunately, their bond was stronger than ever. He shut his eyes tight to hide his emissions, knowing they would instantly give away his and Teo's position. Heightening his receptivity to the cohabitor in the next room's thoughts and emotions, he felt aer distress at witnessing the events through his eyes. Not intentionally had he conveyed the image of aer aged partner skewed to the wall. Suffice to say, ae received it loud and clear, and was so overwrought with worry and anger that he couldn't help but unloose a stifled whimper in response. The pain caused by attaining resonance with an emotionally distressed cohabitor that Hiroki had spoken of—he felt every iota of it now.

Grimacing, he pried his attention away from the cohabitor's growing agitation. The gunmen were within spitting distance now, and if Jonah's objectives were as diabolical as he had begun to suspect, Nanimonai had to be given time to get the children to safety.

Searching for an answer, Teodora's fond recounting of her earlier years digging through scrap replayed in his mind. Specifically, her mention of the emergency trapdoor in the dining room that she regularly used to sneak down to the Vestiges. He brought the trapdoor to life on his synaptic canvas, envisioning himself wrenching it open and making an escape, carrying on his shoulders the infant cohabitor who had taken a liking to him earlier.

I hope you're alright, li'l buddy.

Nothing came back to him through the bond: no imagery, no feelings. He only hoped it was because his empathic partner had left the building and made it undetected out of resonance range.

In a gruff voice, Jonah directed the other two to search the rest of the build-ing; one unwittingly stepped so close that Tobias could smell syn-leather as the man's bootheel grazed the skin of his nose. Teo tensed her body as the other entered the dining room. Tobias held his breath in anticipation of screaming and rapid bursts of gunfire. After a few seconds, however, there was only silence.

Hiroki looked up to face Jonah, his head cocked to the side, blood bub-bling from his lips.

"Don't you fellas know how to knock?"

Jonah showed a sinister grin, the shadows of his face morphing menac-ingly as the remaining intact light jar rocked back and forth in the residual motion of the concussive blast.

"You wouldn't happen to be the owner of this here establishment would you, old-timer?"

Hiroki coughed. "That'd be me . . . Not looking for shelter, are you? I don't normally turn kids away on account of their ugliness, but I think we might struggle to find you boys a forever home." The elderly man gave a grating laugh, but it quickly deteriorated into coarse retching.

Jonah used his tongue to pick something out of his teeth in disapproval. His two accomplices returned from their search and formed up behind him.

"The place is empty, boss. They're not here."

Jonah sighed then pointed at Hiroki's wound with the muzzle of his SMG.

"That looks pretty nasty." He removed a white spray can from one of the utility pouches on his vest and rattled it. "Nothing a shot of med-foam couldn't fix, though. Why don't you tell me where you're keeping all the leechlings and we'll patch you up? That way, you don't have to bleed out, and we get to help you with the little vermin problem you got going on here." Jonah shrugged suggestively. "It's a win-win."

Hiroki spat red-mottled saliva atop the chunk of ragged steel lodged in his gut. Steadying his ladened breathing, a calmness descended over him. His eyes narrowed. "One day, the scales will finally tip, and men like you who use words like 'vermin' to debase and persecute the downtrodden will be judged as vermin by the Almighty Emptiness."

"Wasn't that a nice sermon, boys?" Jonah jeered as the other two broke into biting laughter. "Hate to tell you this, Reverend, but we ain't void wor-shippers like you sternside folk. Keep talking though, maybe you can make converts out of us poor heathens yet."

Hiroki shook his head slowly. "I think you three might just be beyond help in that regard."

Jonah's impatience seeped through his expression. He glanced over his shoulder at the other two.

"Doesn't seem like our holier-than-thou friend here is feeling all that compliant today. Let's get this place rigged up and see if we can't persuade him to be a little more obliging."

"You sure this'll do the job?" one of his men asked, swinging a duffle bag over his shoulder and handing out the contents to his counterpart. "What if they really ain't here?"

"Oh, they're here alright. Probably scurrying about inside the walls. We'll have to smoke 'em out."

Jonah's accomplices disbanded again, going room by room and attaching small devices to each of the main support structures throughout the building. They were black, rectangular objects, each with a blinking red light and a remote receiver—no doubt explosive or incendiary charges of some kind. Evidently, Abernathy had managed to source something a little more lethal than a few concussion charges this time around.

"Last chance, Father," Jonah said, holding his SMG low ready with the sights aligned with his target's chest. "Tell us where the leeches are and maybe I don't burn this festering shithole down to the ground."

Teodora convulsed beneath Tobias's protective arm; he could feel the fear and hatred coursing through her body. This girl, who more and more he found himself seeking to forge a connection with, would forever despise him for forcing her to watch the cruel execution of the man who had raised and cared for her. There was no more time for deliberation—he had to intervene.

Fragments of rubble fell from his head and shoulders as he pushed himself off the ground, raising trembling hands in the air. "Put the gun down, Jonah."

Jonah swung around in surprise, the stock of his SMG pressed firmly into his shoulder, one furious magnified eye staring down the weapon's electric-green holo-sights.

"Tobias? Is that you?" Gleeful surprise painted his thuggish face, quickly overtaken by wary bewilderment. He lowered his gun but kept his finger on the trigger. "Mr. Edevane told us you were being held by DMED. Said that traitorous whistleblowing cop from Amidships was keeping you hostage. What in the hell are you doing with these Mouth rats?"

Tobias took one step forward, showing his palms in submission. "Marshal Wyatt stationed me on a weld and salvage ship to see out a term of community service. I've been doing time aboard the *Assurance*."

Jonah raised an eyebrow. "The *Assurance*? Captain Holloway's hauler?"

Tobias nodded. "Is Caleb with you?"

The man curled his upper lip. "Nah. This job was a little too hot for the hot redhead. She's back home with Mr. Abernathy. Those two are getting *real* comfy, if you catch my drift."

Tobias disregarded the insinuation, knowing it was only an attempt to get under his skin and pleased to find himself generally unperturbed by it.

"Jonah . . . if you know Delilah, then you know she wouldn't be too pleased to find out what you're doing here."

The other two mercenaries returned, the building now sufficiently primed for demolition. Each gave their leader an affirming nod as they formed up behind him. He showed a toothy grin. "Yeah . . . well maybe *Her Majesty* don't rule the roost like she used to no more. Lilah lost the support of the Captain's Guild once she cozied up to that crook Drexen and started harboring an enemy of the NTU on her ship. So maybe I don't give a leech's ass what she thinks about it."

The man's bellicose stare switched to Teodora as the girl cautiously rose to her feet behind Tobias, starting toward Hiroki. Slumped forward, still pinned to the wall, the man was silent and lifeless.

"Don't you move another muscle there, Blue," Jonah barked. Moving like an execution squad preparing to fire, his men synchronously took aim at the girl.

"P . . . please. He needs help," she muttered through tears.

"Unless you're looking to get peppered with holes, I suggest you stay right where you are, li'l girl," Jonah sneered.

Tobias took another step forward. "You don't want to do this, Jonah," he pleaded. "I know you think what you're about to do is justified, but it's wrong."

"Wrong?" Jonah let the word linger in between sharpened teeth. "I don't see how any action could be considered *wrong* when it's for the good of the human remnant."

"You tell me how setting fire to an orphanage does *anything* to benefit the New Terra Union."

Jonah twisted his face in scorn. "These aren't kids, Tobias; they're insects. This ship is diseased, and what Humanity First is doing is the cure. If we don't find a way to stem the tide soon, the blockade will fall and the infestation will overrun the *Novara*. Is that what you want?"

"Of course not." He paused, breathing heavily. "But it's not what they want either. I'm sorry, Jonah, but you've been sold a lie. I know because I bought into it too. I know you're scared, and I know you're angry, but the truth is we've *both* been conditioned to hate these people by a system that practically feeds off our ignorance. You've been conned, but trust me, it's not too late to come back to reality."

Jonah took Tobias in his aim, tightening his posture. "What the hell happened to you? You spend a few days in the Mouth and now you're suddenly a leech sympathizer? You sound like a damned traitor. Mr. Edevane would be ashamed to hear you talkin' like this."

Tobias shrugged. "I bet he would, but he's been played just like the rest of us."

"You aren't stopping me, boy. Mr. Abernathy needs places like this gone. They're making advocating for separation impossible."

"It's already impossible! The *Novara* is a ghost ship without the *Devourer*. If Bhaltair somehow goes through with this insane, genocidal plan of his, it doesn't just mean extinction for the cohabitors, it means extinction for all of us!"

There was a moment of hesitation from Jonah, as if something Tobias had said had finally penetrated the man's thick skull. That was until the sudden arrival of powerful emissions. Incandescence flooded Tobias's field of view as he was imbued by feelings of wrath and anger. Struck by an unquenchable thirst for vengeance, he knew it could only mean that Nanimonai was somewhere in the vicinity.

A look of pure horror swept across Jonah's face in response to the outpour of retinal light. "The boy's been indoctrinated! Put 'em both down!"

The men drew their weapons. Tobias sidestepped to place himself in between Teodora and the execution squad; his unathletic frame would do little to shield her from the incoming hail of bullets, but he made what futile attempt he could with his remaining seconds.

The conical rays of Höllengarten light peering through the blast hole were obstructed by a tall figure. Still wearing aer now-torn apron, Nanimonai charged toward the nearest of the assailants with aer hackles up, unleashing a hair-raising shriek.

Jonah caterwauled a panicked order to his men to open fire. A second later, blinding strobes cast the ruined playroom in flashes of phosphorescent light, muzzle flare seeming to come from every direction.

Evidently, Bhaltair had anticipated that the blunt instruments he'd dispatched to do his dirty work would be targeting cohabs in their infancy—yet to develop their hardened exoskeletons. As such, he had neglected to outfit them with the armor-piercing ammunition necessary to penetrate fully formed chitin. The rounds bounced off Nanimonai's carapace in brilliant zigzags as the three terrified men emptied a full magazine each into the alien.

Demonstrating aer inhuman might, ae swung one massive paw and backhanded the first, sending him cartwheeling across the playroom and into the kitchen to the sound of crashing glass and cutlery.

"Shit! I need to reload!" the other one squawked. Disinclined to allow him an opportunity to do so, Nanimonai raised one hulking leg, and with the power of a railgun, extended aer reverse knee joint. With sharp talons, ae struck the man directly in the chest, catapulting him through the air; a heavy thwack of broken bones and colliding Kevlar rang out as his contorted body impacted a support girder.

By now, Jonah was profusely aware of his physical inferiority compared to the vengeful alien; while his counterparts were being flung about like rag dolls, he had already begun his escape. Only just evading another lethal swing from Nanimonai, he hastened back to the blast hole. He stopped before exiting, laughing maniacally with a small cylindrical implement clutched in his fist—the remote detonator linked to the incendiary charges spread throughout the building.

"Burn with the rest of them, traitor!" He flipped open the detonator's end cap and, with a baleful grin, pulled the trigger.

A rolling inferno consumed the sanctuary. The hanging cloth and tapestries that had been a source of such comfort before transformed the playroom into a molten hellscape, the highly flammable materials igniting instantaneously.

Gasping sharply, Tobias staggered backward, the scorching heat licking his skin and soiling the air with the nauseating stench of his own singed hair. Disoriented, he covered his face with his jacket, frantically scanning the playroom in search of Teo and Nanimonai. While the four walls of the room had been quickly swallowed by a carpet of volatile combustion, there was a small safe zone just below the main staircase where Hiroki had been impaled. There, he found the pair standing by the elderly man's side, both seemingly oblivious to the blaze closing in around them. Teo held the housefather's pale, wrinkled hand in her own while his distraught partner tended to the shard of debris wedged in his belly. It was clear, perhaps only to Tobias, that the housefather was already dead.

Nanimonai turned to face Tobias as he approached, aer eyes glistening and still. He hastily diverted his gaze, conscious that attaining resonance now could prove fatal, for he too would be stricken by such grief that it might completely paralyze him. Closing his mind to any encroaching emissions, he wrapped his arm around Teo's shoulder.

"Teo," he said—not so softly that it couldn't be heard over the roar of the fire. "He's gone. I'm sorry, but we have to get out of here."

"Can't you just give us a damned minute?" the girl hissed through tears, shaking her arm free.

The building moaned, its structural foundations beginning to buckle in the intense heat. There was a thundering crash as a support beam collapsed from the ceiling. Tobias felt growing panic, realizing that all exits to the playroom were now blocked by either mounds of rubble or an impassable wall of fire.

"We don't have a minute!" He tried to pry her hands away from Hiroki's blood-soaked sweater, but the girl clung on as if dangling over the edge of a cliff and holding on to the only thing keeping her from falling.

"Teo! This place is gonna come down on top of us! We need a way out!"

Finally, she stirred to the peril of the situation. Pressing shaking fingers against her lips, she glanced around the burning room, the reflection of the devouring flame scintillating in her eyes.

"We gotta try and get to the roof," she said. "There's an emergency stairwell that'll get us back down to street level."

Tobias agreed, but Nanimonai would not be so easily persuaded; the pair made an attempt to physically drag the alien away from Hiroki, but the combined strength of two humans was scarcely enough to impel aer to move.

Tobias had no choice but to link with aer empathically, exposing himself to a debilitating deluge of intense sorrow and anguish: the sudden and unexpected loss of a companion whom he'd known for decades and cared for dearly, when in reality he barely knew the man. Clenching his jaw, he drudged through the torment, forcing Nanimonai to consider what the fate of the young ones under aer protection would be should ae allow aerself to perish in the fire. Ae understood and in turn presented an image of the junies taking shelter somewhere beneath ground, the older among them helping to calm the little ones upset by the fray. Given some reassurance the kids were safe, Tobias finally managed to rally Teo and Nanimonai to flee.

Battling their way through a dense veil of noxious smoke, they made their way upstairs and headed through the dormitory, passing row after row of bunk beds untidy with countless cherished possessions that would soon be immolated by the spreading flame.

Nanimonai took a running charge at the roof exit. As it slammed open, the fresh air smacked Tobias in the face like a wet cloth. He filled his lungs too eagerly, which caused him to cough and retch as he violently expelled the smoke from his airways.

Outside, all was quiet: no crowds, no emergency-response barge hovering low, dousing the burning building with extinguishing foam, as there might have been bowside of the blockade. In the Mouth, no such infrastructure existed, and the blaze would rage on until Juniper Sanctuary was reduced to nothing but ash.

"Where are they?" Teo spluttered, coming to a stop near the edge of the roof, leaning on her knees to catch her breath. "Are they OK?"

Tobias rubbed his stinging eyes. "They're fine. I showed Nanimonai the trapdoor you mentioned earlier. Don't know where ae took them—somewhere with lots of blankets and cans of dehydrated food—but they're alright."

Teo nodded in recognition. "There's a storage room a little ways down the main passage—sounds like ae took them there."

Nanimonai took two cumbersome steps forward before collapsing to aer knees, clutching aer thorax. Dark purple fluid seeped through the gaps between aer digits.

"Oh no!" Teodora exclaimed, racing to the cohabitor's side. Ae snorted, removing aer paw to reveal what was merely a bullet graze to an area of unarmored flesh. One didn't need to be a cipher to comprehend aer meaning—the wound was painful but by no means lethal.

"You big dope!" Teo said, lovingly wrapping her arms around the crest of aer broad neck. "Why'd you come back for us like that? You could have gotten yourself killed!"

The cohabitor disregarded her, jerking aer head in the direction of the space behind Tobias. Emitting a deep, harmonic growl, ae pushed Teodora aside defensively.

"Safe room, huh?" Jonah repeated. Tobias spun around just in time to catch the man ascending the very same emergency stairwell they had planned to escape down, SMG drawn at the ready.

The menace had removed his helmet, revealing a bald head ripe with beads of sweat trickling down and collecting atop wild eyebrows.

"Sounds pretty nifty" He strafed sideways, taking Nanimonai in his aim. Completely drained of energy, the wounded alien made no attempt to defend aerself but simply bowed aer head in defeat.

Jonah grinned, setting predatory eyes on Teo. "I'm gonna get things wrapped up here, Blue. Then I'm thinkin' maybe you're gonna take me down to this safe room so we can pay your bug friends a little visit. That sound good to you?"

"I'd die before taking you anywhere," Teo spat.

Jonah chuckled in malevolent delight. "On that, we just might agree, Mouth rat."

Tobias sidestepped into Jonah's line of sight. Before he could utter even a single syllable, the man turned the muzzle of his SMG toward the Höllengarten and squeezed off a rapid burst. The deafening flurry of shots cracked in the distance as they echoed around the district. "Don't you move a fuckin' muscle, dude. I've tolerated enough of your treasonous, leech-lovin' bile for one day. If I see your eyes lighting up like that again, or if you say another goddamn word, I *will* put holes in you. Understand?"

"And what do you think my father would say if you did?" Tobias replied with equanimity. "You think he'd be happy you murdered his only son?"

Disgust roiled over Jonah's face. "Hell, look at what they've done to you, boy—I reckon your old man would probably see me putting you down as an act of mercy. Now step aside!"

Tobias shook his head adamantly. "You're wrong about him. My father is a good man—misguided and overzealous, maybe, but even he would understand what you've done here is crossing the line. I mean, Hiroki! Lei-Ghannam, Jonah, you killed him!"

Jonah showed an insidious grin. Bringing the stock of his SMG against his shoulder, he tightened his aim at Nanimonai. "That geriatric shrew was stood in the wrong place at the wrong time; weren't my fault. And regarding your dad's involvement in all this—who do you think it was who told me about this place?"

Tobias betrayed shock in his expression. "And did he tell you to burn it down? You're committing a massacre here, Jonah, so I hope you're sure."

"It was implied. Now for the last time, boy, step aside!"

Tobias shook his head, planting his feet firmly in front of Nanimonai, hands raised in the air. "If you're gonna kill them, you'll have to put your money where your mouth is and kill me too. I'm not gonna let you hurt anyone else."

Jonah's attention was taken momentarily by the distant roar of thruster ignition echoing from the other side of the Mouth. Tobias's heart sank as he realized what the cause of the din was—the *Assurance* taking off from the Cohabitor Ghetto. He and Teo hadn't made it back in time, and Captain Holloway had been forced to return to the Lower Amidships Docks without them. There was no rescue coming; they were well and truly on their own.

Jonah deliberated for only a moment before shrugging off the rising thrum and tightening his shooting stance. "Fine. Have it your way. Like I said: I don't leave the Mouth without getting blood on my knuckles. I'm just sorry it had to be you."

TWENTY-NINE

Delilah closed her eyes as Kahu swung the stolen zero-terrain load lifter around a corner and accelerated into the desolate clearing where the *Assurance* was berthed. She didn't know what she expected to see when she reopened them: a mound of smoldering wreckage resulting from a precise aerial bombardment from Vidalia's yacht, perhaps? Or a fleet of raptors with legions of Monarchs keeping her on lockdown.

The muscles in her shoulders melted like butter once she peeled open her eyelids to find the vessel waiting in all her useless aerodynamic beauty, entirely intact and totally unguarded. Word hadn't gotten to the Governor about what befell his capping plant in the Vestiges yet. But it soon would, which meant there was little time to get the ship and her crew back through the *Devourer* and bowside of the blockade.

The cargo bay door swung open automatically, as if the *Assurance* had been anxiously awaiting the return of her crewmates. Fully extended, the door doubled as a boarding ramp, which Kahu used to maneuver the ZT-LL into the hold. Isaac strenuously lowered himself down from the flatbed as the growl of the repulsor pads spun down, avoiding eye contact, his facial expression and body language weighed by shame.

"Thank you, Delilah. I don't know what I would have done without you."

"You'd be dead," she sharply replied, although the attempt at humor was, perhaps, a little too dry and only acted to worsen the boy's already fragile condition. She hopped out of the passenger side and went to him, lifting his dipped head with a curled finger under his chin.

"We did what we had to, Verhoeven. Don't forget, you're crew—that means you're family."

He gave a meek nod, intimating his thanks and understanding, although his ruminations were as clear as the night was everlasting—he had heard the same spiel a thousand times before, and being asked to consider those he worked alongside "family" made him feel no more at ease with constantly having to rely upon them to save his life. Isaac had had no real family for over a decade now, and Delilah suspected the sentiment, although meant in earnest, was beginning to feel a little bit hollow.

He turned to leave, looking dead set on spending an evening exacerbating a miserable comedown with plenty of self-flagellation. The problem was, she needed her engineer on duty . . .

"That being said, it did get pretty hairy down there," she intoned sternly. He stopped to listen, glancing back at her with eyes clouded by glow exposure.

"I put more at risk coming to pull you out than I think I ought to have. I know this addiction isn't your fault, and I know you're working hard to kick it, but I need you to understand that if you *ever* get yourself into a scrape like that again, there may not be anybody coming for you."

He smiled, seeming happier now that he had been reprimanded for his behavior.

"I know, Captain, and I wouldn't expect there to be. I've taken advantage of your courage and your generosity too many times. I won't endanger myself, or you, or anybody else on this ship, ever again."

She gave a nod of acceptance. "Get yourself to the med cubby: you need rest and lots of fluids. I want you back up to fightin' strength, ASAP."

"Easy, wonder boy," Kahu said, giving Isaac one of his signature shoulder slaps as the boy headed off, then turned his attention to the two reclaimed hydro-ionizers stowed on the ZT-LL flatbed.

"You want me to get these bad boys unloaded, Skip?" he asked, preemptively starting to unbuckle the holding straps.

"No. They're too hot to keep here. Get us over to Lower Amidships, then we'll transfer them somewhere safe after we dock—keep them hidden until things die down a little."

"You think things ever *will* die down?"

Delilah tilted her head, assuming a vacant stare. "Well . . . the Composer has her choir stationed on every street corner now, and Vidalia will be going to war in order to take back control of the district . . . So no, I guess in reality, things are only gonna escalate. It sure as hell ain't our fight, though; he'll have more on his plate to worry about than us. I plan to be long gone before all the killing starts."

"I dunno, Delilah," Kahu said, his brow furrowed. "He sure don't seem like the type to have a short memory span. I bet that bloodthirsty bastard wouldn't think twice about toppling his own empire if it meant settling a score with someone who crossed him."

"Well, maybe you shoulda thought of that before you decided to murder his right-hand cohabitor with a chair."

Kahu snorted mischievously, but then a troubled expression consumed him. Delilah read his battle-hardened face like the pages of an open book: there was a lingering question about the events that took place in the VLF—one that he was carrying a fair amount of apprehension about asking.

"Speak your mind, Heperi," she ordered.

"It's just . . ." He twisted his lips, brown eyes cast to the floor. "Those other glow worms—the ones we rescued along with Isaac. You really think it was a good idea turning 'em loose? Won't they just go straight to the next vent and get stuck all over again? I kinda feel like we shoulda brought them with us, ya know?"

Delilah leaned back in surprise—it wasn't out of character for the old pilot to question her judgment, but showing concern for two random addicts certainly was. She had thought the discussion over and done with back when they parted ways with the pair of vagrants after emerging from the Vestiges. Clearly, the decision still weighed on his mind.

"Honestly, Kahu, I don't doubt that they will go straight to another vent, but they're not our responsibility. We pulled them out of that nightmare and made sure no one gets sucked into it ever again; that's the best we can do right now. We've picked up enough stragglers on this job as it is—I can't afford to have any more souls on this old boat taking up air and resources. Times are gonna get tough. All we need to worry about going forward is making enough nunits to keep the *Assurance* afloat and looking after our own."

He smiled fondly. "That includes Bug and Bug-Eyed, right?"

She shrugged. "I suppose that's up to them. There's no telling how they'll react to news of the trouble we made with Vidalia. Maybe they'll try and kill us, maybe they'll leave. But on the off chance they're inclined to stick around, they're more than welcome to."

"Right on. What about the kid from the Upperdecks?"

Delilah took a deliberative pause. "We'll see."

While Kahu prepped for takeoff in the bridge, Delilah headed to the galley, where Mercy and Null were sitting silently in their usual spot, somehow managing to look even glummer than normal. The pair had returned from their expedition into the *Devourer* to investigate the "urgent matter" that had sent Null into such a swivet. Judging by the solemn expression on the young cipher's face and the dispirited body language of her companion, their efforts, it would seem, had been fruitless.

"Captain Holloway," Mercy said, brushing pearl-white hair out of her eyeline, clutching her brass pendant fervently. Although clearly agitated, Null still made sure to humbly bow aer head as Delilah entered.

"I trust you were successful in retrieving your missing engineer. He is uninjured, I hope."

Delilah made a beeline straight for the coffee machine, not stopping to acknowledge the glum pair—she'd gone thirty-plus hours without sleep by now, and since no rest could be had until they were clear of the Mouth, some synthetic liquid stimulation was in order.

"Isaac is safe," she replied, waiting impatiently for her cup to fill with dark, steaming wake-up juice. "But I'm afraid recovering him was not easy, nor did it come without sacrifice."

"Please elaborate, Captain."

The coffee machine sounded a steady beep. Delilah retrieved her piping hot libation and joined them at the table. She exhaled slowly. "As it turns out, he went down into the Vestiges looking for a fix. He got picked up by the Governor's people and put to work at one of his capping facilities. I doubt Vidalia was aware he had one of my crew members in internment, but once we were privy to what was going on down there, I felt we had a moral obligation to intervene. I'm sorry to say that this led to an altercation with three of his Monarchs, as well as our complete dismantling of his operation." She bit her tongue, stopping herself just short of admitting to severing a conduit—there was a chance Null would react adversely to that point.

Mercy's bland expression betrayed absolutely nothing about her response to the information. Delilah took a quick sip of coffee, affording herself a moment to formulate her next sentence.

"As a result, there's a good chance Vidalia will be coming for us. I understand this creates a conflict of interest for you two, and the last thing I want is for him to think either of you were involved. So, once Null gets us starside, I can arrange for a landing skiff to dock with us that you can then take back through the *Devourer* to rejoin Vidalia . . . *if* that's what you both want. If you and Null want to disembark, now'd be the time to do so—we'll be departing the Mouth shortly, and I should think it'll be a while before we return."

Mercy took plenty of time before responding; she had an irritating knack of turning an awkward silence into a painfully long suspension in conversation.

"Those capping plants are terrible places," she finally replied. "Dangerously alluring to those who abuse the signal recreationally. Few who sell themselves into servitude to satiate their lust ever make it out alive . . . They work and consume until they die."

Delilah had to remind herself that "the signal" meant "glow" in Mercyspeak—it was getting harder and harder to keep track of resonant terminology.

Mercy made stirring eye contact. "If it's true you destroyed this facility, then you have done the people of this district a great service. Conduits are a fact of life for all of us on the Coalescence: they can be a burden *and* a gift, but the vents are sacred to the Prey—they should not be misused, nor should they be profited off".

"The Prey" equals "cohabitors" . . . Got it, Delilah thought, breathing a deep sigh of relief.

"I couldn't agree more. Honestly, I wasn't sure how you two were going to react, given that you're both closely associated with Vidalia. I was worried you'd be furious with us."

Light simultaneously poured from behind the eyes of the interspecies pair. In the dimness of the galley, a faint wisp of luminosity drifted like a thin ribbon between them, connecting their minds through the ether. Delilah understood that she was now being addressed by both the cohabitor *and* aer cipher.

"We are not associates of the Governor," Mercy said. "There was a time, not so long ago, when we were indebted to him, but with no means of financial reimbursement, we were forced to trade our freedom and our abilities to pay our dues. But that debt has long since been paid and we remain under his influence—unable to go where we please or do what we wish. I told you it was our desire to stay aboard the *Assurance*, but I must admit that was very much under the instruction of our master. However, listen as we tell you now: we wish to remain under your employment." She glanced at Null then back to Delilah with heartfelt eyes. "By now you are aware of how useful our skills are to you. We will work tirelessly to pay our fare. Please, Captain, you must get us as far away from that man and his wretched enterprise as possible."

"What I said still stands," Delilah said. "You're both welcome to stay for as long as you like, just as long as you're aware that freeing you is giving Vidalia just another reason to hunt this ship down. By no means is it gonna be a smooth ride from here on out."

Mercy smiled appreciatively. Null bowed aer head in an unmistakable gesture of thanks.

"We are safe with you, Captain. Of this, we are certain."

A cool breeze swept through the cabin as the air filtration turned on. Delilah felt the low rumble of the dorsal pulse engine beneath her diaphragm—Kahu had nearly completed his preflight checks and would have the *Assurance* skyborne within a matter of minutes. The conversation would have to be cut short, but as she stood up to join the old pilot on the bridge, her curiosity got the better of her—she had to ask.

"I hope I'm not prying, but you haven't told me how your venture into the *Devourer* went. Did Null find what ae was looking for?"

Still empathically linked to Mercy, Null answered by lifting aer arm up high and slamming it angrily on the countertop, causing the entire gallery to shake.

"We were . . . unsuccessful," Mercy sorrowfully admitted, patting the vexed alien's thigh in an attempt to calm aer. "The Composer has gained a great many followers in recent weeks. We are unsure how it has been allowed to happen, but her forces have occupied the primary habitat chamber inside the Savior—a place known as the Magnanimous Hollow. We encountered a group of armed zealots who would not allow us access to the core. We do not know the root of the sickness that is beginning to impair the signal, but we are convinced it is a result of their meddling."

"That's terrible . . . Honestly, I didn't think Harmony had the military strength to launch an assault like that."

"It wasn't an assault, per se. Do not forget, Captain: there are many cohabitors in the Composer's ranks too. Those who subscribe to her teachings forced the nonbelievers out of the Magnanimous Hollow and allowed her foot soldiers to invade and fortify. The Prey who were evicted have no weapons to speak of. I'm afraid to say that, for the time being, retaliation is out of the question."

"Are you sure Null wants to leave at such a critical time? Isn't ae needed here in the Mouth?"

Mercy shook her head. "There is little we can do trapped in between the Administration's blockade and the Composer's bastion. There may be a way for us to access the chamber externally, but we must first escape the district before we can formulate a plan."

The sudden ignition of the vertical thrusters caused the rug-covered floor to shudder. Delilah started for the helm access corridor. "Lucky for you, escaping the district is exactly what we're gearing up to do. I need Null to report to the bridge and for you to get yourself strapped in. It's gonna be a bumpy one."

Mercy showed a look of surprise; her peroxide-white eyebrows would have appeared raised were they not invisible against her ghostly-pale skin. "We cannot leave yet, Captain."

"And why is that?"

"Your crewmembers—the ones who ventured into the markets—they have yet to return."

Delilah sighed, exasperated. "I'm gonna kill that girl."

She arrived on the bridge to scenes of pandemonium. Kahu sat strapped into the pilot's seat, flinging his arms around the helm in a hurricane of sweat-glistening muscle and faded tattoos. Emergency klaxons shrieked from the overhead instrumentation panel so blaringly loud that she could hardly hear her own hurried voice as she entered.

"Have you heard anything from Teo and Tobias? Mercy says they haven't checked in yet!"

"We've got bigger problems than that, Skip," Kahu responded, eyes darting frantically over the control pedestal beside him. "The Governor just target-locked us."

Delilah hastened to the windshield, pressing her nose against the glass to gaze out at the empty space above the Copper Swathes, knowing the merciless eyes of Vidalia Drexen were meeting her stare.

"Using that luma-cast stealth tech to hide his yacht, ain't he?" said Kahu. "Crafty bastard. You better get the bug up front. We need a path clearing through the *Devourer*, stat."

Delilah spun around to face the old pilot. "We are *not* leaving without Teo and Tobias!"

"Are you crazy? We're about to get blown to dust!"

"It's just a threat! He isn't gonna fire on this ship when he knows Null and Mercy are aboard. They're too precious a commodity to him."

"How's your poker face, Skip? Are you willing to call him out on that?"

"Just get us skyborne and keep him busy until we can figure out where the hell they got to."

Kahu cracked his knuckles and wrapped his brawny hands around the flight stick and thrust.

"I'll do my best, but it's tight in here—not a lot of space for maneuverability, what with Tycho Block 'n' all."

"It's a pleasure yacht, not a gunship. I'm sure you can outrun whatever he throws at us. Now get a move on!"

A dust cloud obscured the view through the windshield, kicked up by the heavy vertical propulsion required to lift the cumbersome vessel off the ground. Delilah clung to the back of the pilot's seat as Kahu took the *Assurance* into a steep climb, leveling out as the ramshackle rooftops of the surrounding buildings disappeared beneath the ship's nose cone.

"Are you hailing Teo?" she asked, addressing the comms panel to check if there was anything pending or inbound.

"I'm trying, but you know damn well that girl never picks up her feather."

As Kahu banked to the right and wheeled around Tycho Block, Delilah spied a column of black smoke rising from a point low in the distance.

"Smoke!" she exclaimed, staring intently at the ominous plume—darker than the smog expelled by the chimney stacks in the Langrenus Harrow and more like the kind that might be produced by an uncontrolled fire.

"Is that coming from the Warrens?" she asked.

"Looks like . . . Weren't they headed out that way after finishing up at the markets?" Kahu made little attempt to stifle the concern creeping into his tone. Delilah felt it too, hard—an innate understanding that whatever the cause of the blaze was, her troublesome salvage specialist and the Upper-decks brat were somehow involved . . .

"Heads up, Skip. Looks like the Governor's sending out a welcome party."

Delilah followed Kahu's gaze to a location just below the Höllengarten. Two silhouetted raptors seemed to materialize from thin air as they passed through the luma-cast stealth bubble projected around Vidalia's yacht. They tipped their hoods and began to descend, bringing themselves on course to intercept.

"Lei-Ghannam!" Delilah thumped the back of the pilot's seat with her fist. "They're gonna try and force us to land."

Kahu shook his head. "I don't think so—ain't nobody landing this ship but me."

He pitched down, dropping the *Assurance* as low as possible without colliding with the pylons and power lines protruding from the urban sprawl below. They would be harder to follow staying closer to the ground, and the dangerously low altitude afforded a clearer view of the nearing smoke, as well as the burning three-story townhouse it appeared to be originating from. Delilah felt her insides plummet.

"Kahu . . . Kahu, it's Juniper," she stuttered, panic-stricken.

"You're kidding." He reached toward the overhead instrumentation panel and pulled a lever. The windshield turned momentarily opaque before displaying a magnified image of the view ahead, captured by the forward-facing survey cam. The feed zeroed in on the target in question, confirming Delilah's fears—Juniper Sanctuary had indeed been set ablaze. The feed showed in striking clarity a ravenous fire encroaching up the building's walls. Ink-black smoke seeped through the slats of its shuttered windows and billowed from a large, ground-level blast hole, the presence of which suggested that whatever had happened was no accident. On the roof, surrounded by the encircling inferno, were four figures. One—clearly a cohabitor—lay on the floor, apparently injured. The identity of the girl crouched beside them was telegraphed by her metallic-blue hair, while the unmistakable profile of Tobias stood protectively in front of them. The boy had his hands in the air, facing down a Phalanx enforcer with an intimidating physique and his weapon drawn.

"What is it with these suicidal kids tryna get themselves killed all the time?" Kahu bellowed, sharing his captain's disbelief. In truth, she couldn't help but laugh at the sheer insanity of it all. With two of her crew members currently held at gunpoint atop the roof of a burning building and the Governor's raptors on hot approach, she didn't know how the situation could get any worse.

"Who the hell is that?" Kahu asked, squinting in an attempt to identify the mystery gunman.

"I have no idea, but he isn't messing around. You got anything for me, big guy? A card hidden up your sleeve?"

"I'm thinking I take the *Assurance* up as high as she can go without scraping the hell garden. You go open the cargo bay door. Then I send her into a nosedive—all hot and nasty like—as steep as I can without passing out. The raptors won't be able to track us at that velocity on standard repulsor pads, so hopefully we'll lose 'em. I bring her to a dead stop over the roof, and if the g-force don't kill us, the kids can hop up the boarding ramp and we'll get the hell outta here."

Delilah felt a slightly insane grin appear on her face. "Nebula. Sounds like my kind of reckless. You ever done it before?"

"Skipper, you know every time you make me pull one of these batshit crazy maneuvers it's gonna be the first, and last, time I ever attempt it."

"Atta boy."

Using her concussion repeater as a crutch, she stumbled back down helm access and headed through the galley, her limbs growing heavy as Kahu swung around the district and began his ascent. She barked an order at a startled Mercy to send Null to the bridge and get secured, then made her way below deck. Down in the cargo bay, she punched the permissions code into a console. Brash amber light flooded into the hold as the cargo bay door opened, allowing a powerful gale to blow into the belly of the *Assurance*.

She staggered past the dormant ZT-LL to a wall-mounted jump seat, almost completely blinded by the frenzied bird's nest of hair blowing about her face. Buckling herself in, she heard Kahu's voice over the intercom.

"Hey, Cap! I just checked the Nov-Net to see if I could get an ID on whoever it is down there with Teo and Tobias. Turns out it's that freighter captain Jonah Sinclair."

"Sinclair? Flies a pugnator class?" she shouted over the bluster. "Son of a bitch! Well, that's definitely *not* a genuine Phalanx uniform he's got on."

"Hell no, which means whatever he's up to down there ain't *sanctioned*, if you catch my meaning."

Jonah Sinclair . . . Delilah recalled finding the unruly thug starting trouble with Eamon Wyatt in the Weary Navigator. She had called him harmless at the time, which, beyond starting scraps in dive bars fueled by syn-beer and differing politics, was largely true. Whatever he'd embroiled himself in now, though, was a severe escalation from the drunk and disorderly behavior he was renowned for. She slung the strap of her repeater over her shoulder and flicked the trigger lever to charge a round. If that belligerent menace of a man laid a finger on either of those kids, taking a blast of concussion energy to the face would be but an appetizer to the pain and suffering she would incur upon him . . .

The *Assurance* jolted sideways. A cacophony of crashing, screeching metal exploded through the fuselage. The sudden motion caused Delilah to crack the back of her head on the cladding behind her.

"Kahu! What the hell are you doing up there?" she screamed, rubbing her throbbing scalp.

The old pilot's distressed voice came blaring through the intercom again. "One of the raptors just rammed our starboard side—they're right on us!" His voice went quiet, as if he were turning his head away from the comms panel. "You better not have scratched the paintwork, dickhead!"

The ship banked sideways sharply—a final, clumsy course correction.

"Alrighty, Cap. I hope you got yourself strapped in!"

Through the open cargo bay door, Delilah saw the cityscape below rear up to face her as Kahu nosed down. Her heavy concussion repeater became weightless, her arms free-floating before her in zero gravity. She glanced over at the ZT-LL, grateful that her intrepid pilot had remembered to engage the vehicle's magnetic locks. Without them, the half-ton hunk of machinery would have been bouncing around the cargo bay like a frightened bovine in a confined enclosure.

The *Assurance* dropped the one-kilometer height of the Mouth in a matter of seconds; the extreme forces of such a rapid descent began to take hold. Delilah felt consciousness slipping away, her perception of the world around her dissolving to blackness. Just as she thought she might succumb to the urge to pass out, Kahu leveled off, taking the thrusters to full burn to quickly kill the ship's downward momentum.

Slowing to a stop over Juniper Sanctuary, he unintentionally slammed the boarding ramp into the roof of the building. Had Jonah or either of the kids been standing beneath, they would have been reduced to a steaming pink puddle; had he misjudged the maneuver by another meter or so, the building would have been instantly demolished.

Delilah couldn't waste any time allowing her body to recover from the trauma it had just sustained from the abrupt deceleration. She unbuckled herself from the jump seat and sprang to her feet, concussion repeater ready to fire. With legs like jelly, she lumbered out of the cargo bay and headed down toward the group of startled individuals waiting at the bottom of the boarding ramp. Tobias and Teo stood mouths agape, staring in shock at the familiar ship that had just fallen from the heavens before them.

With Kahu idling the vertical stabilizers to hold steady over the building, Jonah stood shielding his face from the propulsion cascading onto the rooftop, a bewildered look on his thuggish face.

Delilah stepped off the boarding ramp, struggling to breath in the smoke-laden air. She felt the heat rising from the fire raging beneath her feet. It wouldn't be long before the building's foundations began to crumble and the sanctuary collapsed in on itself.

Approaching the dumbfounded bunch, she recognized the downed cohabitor as Nanimonai—one of Teo's caregivers back when the girl was a resident at Juniper. Ae was injured, as she had suspected from what she'd seen on the survey cam feed. Worryingly, the alien's crotchety old partner, Hiroki Sato, was nowhere to be seen—not to mention the twenty or so children supposedly under their care.

Jonah . . . what have you done?

"Captain Holloway?" the bruiser asked, shaking off his stupor. Intentional or not, he made the unfortunate mistake of allowing the muzzle of his viperinae SMG to drift in her direction. She didn't have time for a standoff, nor did she have the patience to try and talk him down. As Kahu had predicted, Vidalia's raptors hadn't been able to follow at such a steep angle of descent, but the maneuver had only bought a few extra seconds; they were circling back over the Cohabitor Ghetto and making their final approach.

"Holloway!" Jonah repeated. He flicked a minatory look at the bridge of the *Assurance*, then back to Teo and Tobias.

"Makes perfect sense this leech-sympathizin' scum would be serving on your crew . . . You always did have a soft spot for—"

Delilah fired from the hip. A cone of displaced reality fulminated from the barrel of her repeater, walloping Jonah in the legs and sweeping him off his feet. He somersaulted in the air before hitting the rooftop with a stomach-turning crack. Then he was still.

There was a moment of calm. She stood over his contorted body, feeling no guilt, and no remorse, watching a pool of dark crimson gather around his broken, misshapen nose.

She felt a small, trembling hand sliding into her own. It was Teo, standing at her side, looking up with teary, guilt-ridden eyes.

"What did I say?" she spat angrily.

Teo's bottom lip quivered. "Get back to the *Assurance* by oh one hundred hours."

"That's right! Now, get your butt back on that hauler right now, or stars help me, I'm leaving it behind!"

THIRTY

With the Governor's raptors drawing ever nearer, Delilah helped Teo and Tobias up onto the boarding ramp and ushered them into the ship. She offered a hand to Nanimonai, but ae stubbornly refused, using Tobias as aer empathic vessel to explain aer intent to retrieve the children, who were hiding in a safe location nearby, and to seek shelter with aer sibling out in the Cohabitor Ghetto. Delilah was impressed by the ease with which Tobias used his burgeoning abilities, considering the last time she saw him attain resonance it was a complete accident and had knocked him on his ass. Now, anyone could be forgiven for thinking he had been doing it all his life.

Clutching aer bleeding abdomen, Nanimonai bowed aer head in thanks, staggered over to an emergency stairwell, and disappeared.

Delilah slammed the intercom with the heel of her hand. "We've got a full house, Heperi. Now, get us the hell out of here!"

The boarding ramp folded into itself, hermetically sealing the cargo bay shut. As the *Assurance* pitched up and began to ascend, she gazed down through a porthole dripping with condensation at the shrinking rooftop of Juniper Sanctuary, where Jonah Sinclair lay dead or unconscious. Part of her wondered whether the decent thing to do would have been to lug his ignorant ass onto the ship, but she eventually answered that quandary with an unpitying mental shrug.

The building collapsed, swallowing the man in a molten vortex of rubble and smoke—consumed by a fire that Tobias would go on to explain Jonah had started. Fortunately, Teo had already left for the med cubby and wasn't present to witness the demolition of her childhood abode. There hadn't yet been an opportunity to ask about the fate of Hiroki Sato, but the fact that Nanimonai hadn't gone back into the fire at the earliest opportunity to rescue him spoke volumes. Teodora was resilient—she would hold it together for as long as Delilah needed her to, but there would be some serious consoling to do once they made it bowside.

Kahu swung around and aligned his trajectory with the *Devourer*. The black shapes of the two raptors in pursuit flashed past the porthole, close enough that Delilah could briefly make out the scowling faces of the Monarchs piloting them. It would take some masterful flying to stay out of range for long enough to enter the core, so she started for the bridge to offer what tactical guidance she could. Tobias, reeking like burnt toast, followed as she shuffled through the galley, struggling to keep her center of gravity as the ship jerked left and right sporadically. She hadn't forgotten about what she'd seen on the survey cam feed: the boy standing protectively over Teo, bravely facing down an unhinged gunman with scarcely any means of defending himself. Admittedly, that took more guts than she'd thought him capable of. How the pair of miscreants had managed to get themselves into such a predicament she could hardly fathom, but undoubtedly she had Tobias to thank in some part for getting Teodora out of it alive.

"Captain," he wheezed, spluttering from severe smoke inhalation. "You . . . you just saved us."

The helm access corridor rolled sideways as one of the raptors took another swipe at them, which Kahu counteracted with an abrasive avoidance maneuver.

"Don't thank me just yet, Edevane. Let's see if that old dog can get us out of the Mouth in one piece first—then you can kiss *both* our asses."

On the bridge, Kahu grumbled profanities as he grappled with the helm, while Null stood entranced by the windshield, one arm outstretched with aer paw splayed against the glass.

"How we doing, big guy?" Delilah asked, vaulting into the copilot's seat beside him.

"Can't fault these crooks for their persistence, Skip. I ain't planning on slowing down, so the bug better open us up a way through or else we're gonna be nothin' but a scorch mark on that big ugly hull."

Like plunging into a tornado from directly above, the oppressive exterior of the *Devourer* neared through the windshield. Tobias ran to the front of the bridge to get a better look, shoulders squared with his head held high. The arrogant, feebleminded narcissist who ventured out earlier that day had returned almost unrecognizable from his prior self. Standing beside Null, the boy exhumed confidence, awareness, empathy—qualities that had been sorely absent before but now radiated off him like sunshine. Delilah couldn't wait to hear about what had happened to trigger this incredible transformation, but the debrief would have to wait for now.

"What are we doing?" he asked calmly.

With a wild grin, Kahu relinquished the flight stick and threw his hands in the air, sending the *Assurance* into a listless drift. "Just you watch, kid. This shit'll blow your mind."

Null's timing was impeccable. Through esoteric sorcery that Delilah didn't think she would ever comprehend, her mute navigator willed the wall of manufactured viscera ahead to unfold like origami. The invisible forces residing within the core reached out and caught the careening hauler like a bird in hand, pulling her inside as bands of opalescent light danced excitedly around her nose cone, illuminating the way home down dark, organic passageways.

Tobias stood frozen in place with childlike awe slathered across his stubbled face. Joining him by the windshield, Delilah said, "Honestly, I thought you would have been a little more freaked out by . . . well, whatever that is out there."

"Not what, Captain," he absently replied, "but who. It's the light of the Savior. What I've been calling the *Devourer* all my life is really just a protective shell." He motioned toward the light show outside. "And this is what it protects. An ancient, cosmic entity—or a collection of entities; I'm not quite sure. In the decades since the Collision, it's been trying to unite us with the Prey—to help us understand that we are all one people now. The more we resist, the more it seeks to build a connection, because it needs us—our fighting spirit—for the hardships that lie ahead for us all."

"Great," groaned Kahu, rolling his eyes. "Now we got Bug, Bug-Eyed, and the Bug Kahuna aboard. You planning on turnin' my ship into a circus, Skipper?"

"It ain't your ship," Delilah rebuked. "Now quit your wisecracking and tell me if those Monarchs are still on our tail."

The old pilot studied the control pedestal beside him for a pensive moment, then relaxed in his seat. "We're in the clear—they didn't follow us into the core."

She ran fingers through her untameable curls in relief. "That's a shame. Would have liked to see how those raptors would fare in here without Null guiding them. Someone better tell the Governor his ruthless lackeys are afraid of a little turbulence."

"Why don't you tell him yourself?" Kahu gestured nervously toward the pulsating inbound call notification appearing before the windshield. Delilah hoisted herself out of the copilot's seat and hastened to the comms panel, pausing for a moment to summon from within herself the fearless, venturesome alter ego she normally assumed for dealing with ship captains and the like. Vidalia would make sure his strength was her weakness; she couldn't let her countenance betray just how rattled the pursuit had left her.

Drawing a deep, spurring breath, she accepted the call. Vidalia's image was cast just forward of the helm, the harsh angles of his face forming a virulent expression. With elbows resting on his stone desk, he turned and manipulated his moisturized hands, allowing a butterfly to crawl freely between his fingers, black-and-orange wings opening and closing hypnotically.

"You disappoint me, Captain Holloway," he said, dipping his head like a feline readying to pounce on its prey, his deep, resonant voice booming throughout the bridge. "I saw great promise in this new partnership of ours—not something I say lightly to those with whom I do business. You and your crew were destined for great things. What a shame that it has, instead, come to this."

Delilah formed a snarl, showing fangs. "You had my boy, Vidalia. We were getting him back, no matter what it took."

The veins on the man's temples throbbed angrily; the Governor of the Mouth wasn't one to lose his cool, but the cracks in his calm, collected facade were beginning to show.

"And had you simply called to appraise me of the situation, then of course I would have arranged for his release. But instead, you decided to launch an unwarranted attack on one of my most lucrative facilities, not to mention assault three of my employees."

"It did occur to me that there might have been a more amicable way to resolve the situation. But what good would that have done for the other two you had chained up to that vent like animals? Isaac might have been our priority, but their lives matter just as much as his."

"I reject that insinuation, Delilah. The individuals I employ at my capping facilities—your engineer included—are there by choice; they are not prisoners. They are given full control of their own consumption and are made well aware of the risks. They are free to leave whenever they wish."

"Tell me—if it is, as you say, by choice, then how many have actually chosen to leave? Was there ever a single one, or do they all work themselves to death, hands red raw with that dopey grin on their faces? You might not have pulled the trigger, Governor, but you sure as shit handed them the gun."

Vidalia's nostrils flared. The creatures in the aquarium behind him flicked their tail fins, seeming to match his seething temperament.

"I will make one attempt, and one attempt alone, to edify you, Delilah. Second chances are not something I offer readily, but you and your crew have done exemplary work for me thus far. You are owed an opportunity to atone. You see, I believe the people of the Coalescence are undergoing a transformation—a kind of metamorphosis, if you will." He raised his hand, staring fondly at the insect currently cleaning its antenna on the end of his thumb.

"The Collision was no happenstance: it was, in fact, fate—the mechanism that would deliver to us, the remnant of humanity, the very key to our salvation. We must reshape ourselves in order to wield this key, and there can be no growth without pain, no transcendence without sacrifice. I understand if what you saw at my facility was . . ." he paused, "distressing to bear witness to."

"That's one way of putting it," Kahu remarked.

"But let me assure you that what you saw is entirely necessary. I have come to realize that the cohabitors are more than just spacefaring vagabonds, dropped on our doorstep by some mathematically impossible coincidence: they are tools—tools that only a few among us presently have the genetic means and power of comprehension to utilize. If people like you and I ever hope to join the resonant in being able to commune with these creatures—if we aspire to brandish the power bestowed upon us by the cosmos—then the glow *must* be harvested and consumed by every human on this ship. Only *then* can we ascend from purgatory and claim the mantle that is rightfully ours."

Delilah tapped her lips with a finger in feigned contemplation. "I see. And I guess it's just an added bonus that you get to make a pretty penny in helping us all achieve this 'transcendence'—is that right?"

"I did not take you to be one for petulance, Captain. Again, you disappoint me."

Delilah leaned on Kahu's shoulder, arms folded in a show of insolence. "Forgive me, Governor. I'm just growing a little weary of hearing you yammer on like you're some kind of messiah while I watch you slowly tightening the shackles you have around people's necks. Dress it up however you like. Won't change the fact that what you're really doing is employing slave labor to industrialize your poison pedaling. We risked our lives retrieving those hydro-ionizers, and instead of giving them to the community like you promised, you've just found another way to exploit and extort people."

The butterfly flapped its wings and took flight, making a fleeting escape before Vidalia ensnared it in a cage of perfectly manicured fingers. Watching with a cruel expression as it struggled to break free, he said, "Have it your way, Delilah. But know that there isn't a dark hole on the Coalescence where my Monarchs will not hunt you down. If you have any regard for the lives of those who serve you, you will turn around at once. I will, of course, be requisitioning your balaener class as a means of reimbursement for the trouble you have caused me, but if you agree to return what you purloined posthaste, then I promise to spare the lives of you and your crew."

Delilah glanced at Null through the luma-cast projection of aer master. Ae was still laser focused on guiding the *Assurance* through the core, but ae was trembling—violently so. The mere sound of Vidalia's voice was enough to send a surge of crippling fear crazing through aer Herculean body.

Emboldened by an almost maternal urge to protect aer, she said, "That's a very kind offer, but Null and Mercy are staying with me."

Vidalia's face became a twisted visage of wrath, his smooth ebony skin stretched tightly over angular bone structure. "I was referring to the hydro-ionizers, but if you think for a second that I will sit idly by while you kidnap two of my most valuable assets, then I fear you have gravely underestimated me."

"It's their decision—not mine. If you want your people to stay loyal to you, I'd suggest you try treating them like more than just commodities."

Without so much as a word of warning, Vidalia formed a tight fist, crushing the butterfly inside, its twitching legs poking through the gaps between his tensed fingers. He unfurled his hand, allowing its crumpled remains to slide off his palm and onto his desk before sweeping them away in remorseless indifference.

"I will not be lectured, nor have my integrity questioned, by the likes of you—a petty plunderer, a lowly scavenger picking at the bones of the *Novara* for scraps."

Personal insults, Delilah thought. *Now you've really ruffled his feathers.*

"I do hope you've gotten everything off your chest," he continued. "Because this will be the last opportunity you will have to speak to me before your demise."

Delilah cast her eyes to the floor, taking on an air of sincerity. "Well, threats of bloody revenge aside, I did want to express how truly sorry I am for what happened to your cohabitor associate, Naught . . . I told you I was prepared to do whatever it took to retrieve Isaac, but it was never my intention for anybody to get killed."

Vidalia showed a sinister grin, baring pearl-white teeth and dark, depigmented gums. "I'm sure you will be delighted to hear that Naught is, in fact, alive and well, Captain."

"Is that so?" she asked, having to stop herself from fiddling with the concussion rounds in her gun-belt, aware that she was practically broadcasting her concern.

"Oh yes . . . As it happens, ae survived aer unfortunate encounter with you in the Vestiges. Naturally, ae will need time to heal, but save for one missing arm, my exo-physician informs me ae is expected to make a full recovery." Speaking in a chillingly affable tone, he leaned forward, clasping hands on his desk. "Do you know, Captain, I once saw a cohabitor rip the spinal column clean out of a man's back? An incredible display of strength and brutality—harrowing, I can assure you, but undeniably impressive. Imagine what horrors such a specimen could inflict upon the human body when aided by the finest prosthetic enhancements money can buy."

With that final discomfiting anecdote, the transmission went dead. Vidalia's image evaporated, and with it, so too did the air of triumph brought about by their successful escape from the Mouth.

Delilah collapsed into the copilot's seat, bringing her forehead to rest on her knuckles. Naively, she had hoped expressing her sincere condolences might have helped defuse the situation. Not for a moment did she think it would backfire quite so spectacularly. Though she had expected Vidalia to pledge vengeance, she had to admit that she had never really considered the ramifications of—nor prepared a contingency for—that eventuality. She had managed to keep a brave face throughout the call, but ultimately, Vidalia was right: in spite of its colossal size, the *Novara* was really no more than a tiny desert island in an ocean of infinity. Even with their new route in and out of the Mouth, there were very few places she could hide where he could not find her.

They completed the remainder of the journey to the Lower Amidships Docks in brooding silence, the Governor's threats having struck a serious blow to morale. Content that ae was no longer needed on the bridge, Null released a long, whistling exhalation and started for the galley. Tobias followed eagerly, and it was only when the boy turned his attention away from the windshield that Delilah caught the faint glow radiating from his irises. She displayed a tilted smile, delighted to see them getting along but unsure of how she felt about clandestine conversations taking place between her crew. She could be sure they weren't plotting mutiny or anything so absurd, but still, secrets made her uncomfortable.

Kahu sailed the *Assurance* through the fission field, taking her into the docks as gently and inconspicuously as he could to avoid drawing any unwanted attention. Their arrival was way overdue, but that was nothing gracing the harbor master's palm with a few loose nunits couldn't normally solve. She would likely have to sit and endure a prolonged diatribe about the importance of docking bay traffic regulations. Although, truthfully, she looked forward to the opportunity to stare blankly and switch off for a while.

A klaxon sounded from the overhead instrumentation panel.

Great. What now?

"Warning!" blurted a synthesized voice from the bridge speakers. "Autodock disabled. Docking clamp obstruction detected."

Kahu hastened to manually engage the landing gear, growling, "Lei-Ghan-nam!" in the back of his throat.

"What's the problem?" Delilah asked.

"Agh! There's some drunken bum comatose out by the docking clamps." He pushed himself up from the pilot's seat to glare through the windshield. "Hey! Why don't ya sleep it off somewhere else, pal?"

Delilah strode to the front of the bridge to investigate. Sure enough, a man lay slumped against the docking clamp actuators. Not just some random bum, but Eamon Wyatt. Head drooped to the side with the color drained from his cheeks, that scruffy aviator jacket he refused to wash or replace soaked in blood. The marshal was clearly in need of urgent medical attention.

Engaging the ship-wide intercom, Delilah released a sigh of both physical and mental exhaustion.

"Isaac, Teo! Prep the med cubby and get a stretcher ready. We've got wounded!"

THIRTY-ONE

amon awoke in the claustrophobic medical cubby of the *Assurance*. Not since infiltrating a gang of Portside Ward moonshiners had he come to with such a fuzzy head, although the current hangover wasn't the result of fermented molasses spirits, as was usually the case then, but the high-strength pain meds circulating within his battered body.

The unidentified marksman who nailed him from across the Canyon had only grazed the skin, but the high-caliber ammunition meant the near miss had resulted in devastating trauma to the surrounding tissue. Thankfully, Captain Holloway had chosen *not* to let him bleed out on the landing pad and instead had him hastily brought aboard so her young medic could plug the grizzly wound up with med-foam. The gunk had solidified now and sent sharp pangs radiating through his abdomen if he breathed too quickly or made any sudden movements. Laughing was especially painful—unfortunate, given just how much it amused him to hear of Lilah's recent hijinks down in the Vestiges. He hated the thought of anybody close to him ending up on the wrong side of Drexen, but knowing such a terrific blow had been dealt to that ruthless despot's operation brought no end of satisfaction.

For his sanity's sake, he allowed himself to revel in this one small victory but couldn't overlook the potential ramifications of it coming hot on the heels of the botched assassination attempt in the Çorak. With more of his turf falling into the hands of the Composer, Drexen would be growing desperate, and, like an animal caught in a trap, that made him even more of a danger than usual. Delilah had proven the Governor was mortal after all. Now, Eamon just needed to figure out where to stick the knife in to strike a killing blow . . .

After drifting in and out of consciousness for a while, he abandoned the harsh fluorescents of the med cubby and retreated to the galley to bask in the soothing warmth of Holloway's rustic array of decorative illuminations. He lay on a moth-eaten sofa with his bloodied shirt unbuttoned, exposing the wraps of gauze wound haphazardly around his midriff, light gray clumps of dried med-foam coagulating beneath like two-day-old protein porridge.

The crew gathered around him, listening patiently as he recounted in slurred and occasionally confused speech the chain of events that had led him to their docking bay in such a state. Holloway was predictably dubious of it all, but having been initially dismissive of Dr. Faye Lucero's prognosis of government corruption, he couldn't say he blamed her in the slightest.

"I don't buy it," the captain asserted, gentle lamplight dappling through beige fabric and softening her taut expression. "Don't forget, I grew up in Quarterdeck—I knew Madeline Vargos personally. She was a lecturer at ACS long before she took to politics. Sure, she can be a tad unpleasant at times, and maybe her methods of governance a little draconian, but not for a second do I believe she's capable of having someone assassinated—especially not a retired official like Anaya Lahiri, or an ex-Phalanx detective, for that matter."

"Trust me," Eamon said, wincing at the subsequent jab of abdominal pain. "Having troublemakers like me and Anaya offed is the least of what Vargos is *capable* of. She's been pulling the strings on both sides of the blockade from the very beginning, whispering in the Composer's ear while making sure Humanity First has all the funding and publicity they need. She's engineering a civil war—the biggest conflict since the Antonelli expansion. You better believe she's prepared to silence anyone who cottons on to what she's doing." He pressed a finger to his forehead, signifying the dot of a laser sight. "I was a dead man the second I set foot in that apartment. Had I not seen the muzzle flash, I'd be a goner for sure."

Teodora Brižan, Holloway's bright-eyed salvage specialist and part-time medic, stepped forward, peeling open a pouch on her utility belt.

"You might still be, if you don't get back to your gurney and let yourself heal like I told you." Pinning him with a knee on his chest, she produced a length of surgical tape and used it to fasten down an unruly corner of the gauze dressing. "Carry on stumbling around like a drunk and you'll snag that foam on a door handle and disembowel yourself—I'm only good for light patchwork."

Got a lotta spirit, this kid, Eamon thought. There had been a few hushed words spoken while he was recovering in the med cubby regarding a terrible tragedy that had recently befallen her. Something about a gunman, a fire in the Warrens, and the death of someone dear to her. If true, and she was presently conducting her duties in the wake of a devastating loss, she was hiding it remarkably well. By all accounts, she had the same grit and determination as the captain herself and was apparently no less of a hard-ass.

"I'll be careful, young miss—you have my word." He offered a wink; she returned an eye roll that was more endearing than it was probably meant to be.

There was one other development he'd managed to glean fragmented information about in his semidelirious state—this one so bizarre and unexpected that he half suspected it to have been a hallucination. "Tobias, hyper-resonant"—the words couldn't possibly have held any bearing to each other but for some reason were stuck in his mind like the abstract, nonsensical lyrics to a song with a naggingly familiar melody. He strenuously shifted onto his side to face the councilman's son, whose uncharacteristically haggard appearance, in his humble opinion, suited him much better than the usual trench coat and mounds of pungent hair product. The boy sat perched on the opposite sofa, practically shoulder to shoulder with Holloway's nonhuman crewmember, Null. Eamon had hoped spending a little time on the *Assurance* would help drill in a little tolerance and understanding, but Tobias becoming as thick as thieves with a cohabitor was a stretch beyond his wildest hopes for the judicial experiment.

"So, Tobias. You gonna show me this new party trick of yours, or what?"

The boy smiled, turning his eyes into two miniature Edison bulbs on demand, drenching the galley in faint starlight as Null followed suit.

Eamon chuckled in amazement. "Well, would you look at that. The son of Councilman Edevane—a cipher."

Delilah scoffed and shook her head. "Wyatt, you really are a lousy cop. It's no wonder Madeline fired your ass. You mean you dropped this kid off on my ship—the *only* ship in the fleet with a cohabitor serving aboard—without knowing he was hyper-resonant?"

"I can honestly say I had no idea."

"I should really thank you, Marshal," Tobias chirped up. "Had you simply handed me over to the bowside authorities, I never would have found out. I know I'm probably the last person on the *Novara* deserving of these abilities; nevertheless, I'm not going to squander them."

Eamon dipped his head, engaging the boy in a peremptory stare. "Don't take this lightly, Tobias—carrying the responsibilities of a cipher is nothin' to sniff at. They've helped keep relative peace between our two species since the Collision. Nowadays, there aren't nearly enough out there doing their part; that's why things are deteriorating so rapidly—a breakdown in communication. We need people like you stepping up to help us all understand one another. There's plenty you've got to reconcile for, but if you promise to put your resonance to good use, I reckon you and me will be just about square."

Tobias gave a nod charged with determination. "You can count on it."

"I hope so. Cuz the only other hyper-resonant I know is Marshal Jyn Sato, and she's gonna be a mighty tough act to follow."

"Is that who you left Abraham with?" Delilah asked with a worried pout.

"Should have known you'd be more fussed about the mutt than me, Lilah . . . Yeah, he's safe with Jyn."

At the thought of the deputy, he felt a stab of guilt that was somehow even more uncomfortable than the pain caused by the med-foam, his chest sinking in regret. "I have to get a warning out to her—I don't know what Vargos is planning, but right now, Harmony, Humanity First, and the whole ruttin' garrison are gearing up for a showdown, and it's lookin' like the Administrator is the hand directing all three."

"But that still doesn't make any sense!" The impassioned objection came from beyond the lounge, in the darkest corner of the galley, where the lamplight could only just touch. Holloway's mercurial engineer, Isaac Verhoeven, sat with his back against the wall and his legs tucked into his chest. With bloodied hands, he held a coolant pack to his forehead, his entire body trembling uncontrollably. Eamon had spent enough time around glow addicts in the force to recognize he was suffering from withdrawal symptoms. Holloway never did say what precipitated her perilous descent into the Vestiges—to a capping plant of all places—but he had no problem connecting the dots.

Isaac removed the coolant pack and met Eamon's stare, his pupils almost imperceptible beneath the milky lenses of his eyes. "Don't get me wrong, I'm no unionist—my parents were incarcerated on erroneous mutiny charges when I was very young, so there's nothing I'd like more than to see the Administration eat itself alive. Even still, I don't see what Vargos has to gain from starting a war."

"Separation," Tobias submitted. "That's what this is all about. If the Administrator is in league with Bhaltair Abernathy as well as instigating the unrest in the Mouth, then her intent is to sway public opinion *toward* separation from the *Devourer*. It's all Humanity First cares about."

"Surely Abernathy's followers aren't moronic enough to really think that could ever be a viable option?" Isaac sneered, sending just a suggestion of acrimony Tobias's way.

"Oh, but they are," Holloway countered. "Well . . . perhaps not moronic, but impressionable enough—definitely. Whatever vitriol this Abernathy guy is spewing is potent enough to turn regular folks into devout believers." The captain hung her head. "You remember that drunken ogre you nearly got yourself shot up by in the Weary Navigator?"

"I do," Eamon replied. "Although I think you'll find it was Sinclair who was spared from catchin' holes."

Holloway tightened her countenance, her next words seeming reluctant to leave her lips to the point where she almost had to physically force them out. "He burned today, and I let it happen . . . I *watched* it happen. He snuck into the Mouth with a couple of Abernathy's finest fixing to do something . . . unconscionable."

"The sanctuary," Teodora said, batting away encroaching tears. "Those hateful bastards burned it to the ground."

"Lei-Ghannam," Eamon hissed, an agonizing concoction of sadness and rage roiling in his chest. "They torched Juniper? What about the kids? And the old pair who ran the place—what happened to them?"

Tobias cast his eyes to the floor. "We managed to buy Nanimonai and the little ones enough time to escape, but we couldn't save Hiroki."

Holloway flicked Eamon guilt-ridden eyes. "Jonah was ready to execute these two when we showed up to intervene. I had no choice but to put him out of action."

"You did the right thing, Skipper," Kahu Heperi reassured her. "These two bright kids are breathing right now because of the decisive action you took—don't go beating yourself up about it."

Holloway smiled appreciatively. "I won't. But do you see what I'm saying here, Wyatt? I ran with Jonah for a spell back before I bought the *Assurance*. I considered that man to be a friend . . . Sure, he always was a blunt instrument—pigheaded, blameful—but a bloodthirsty militant? Never! Humanity First twisted his mind and filled him with so much antipathy that it consumed him. They blather on about separation being the salvation of humanity, but really they're just using it as an excuse to kill cohabitors."

Teodora's pretty features creased in pure detestation. "Population control, he called it, like they was nothin' but insects."

Eamon scanned the grieving and vengeful faces of those around him, feeling for the first time in a while that perhaps he wasn't alone in this fight.

"Separation might be what Vargos is using to spur on the conflict, but it's not her end game. Anaya suggested in her message that the leadership have a lot to gain from symbiosis with the *Devourer*, which means we should assume every move she makes is designed to keep herself in power and the status quo maintained."

He swung his legs around and propped himself up against the backrest of the sofa, readying to stand.

"For the love of the Abyss, will you please sit still," Teodora grumbled. He raised a pacifying hand, determined to allow his train of thought to reach its destination.

"Harmony, Humanity First—she doesn't care which side comes out on top, because at the end of the day, she governs both and will ensure that when the dust is settled, the Administration still reigns supreme. She's not so interested in the war itself but the technology born from it. Technology she can use to tighten her grip on the district and make sure the segregation is never broken. Think about it—every conflict in human history has been the catalyst for huge advances in technological development. The great wars of the twentieth century brought us computers, jet engines, and radar technology; the Lunar Colony Rebellions necessitated the advent of ripple-space propulsion and repulsor tech. The civil war that's coming will be no different."

Holloway's crew stared at him silently, their collective incredulity as plain as night. Guessing he could only convince them with a little show and tell, he rose to his feet and limped barefoot toward the countertop at the center of the galley, every cumbersome step triggering explosive waves of pain in his abdomen. He dug his hands into the crumpled pile of his effects on the countertop and removed the spliced cable from his jacket.

"This is hybridized tech," he explained. "Human and *Devourer* engineering spliced together. The stuff has been cropping up all over the district: mainly used to augment weapons, but I've seen a number of different applications now. The Administration can't be seen touching this stuff publicly cuz of their stance on the cohabitors, so Vargos created this whole insurgency to secretly accelerate research and development in this new frontier. Right now, Harmony is keeping the results close to their chest, but eventually she'll have them wiped out. Then she'll seize the fruits of their labor and use it to rule with an iron fist."

"But *Devourer* tech is light-years ahead of us," Isaac said. "Sure, the cohabitors might have a rudimentary understanding, but it might as well be magic to us. It doesn't seem plausible that someone could have figured out how to reverse engineer it, let alone *hybridize* it with human tech."

Eamon thrust the cable toward the dumbfounded group. "That grenadier I told you about—the one that came within a hair's breadth of ghosting me—this cable was used to install some kind of illicit subroutine that played hell with its friend or foe recognition."

Exercising his extensive knowledge of grenadier maintenance and operations acquired from his ACS schooling, Tobias said, "You can't hack a grenadier—their neural cortex safeguarding is infallible."

"Believe me, when you've got this hybridized tech in your toolbox, anything's possible. It's formidable stuff: versatile, robust, and incredibly dangerous in the wrong hands."

Holloway joined him at the countertop, still skeptical but gradually coming around. "If what you're saying is true, wouldn't Madeline be more concerned that this technology she was outsourcing was being used to hijack her own infantry?"

"You always were a smart one, Lilah. Thing is, whoever she's delegating the work to, I believe they hacked that grenadier in secret. When I broke into the apartment in Tycho Block, I think I stumbled onto something not even the Administrator is aware of—a plot to hijack the whole damned garrison and instigate the largest mutiny the *Novara* has ever seen. Vargos might think she's got the Composer on a tight leash, but soon enough, that dog's gonna break free, and it's gonna bite back."

Glancing down at the countertop, he began clearing away the mounds of cutlery, tools, and loose items of clothing piled on its tempered-glass veneer.

"Is this luma surface connected to the Nov-Net?"

Isaac stood up from his dark corner and staggered over. "No reason to suspect it isn't."

Resting on folded arms, Holloway looked up at Eamon with fierce scrutiny. "Wyatt . . . what are you looking for?"

"There's only two things I know about the splicer who's been hybridizing this tech: they're nonhuman, and at some point, they were processed by Phalanx, which means they were given a serial number. The *Assurance* is still commissioned by the Administration as a weld and salvage vessel, right?"

"Right."

"So you should have access to certain low-clearance government databases, the *Novara's* manifest being one of them."

Isaac ceased his tinkering and the luma surface hummed to life. An embedded emitter cast the Sinegex Systems logo above the countertop, painting the galley in electric shades of cyan and gold.

Holloway pressed her fingertips to the glass, triggering the illumination of a touch screen keyboard.

"I don't know if this will work," she said. "We have limited permissions. The Administration doesn't go handing out classified systems access to every scrap captain who asks for it."

"Please, Lilah—just humor me," Eamon said defeatedly. "This is my very last shot. If this serial number doesn't come up with anything, I'm done."

"And what if it does? You aren't exactly in prime condition—certainly not in any state to be launching a one-man assault on Harmony or taking down a corrupt government. Even if this does help you figure out who the Composer is, it won't help you stop her."

"You're right, I ain't in fightin' shape. But we'll cross that bridge when we come to it."

The remainder of Holloway's crew gathered around the countertop to watch as she navigated through endless luma-cast menus, finally arriving at the manifest—a comprehensive database identifying every person who had ever lived or died on the *Novara*, going all the way back to launch.

"Filter by nonhuman persons," Eamon said, scanning the list of names and profile pictures suspended in the air before him.

Holloway hammered a few keys on the glass, prompting the list to recompile itself to only display the cohabitors unfortunate enough to have become "known nonhuman persons of interest" to the Administration. After a moment of buffering, the profile pictures became mug shots, depicted in tandem with each individual's given serial number, known alias, and last known location.

Eamon felt excitement building as answers to questions that had driven him to the very cusp of madness drew tantalizingly close. Heart pounding in his chest, breathing hurried and shallow, he said, "Punch in serial number 241089RB."

Holloway complied, and the manifest reshuffled itself once again until only a single listing remained.

SERIAL NUMBER: 241089RB

STATUS: DATA CORRUPTED

LAST KNOWN LOCATION: DATA CORRUPTED

KNOWN ALIAS: DATA CORRUPTED

Eamon hung his head and let loose a sigh of total despondency, the crushing weight of his failure bearing down on his shoulders. Of course, the data hadn't been corrupted as the manifest suggested. Much like Anaya's apartment, somebody had plundered the database, anticipated his exact line of inquiry, and surgically removed any information pertaining to the cover-up, erasing the very last crumb of intel that might have led him to the truth.

Always a step behind, forever playing catch up . . . You're a washed-up has-been, Eamon. No good for nothing or nobody.

Feeling the spliced cable in his hand, he was struck by a sudden repulsion to the object; it represented his complete and utter ineptitude, and he found that he utterly detested it.

"I'm sorry, Wyatt," Holloway murmured, placing a consoling hand on his back. "It was worth a shot."

He raised his arm up high and hurled the wretched contrivance with as much might as his broken body could muster. But it didn't collide with the wall and shatter into a thousand sinewy pieces as he had wanted it to. Instead, it was caught in midair by a massive, four-digited paw. Null brought the cable before aer snout for closer inspection, eyes blinking asynchronously and mandibles squirming in intrigue. Ae stomped around the countertop to the spot where Holloway stood, practically barging her out of the way to commandeer the console's interface. Alarmingly well versed in human computronics, ae directed the manifest back a page then began sifting through countless rows of ID cards, studying intensely the faces of each cohabitor listed. After another minute of frantic scrolling, ae bleated sharply, taking a step back from the console. The currently highlighted listing expanded—framed beside a cluster of identifying information was the mug shot of the cohabitor in question, aer face bruised pink, aer demeanor broken and defeated. Eamon gazed into those eight piercing eyes, knowing innately that they belonged to the individual responsible for the weapons wielded at the blockade massacre.

I found you, you son of a bitch.

Satisfied the suspect's solemn countenance had been committed to memory, he glanced across at the identifying information. *Now let's put a name to that pretty face.*

SERIAL NUMBER: REDACTED

STATUS: DECEASED

LAST KNOWN LOCATION: REDACTED

KNOWN ALIAS: ABSENCE

Absence . . . Absence.

Eamon let the word rest on his tongue; he knew it held extreme personal significance, but the reason why was obfuscated by the impenetrable cognitive fog caused by pain meds lingering in his addled brain.

"Deceased," Teodora recited, leaning in toward the projection. "Another dead end?"

His insides plummeted as he realized exactly why the name Absence was so gnawingly familiar. Stumbling backward from the countertop, his stare distant and dismayed, he said, "No . . . unfortunately, it's not."

"So it's a mistake then—the cohab you're lookin' for isn't dead after all?"

"No, I reckon ae's alive and well. What's a mite troubling, though, is that Marshal Jyn Sato, who was previously ciphered with a cohab named Absence, told me with absolute certainty that ae died in internment after being arrested by Phalanx years ago. She's a vehement defender of cohabitor rights, downright lethal in a firefight, and she also tried to deter me on multiple occasions from investigating Harmony."

"So you think your successor as marshal might secretly be the Composer?"

Once Eamon took a moment to actually confront that terrifying possibility, the realizations came thick and fast. From Jyn's bizarre reaction in the two instances when he'd presented her with hybridized tech to her stalwart insistence that Devruhkhar would be a dead end to the oddly pleasing scent he'd picked up in apartment 2801, which it now dawned on him was Jyn's sweet, citrusy perfume—so much suddenly made sense.

He recalled how peculiar it seemed that Devruhkhar had voluntarily opened the door to his killer. In life, that slimeball was as neurotic as they came, but he always did have a soft spot for Jyn; she would have had no trouble sweet-talking her way inside. Only now was it obvious that she'd slaughtered that poor bastard in an attempt to cover her tracks after being shown the augmented pistol at the diner in the Amaali Bazaar. Clearly, she didn't count on Drexen sharing intel; otherwise, the trail would have gone cold at the gunsmith's workshop as she had likely intended it to.

Shock gradually morphed into fury as Eamon realized the person who had been his closest ally had been allowing him to run around the Mouth like some boy scout on a scavenger hunt, watching from the sidelines while he got himself into all manner of potentially deadly scrapes. Now the biggest threat the district had ever faced was also in charge of the law, and the innocent civilians caught in the middle of this pointless tussle for power would be left entirely defenseless.

These developments, while deeply concerning, would be meaningless without proof. As unlikely as it seemed to him now, there was still a remote possibility that Jyn's history with this Absence was just an unfortunate coincidence, and that the connections he'd made were really just him clutching at straws, desperately trying to find patterns in the storm.

He snapped his head in the direction of Null and aer fair-skinned cipher, gesturing toward Absence's holographic mug shot.

"Mercy . . . I need you to ask Null how ae can be certain *this* is the cohab I'm after. See if you can find out how ae's acquainted."

The girl nodded, turning to her companion and submerging herself in the murky waves of aer consciousness.

Oh, Jyn, Eamon thought, anxiously watching the silent exchange. *I hope like hell I'm wrong about this. Maybe one day we can sit together in the Drunken Shovel, get loopy on Hades sisters home brew, and laugh at this outlandish hypothesis of mine.*

He clung on to that thought as Mercy emerged from her trance to report her findings. Eyes still aglow, she said, "Cohabitors with knowledge in this field may not be as uncommon as you think, Marshal. Indeed, there are many among the Prey who seek understanding of the Savior's anatomy. For some, learning to dismantle and construct using its sacred material is, in a way, a pilgrimage—one of spirituality and science. Null has been on one such journey for a while now—ae too strives to gain comprehension, to improve aer craftsmanship, so that ae might find ways to better the lives of aer people."

Holloway leaned into the exchange. "Null was a dab hand with those hydro-ionizers. I doubt hooking them up to the conduit in the Çorak was easy work, but ae certainly made it seem that way."

Mercy smiled fondly. "It's true—ae has become quite accomplished in aer studies. But even still, this 'hybridization' is far beyond aer capabilities. We know of only one cohabitor proficient enough to have engineered something like the cable in your hand." She gestured with a nod toward the projection above the countertop. "The cohabitor named Absence was a pioneer of this movement—something akin to a shaman paired with a skilled technician, completely unmatched in aer faith and expertise. Like many others, Null learned everything ae knows from aer teachings."

Kahu made an incredulous grunt. "You can translate all that from one little staring contest?"

Eamon spurned the remark with a quick wave of the hand. "What happened to aer?" he asked, the answer already firmly rooted in mind.

"Ae was apprehended by Phalanx for inciting subversion. Aer exact fate is not known, but ae is assumed to be dead." A stern expression took her, the incandescence from her eyes spiking sharply. "It would seem what *we* know of this individual is consistent with your friend's version of aer story, but this hybridized technology has aer signature all over it, and its appearance undoubtedly throws that truth into question. If Absence *has* chosen to dedicate aer skills to the Composer's cause, then she has gained a powerful ally. Absence's followers were, and still are, many; this would explain why the Prey are now pledging themselves to Harmony in such high numbers."

Null became suddenly agitated, aer hackles risen and breathing sporadic. Doing her best to placate aer, Mercy continued, "Harmony has fortified themselves within the core. They are desecrating the Magnanimous Hollow and meddling with the light of the Savior. We do not know what their intentions are—only that they have become a very grave threat to all on the Coalescence. They must be stopped at all costs."

Eamon pushed himself away from the countertop; he had heard enough. While the pair couldn't explicitly confirm what he suspected, what they *had* provided was more than enough to fill in the blanks. The confused nebula that was his understanding of the situation had now funneled itself into a concise, coherent stream; no doubt remained in his mind about Jyn's involvement: with Vargos, with Harmony, with everything—she was the nucleus at the center of the whole damned conspiracy.

Holloway and her crew were silent, presumably awaiting some form of guidance or reassurance. Regrettably, he had none to offer.

He crouched down to collect his personal effects, swinging his aviator jacket over his aching shoulders and buttoning up his shirt.

"Wyatt, if you don't get back to that med cubby right now, I'm gonna drag you there myself," Teodora snapped.

"I'll be fine, li'l miss. You've done a fine job of putting me back together, but I need to take my leave. Mr. Edevane." He turned his attention to Tobias. "I've heard tell through the grapevine that your sister might be showing some very slight signs of recovery. Ain't nothing to get your hopes up about just yet, but if you want to consider your community service on hold to go and be with your family, that's fine by me."

The boy glanced around at his crew members, lingering on Teodora for a moment longer than the rest.

"Thank you, Marshal. I will. In the meantime, if there's anything I can do to help, please don't hesitate to ask."

Eamon shook his head, readying to leave. "It ain't marshal no more, just Eamon. And I appreciate the offer, but this ain't your fight." He paused, tilting his head slightly. "Suppose it might be soon, though."

"Wyatt, you can't seriously be leaving in this condition," Holloway protested as he turned and headed for the door. "Where are you going?"

He stopped, glancing over his shoulder. "To get my dog back."

THIRTY-TWO

arshal Wyatt's stark warning about keeping tempered expectations concerning Hazel's condition was not unwarranted; her signs of improvement were marginal—definitely *not* the kind of progress to raise one's hopes about. She was managing to breathe without assistance and, according to the on-duty nurse, would stir occasionally to utter a few words, if usually confused and relatively incomprehensible. That, unfortunately, was the extent of her recovery.

In true fashion, Atherton had spent a fortune securing a private room in the trauma ward that had all the trimmings of a luxury penthouse suite—an entirely redundant gesture, considering Hazel was hardly able to appreciate it.

Tobias sat by her bedside, his pounding forehead resting on the heels of his blackened hands, catching looks of disapproval from people passing the open door, mainly in response to the workwear he'd neglected to change out of before leaving the *Assurance*. Aegis Infirmary was situated just off Chennai Plaza; he was in the very heart of the Upperdecks—the region in which he had spent the majority of his life, where his father's influence was ubiquitous and his family name respected and revered . . . and yet, he felt so out of place.

The alienation bubbling in his stomach stemmed not from chagrin surrounding his disheveled appearance but from the realization that his perspective had become so drastically unaligned with that of the people around him. They didn't know it yet, but he was everything they feared, everything they despised. He had no intention of hiding the truth about his hyper-resonance—he would do everything in his power to ensure it was properly nurtured and put to good use, just as he had promised the marshal. The moment those in his circles caught wind of his "affliction," he would become a social pariah, scorned and ostracized, exiled from the high society he once prized so fervently.

Scanning the busy stream of patients, visitors, and medical staff bustling about the hallway outside, he saw in them fragments of his prior self: his arrogance, his willful blindness, his contempt. He pitied them, wishing they too could be afforded the same experiences that had pushed him to see the light . . . *The light of the Savior.*

Taking his sister's limp hand in his own, he opened his mouth to speak. There was so much he needed to say, and though any confession he made to her would almost certainly go unheard, he had to believe at least some part of her was still there, listening intently beneath her pale, lifeless shell.

"You never liked Caleb." He paused for a response, dropping his shoulders in sorrow when met with silence.

"Remember when Dad hosted that fundraiser? The one me and Caleb showed up to blind drunk? We were goofing around by the buffet table, and I tripped up and catapulted a whole tray of hors d'oeuvres onto Admiral Coombs. You were so pissed off at me; I remember we had a blazing fight the next day." A rueful chuckle slipped out. "You always knew I'd get myself in serious trouble tagging along with her. Used to say I'd follow that girl to the end, whether it was a jail cell or an airlock burial. I guess you were right. Although, I can't give her all the credit—this one was on me too."

He squeezed her hand tighter, turning introspective. "You never said so, but I know you were starting to worry about me—I was getting all worked up, just like Dad: hateful, opinionated. I couldn't see it at the time, but after what happened to you, I let myself get all twisted up inside, ended up doing something absolutely unforgivable. I didn't hurt anybody, but it wasn't exactly a victimless crime, either."

Silence endured, broken only by the slow and steady beeping of her heart rate monitor.

"I got caught instantly—hapless oaf that I am. Luckily, my fate was in the hands of somebody who wasn't interested in making an example of me, which is what I probably deserved. This guy, a marshal, he knew I could be better and decided to give me a second chance. He dumped me in a situation that I never would have dreamed of putting myself in voluntarily. As a result, I met some incredible people, had some unforgettable experiences, and I found out something about myself that I'm still struggling to believe even now." He stared into the distance, overwhelmed by his own brief recounting of the journey he'd taken. "The *Novara's* been turned upside down for me—nothing is like it was before. Not in a bad way, though: in a way that's given me meaning and purpose." He drew a deep breath, determined and resolute. "I guess what I'm saying is, you don't need to worry about me anymore. I found a new path; I'm not sure where it leads, but I know it'll be a damn sight less destructive than the one I was on."

He glanced at the monitor to check her bio readings, noticing a small spike in brain activity. He returned his stare, studying her face for any minute signs of recognition: a twitch of the lip, a burst of rapid eye movement. But no, she was still. He shook his head solemnly and sighed.

"I'll be here for you when you need me . . . but beyond that, I don't think there's much left for me here in the Upperdecks. It's funny thinking about how livid even just the thought of what lay beyond the blockade used to make me. Now, even in the midst of everything that's going on, I can't wait to get back. It has me wondering if Mom was driven by a similar compulsion—an irresistible pull to the Mouth, a need to be there, boots on the ground, to help in whatever capacity possible . . . I certainly like to think she was. It's nice to be able to say with absolute confidence that I think she'd be proud of *both* of us. There was a time when I wasn't so sure I could say so for myself—honestly, I couldn't have cared less—but now I know she would be."

He squeezed his sister's hand a final time, then rose to his feet. Before he could take his third step toward the door, his ears were graced with a sound sweeter than any he'd heard before.

"Tobias?"

He spun around to find Hazel semiawake, eyeing him with a look of warmth and mild confusion. She smiled. "Oh, you look so handsome in that suit."

He glanced down at his rumpled jumpsuit and ash-stained canvas jacket, recalling what the nurse had said about Hazel's intermittent speech. In truth, she was merely repeating one of the last things she'd said to him on Capella Promenade. It wasn't much, but it was something—his heart swelled with relief and gratitude.

"You think?" he replied meekly, savoring every second of the exchange.

Hazel's attention drifted. She furrowed her brow, eyelids fluttering as she struggled to formulate her next thought.

"Mom was here earlier," she croaked. "She was here . . . I saw her."

Tobias was unsure whether or not this was just another instance of her scrambled synapses triggering a random memory again, or if there was, perhaps, a less prosaic explanation. Had the connectivity between Null's mind and his own over the past few days somehow extended to her too? And if so, did that mean she had been visited by the same empathic manifestations while unconscious? He wasn't sure if hyper-resonance was hereditary or not, but if Hazel had been born resonant as well . . . He shook his head, acknowledging that she was hardly in any condition to be probed on such matters.

"I know; I saw her too," he said, nodding reverently. She smiled affectionately, her focus waning, then she was gone again.

Tobias exited the hospital lobby and found his father's swoop waiting for him in the loading area, its recently waxed red finish shining brighter than the emergency lights of a nearby ambulance. He was remiss to accept the offer of a lift from a man with whom he had so many grievances, but with his temples throbbing from mental and emotional exhaustion, he knew every meter he trudged would feel as arduous as a mile should he choose to walk. Reluctantly, he boarded. Hypatia greeted him warmly, then set course for the financial district.

Smothered by the sickly-sweet scent of the synthetic leather interior, he sat with his forehead pressed against the passenger-side window, the Canyon speeding by in dazzling streaks of neon and glass, fogged by the condensation of his breath. Hypatia habitually set the viewscreen to display mode and tuned to the NTNN broadcast; he immediately barked an order to switch it off.

As an oppressive silence filled the cabin, Captain Holloway's final words echoed in his mind.

"I know we had our issues when Wyatt first dropped you off," he remembered her declaring. "But I don't reckon Teo would have made it back without you lookin' out for her at Juniper. That matters a minute to me—a heavy minute. Now, I know you got your own things going on bowside that need your attention, but just know that no matter how rocky things get, there's always a place for you here on the Assurance."

Perhaps even more difficult to dispel from his mind was the image of Teo as he left her in the cargo bay, standing intoed, her face weighed by betrayal and disappointment. It was as though she'd never even considered the possibility he could want to leave so soon after the ordeal they'd pulled each other through.

"I'll be back," he'd tried to reassure her, which, as much as she chose to disbelieve him, was meant sincerely.

Leaving the Assurance and her crew behind was proving bittersweet; coming back to his old stomping grounds didn't quite feel like the triumphant return home he'd envisioned. In truth, it wasn't obvious where "home" was anymore—where the heart is, the ancient adage goes, which he supposed meant somewhere one could find feelings of safety, acceptance, and love . . . Worryingly, there wasn't anywhere he could think of bowside of the blockade that fit that description. If it was a sense of belonging he sought, then he couldn't help but think that home was a few kilometers back the way he'd come, berthed in the Lower Amidships Docks.

He would return to the *Assurance*—in that, he was steadfast—but Captain Holloway was right: there were a few things he needed to deal with first. There was music to face, an entire symphony's worth.

Entering his father's apartment, Tobias found a luma pad waiting for him on the foyer coffee table with a note written on it.

Tobias, it's good to have you back home with us in the Upperdecks. I'm away on an engagement at present, but I shall be home for dinner. Get yourself tidied up and I'll see you at 1900. Atherton.

As much as he desired to be sickened by the obscene luxury of his father's amenities, the high-pressure rain shower in his lavish bathroom was a sight for sore eyes. The powerful hail of steaming water eroded away the rind of mouthian residue caking his skin—a chalklike mixture of soot and dried blood fall gathering at his feet in swirling pools of umbra and gray. He was visited by the harrowing image of a mass of gasping people lunging toward a tapped conduit to collect their pitiful ration of water, forcing him to cut short his obscenely indulgent bathing ritual.

A stack of neatly folded clothes had been left for him atop the linen basket. Brand-new beige pleated trousers and a fine pastel-blue shirt. Despite being perfectly tailored, he found the garments strangely ill-fitting. It hadn't been long enough for him to have lost or gained any significant weight, but something had definitely changed . . .

Bathed, shaved, suited, and booted, he eyed his reflection in the bathroom mirror, gazing through a window in time at his meretricious self. He drew a deep, spurring breath, preparing himself for what would undoubtedly be a politically and emotionally charged reunion with his father.

Not *just* his father. As he left the bathroom and turned into the main staircase, a familiar voice fluttered up from the parlor: soft and melodic, yet commanding and austere. He arrived downstairs to find his father busying about the kitchen, leaving his two guests to mingle on barstools at the dining counter. Caleb sat with rigid posture in the same black, skintight dress she'd worn to the Promenade, her titian hair pulled back in a tight crown bun. The luma bracelet on her wrist that had once cast white vine leaves on her fair skin now projected the interlinked rings of Humanity First in a spiraling pattern up her arm.

Bhaltair Abernathy sat beside her in his loudest suit yet—a lurid two-piece in sky blue embellished with large green polka dots, presumably representing the Grasslands of Pasture—his holy mecca.

He said something that made her laugh; she leaned in close and playfully rested her head on his shoulder. The flirting pair noticed Tobias approaching and snapped away from each other. Caleb launched to her feet and bounded across the kitchen, wrapping her arms tightly around his neck as she cooed his name.

Indignation jounced in his rib cage. After goading him into joining Abernathy's damning crusade, tossing him to the mercy of the local authorities the moment things went awry, and leaving him to stew for a week with zero attempts to communicate, she had the audacity to show up wholly oblivious to the anguish and turmoil she'd wreaked upon him. Worse still, she'd come to welcome him home hanging off the arm of this conniving, murderous son of a bitch—a man who had manipulated the fears and insecurities of so many, himself included. Caleb likely wasn't aware of the true depths of Bhaltair's character; at least, Tobias hoped she wasn't. Before the evening was over, he would make sure she knew exactly whose cause it was she had blindly rallied to; he owed her that much at least.

"Is everything OK?" she asked, holding him at arm's length by his shoulders, her face beset with worry.

He smiled thinly. "Better than ever."

A few uneasy minutes of vacuous small talk passed as Atherton plated up dinner. Tobias was presented with a miserly portion of synthesized meat and potatoes—the usual four or five proteins rearranged molecularly into variations of the same bland, tasteless crap, paling in comparison to the homegrown produce available in the Mouth.

Is it possible to be homesick for a place you only spent a day or two in? he pondered, picking artificial gristle out of his teeth with his tongue.

Atherton swanned over to his drinks cabinet and retrieved his ancient bottle of single-malt Scotch, then placed four tumblers onto the counter and poured a measure into each.

"A toast!" he announced, distributing the priceless libations to his guests. "To my son, and to his much-anticipated return!"

Tobias quickly knocked back his pour and slammed the empty tumbler on the counter. Caleb and Bhaltair shared a puzzled look. She leaned in surreptitiously and whispered something into his ear. The man nodded, then turned to Tobias, his countenance revoltingly sincere.

"I imagine you might be a little upset with me, comrade. I was hoping we could take a moment to clear the air."

Tobias tilted his head in surprise, not thinking for a second that a polite apology was how the attempted murder of a dozen kids and the burning down of the sanctuary his mother had helped to build would come up in conversation. Sooner than he'd expected, which was ideal considering how much he was looking forward to slugging it out.

"Upset? Why is that" he asked reservedly.

"Well . . . your father was furious with me when he found out that I let you get involved with our *off-the-record* operations without his blessing. I suppose I'm to blame in part for your arrest—the plan was nowhere near as airtight as I initially thought, and for that I apologize."

Tobias stared blankly, stunned by the realization that the oblivious idiot grandstanding before him had absolutely no clue about the fate of the three men he'd sent to Juniper. Feeling the animosity seeping through his expression, he wanted nothing more than to grab Abernathy's detestable face and scream *"Murderer!"* as loud as he could . . . Instead, he drew a deep, calming breath; it wasn't yet time to show his hand.

Bhaltair tapped expectantly on the rim of his glass, demanding another pour of Atherton's liquid treasure. "While the destruction of that slop refinery was entirely necessary, we had to change our strategy once you got caught."

"Needless to say," Caleb put in, "we feared letting it get out that Humanity First was involved could potentially deter moderates from joining our movement." She straightened her slender neck and tipped her chin forward, taking on an air of elegance and austerity; Tobias could hardly recognize her. "We saw an opportunity to use the demonstration to put a spotlight on the growing leech insurgency in the Mouth, and to use it to emphasize the necessity for stronger segregation. After Bhaltair appeared on the NTNN broadcast to discuss the incident, Humanity First's approval went up by an estimated fifteen percent."

"You see, Tobias?" Atherton said, proudly pouring him a second measure. "Though it may have been regrettable how things turned out for yourself, there were some positive outcomes. Now that you're home, we can get straight back to work. Bhaltair and I have some big ideas concerning your role in the organization going forward."

Tobias felt a sardonic grin stretch across his face. He raised his glass and led another toast, this one in the name of Humanity First—the sociopolitical cancer eating its way along the *Novara*, the eradication of which, he was beginning to suspect, would have to be his cross to bear. For now, he would let the evening progress in mild-mannered and trivial conversation. He would lure them into a false sense of security, then strike.

"So, Tobias." Atherton began cutting into his synthesized meat, struggling to get through it even with his serrated steak knife. "We're all chomping at the bit to hear about your time serving in the Novarian fleet."

"Oh yes," Caleb concurred. "Tell us how it was."

Tobias paused, beckoning from within the strength to keep himself poised and civil.

"It was transformative," he began affably, going on to describe in broad strokes to faces of questionable interest what role the *Assurance* played in the fleet and what the day-to-day responsibilities of her crew were.

"Remarkable!" Bhaltair declared; the lack of condescension in the man's tone did not signify the absence of it. "What a versatile little ship."

Tobias set fierce eyes upon the man. "What's *remarkable* is that there are currently around ninety thousand souls inhabiting the Mouth who depend on that *little ship* with their lives. The *Assurance* is literally the only preventative measure in place to stop a major decompression event." He turned his glower toward his father. "The situation is being criminally neglected by the Administration. The experience highlighted the complete ineptitude of the council and demonstrated the blithe disregard Madeline Vargos is willing to show toward the lives of so many."

"Come now, Tobias," Caleb interjected diplomatically, his father reeling beside her, aghast at his son's insubordination. "You know just as well as I do that the District of the Mouth exists outside of Union sovereignty. I'm sure the plights of the people who choose to live there are many, but they're hardly the concern of the Administration, are they now?"

"That's quite right, Miss Callaghan," Atherton chimed in, fighting to regain some of his lost stature. "We have enough on our plate to worry about without fretting over the safety of our adversaries."

Tobias shook his head impatiently. He turned to Bhaltair. "Look . . . I know the plan is to make the blockade airtight and the *Novara* ripple space worthy again, but until such repairs can be carried out, a rupture in the Mouth means decompression throughout the entire Coalescence. This could be a crisis on a cataclysmic scale. Your feelings about the inhabitants of the Mouth aside, more resources and funding *must* be dedicated to refortifying the hull."

Bhaltair rapped his brass rings on the countertop. "I appreciate your enthusiasm in the matter, but I hardly see the point in wasting public spending on keeping the *Devourer* attached when we're working so hard to free ourselves from its clutches."

The ensuing silence was thick with tension. The signs of Atherton's growing exasperation showed in the form of quick clenches of his fist and bursts of rapid blinking. Tobias smiled to himself—the man had absolutely no inclination of just how furious he was about to be.

Caleb cleared her throat in an attempt to dispel the simmering enmity.

"Regardless—I'm sure it was an experience you'll not easily forget. Tell us more about the crew. I imagine there were one or two eccentric characters aboard. Did you meet anybody interesting?" She dipped her head and smiled presumptively. Tobias had known her long enough to recognize the ingratiating undertone to the question, as if she expected him to start reeling off about how unsavory they all were. Perhaps he might once have obliged her, but now she wouldn't get the satisfaction.

"They happen to be some of the finest individuals I've ever had the privilege of acquainting myself with. Captain Holloway has assembled an outstanding crew, bringing together people from all over the *Novara*."

"Ah yes, Miss Holloway!" Atherton hastily swallowed a mouthful of food, hell-bent on providing further interruption. "I once worked with her father. A terrible shame about that girl. She had a promising career lined up in the Department of Welfare before deciding to throw it all away in the name of pursuing this silly welding business."

Tobias shrugged. "If it was her intention to find vocation in protecting vulnerable people, then I'd say she's doing just fine."

"I suppose," Atherton wryly intoned. "And who does she have flying this miraculous boat of hers?"

"A veteran of the NTSC by the name of Kahu Heperi. He flew a kestrel during the Antonelli expansion."

Bhaltair raised his glass. "Ah! A true Novarian hero." Caleb and his father followed suit.

Tobias took a deliberative pause, scanning the tipsy, contented faces of his captivated audience. Atherton's pre-Collision whisky had warmed their bellies just right—their guard was down, and the time to dig his claws in had arrived.

"There were a few others worth mentioning: an engineer from Lower Amidships, a young salvage specialist from the Mouth. The most fascinating among them, however, was an individual called Null."

"Null?" Caleb asked, hovering a hand over her lips to stifle her scornful amusement. "What kind of ridiculous name is Null?"

Tobias overcharged his smug demeanor. "Well . . . it turns out cohabitors don't really *have* names—not in the traditional sense anyway. Null was the moniker given to aer by aer cipher, Mercy."

Atherton dropped his fork, his mouth hanging agape. Bhaltair nearly choked on an inopportunely timed sip of whisky. Only Caleb managed to stay composed.

She breathed Tobias's name, calm but stern. "Do you mean to say this Captain Holloway has a leech serving aboard her ship?"

Tobias gave an apathetic nod. "It's really not very polite to call them that, but yes, she does."

"This is an outrage!" Atherton rasped, his face glowing red. "She ought to have her docking license revoked and her ship impounded!"

Bhaltair jousted his fist forward. "She's harboring an enemy of the NTU—she should be arrested for treason. We need to inform the Captain's Guild immediately."

Atherton turned to his son, incensed. "Why did you not report this to the harbormaster as soon as you boarded?"

"Well, with the confiscation of my feather I had no means of communication. And we returned to the docks for the first time just a few hours ago, so I didn't have an opportunity." Tobias pinched his shoulders together defiantly. "Plus, I can't say I had any desire to."

"I don't understand." Caleb shook her head, eyes trained on him intensely. "You've been gone for days . . . If you weren't docked even once all this time, then where exactly have you been?"

"The Mouth."

A shared gasp faded into a capricious silence.

"That's impossible," Bhaltair said, just louder than a whisper. "The transfer checkpoint's been locked down since the explosion. There's no way some run-of-the-mill weld and salvage captain could have been granted passage."

"Comrade," Tobias said with a mimicking sneer, "you know perfectly well that just because the blockade is closed, it doesn't mean people with the right connections can't find a way to cross." He sat back, clasping his hands in his lap conceitedly. "Anyway, turns out there are other means of getting yourself sternside nowadays. We flew into the Mouth and parked up near the Cohabitor Ghetto. Delilah and her crew were kind enough to give me a little sightseeing tour around the district. I got to go to the markets, see some of the culture, try some of the food." A loathing expression came over him. "I went to a place called the Çorak and got to witness people living in poverty and destitution that made me sick to my stomach with guilt. I also visited a little place called Juniper Sanctuary—Dad, maybe you've heard of it?" He targeted his father with an accusatory glare. The man drew a quick, panicked breath, turning his head away in shame.

Caleb's eyes were trembling and wide. Tobias met them with his own for the first time since the evening began. "I got there about an hour or so prior to Jonah Sinclair showing up with two other degenerates, who then proceeded to murder the owner of the place before burning it to the ground."

Just as he thought his father might explode with rage, Atherton suddenly stood up, bearing down on the countertop with quivering arms but channeling his anger at Bhaltair.

"What is the meaning of this?" he demanded. "You gave me assurances the establishment was no longer in operation. You told me your men were only going to confirm it was still unoccupied and make sure it stayed that way."

Bhaltair showed his hands defensively. "Well, yes, that's true, Mr. Edevane, but you never specified what should be done in the event we found it still up and running."

Atherton slammed the counter with his fist, causing a loud clank of cutlery and glassware. "Well, obviously I didn't intend for your men to *kill* anybody. This is too far, Bhaltair. By the stars, what have you done?"

"Please, Councilman. You wouldn't think twice about me sending someone to the ass end of the *Novara* to fumigate an insect hive. This was no different."

"Children, Caleb." Tobias had his eyes still fixated on hers. "Kids, human *and* otherwise, but children nonetheless. And this waste of skin whose toxic bile you've spent the last week regurgitating to gullible crowds sent an execution squad to terminate them."

Caleb's face sank, but not in a way that pronounced shock or surprise—it was mortification. She'd known about Jonah's mission all along, but the true abhorrence of it had only just struck her. Bhaltair's mendacious talk had swayed her too, but unlike Jonah, she could finally see the man's "population control" for the infanticide it really was.

Desperate to escape Atherton's interrogating stare, Bhaltair stood up and began fumbling nervously with his feather.

"Please, Councilman. Just give me a moment to speak to Jonah—I'm sure it's not all as bad as your son is making it sound. We'll get this straightened out."

"Jonah isn't picking up," Tobias said, his voice grave and severe. "Thankfully another crew member and I managed to get the little ones out safely, but your man wasn't too happy about that, so he chased us to the roof, which is where he planned to execute us both in cold blood."

Atherton slammed the counter a second time, screaming a demand for Bhaltair to explain himself immediately. Tobias seized Abernathy's stunned silence as an opportunity to push him further.

"Captain Holloway showed up just in time to put Sinclair out of action, then we left that heinous scumbag to burn along with the other two in the fire they started."

"Do you realize how serious what you're saying is, Tobias?" Bhaltair snapped his head to the side. "Did you hear that, Atherton? Your son just admitted to his involvement in the deaths of three NTU citizens—valued supporters of Humanity First. Are you going to let this stand?"

"It's far more concerning to me that the bumbling amateurs you have doing your groundwork murdered an innocent civilian and made an attempt on my son's life! We are a political organization, Bhaltair, not terrorists! If we resort to violence, then how are we any better than the leeches? By doing this, you undermine everything we're striving for!"

Atherton stormed across the parlor, his collection of hanging artifacts clattering in sync with his pounding footsteps. He wrenched the front door open and gestured angrily through it.

"It's time for you to leave. I think we need to have a little discussion about your conduct, but we shan't be doing it here and now."

Bhaltair shot Tobias a venomous glance before collecting his things and heading to the door. Caleb timidly hurried after him, making it abundantly clear where her loyalties lay. Before leaving, she brought herself before Tobias, touching his wrist with her fingertips.

"What happened to you?" she asked. "What happened to us?"

"Nothing is how we thought it was, Caleb. If you spend ten minutes beyond the blockade with an open mind, you'll realize that." A wanting expression took him. "I'm going back as soon as I can—you should come with me. See it for yourself."

She shook her head. "My place is here. And so is yours. I can't say I'm not deeply troubled by what you just told us, but it doesn't change anything. My allegiance is—and always will be—with Humanity First."

"This isn't about humanity, or progress, or whatever bullshit that snake's been feeding you—this is about revenge. You let your grief over the loss of Jade take over your mind. It's controlling you!" She glanced off and to the side, tears welling in the corners of her eyes. "Jade loved you, Caleb. She loved you for the same reasons I do: because you're brilliant, fierce, nurturing, and resourceful—and right now you're using those strengths to assist an organization that's targeting people who had *nothing* to do with her death. I just need you to understand that it doesn't have to be this way. It's not too late to turn back."

There was a moment of tormented introspection, then sorrow turned to anger, her trembling frown tightening into a rancorous snarl.

"I would suffer Jade's death a thousand times over before I let myself turn into a leech sympathizer." She flicked her hand away from his. "You disgust me, Tobias. Run away to that festering piss-hole if you must—if it means I never have to see your face again, then that suits me just fine!"

"It sounds like you've been through quite the ordeal," Atherton said, perched on the armrest of his sumptuous sofa. "You weren't hurt at all, were you?"

"A little smoke inhalation, but otherwise I'm fine."

Atherton sighed, ushering in a long, oppressive quiet, broken only by the gentle crackles and pops of the cast-iron hearth.

Tobias found himself surprisingly relieved to have learned that his father was not as complicit in the incident at Juniper Sanctuary as he had first suspected. Atherton was a stubborn, overbearing bigot of a man, but he wasn't a killer.

Eventually his father was forced to do the only thing he knew how to when there was something unspoken that he couldn't bring himself to say: he hastened to the kitchen and retrieved his treasured Scotch, placing it in the center of the mahogany coffee table.

Tobias glared at the half-empty bottle—a symbol of so much that he sought to distance himself from: obscene, unnecessary wealth, a slavish attachment to an unhealthily glorified past. He despised it.

"I expect you'll be wanting to talk more about this Juniper Sanctuary."

Tobias ignored the question, casting his eye around the surrounding memorabilia.

"Look at this place," he mumbled absently. "You've got trinkets and treasures from every corner of Earth Before, relics from every period in human history on display . . . and yet, not a single picture of my mother."

Atherton froze, the rim of his bottle resting on Tobias's tumbler, a moment of reverent cogitation. "I don't need Tabitha's portrait hanging on the wall to keep her alive in my memory, son," he said, proceeding to pour yet another measure.

Tobias watched his glass fill with golden fluid. A hot rage flurried in his chest as he realized his father would continue to use the substance as a scapegoat to skirt around every uncomfortable topic of conversation. He stood abruptly, snatched the whisky from his father's hands and launched it into the fireplace. The neck caught the heat guard, and the bottle exploded. The flame swelled, discharging a surge of broken glass and alcohol.

Tobias stood motionless, staring into the blaze.

"I learned more about my own mother spending two days in the Mouth than I did from a lifetime spent with you. There are monuments to her! Commemorative plaques left in remembrance, scattered all throughout the district. She's celebrated like a saint for the work she did."

His father nodded solemnly, surprisingly unbothered by the obliteration of his prized possession. "I know . . . It was by my design that they were placed there."

"Explain to me then—when she did so much good for so many, why was it your response to discredit her achievements and bury her legacy! Hazel and I spent our entire childhoods thinking so little of her thanks to you."

"Legacy?" Atherton repeated. "Your mother's legacy was the destruction of this family. Let's not forget that it was her misguided compassion for those demons that got her killed, leaving her two children mother-less and her husband in ruins. Do you really want to know why I down-played Tabitha's humanitarian efforts to you and your sister? Why I did everything in my power to give you as much cause as I had to hate the leeches, making sure you never desired to set foot beyond the blockade? It's because I was afraid—terrified you would follow in her footsteps. I thought you'd go wandering off in search of duty and meaning, only for you to get swallowed up by that slum. I lost your mother to that place; I wasn't going to lose you too."

Tobias paused. He leaned over and placed a hand appreciatively on his father's knee.

"That, I can understand . . . but what I don't get is why you thought it nec-essary to cut funding to all her relief centers. You denied untold numbers of at risk people a better quality of life. Why?"

"And continue hemorrhaging nunits to a cause I didn't believe in—money that could have been spent on yours and Hazel's education? I loved your mother dearly, Tobias, but just because I funded her work, don't think for a second that I *ever* shared her beliefs. After her death, I wasn't going to waste another second on it."

"You may not have deemed their lives a worthy cause for charity, but I do. That's why I'm returning to the Mouth to carry on with Mother's work. I will restore her legacy and bring humility, empathy, and compassion back to the Edevane name."

Atherton's eyes nearly popped out of their sockets in his rage. He stood up suddenly, staring down at Tobias, his face furious and red.

"You will do no such thing! I absolutely forbid it! You will return to the Academy to continue your education or so help me, Tobias Cole Edevane, you will be cut off!"

Tobias stood to calmly straighten his father's tie, just as the man had done for him countless times before.

"I'm resonant, Dad. I doubt you know what that means; all you need to know is it means I can't stay here. I know you have big ambitions for me and my place in the Upperdecks, but I'm called to the Mouth—just like Mother was. I'm going to do great things. It may not seem that way now, but I believe one day you will understand."

Tobias headed for the door as his father's vociferation degraded into pleading whimpers.

"Please, Tobias. You can't leave. Think of your sister! She needs you."

Tobias turned to face the man, who almost appeared to have shriveled to half his size.

"Hazel will be waking up soon. And when she does, it won't be me she needs but you—not a councilman but a father. I suggest you take all the time and effort you've been wasting on Humanity First and channel it into her recovery. If she is to ever get back up on her feet, that's what it's going to take."

EPILOGUE

The streets of the district were all but deserted. Tinji Marketplace, once a vibrant hub of life and culture, was now nothing more than a barren clearing, the oppressive quiescence broken only by the muffled pops of distant gunfire.

The insurgents and the Glow Syndicate were moving against one another, their long struggle of attrition finally taken to the streets. Denizens anxiously took shelter in their homes, praying in countless tongues to countless deities for the bloodshed to abate and for peace to resume, even the most hopeful among them knowing that to truly expect respite was a fool's pursuit. In the Mouth, violence only heralded further violence. Retaliation meant escalation, and such would be the case until the eventual engulfment of war.

Despite the completion of repairs to the transfer checkpoint, the enclosing Phalanx compound remained under grenadier control. A garrison of tireless automatons waited vigilantly as the fighting crept ever closer. Their directive, issued to them by the highest levels of the Administration: to hold fast until the conflict encroached upon NTU sovereignty. Unbeknownst to their self-assured masters, that very directive would soon be rewritten, and the infantry manufactured to protect the interests of the Novarian elite would soon serve a new purpose, ushering in a new era for the Coalescence and all who inhabited it.

Nestled high above the compound, Antaeus Gateway, which had been sealed shut since the deadly terror attack, awoke from its slumber. Hulking slabs of reforged hull metal parted like the jaws of a colossus, gear wheels and drive chains squealing and clunking as they crawled to life. A vehicle slid through the newly revealed aperture like a shadow, a limousine on cobalt-encased repulsor pads and reinforced with titanium body plating. Flaunting a pearl finish as black as the endless night, it nosed down and accelerated, the vehicle's occupants seemingly undeterred by the plumes of smoke rising from the many firefights raging below.

A heavy blood fall descended on the district. Windscreen wipers flicked back and forth furiously, wrestling with the riot of crimson precipitation unleashed by the layer of lambent moss above.

The limo scudded over the Copper Swathes and descended toward the Langrenus Harrow, coming to a quick stop over the roof of a dilapidated warehouse.

The passenger-side door swung open vertically. Administrator Madeline Vargos emerged, dressed in her signature red, wearing a bulletproof vest over her double-breasted suit jacket. Three compact hover drones raced to form up above her, casting between them a thin triangular fission field, keeping her dry from the deluge.

A heavily armed security detail disembarked—two Phalanx enforcers flanked by two grenadiers. They fell into step behind Madeline, each surveying a sector of their surroundings for potential threats, weapons drawn and held at the ready.

Jyn Sato stood awaiting their arrival. Her new companion, Abraham, sat obediently by her side, growling softly at the nearing figures, his brindled fur coat sodden and discolored by the torrential blood fall. Madeline glanced over Jyn's shoulder as she approached, her wrinkled face shriveling into a look of revulsion, disdainful eyes scanning the ravaged exterior of the imposing alien warship beyond.

"There are many things to utterly detest about that parasitic derelict, but none so much as this accursed rain." She clawed obsessively at her right shoulder pad, attempting to brush away the stray globule that had breached her automated umbrella and blemished her attire. "I don't know how you can stand to have it all over you like that."

Jyn reached out, allowing the organic substance to pool in the palm of her hand, eyes wide and wistful. "You get used to it after a while. Some of the locals think it brings good fortune; others say it's a sign of great change on the horizon."

Madeline made a sneer of impatience as she came to a stop. "Come now—I sincerely doubt you summoned me to this dreadful place to discuss folklore and superstitions, did you, Agent Sato? Now give me your latest report. How are operations in the District of the Mouth going?"

A well-timed explosion sounded from somewhere in the Copper Swathes, reverberating chaotically around the mountainous walls of the chamber. Abraham jolted his head in the direction of the blast, ears raised and alert.

Jyn leaned on her hip. "Well, as you can probably hear, the Monarchs are putting up more of a fight than we originally anticipated. We took the Warrens in our initial advance, but they've since pushed us back toward Tycho

Block. I don't think the Governor's gonna let go of his hard-fought territory, not willingly anyway."

Madeline shrugged. "Vidalia is a businessman. He can play warlord all he likes, but ultimately there's only one language he's truly fluent in. It may be that we need to consider offering a financial incentive in order for him to think about loosening his grip. I'll speak to the treasurer and see what can be allocated."

Jyn sighed. "I fear any hope of an amicable resolution may have been scuppered when one of my followers took it upon themselves to try and assassinate the Governor—now I'm hemorrhaging resources keeping him engaged, both my own and DMED's. Fighting him on two fronts like this is causing pandemonium throughout the district."

Madeline raised an eyebrow. "But 'pandemonium' is precisely why you're here, is it not? Remember, Jyn, your goal is and always has been the destabilization of the Mouth. So far, the actions of your organization have helped generate tremendous sympathy for Humanity First and their mission, but dissent continues to grow in lower-income areas, especially the Portside Wards. We must continue our efforts to sway public opinion for continued and strengthened segregation. It's paramount to the future of the New Terra Union that people rally behind Mr. Abernathy's campaign. His talk of *Devourer* separation is all bluff and bluster, of course, but it will give us the funding and approval we need to refortify the blockade and enact tighter control over this district."

"I understand, Administrator." Jyn bowed her head subserviently. "But you don't need to worry. I'm happy to report there's been a significant breakthrough. Absence is getting close to figuring out a way of harnessing the *Devourer*'s power—one that will ensure Harmony dominance over the region for the foreseeable future. The citizens of the NTU will have plenty to fear about the Mouth and its inhabitants. Abernathy will have his followers."

"Excellent news!" Madeline exclaimed, clasping her hands in delight. "That creature of yours is most resourceful, I shall give you that. Can I assume this had something to do with your recent infiltration of the . . . What was it called again?"

Jyn cleared her throat. "The Magnanimous Hollow, ma'am."

"Ah yes, the Magnanimous Hollow," Madeline echoed derisively. "The very nexus of the *Devourer* itself—what an absurdly regal name for what I presume is an absolutely dismal place. Not too much of a struggle getting inside, I hope?"

"Not at all." Jyn cocked her head with aplomb. "Absence's influence among the natives meant we were met with very little opposition. There were a few scattered loyalists standing their ground, but they were hardly equipped to defend themselves."

Madeline feigned sorrow, dropping her shoulders. "Yes . . . I'm afraid that voracious fighting spirit was all but beaten out of them during the Antonelli expansion, but my constituents certainly don't need to know that." She clapped her hands. "Well then! I should like to see this new breakthrough in action! I must warn you though, Jyn, your last *demonstration* might be a tough act to follow—Admiral Coombs was most impressed by the performance of the two kestrels he donated to our cause. Jasper was being a stubborn old fool, obtusely cynical of our vision of a future empowered by exo-tech hybridization, but seeing your augmented fighters in action almost certainly helped him see the light." Madeline's tepid smile straightened into an austere look. "I, on the other hand, would have appreciated a little more attention to detail from you. The young trainee who survived your little weapons test is, thankfully, still unresponsive, but should she recover, I imagine she'll have quite the story to tell." A Machiavellian grin swept across the Administrator's face. "I trust that in the event she *does* show signs of improvement, you will be on hand to tidy up any loose ends."

"I've been monitoring the situation closely, ma'am. It won't be an issue."

Abraham made a whine of discomfort, then shook himself dry, dispersing an explosive surge of grubby vapor into the air. Madeline's security detail synchronously flinched in response to the sudden movement, briefly tightening their shooting stance before standing down. The Administrator's hatchet face was again visited by a look of disgust; she turned her shoulder to protect her expensive regalia from the canine-triggered cloudburst.

"I hope you don't plan on bringing this rabid animal to all of our meetings like your predecessor insisted on doing. The stench is overpowering!"

Jyn ruffled the fur on the nape of Abraham's neck. "I don't think I have a choice. There are a few fossils down at the precinct house who aren't too happy about my expedited promotion to marshal, considering how green I am to the force compared to some of the relics gathering dust there. I think there might be a growing suspicion that I had something to do with Wyatt being discharged, and they've already been pretty vocal about my soft-handed approach in dealing with Harmony. I need to get this mutt as sweet on me as he was with the last marshal—it's the only way I'm gonna win them over."

Madeline clucked her tongue in disapproval. "I see . . . well, let's just hope this gambit of yours pays off. I'm sure you're aware that I would have preferred a more *permanent* stratagem for removing that meddling fool from the frame."

Jyn nodded affirmatively. "I know, ma'am. Eamon is fiercely dedicated to doing what he believes is right. His relentless snooping caused him to have a near miss with one of Absence's prototypes—he was nearly killed. I don't want him hurt in all this, but I understand that he needed to be removed. This was the appropriate course of action; I have every confidence he won't be a problem."

The Administrator twisted her lips. "I wish I shared your optimism. While the way in which you dealt with Anaya Lahiri may have been a tad heavy-handed, at least we can rest easy knowing she's silenced for good. Of course, I will honor your request to keep Eamon out of harm's way as much as I am able. At the end of the day, though, he's now in my jurisdiction, and if he starts to become more trouble than he's worth, I will not hesitate to take matters into my own hands."

Jyn took a sharp breath of anger and surprise. "Vargos, I swear by the Abyss, if you lay a single finger on that man I—"

The two grenadiers took a coordinated step forward. Vargos raised a finger to quietly dismiss them.

"That's 'Administrator' to you, Agent Sato," she spat. "And I think you'll find you're in no position to be threatening or making demands of me. I'll remind you that were it not for my swift intervention, that ailing varmint Absence, who is the subject of such misplaced adoration from you, would have been executed long ago, and you would have been charged with sedition for conspiring with an enemy of the NTU. It was by my grace that you were *both* allowed a second chance and by my generosity that you were given an opportunity to serve something much greater than yourselves." Madeline placed a hand on Jyn's shoulder, simpering disingenuously as she began to squeeze tighter and tighter.

"You've done exemplary work so far, my dear. I'm really starting to see the potential in you, but you mustn't become complacent in thinking that I won't revoke the freedoms I have afforded should either of you choose to disobey me. You belong to *me*, and you would do well to remember that."

Jyn cast her eyes to the floor, her body language intimating understanding but her trembling, tightly curled fist suggesting otherwise.

"My apologies, Administrator: I did not mean to speak out of turn." She glanced at her wristwatch then over her shoulder at the *Devourer*. She met Madeline's scrutinizing stare once more, the corners of her lips pinched in a subtly devious smile.

"Please allow me to make up for my impertinence by showing you exactly what Absence and I have been working on: the start of a new future for humans and cohabitors alike, one of security and prosperity for all who are willing and of swift judgment for any who oppose."

She turned away, waving an arm to beckon the Administrator forward—to join her in observing the sweeping vista stretching beyond the rooftop.

The *Devourer* bellowed a deafening chime—a discordant fanfare of woodwind and brass that rattled the entire district. Abraham darted behind Jyn, tail tucked between his legs, cowering from the otherworldly cacophony.

All throughout the Mouth, residents heeding the announcement gathered in their domiciles, settling in for what would be a brief escape from the carnage outside—an opportunity to receive a blessing of warmth and knowledge from their Savior.

Wavering vines of light emerged from deep within the serrated, spiraling orifice occupying the *Devourer's* hull. They dispersed across the district, floating daintily over the cityscape like paper ribbons caught in an air current before connecting with antennas and pylons standing tall atop the roofs of buildings.

"Fascinating!" Madeline declared. "The dissemination, I presume?"

Jyn flicked a look of surprise; the Administrator tutted in response.

"Oh, come now, Agent Sato. I'm not completely oblivious to the nature of this place. It's a quite ingenious solution for supplying the addicted with their coveted hallucinogen, isn't it?"

"Very true, although the signal is far more than just a glow delivery method, ma'am."

"How so?"

"Well, what we've discovered is that much like the *Devourer* itself, the signal is both organic *and* artificial. What you see before you is essentially a form of data transmission—resonant frequencies consisting of strains of code combined with something that, remarkably, resembles DNA. Absence found a way to tap into these strains, enabling us to reprogram the signal itself and coerce it to perform new functions. Our testing has revealed that its semi-biological composition gives it a certain fluidity that enables it to bypass even the most rugged encryption."

Madeline turned her nose, making no secret of her growing disinterest. "That all sounds very impressive, but I still don't understand what you think we can hope to benefit from all this."

"I think it would be easier if you saw it for yourself, ma'am."

The two nearest vines made a sudden course deviation; they began to twist and undulate, their gentle amber hue transmuting into a volatile pink as they snaked toward the rooftop. Madeline Vargos's frail body tensed as they approached; her security detail jolted into action and moved to form a protective perimeter around her. The status lights on her two grenadiers switched from docile blue to sharp yellow. They held steady, cautiously assessing the threat level.

The vines slalomed closer to the two primed androids then reared up and lunged toward them, burying into the back of their faceless heads like worms into the dirt. The machines recoiled and convulsed as the repurposed signal penetrated their neural cortices. Madeline stood motionless, awestruck and terrified, watching her indomitable protectors reduced to helpless, writhing marionettes by nothing more than tenuous strands of luminescence.

"Agent Sato. Explain yourself immediately!" she shrieked, her implacable demeanor quickly unravelling.

Jyn didn't respond. Firmly holding Abraham's collar to prevent him from bolting, the marshal stood quietly, watching the scene unfold, the lines of her face drawn in baleful intrigue.

Seconds later, the ethereal vines had evaporated. The grenadiers straightened their posture, going rigidly still. They began to recalibrate, and after a suspenseful moment, their status lights turned red. They snapped to attention, then drew their rifles ready.

"G-units one and two are compromised!" one Phalanx enforcer barked at the other. Before either could take preemptive action, their mechanical squadmates executed them with callous precision. Two quick bursts of fire rang out. Muzzle flare ignited the blood fall, the murky atmosphere torn asunder by jagged, phosphorescent streaks. Two lifeless bodies hit the deck with heavy thuds, identical bullet holes placed dead center between their eyes.

Gun barrels smoking, the grenadiers stood down, pending receipt of new directives.

"Apprehend the Administrator," Jyn said coolly.

They turned their attention to Madeline, who let slip a whimper of shock and horror, staring down the armor-plated visions of death marching toward her. Each took one of her arms in servomotor-driven fists. With feet like the armored tanks of wars since passed, they applied pressure to the back of the woman's legs, forcing her down to her knees before Jyn's unmerciful gaze.

Panic consumed the Administrator; her enfeebled body began shaking violently and her face became a grim visage of despair, betraying the sudden realization of one simple fact—by giving Jyn the funding and resources to wage war on her behalf, she had ultimately brought about her own demise. She had been bested, and now her lack of foresight would be her undoing.

Abraham broke free from his master's grip then, wholly confused by the situation, began licking the tears flowing down the Administrator's face. Jyn slapped her thigh, throwing her head back in amusement. She leaned over, bringing her face before that of her fear-stricken captive.

"You know what? I didn't think there was a chance in the Abyss that would actually work. I thought surely you—the ruthless strategist and master tactician—would anticipate this very play. I thought for sure you'd have all manner of countermeasures in place to thwart me. And yet, here we are." She shrugged suggestively. "Funny . . . I'm almost disappointed."

"Jyn. P-please," Madeline gurgled through tears, her grenadiers tightening their grip on her fragile physique. "What do you want? You know I can give you anything! Please, just let me go!"

"I don't think so," Jyn replied calmly, her mirthful bearing starting to wane. "There isn't a thing on the *Novara* you can offer me that I'm now not in a position to take for myself. You've seen what I can do with just two hijacked grenadiers—imagine what I can do with the entire garrison."

"But I don't understand! After all I've done for you! Why are you doing this to me?"

"After all you've done?" Jyn repeated, the words crawling out from between bared teeth. "You don't have the faintest idea what you've deprived me of, do you? You don't know what it's like to live with a knee pressed against your throat, to be stripped of your liberties and forced to commit the most heinous atrocities under threat of incarceration and death. To be made to throw the home that you love into chaos just to satisfy the power lust of a decrepit old gargoyle in return for your freedom and the lives of those you hold most dear."

Madeline drew a quick breath, regaining a modicum of her lost composure. "So this is payback then, is it? Forgive me, Jyn, but I didn't think you so petty. I thought you understood what we were trying to accomplish here. If you really believe that I'm not acutely aware of the sacrifices you've made in service of my vision, then I apologize, but you cannot throw it all away now when we are so very close to victory."

"Victory?" Jyn sneered. "Another century of Union rule? Generations of my people treated like vermin, oppressed and strangled, left by the wayside to suffer and starve while the wealthy reap the benefits of our subjugation—does that sound like a victory I'd want to pursue to you?"

Madeline became enraged, her cheeks turning the same red as her garish suit. "Everything I did, everything I asked you to do, was for the good of the human remnant. Hybridization is the key to our survival!"

"You think so small, Administrator," Jyn said, smiling cruelly. "The Divine Abyss bestows upon you the means of our ascendance, and your first inclination is to weaponize it? It's clear to me you don't know the first thing about what's good for us. You and your ilk have led the human remnant astray since the Collision, squandering and abusing every resource and opportunity afforded us by the Savior, and for what? Wealth? Superiority?"

Madeline sniveled, succumbing to panic again. "I only wanted to provide a safer future for our descendants."

Jyn placed a hand on the woman's cheek. "Our future lies with the cohabitors, Administrator. I'm sorry I can't make you see that. We found each other in the dark. The fates of our two species are inextricably interwoven, and all you and your precious Union have done is pull us farther apart from one another." She stood up, towering over the downed woman. "The celestial ties that connect us can only take so much strain; it's now up to me to Quell the Dissonance. To repair those bonds and get us back on course."

"And what will become of me?"

Jyn took a thoughtful pause. "Well . . . part of me laments that I can't spare you long enough for you to see the blockade fall and watch Harmony take the *Novara*, but sadly, the future I endeavor to bring about has no place for relics of the past like you."

Madeline's pleading expression became one of seething hatred. "Do what you must, you traitorous cockroach, but know this: grenadiers or not, this revolution of yours will be short-lived. The people of the NTU will *never* accept Harmony control. You, that wretched leech, and all who follow you will be executed, your very existence erased from the compendium. The Mouth will be sealed for good, and the Administration will reign supreme, just as it always has and always will."

Madeline's furious face melted into a look of anguished confusion as Jyn casually reached into her pocket and fished out a crumpled bag of synthetic beef jerky. The marshal removed a chunk of the gamy meat, briefly waved it before Abraham's nose, then tossed it across the rooftop. The dog exploded into action and bounded off in search of his treat.

Jyn locked eyes with Madeline. "New directive."

The grenadiers stood at attention.

"Kill the Administrator."

AUTHOR'S NOTE

Thank you so much for reading my debut novel, *Insurgency Harmony* (The Collision Book 1). This book has been a labor of love for the better part of three years. I didn't plan on taking quite so long to complete it, but balancing family life and full-time employment while writing a sprawling, high-concept science fiction novel has been a mammoth task. I'd love to tell you *Insurgency Harmony* was written from my home office in a structured, orderly fashion, but that would be a lie. The truth is that it was written in feverish dribs and drabs during my lunch breaks at work, composed in my head as I showered or did housework or went food shopping, scribbled down as barely comprehensible notes in Google Documents to be later transcribed into the cornucopia of manuscripts sitting on my desktop named "NEW VERSION. EDIT CURRENT. NEW EDIT." I really must get better at version control.

There were times when I would be out with my partner, Emma, walking our little dog, Poppy, around some reservoir in the UK's beautiful Peak District. She would catch me staring into space, leaving something she had said unanswered, and ask me . . .

"You're thinking about your book, aren't you?"

Emma has been my rock throughout the entire process, telling me to "shut up" when I began doubting myself, or cracking the whip when I let my writing stagnate.

"What chapter are you on?" she would often ask me.

"Nine," I would reply feebly for the fifth time in two weeks.

Not only did she have unwavering faith in me and the quality of my writing, despite having never read a sci-fi book in her life, but she was also instrumental in making sure the financial resources were set aside to have the novel professionally edited (by the wonderful Toby Selwyn) and illustrated with a fantastic cover (created by the visual magician, Tom Edwards). I have always struggled terribly with self-esteem, and so I can confidently say that I never would have completed the book were it not for her strength and tenacity, and certainly never would have had the confidence to publish it.

I've been trying to write for as long as I remember, but nothing before the Collision series had ever really stuck. My dad, who is an avid reader and ravenous fan of science fiction, used to tell me, "Everyone has a book in them, you just have to figure out what yours is." I think it's safe to say that I finally found my book . . . The Collision series is named as such because that's precisely what it is—a collision of everything that inspires me, everything I think about: my thoughts, my fears, my hopes, and aspirations. It's everything I love and hate about the world, presenting a microcosm of the current state of western society within the boundaries of a dystopian future, inspired by the gritty, kitbashed worlds presented in the science fiction films of the '80s and '90s on which I grew up.

The Collision series is also named as such because it is about a collision of cultures. It's a cautionary tale positing a simple question: looking at how galvanized and divided we have become, how vitriolic the discourse has turned over everything from climate change and the pandemic to racism and gender equality, what would *really* happen if we were to come across another sentient species and were forced to share a claustrophobic space with them? How tolerant would we be of their culture, their traditions, and their unfamiliar anatomy? How willing would we be to impart knowledge and resources or assist them in a time of crisis?

Call me a pessimist, but I think, despairingly, that if we were one day to encounter an alien civilization, organizations like Humanity First would be somewhat inevitable. Afterall, how could we ever trust ourselves to reconcile the cultures and eccentricities of an extraterrestrial species when many of us struggle to tolerate different cultures from our own planet? I only hope that, should such a meeting occur, we have managed to pull ourselves out of the primordial sludge of hatred and xenophobia that we are apparently *still* stuck in.

Hopefully I have successfully conveyed these messages, because beneath all the sci-fi high jinks, it's the core of what the Collision is about, the very foundation upon which it's built. Whether you think I've succeeded, failed miserably, or if something in this book resonates with you, or even if you just want to ask something about the *Novara* and the folks who inhabit it, then please email me at tom.clayton@accipiterpublishing.co.uk—I will endeavor to answer any correspondence I receive, even if you just want to tell me this was the single worst book you have ever read. It is, after all, my debut novel, and I welcome any feedback and constructive criticism.

Right now, I'm cracking on with the second installment of the Collision saga. It's working title is *Crisis Horizon*, and I promise not to take three years with it. This story has been in my head long before I began typing, and I'm incredibly excited about where it's headed next. It's going to be one hell of a journey, and I hope to have you along for the ride . . .

I couldn't possibly wrap this up without giving a special shout-out to Philip C. Quaintrell of Echoes Saga acclaim. Phil is a fantastic fantasy author who has been a veritable font of knowledge and advice throughout this process. He has been immensely helpful in not only assisting to improve the quality of my writing, but also in lighting the way through the murky woods of publishing. There was no question he wouldn't eagerly answer, and I can honestly say that I would have been utterly lost without his guidance and friendship. Cheers Phil. Couldn't have done it without you.

Finally I'd like to give special thanks to the wonderful people at Podium for taking a chance on me. I really didn't have any hope of self-funding and producing an audiobook any time in the near future, and now, thanks to their faith in me and my work, it will be available to an entirely new audience—one whom I would have had little chance of reaching were it not for their help. With two Collision sequels on the horizon, this is only the beginning of my friendship with Podium, and already I can tell that it will be a beautiful one indeed . . .

ABOUT THE AUTHOR

T. M. Clayton is the author of the groundbreaking Collision series. Growing up in Manchester, UK—otherwise known as "Rain City"—Clayton developed an inextinguishable love of science fiction while stuck in the house on wet days, utterly devouring anything and everything from his parent's VHS collection. His infatuation would manifest in young adulthood as an irrepressible desire to create his own fantastical worlds, inspired by the dystopian, "kitbashed" sci-fi cinema of the '70s and '80s. Though he works full time for an engineering company, Clayton devotes every spare minute to his mission of crafting emotionally resonant stories, interweaved with contemporary sociopolitical commentary and set against a backdrop of gritty, mind-bending science fiction.

tom.clayton@accipiterpublishing.co.uk
https://www.facebook.com/ThomasMichaelClayton/
https://twitter.com/T_M_Clayton

DISCOVER
STORIES UNBOUND

PodiumAudio.com

Made in the USA
Middletown, DE
03 November 2022

14040162R00222